DARKER THAN THE STORM

Gregardreos raised a hand, interrupting her. 'There is something much more important than the Sphere, and that is human responsibility. When you achieve your white mantle in ten years' time, Drey, you will take an Oath, by which you swear only to use your powers for good, never for the purpose of deception or aggression of for any other wrong purpose. The School's purpose in training a Sorcerer is not so much to teach power as self-control. Many find that the hardest thing of all, and fall by the wayside because of it. If you fail as a student no shame will attach itself to you, but once you are a fully-fledged Sorcerer it will be a different matter. Break your Oath and your white mantle will be stripped from you, your power burned out of you. Do you understand this?'

His voice was resonant and grave. The young man stared at him with wide eyes. 'Yes – yes, Master.'

'And you still wish to join us?'

'It's all I've ever wanted.'

'Then I welcome you to the School of Sorcery.'

Also by the same author, and available from NEL:

A BLACKBIRD IN SILVER
A BLACKBIRD IN DARKNESS
A BLACKBIRD IN AMBER
A BLACKBIRD IN TWILIGHT
THE RAINBOW GATE

About the author

Freda Warrington is the author of the four-novel fantasy sequence which began with *A Blackbird in Silver*. Born in Leicester, she grew up in Charnwood Forest. After leaving school she studied graphic design; as well as being a writer she is also a designer and illustrator. She now lives in Derbyshire.

Darker than the Storm

Freda Warrington

NEW ENGLISH LIBRARY
Hodder and Stoughton

First published in Great Britain in 1992

An NEL paperback original

Printed and bound in Great Britain for Hodder Christian Paperbacks, a division of Hodder and Stoughton Ltd., Mill Road, Dunton Green, Sevenoaks, Kent TN13 2YA (Editorial Office: 47 Bedford Square, London WC1B 3DP) by Clays Ltd., St Ives plc. Typeset by Medcalf Type Ltd., Bicester, Oxon.

ISBN 0-450-53817-6

Contents

This book is dedicated to Keren Woods
with love and thanks . . .
for dreams as close as gold, and silver in the sun.

The rocks remain . . .

1

The Silver Sphere

Night lay on the School of Sorcery, and starlight falling through the crystal walls made the chamber resemble the interior of a dim blue diamond. All around, the corridors were silent. The Sorcerers and students had gone to their beds, but the High Master still lingered in the Chamber of Sight, brooding.

Walking to the chest-high marble column that stood in the centre of the chamber, he hesitated a moment, then began to summon an image. Nebulous light swirled above the column. The High Master, Gregardreos, breathed more power into the vision until it became as clear as life.

The image was of a face framed by long black hair, an aristocratic face with arrogance and cruelty bred into the finely carved lines of the bones. The skin was bitter-brown sheened with violet, the green eyes narrow and cold yet possessing the luminous magnetism of a cat's. Suffering had abraded some of the harshness and cast permanent shadows there, but Gregardreos could feel no empathy with the baneful visage. He looked on it with an emotion that he tried to convince himself was not hatred.

'Ashurek,' he said softly to himself. 'Prince Ashurek of Gorethria.'

He dismissed the vision, but it faded slowly, and the eyes remained. Hooded under the fierce brows, they seemed to pierce right into him. He turned away abruptly, cursing.

'Seven years. That is how long I have borne this,' he murmured. 'Of all the people Silvren could have chosen as her lover, why did it have to be *him*? Oh, Silvren, it's not my fault I love you, I've tried hard to be a perfect High Master but I'm not made of stone . . . I know, after all this time I should have risen above these feelings, but they only seem to grow worse, not better.'

Gregardreos walked slowly around the chamber, violet-blue lozenges of starlight sliding over his white robe, glinting on his blonde hair and beard. 'Dearest Silvren . . . for your sake I must tolerate him, for your sake I *cannot* tolerate him! Why can't you see that he's evil? If only he'd do something wrong, just one thing to prove his true nature and give me a reason to exile him – but his behaviour on Ikonus has been exemplary. Exemplary, damn him!'

Few days went by when Gregardreos did not brood about Silvren and Ashurek. He had worked hard to be a perfect High Master of Sorcery, rooting out his own faults one by one, but this remained stubbornly beyond him; simple, human jealousy. The more he tried to overcome it, the more of an obsession it became.

He pressed his knuckles to his forehead, trying to calm himself. 'No, no. I must be detached about this. I have overcome obstacles far greater than this . . .' But that thought only brought a tide of unpleasant memories and he shut his eyes, forcing them out of his mind. 'Go away! What I used to be has nothing to do with what I am now, and I will not listen to your voices!'

And the voices slid away – not even memories but formless shadows of the things he had trained himself to forget. Gregardreos relaxed slightly. He knew that in his present mood it would be a waste of time retiring to bed, so he sat cross-legged on the floor, hands resting on his knees, trying to send his mind into the meditative state that would bring him rest and peace of mind. But a few minutes later his large frame shook with anger and his eyes flew open.

He looked up at the column. The image was gone but it seemed Ashurek was still in the room, a persistent, haunting presence.

'Do something, damn you!' he exclaimed. 'Prove my suspicions right, then at least I could hate you with good reason!'

Gregardreos was glad when morning came, and life returned to the School like the gradual sweet crescendo of a dawn chorus. He left the Chamber of Sight and went to his office, a crystal-domed room furnished with a desk and chairs of light red wood. There he watched the first glimmer of light brightening until it splashed through the walls in a glory of coloured fire. Then he smoothed out his robes, combed and rebraided his hair, and waited for Silvren.

She came to him through the shattered light, as she did every morning, her sleeveless robe very white against the deep gold of her hair and skin. Her face was oval and slim-featured, her eyes guileless. She was all golden warmth. No Sorcerer was ordinary, and he had seen hundreds pass through the School in his time, but he had never met anyone to compare with Silvren.

'Have you been here all night?' she said, frowning.

'Is it so obvious?'

'I can always tell when something is worrying you, Gregar. And that's human instinct, nothing sorcerous.' She smiled faintly.

He could hardly say, *'I have spent the night pondering how much I hate the man you love, that's all.'* The only consolation to his pride was that Silvren knew nothing of his feelings, and never would. Ashurek could not be removed without just cause, nor without hurting Silvren deeply, and Gregardreos had always considered her feelings before his own.

'There's nothing wrong,' he said rather brusquely.

'I believe you,' she said, as if she did not but would let it rest. She sat down opposite him and they began to discuss the business of the day, but his mind was wandering. *These banal words are leaves floating on the surface of my thoughts . . . and below are the dark waters of what I am really thinking, the words I can never say . . .*

He vividly remembered the day, more than twenty years before, that she had come to him from another world; hardly more than a child, completely alone and terrified by the strange powers that had made her an outcast in her own land. He had taken her under his wing and for ten years she had been his best student, his beloved protégée. When she had eventually left to return to her own troubled Earth, he had resigned himself to never seeing her again.

He had never declared his love, and for a long time had not even acknowledged it to himself. She had been so young, and the High Master was allowed no relationship with students other than that of pupil and teacher. He thought he would forget her but she remained in his thoughts and he had dreamed of seeing her again. Years later she did come back to Ikonus, but his dream, which so nearly came true, turned bitter and dark when she brought a lover with her; not even a man of whom Gregardreos could approve, but a warrior with a turbulent and bloody past. The damnable outcast Prince of Gorethria.

I accept the situation or drive her away, he thought. *I've always known that. To have her working at my side is worth the pain I suffer, day after day, knowing she loves that man . . . or is it? That's the point, nothing changes, nothing will ever change unless I act – but I cannot, cannot hurt her!*

'Gregar, are you listening to me?' she said.

'Of course I am.' He felt his face turn hot, and thought, *Thank the Sphere she does not know what I am thinking!* Even sorcerers could not read each other's minds – at least, not without consent.

'You seem to be a million miles away. I was just saying

that the new student, Drey, arrives this evening. Aflouel and Terarct will bring him to see you.'

'Good. I should like you to come too; you have a way of making newcomers feel at home. And I'd like to leave the talking to you, if you don't mind.'

'Of course not, but why?'

He tried to smile. Latent power tingled in his fingertips, and he thought, *Power? What is that, when I cannot even break through the barrier of Silvren's blindness, make her see Ashurek for what he really is? All the sorcerous skills in the world cannot overcome this lack of communication between us.* 'Because I am tired and I feel lazy. Indulge me. You were the best of my students and now you are the best of my tutors, my most valued Sorceress.' *And because I love the sound of your voice and watching you charm others . . .*

'No need to flatter me into it! I'll see you later, then.' She walked to the door, smiling at him over her shoulder. Her beauty was an ache that went right through him. It was not that she was indifferent to him; far from it, she *did* love him, but in absolute innocence, as a daughter loves a father. Not as he wanted her to love him. *And that,* he thought, *that is the worst thing of all.*

The young horse reared and plunged, fighting its rider, Its coat was sweat-smudged grey against the darker grey of the hill, but the last blaze of sunset sent silver light rippling through the mane and tail.

Ears flattened, eyes wild, the horse twisted through every possible contortion to unseat the man on its back. Ashurek, however, stayed firmly in the saddle. His hands were steady on the reins and he flowed with every movement, his green eyes alight with something of the horse's fire.

'There is nothing you can do, my friend,' he said softly. 'My old war-mare was trained to do far worse than this in the course of battle.'

The young stallion made one final, sideways leap, set its mouth against the bit, and bolted. Ashurek leaned forward, giving the animal its head. The hillside was clear of trees, a gentle scarp rising against the silver glow of the sky. The only sounds, filling his head, were the low drumming of hooves, the horse's quickening breath, the creak of leather. The landscape was deserted. The wind swept his hair into rats' tails and flattened the thin material of his tunic against his skin.

At such times he could almost imagine himself on his own Earth, leading an army into battle, or fleeing demons across Tearn. He felt no fear for his own safety, only exhilaration – not joyous, but piercing and sad.

The horse had been badly broken-in and was ill-tempered and intractable. Its new owner had brought it to be reschooled by Ashurek, whose skill with horses was becoming well-known across Ikonus. He used no force with the animals he schooled, only a sure instinct and determination. The more wayward the horse, the better he liked it. The battle of will brought him to the edge of the abyss of chaos, the knife-blade on which he had once thrived. Sometimes it was the only thing that saved his sanity.

The horse pounded towards the skyline. It was fit as well as strong, Ashurek noted with approval. An observer would have thought he sat on the bolting horse in a daydream, too relaxed, his gaze distant.

Finally the grey's breath gave out and it responded reluctantly to Ashurek's hands as he slowed it to a canter. By the time they reached the peak of the hill it was content to walk. Ashurek let it stride along the ridge to cool down. The stallion went uneasily, rolling its eyes as if warning him what would happen when it recovered its energy.

Ashurek slapped the sweat-greasy neck. 'There's no shame in defeat, lad,' he said. 'Only in failing to fight.'

He looked out at the landscape of Ikonus with detached appreciation of its beauty. It seemed an ornamental garden, sketched in watercolour; tiny fields and lakes, narrow tors like fingers gloved in foliage, all floating in violet shadow. Only the School of Sorcery, on the horizon, cupped the last of the light and blazed it back like a prism.

Far above the School, a mercury-silver Sphere floated like a tiny moon. It had been created by sorcery and its purpose, as Ashurek understood it, was to purify the energy that made sorcery possible. He looked on this intention with utmost cynicism; evil ultimately lay in the way the power was used, not in the power itself.

He felt little affinity for the world on which he and Silvren now lived. Ikonus was a smaller world than their own, lying in another dimension like a green jewel in a filmy plane of ether. Its sun was silver-blue, its vegetation a lush and delicate shade of green. There was one modest continent, a few large islands, all under the benevolent restraint of the School of Sorcery. Sorcery permeated everything, a rich and golden warmth sparking in the air, heating the very soil, ready to be tapped by those, like Silvren, who had the ability and knowledge to use it. The world had had its troubles in the past, but those had long been solved. Now the power was tame, like Ikonus itself; a beautiful but overpruned park.

Ah, but Silvren and I have found peace here, when escape and tranquillity were all we craved. Seven years of peace should not seem too much . . . Yet I cannot shake off this restlessness.

Ashurek recognised the onset of the black mood, but as always he could do nothing to stop it. It washed through his mind like a slow, persistent tide, a sea of tar under an ancient moon. He dismounted and led the stallion, which instantly tensed as if it sensed a darkness it could not comprehend.

Ashurek came to a lake, hardly more than a pond, with trees weeping into the water. Now the grey had cooled down he let it drink, and looked down at his own reflection. His clothes were deliberately nondescript – grey tunic and breeches, dark riding boots – but they could not minimise the power and presence of what he had once been.

Prince Ashurek of the House of Ordek in Shalekahh.

Twin brother of the late Emperor Meshurek; High Commander of Gorethria's Imperial Army. The scourge of the Earth, loathed and feared the world over. But no more.

The violence and horror of those years had brought him nothing but suffering, self-hatred and despair. Silvren had been his only light, still was. In her, always, was the sweet fire of morning and the hope of redemption. Once their last great struggle against the Serpent was over, all he had desired was to leave the Earth behind and start a new life with her.

To a certain extent, they had succeeded. They had known times of incredible happiness on Ikonus. They had a small daughter, Mellorn, although Ashurek's delight in her was tempered by the knowledge that she was too much like himself. Silvren was still the centre of his life, although he was sometimes unsure whether he was completely the centre of hers. He tried not to resent her loyalty to the School, because he understood her need for the security that the School gave her. She belonged there as she had never belonged anywhere else. Thus his love for her bound him to Ikonus, but no amount of love could change the essence of who he was.

He had been born to lead men. All his life, he had never known a time when there was no conflict and no challenge. He remembered how it had felt to be proud of being Gorethrian, to revel in warfare. That had been in his youth, before he had come to understand that war was wrong. Innocence, of a sort. Even after that, when he had been possessed by the Egg-Stone in full knowledge of its evil power, there had still been the blood-red edge of exaltation, a mania that had given him a taste of how it must feel to be a demon, glorying in its own wickedness.

In the midst of the self-hatred he had found diabolic joy. And through the joy, always, self-hatred.

He wanted no more of it. And yet, without it, what was he?

He had made a vow to the Lady of H'tebhmella that he would never again wield a weapon. That was as much to protect others as to appease his own conscience. He wanted no forgiveness for the evil deeds he had perpetrated, and cared even less to be remembered as a hero for slaying the Serpent M'gulfn. They were all reasons for him to have left the Earth behind forever.

Yet it was Earth's savagery and wildness that he missed. *I am insane,* he thought, staring down into the lake. *All the years Silvren and I spent struggling to end the evil . . . The terrible prices we paid, sacrifices that almost tore the souls out of us . . . In spite of all that, is there still some demon inside me, telling me that I desire those horrors again?*

There is no demon, his reflection seemed to reply. Only you.

Can I never find rest?

He had never known the wild mood descend on him with such intensity before. It was like a fist grasping his brain. The landscape seemed to distort under the pressure, every detail becoming as sharp and clear as glass while vibrating behind a veil of unreality. It was like a call, a possession, but it came from inside himself.

Looping the stallion's reins through his arm, he reached into his pocket and drew out three small, pointed lodestones. He had no innate aptitude for sorcery, but there were other, related arts which could be learned rather than inherited. One was the art of finding the Ways between Worlds.

Soon after arriving on Ikonus he had asked Calorn, an Ikonian woman who was a master of the art, to teach him the finding of Ways. He had never put the knowledge into practice. It had simply been an automatic precaution, like noting the exits from any building he entered.

But now, without clearly considering what he was doing, he placed one of the stones on the grass and held the others, one in each hand, to form the points of a triangle. He moved them slowly in relation to each other, sensing the magnetic pull between them, changing the angles until the correct configuration was achieved. It was a delicate process, one of instinct rather than mathematical rules. He felt the ion-streams moving softly across his hands, trapped into a slow rotation between the lodestones. His muscles twitched in the strange electric flow.

He did not intend to use the Way. He did not even know where it would lead. He merely wanted to look on another world, to cauterise his restlessness by tasting chaos.

There was something about the lake . . . It was as if the Way had been here all the time, drifting like a ghost, calling silently for someone to summon it, make it tangible. *Come back. Fulfil your obligation. We are in peril and you have deserted us . . .*

Like a whirlwind becoming visible as it sucks up earth and water, a dark tube began to spin between the lodestones. Cord-thin at first, it began to expand, spitting flashes of blue and red fire. He could still see the water and trees around him, and he was aware of the solid ground beneath his feet, but within the tube the world ceased to exist. He gazed on a whole universe, held within the circle of his arms. He saw an infinity of radiant blackness, across which giant shadow-figures moved in conflict. He heard the clash of weapons, the echo and re-echo of a million voices shouting and weeping . . .

He screamed.

The Way thickened and fountained towards the sky. He lost his balance and began to fall.

In the same instant, he was suddenly jerked backwards and almost off his feet. The stallion towered above him, rearing in terror. Its eyes were rimmed with white, its mouth open. The flailing hooves barely missed Ashurek's skull.

The Way vanished. Reality rushed back in and for a few minutes there was only the pure physical struggle with the horse. He held grimly onto the reins, pulling the animal back to the ground and moving with it as it dashed in circles around him. Only when he led it away from the lake did it begin to calm down, its ears flat and its neck frothing with sweat.

Ashurek had dropped the lodestones, but he did not go back for them. The shock of what had happened settled on him very suddenly. Had he really risked everything, just to indulge a transient depression? If he had wanted proof that safety was only a thin skin stretched over the pit of chaos, he had received it.

The grey looked at him balefully and sank its teeth into his arm. Ashurek slapped its head away in annoyance, then relented and scratched the damp neck.

'I have you to thank for saving me,' he said thoughtfully. 'If my life here is pointless . . . how much more pointless to return to the madness that created me. No. I'll keep my vow.'

'Sorcery is a wild energy that circles the world like the wind, unseen and unfelt except to those who are sensitive to it,' said Silvren. The student, Drey, listened intently to her, dark-eyed and serious. Two senior tutors flanked the newcomer; Aflouel, a plump, smiling woman who was a close friend of Silvren's, and Terarct, an austere man who kept himself to himself. His face was very pale, his hair black and sleek, in contrast to the High Master's leonine magnificence. Gregardreos sat behind his desk, seeming, to Silvren's relief, rather more cheerful than he had been that morning.

Darkness was falling. Silvren would have preferred to have gone home to Ashurek and her daughter than stay late at the School, but Gregardreos had insisted that she was needed.

Smiling at Drey, Silvren went on, 'Only a few humans have the ability to tap into the energy. We are privileged, you and I, but it is also a very great responsibility. Power can be used for evil as well as for good.'

She raised a hand above her head and a thread of light

streaked out to crackle on the crystal ceiling. A translucent pane opened, revealing a square of violet sky and the silver Sphere gleaming against it. 'I expect you have often seen the Sphere before, and wondered what it is.'

'All my life,' said Drey. He was very young; his voice had hardly broken.

'It is not easy to explain, but it acts as a kind of filter. The raw power is drawn through it and the Sphere takes out the darker aspects, the negative elements that could cause corruption and evil. Thus the power comes to us purified.'

Aflouel squeezed Drey's arm and said, 'Don't be afraid to ask questions. We don't bite!'

He cleared his throat. 'Did the . . . the Sorcerers make the Sphere?'

'Yes, it was made centuries ago,' Silvren replied. 'The power can be destructive as well as beneficial, so they had to find a way to tame it. But it happened that . . .' She hesitated. She had reached an event that still caused her pain to relate, even though she had not been to blame. It could be both a virtue and a fault, Gregardreos had said, that she was too willing to take responsibility for the actions of others. 'Some years ago, a misguided person thought they could steal power from the Sphere. All they achieved was to unleash a terrible darkness which almost destroyed Ikonus. It was only then that we understood that the Sphere could be dangerous as well as beneficial. However, Gregardreos rebuilt it with safeguards to ensure that such a disaster could never happen again.'

Drey's interest got the better of his nervousness. 'So the bad side of the power is stored *inside* the Sphere?'

'It used to be.' Silvren glanced at Gregardreos with the shadow of a smile. 'But the High Master reconstructed it so that the negative power, the Flux, is filtered into another dimension, where it can harm nobody. That's one way we keep the power of sorcery uncorrupted, and –'

Gregardreos raised a hand, interrupting her. 'There is something much more important than the Sphere, and that is human responsibility. When you achieve your white mantle in ten years' time, Drey, you will take an Oath, by which you swear only to use your powers for good, never for the purpose of deception or aggression or for any other wrong purpose. The School's purpose in training a Sorcerer is not so much to teach power as self-control. Many find that the hardest thing of all, and fall by the wayside because of it. If you fail as a student no shame will attach itself to you, but once you are a fully-fledged Sorcerer it will be a different matter. Break your Oath and your white mantle will be stripped from you, your power burned out of you. Do you understand this?'

His voice was resonant and grave. The young man stared at him with wide eyes. 'Yes – yes, Master.'

'And you still wish to join us?'

'It's all I've ever wanted.'

'Then I welcome you to the School of Sorcery.' Smiling, the High Master stood up and shook Drey's hand. 'Enter your training with a glad heart and don't be afraid of failure. Even I have made my mistakes in the past, but you learn to put them behind you.'

When Terarct and Aflouel left to show Drey to his quarters, the High Master turned to Silvren, looking pleased. 'He will do well,' he said.

'I think so,' said Silvren. Teasingly, she added, 'But mistakes, Gregar? You?'

He grinned, a touch of self-mockery. 'A very long time ago, even I was not perfect.'

She laughed, began to say something else, stopped in mid-word and looked around the room in bewilderment. She felt a strange shivering of the air and knew that Gregardreos also felt it, as did every Sorcerer and student in the School. Somewhere on Ikonus, a Way to another world had opened. To their sensitive minds it was as tangible as the pressure of an approaching thunderstorm, and the more adept the enchanter, the more vividly the burst of far-sight came.

Every Way had its own peculiar ambience; this one brought echoes of stone and dark fogs, a taint of burning at the back of the throat. It hit Silvren hard, but she was astonished to see the High Master staggering forward and collapsing to his knees on the floor. Hoarse cries burst from his throat as if he could not stop them.

'No! Jhensit!'

'Gregar, what's wrong?'

The shock was already beginning to recede. He let her help him up and he slumped heavily into his chair, taking deep lungfuls of air. *Thank the Sphere I was the only one with him,* she thought. *He would have been mortified if the others had seen him lose his dignity, especially a student.*

'Silvren, the Way . . .' he said hoarsely.

'I saw it. It's fading now.' She closed her eyes and began to probe for the last thread of supernatural energy. 'I'll try to hold the vision . . .'

'No, don't,' he said, clutching her arm so hard that she jumped. 'There may be harm in it.'

She was about to protest, but Gregardreos was already sliding into the trance of far-sight, his eyebrows furrowed and his large hands resting on his knees. A few seconds later, Terarct rushed into the office, closely followed by a breathless Aflouel. Silvren sighed to herself; now she could not ask why Gregar had reacted so violently, without revealing to the others that he had.

'Did you sense it?' the dark-haired sorcerer said.

Silvren nodded, and looked at Gregardreos. Presently his eyes flickered open and he drew a breath and released it in a long sigh. 'Ashurek summoned the Way,' he said.

'I know. I sensed that much,' said Silvren.

'Why would he do such a thing?'

'I've no idea,' she said faintly.

'The Way has gone now, but I felt there was danger in it.'

Terarct said, 'I caught a name, "Jhensit".'

'What? No, you could not have done!'

Gregardreos sounded almost demented and Terarct stepped back, looking shocked. 'I assure you, I did, Master. Why, is there some reason it should mean something to us?'

'No!' Gregardreos pinched the bridge of his nose and sighed again. 'No. The name means nothing, nothing.'

'Perhaps it's the name of the other world,' said Aflouel. 'I had the feeling that a part of this Jhensit was probing into Ikonus. If that indicates some kind of sentient intention, Ashurek may have opened up a Way for something very terrible . . .'

'Please be quiet!' the High Master snapped. His tension and over-reaction were so uncharacteristic that Silvren began to feel afraid. In the glow of sorcerous lamps, he looked ten years older. More calmly, he said, 'I need to think.'

'Did you find something out about Jhensit?' Silvren asked. 'I only saw . . .'

His head jerked round, and his eyes were as intense as Ashurek's. 'What? What did you see?'

'Nothing really. Just layers and layers of mist, and a feeling . . .' She frowned. The memory was not pleasant.

'What sort of feeling?'

'I don't know. Not of evil. Here . . .' She pressed a hand over her diaphragm. 'A feeling of loss.'

'That's what I felt, too!' Aflouel said eagerly.

The High Master lifted his hands, and his tone was imperative. 'Far-seeing to another world is always difficult. I only tried briefly, but I had the feeling that Jhensit may be impenetrable. Until I have decided what to do, I forbid all of you to seek far-knowledge of Jhensit. Put it from your minds.'

Silvren and Aflouel exchanged anxious looks as he went to gaze out through a clear pane in the glassy wall. Silvren thought of Mellorn, who was at that moment with Aflouel's young daughter, Netaya. A vague but deeply uneasy presentiment made her say, 'Aflouel, would you mind if Mellorn stayed with you tonight?'

'Of course not, Netaya will be thrilled and so will Mellorn, I should think.' And Silvren was glad that Aflouel did not ask why. She could hardly explain the feeling of foreboding she had as she watched Gregar, the square lines of his shoulders, the proud set of his head. His hair was sandy-fair and worn in the style traditional for the High Master, scraped back from his face and hanging down his back in a long braid.

The affection she felt for him was different from the love she had for Ashurek, though no less real. She had never really known her own father, who had died when she was a child. Gregardreos had taken his place in her heart. He was her rock, and she saw through his harsh manner to the tenderness that lay underneath.

Eventually he turned round, looked at the expressionless Terarct, then Aflouel, and finally at Silvren. 'You know, of course, that what Ashurek did is strictly against Ikonian law.'

A soft fist struck her stomach. 'Well, yes, but . . .'

His face had the grave expression he usually reserved for transgressors. His hands were shaking slightly, she noticed. 'It's a very serious offence, to create a Way without permission. The penalty is exile from Ikonus.'

Silvren's eyes widened. She was only too familiar with his rigorous attitude towards the law, and he never said such things lightly. She felt the blood rushing out of her face. 'Gregar, wait – you can't be telling me that you would exile him!'

He studied her for a moment, as if her distress at the thought of losing Ashurek turned in him like a knife. 'I can't make exceptions. At least, I shouldn't. But for you, Silvren . . .'

'What?'

He paused, then said, 'He brought this on himself. In a way, I am not surprised. His wild nature was bound to resurface eventually . . .'

Silvren was dumbstruck. 'Wild nature? Don't speak of him like that, as if he's a stranger. I know you weren't happy about his coming here at first, but I thought that was all in the past. He's done nothing wrong until now. What were you going to say about making exceptions?'

'I have to think for a time.' He turned his back on her, shutting her out. 'There will have to be a tribunal. Go home, Silvren. Say nothing to him tonight. I will come in the morning and speak to him.'

Silvren felt Aflouel's eyes on her, concerned, but she was so shocked that she could not speak, let alone argue with the High Master.

It was only as she walked home, a white ghost through the dusk, that the sense of outrage began to burn inside her.

Ashurek and Silvren's house was on the fringe of the village that lay beyond the School's exquisite gardens. It stood slightly apart, backing onto the stables and fields where Ashurek kept his horses. Like the other dwellings, it was built of pale red wood, plain except for carving round the windows, doors and eaves.

It was dark when Ashurek arrived home. He took his time stabling and grooming the young stallion. When he entered the house he found Silvren sitting by the light of a single lamp. The polished wood floor, rugs and tapestried chairs glowed in the creamy radiance, which turned one side of her face to molten gold and left the other side in shadow.

She sat still for a moment, watching him.

'Is anything wrong, beloved?' he said. She stood up and slid her arms around him and he embraced her, kissing her hair.

'I – I was waiting for you, that's all.'

'Is Mellorn in bed?'

'No, she's staying with her friend Netaya tonight. Aflouel didn't mind. Mellorn's the most independent six-year-old I've ever known. I think it's right to encourage her.'

'In case we are ever not here to look after her?' said Ashurek.

Silvren pulled back, looking at him, and he sensed the tension in her slim body. 'What made you say that?'

'You're right, it's a sensible precaution. But I would rather she didn't spend every spare moment in the company of Sorcerers and their families.'

Silvren crossed the room to light another lamp. The light shone through her hair and through the edges of her white robe, rimming her with silver. 'I am a Sorceress and so will she be, in case you'd forgotten.'

'I wish I could forget.' Ashurek sat down and stretched out his long legs. 'The School seems to engulf both of you. I think the High Master and the others will only be content when they can keep you there permanently. When they can possess you completely, body and soul.'

Silvren rarely grew angry, even with him, but there was a touch of fire in her expression as she turned to reply. 'That's nonsense and very unfair.'

'You always think the best of people. I love you for that, but it can be dangerous. Of course the High Master wants to possess you; he's in love with you.'

Her mouth fell open. 'That's ridiculous! Gregardreos was like a father to me, when I had no-one else, and he still is!'

'If you insist. But I still say you give too much of yourself to them. They use you.'

'Ashurek, don't. They need me. I owe the School so much.'

'Indeed? Even though it was sorcery that almost destroyed you, not once but several times over?'

'But that's why I have to teach others – so that they never, ever have to go through what I suffered! Anyway, you're just the same.' She waved a hand at the desk that stood under the window, strewn with papers. 'You sit there, brooding, writing reams of Gorethrian history. It must be for a similar reason, though I'd give anything for you to forget!'

'I cannot forget,' he said quietly. 'Gorethria's history is part of me. I can only exorcise it by writing it down. But I do not devote each and every day to it. Ikonus was meant to be a place of respite, where no-one knew us.'

'But wherever we go, the memories will always come with us.' She shook her head in exasperation. Lamplight glittered in her golden irises. 'Ashurek, I am not a dove in a cage, a creature you can look at to bring you tranquillity!'

He stared at her, shocked. 'Do I make you feel that?'

'I know you want to protect me. Sometimes, you cannot.'

'What do you mean?'

'You're keeping something from me. This restlessness that falls on you sometimes, it makes me feel so helpless. You summoned a Way today, and you were not going to tell me. Would you have gone through it?'

'How on earth did you know that?' He stood up and clasped her arms.

'How do you think? I sensed it. All the Sorcerers did, because we are Sorcerers! Answer me, would you have gone through it without me?'

'No, Silvren. No, never,' he said in a low voice. 'And I do not ask for understanding or forgiveness. I acted on a selfish compulsion. The vow I made is sometimes difficult to keep . . . but I didn't expect or want it to be easy.'

He kissed her, his hands tangling in the halo of her hair, and she clung to him with equal fierceness. And as always, the passion was all that could burn the darkness out of him. 'No, I could never leave you, beloved,' he whispered. 'To lose you would kill me.'

2

The Way Between Worlds

In the lavender glow of dawn, the horses were no more than wraiths, grazing or sleeping under the trees. Ashurek and Silvren leaned on the fence, arms round each other, watching them.

Ashurek said, 'Don't go to the School today.'

'The horses can't spare you for a day, and my students can't spare me.' She half-smiled. 'But I needn't go until later, when it's time to fetch Mellorn.'

Ancient trees fringed the field, obscuring the view of the hill on which the School stood. As the first spear of sunlight burnished the leaves, a figure appeared from the trees, walking from the direction of the School.

'That looks like the High Master,' said Ashurek. He felt Silvren tense, as if holding her breath.

'It is.'

'I've never known him to honour us with a visit so early . . .' Then he saw the look on Silvren's face; anxiety, almost guilt. 'Don't tell me. He was listening to our conversation and has come to drag you to the School bodily.' He spoke drily, but he felt the grim mood beginning again, a tightening of the air.

Gregardreos approached them, raising a hand in greeting. He was as tall as Ashurek, heavily built, with a face as harsh and handsome as granite. He wore a robe and a long-sleeved coat of white wool over it, tied with a silver cord. Ashurek had no particular feelings about him, although he could see (as Silvren could not) that Gregardreos loathed him. The sight of the High Master induced only a mild sense of weariness in him.

'Good morning,' said the High Master, nodding politely to them. 'Please forgive me for disturbing you so early.'

'I will leave you alone,' Ashurek said brusquely, but Silvren gripped his arm.

'No, don't go, Lord Ashurek,' Gregardreos said gravely. 'It's you I wish to speak to.'

'Do you have to do this?' Silvren said. 'It's over now, and it was nothing, it won't happen again.'

'It's unavoidable, I'm afraid.' There was a hard glow of determination in the High Master's eyes. Ashurek suspected the reason for his visit, and he read the look accurately. Now that Gregardreos had a crime to hold against Ashurek, he was not going to let it drop.

There seemed no point in observing the usual courtesies. 'What do you want?' asked Ashurek.

The High Master's expression darkened. 'I'll come straight to the point. Last night you opened a Way to another world.'

'If I did, what of it?' Ashurek's tone was cool, his eyes freezing.

'You know full well that the creation of such Ways is forbidden, except by Sorcerers or Way-finders with the approval of the School. To do so without proper controls is unspeakably dangerous. Your foolish action may have put the whole of our world in danger.'

'I think you exaggerate. I closed the Way behind me,' Ashurek said unrepentantly. 'Now if you will excuse us –'

'That is not the end of the matter! Your presence here is tolerated for Silvren's sake, but I will not tolerate disregard for the very rules on which we structure our lives. You learned the art illegally and no Oath binds you to its correct use. That is all the more reason, if you flout our laws, for you to pay the penalty.'

Ashurek could feel Silvren willing him to apologise. If he had done so, it would have more or less have disarmed

Gregardreos. But he could not. 'It seems to me I have done no harm, except to your pride. I take very unkindly to threats.'

'That, if I may say so, is your problem,' said the High Master. 'The inhabitants of this world are under the School's protection, and my only concern is their welfare. I must uphold the law. If you will not obey, you make life extremely difficult for Silvren as well as for yourself.'

Ashurek leaned back against the fence, his lips thinning. 'You have always made it clear that I am not a welcome guest here. You seem to see me as a wayward element that you can't fit in with your well-ordered society. But I made a vow when I left Earth to live a peaceful life, and that is what I've done. I may even have been helpful to Ikonus in some small way. In return you apparently spy on me in the hope of finding a good reason to hound me.'

'It was not necessary to spy on you! When a Way is created, it cries out, it screams for the attention of any who have the far-sight to perceive it. All my Sorcerers were aware of it. There was something malevolent about it.'

Ashurek held his gaze. 'Go on.'

This response seemed to disconcert the High Master, as if he had expected a contradiction. 'We could discern no more than that. The Way vanished too quickly.'

'Forgive me. I would have held it open longer, if I'd known.'

'The point is this,' Gregardreos said heatedly. 'You are a dangerous man, Ashurek. I don't hold your past against you. I accept that you have tried to reform. But there is something in your nature that attracts trouble. Who knows what evil you may have brought to Ikonus? It is within my power to exile you for this!'

'If I leave, Silvren will go with me.'

The High Master glowered at him. 'I'm not issuing empty threats. There will have to be a tribunal and I say again, the penalty is exile from this world.'

Silvren stared from one to the other, distressed, but waiting for Ashurek's reaction. He said, 'Don't be too hasty. I understand the disappointment you must have felt when Silvren brought me back to Ikonus with her. But I am the price you must pay for keeping her at the School. Ask yourself which is worse, tolerating me or losing her?'

For a moment there was such venom in the High Master's expression that Ashurek thought he would explode into anger. But he controlled himself, and said thinly, 'I suggest we let Silvren speak for herself.'

Silvren stared at them helplessly. 'Ashurek, the High Master's right – about the Way, I mean. A Way does not just appear and vanish, it can have deeper repercussions which we can't even begin to calculate yet. You know that, for the Lady's sake! Didn't you give a thought to Mellorn? How can I leave her?'

'You left her with Netaya's family last night. You knew this was going to happen and you knew she'd be safe there . . . Just in case?'

'How can you speak to me like that?' she exclaimed. 'Gregar, please think again, Ashurek meant no harm –'

'Don't defend me, beloved,' said Ashurek. 'I'll ask no mercy or favours from anyone. The fact that you find it necessary to plead on my behalf suggests that you are on his side.'

He spoke quietly, but Silvren pulled away from him and glared angrily at both men.

'You put me in an impossible situation! I'd come with you wherever you go, but how can I desert my students and drag Mellorn to a strange world? And you –' She turned to face Gregardreos, 'You're forcing me to choose between Ashurek and the School. How can you thrust that choice on me? I thought you cared about me. I thought you both did.'

She stormed away from them, a small, straight-backed figure, and went into the house.

The two men faced each other. Ashurek said, 'If I had a sword, I'd break my vow for you.'

'And the blade would run liquid before it ever touched me,' Gregardreos replied. 'You seem to think there is a personal element in this. There is not. I am obliged to punish you by law. However, I can offer you a choice, other than exile. The tribunal have the final decision, but they will not go against a sensible suggestion.'

'Ah. Something to prevent you from losing Silvren completely?'

'Perhaps I've lost her already. Perhaps we both have.'

The look in Ashurek's eyes would have terrified a lesser man. 'I'd rather go into exile this moment than bargain with you over my fate. But for her sake, tell me what the choice is.'

There was a barely perceptible change in Gregardreos's face, a hint of vulnerability behind the façade of authority. He almost stammered as he spoke. 'I – need to know more about the world to which the Way led. All I could discern was its name, which – which is Jhensit. Sometimes it is impossible to far-see into another world. I must know what sort of place it is, so I can judge whether or not it is any kind of threat to Ikonus. Someone must go and study it at first hand. As this is your fault, it might as well be you.'

Ashurek considered this. 'And when I return – assuming I do – I will have paid for my "crime"?'

'Exactly. Your life can return to normal.'

'My life had never been that,' Ashurek murmured. He was tempted to tell the High Master to take his bargain to hell. He would not mind leaving Ikonus, and Silvren and Mellorn would go with him – but he knew how much the School meant to Silvren. It would be heartbreaking for her, and she was the one person he was determined not to hurt. 'Very well. The irony is, Gregardreos, that whatever enmity you feel for me, I trust you. I know you'll keep your word and give me the means to return to Ikonus when my task is over. You are too noble to be good at hating.'

* * *

The tribunal was a formality. It took place in the School's Central Chamber, a huge polyhedron like a faceted jewel, where Ashurek faced a semi-circle of senior tutors who looked on him with a variety of expressions: hostility, indifference, unease. Rainbows flared across their dazzling white robes. A few curious students lined the audience gallery, but Silvren was not allowed to be present.

The tutors were powerful sorcerers, haughty, self-contained men and women. They were radiant with the golden fire of their power, yet it was Ashurek who dominated the Chamber. In the midst of the brightness he was like the dark, magnetic presence of death, silently scorning their presumptuous attempt to judge him. The Sorcerers would die before they admitted it, but all of them, except Gregardreos, were afraid of him.

A few of them were friends of Ashurek, but they were in a minority. Only Aflouel spoke in favour of not punishing him at all. The ones he had expected to demand his instant exile, such as Terarct, remained silent, and the rest deferred to the High Master.

'This is our decision,' Gregardreos pronounced eventually. 'Lord Ashurek shall be sent through a Way to Jhensit. He is only to observe the world, not to become involved. When he has discovered the nature and intentions of the place to our satisfaction, he shall be permitted to return to Ikonus.'

Ashurek grimaced. By the terms of the sentence, he could be sent to and fro from Jhensit for ever more. The High Master was clever. He had succeeded in disposing of Ashurek, at least temporarily, at the same time appearing to be impartial and benevolent.

Yet Gregardreos did not look triumphant. Perhaps he was weighing the cost of trying to fight fire with fire.

Ashurek had chosen to wear breeches of heavy, dark grey cloth, a tunic with a high collar and full sleeves, and under that a buff-coloured shirt. His cloak was also grey, his long riding boots of black leather. In a pouch on his belt was a small amount of food, a knife, and three lodestones which would enable him to return to Ikonus. He preferred to travel light. Those who weighed themselves down against any eventuality, he considered, should think twice about their fitness to make the journey.

He fastened the ornate buckle of the belt and finally, with great reluctance, strapped on a sword and settled the sheath comfortably against his hip.

It felt strange, after all this time. Yet it felt as if it had always been there.

Silvren looked at him, her face solemn with regret and apprehension.'So, I must break my vow after all,' he said softly. 'And it is my own fault. I am sorry. Silvren.'

'You swear that you can't bear to leave me, that you find it loathsome to wear a sword again . . . but I think in your heart you are glad to be going to Jhensit. Isn't that why you summoned the Way in the first place? Boredom?'

He did not reply. He kissed her, then said, 'I wish you were coming with me.'

'I would, if it wasn't for Mellorn.'

'Look after her. Tell her I will be back as soon as I can.'

She nodded, biting her lip. 'I don't care what you do, Ashurek, I'll forgive you anything, if you only come back to me.'

They kissed again. With great reluctance they slid out of each others' arms, and went out of the house to the field where Gregardreos was waiting for them. Aflouel and Terarct stood some distance away to witness Ashurek's departure; Aflouel small and round yet radiant with her power, Terarct all angular whiteness, unsmiling.

'Are you ready?' said Gregardreos.

'Yes.' Ashurek had not wanted to go, but now the moment was here he felt an incandescent excitement. Silvren had been right, though he would not admit it. Gregardreos, still showing no particular sign of pleasure at his departure, lifted a hand and placed his fingers on Ashurek's forehead.

'No, don't pull away. This is essential, if you are to understand and speak the language of Jhensit.'

'But you do not know the language yourself.'

'That doesn't matter.'

Ashurek felt the faintest sensation within his skull; a coolness, like a raindrop falling and dispersing. The High Master withdrew his hand, but again Ashurek sensed anxiety beneath his stern exterior, and said, 'I hope you are not keeping anything from me.'

Gregardreos's expression became guarded. 'Of course not. Surely even you can accept the word of the High Master.'

'I trust you implicitly,' Ashurek said with only a trace of sarcasm, which Gregardreos chose not to hear.

'Then ready yourself to go, but remember; you are only to act as an observer.'

Ashurek caught Silvren's eye. Despite the sadness of her expression, her bright courage shone through, as it always did in times of trouble. Remembering other, more terrible separations, he thought, *At least this time she will be safe.*

'Let us get this over with,' he said. 'The sooner I go, the sooner I'll be back.'

Gregardreos lifted his hands and began to summon the Way. He needed no lodestones to act as a focus; his mind and fingertips formed the triangle, calling in the energy streams and shaping them into a supernatural whirlwind.

The Way was invisible at first, but its presence could be felt as a rippling column of heat. Static furred the air. Ashurek found himself being pulled forward, as if into a vacuum.

'Wait until I give the word,' said the High Master. 'The Way's forming too quickly . . .'

'As if it had been here all the time, waiting for you to call it?' said Ashurek. 'That is what I sensed about it, and I am no Sorcerer.'

Gregardreos did not reply. He closed his eyes, and the muscles of his jaw bunched up with tension. Strands of darkness appeared between his hands. The Way thickened until it became a cone of smoke and light, spinning dizzily on the grass.

The High Master's eyes flew open and sweat trickled down his temples. His arms became rigid, as if he were fighting to contain the power. The Way spun faster and faster, its dark and bright striations searing their eyes. 'I can't control it . . .'

'What's wrong? said Silvren, starting forward. Strands of golden light ran over her body; she was summoning power to help.

'No, stay back,' the Sorcerer gasped. 'Now, Ashurek!'

The vortex stretched into the ground and the sky, coiling itself round a sickening nothingness in both directions. It seemed voracious. Ashurek stepped forward eagerly, but in that instant the High Master lost control. The Way flashed out to meet them, expanding around its circumference with a soft *snap* that was felt rather than heard.

The smoky barrier broke over Ashurek like a breath of air and a sudden, horrible numbness crept into the centre of his bones. He was inside the Way – but Silvren was in there with him.

Her face was pale with shock, and the sparkle of her power turned colourless and vanished. For a split-second Ashurek met her eyes, then the earth dropped away beneath his feet and his mind filled with swirling colours.

As he fell, he could hear the voices of Terarct and Aflouel, shouting in alarm. They were too late to do anything. He reached out in the futile hope of finding Silvren's hand, but he could not feel or see. Pressure was crushing him. He was being pleated like a fan, cracked and scattered like ancient paper. And the echo of voices followed him, disintegrating into a waspish buzz that persisted throughout the endless journey.

3

The House of Neatru

Shai Fea woke in the certain knowledge that something was wrong. Her eyelids lifted but she could not move. The bed-curtains of fine silk were open; between them she saw faint light falling through the balcony windows, scattering spidery shadows across the floor. Everything was in monochrome and the chamber seemed twice its normal size, eerie and dream-like.

A figure stood by the bed. That proved she was dreaming; it was her mother, dressed in the same pale, elaborate garments in which she had been buried. Her eyes were wide, staring at nothing.

Shai Fea drew a breath, but she could not make a sound. Her mother raised a hand to point at the window. '*Beware,*' she whispered, her mouth a grotesque square of anguish. '*Help . . .*' Then she turned towards the bed and Shai Fea saw the wet black stain covering her garment from throat to ankle.

The bud of terror in Shai Fea's stomach began to unfold, choking her. She gagged with the effort of trying to cry out. Suddenly the paralysis broke and she sat up violently, panting, soaked in sweat.

The apparition had vanished. Shai Fea was truly awake now, but everything still felt wrong. The tall balcony windows were shut, yet the blinds of paper-thin silk and the gauzy curtains were billowing like clouds on an unfelt breeze.

In panic she turned to her husband, expecting to see his sallow face slack with sleep, his hair spread out like watered mud across the pillow. But his side of the bed was empty.

'Lan?' she called softly. She climbed from the bed and padded slowly round the room. There was no sound from the dressing rooms or living chambers. She looked in each one, hating the childish terror, but powerless to control it. Finally she approached the windows.

The draperies, floating like ghosts, stilled at her touch. The night sky glowed dimly through the little flower-patterned panes. She looked through them and on the balcony she saw her husband.

He was stretched out on his back, his nightshirt falling in neat folds as if he had been laid out for the funeral bier. His face was bleached, and his eyes stared up at the sky like white jewels.

Her cries brought guards and bleary-eyed maids rushing from the outer chambers. Lamps dazzled her. The nightmare went on, but she felt distant from it now. Someone was guiding her away from the windows while a guard rattled the handles, and announced that they were locked.

Shai Fea became aware of something small and cold pressing into her right palm. They were all watching her as she uncurled her fingers and saw what lay there. A key.

While the under-city lay swamped in the shadows of dawn, the over-city, Niankan-Siol, glowed as if it were immune to darkness. Raised high above the ground on impossibly delicate stilts, the buildings were like egg-shell lit from within, luminous against the sky. The palace of the Hyalon seemed to touch the clouds and its walls gleamed a pale blue-green. The Hyalet Shai Fea Neatru, the Hyalon's sister, leaned on the balcony rail and filled her lungs with the cool air.

Niankan-Siol looked sublime, giving no hint of the grim

atmosphere inside the palace. But the city was busy unusually early. She could see servants and nobles hurrying along the distant walkways that threaded through the buildings. She imagined their hushed voices, the whisper of their silk-slippered feet.

Then she looked down at the long, long drop to the under-city, Niankan-Pel. Her body jerked with sudden dizziness. *Did mother stand on her balcony, that last morning, wondering how it would feel just to tip forward and fall?* Unable to halt her imagination, Shai Fea imagined herself plummeting through the air, robes flapping, hitting the stone flags . . . dying on the filthy ground, the earth from which all foulness came, all the crawling creatures, the consuming evil of the devil, Flaim . . .

No. She could not bear to die that way. She wanted to stay in the palace in the sky, the domain of the silukians and the bell-birds, of the purity of Eyos. She wanted to live.

Why was she so afraid?

There was a gentle hand on her arm, drawing her back into the room. 'You'd better come back in now, Your Highness.' One of her guards, worried that she might have intended to do more than take a breath of air.

Shai Fea did not argue with him. She returned to her chair and sat staring blankly out of the windows at the spot where they had found her husband. They had tried to make her sit in another chamber, but she had refused. She needed to find a way to face what had happened.

Three maids moved quietly around her, dressing her as best they could, but she was oblivious to them. Last night the chamber had seemed too big. Now it seemed suffocating, like the bosom of an over-protective aunt. The blue and silver opulence, even the spun-glass sculptures which she loved, now turned her stomach. It all looked like icing sugar, so sickly.

Her kitten, a long-legged, hairless creature with huge blue eyes, leapt onto her lap. It was a very young silukian, a long way from developing its wings and leaving her.

She stroked it absently, tracing the pink and grey patches on its baby-soft skin.

Wedren Lan died last night. Just there. She mouthed the words but did not voice them. In the palace, there were many layers of questions and insinuations in the word 'died'. It tasted sour and dusty on her tongue. As an isolated tragedy it would have been hard enough to bear, but it was the twentieth unexplained death among the Ruling House of Neatru in half as many years. News of Wedren Lan's demise had permeated the upper city within an hour. The palace was shrouded in terror, while members of the Hyalon's household looked on even their closest friends with suspicion.

No-one had said the word 'murder' to Shai Fea. She knew how the circumstances must have looked. But there had been too many other equally strange killings for anyone to be certain that she had murdered her own husband.

Why should Wedren Lan mean more to her in death than he had in life? Her marriage had not been particularly happy, but she had entered it with no expectations. It had simply been her royal duty. Wedren Lan might have been plain, humourless and largely indifferent to her, but he had never been cruel. Their life had been peaceful. He had not deserved to die.

Thank Eyos we had no children.

'Your Highness?' One of the maids was holding up a mirror to her face. 'Have we arranged your hair as you wish?'

The Hyalet Shai Fea stared into the glass. The round, youthful face she saw was the off-white of candlewax, all beauty vanished. The eyes glared at her, like the eyes of her mother in the nightmare. Horror welled up in her again.

'Take it away!' she hissed. She leaned forward in the chair, hugging the kitten. 'Why is it taking so long to get light?'

'I'll fetch another lamp, your Highness,' said the maid,

backing away. She was a young cousin of the Hyalet's, slender and self-assured. This morning, though, she seemed as vulnerable as a child. A glass rim of tears appeared along her eyelids, but Shai Fea could not cry with her. She felt dried up and fragile, like a dead leaf.

'No, not those awful lamps! More candles.'

'Yes, Highness. It's a dark morning.'

'I'd go back to bed, if I thought I could sleep. I'd like to sleep forever.' Shai Fea sat back in the azure chair, pressing a hand to her hot forehead. All her life she had tried to be strong, following her parents' example, but inside she knew her strength was only a mask she put on with the elaborate court clothes.

Her gaze slid to the window. In the glimmer of dawn, the city's translucent walls were becoming opaque, like clouded glass. She could see figures moving along the walkways, vehicles sliding along the cables. What would her guards do if she tried to go out? No-one had told her she was under arrest. The possibilities circled round her mind, but she did not move. She remained rigidly in the chair until she heard the inevitable knock at the door.

Her cousin ran to open it. Lord Tean Mon stood on the threshold, his expression grave.

'Come in, Uncle,' Shai Fea called, suddenly finding she could not stand up. He crossed to her, his pleated silk robes rustling, his grey hair floating like cobwebs. She held her hands out to him and he bent to kiss them.

'Your Highness, the Hyalon has sent for you,' he said.

Her heart sank. 'Can't he wait? I'm not ready.'

'I'm so very, very sorry at your loss, my dear. I tried to dissuade him, but he insists.' Her Uncle's eyes were sympathetic, but the solemnity of his lined face filled her with foreboding.

She took a breath and composed herself. It was hard to pretend this morning, but years of practice came to her aid. 'Very well. We mustn't keep the Hyalon waiting.' She let the kitten down onto the floor and took Tean Mon's arm, managing to control her shaking legs enough to stand up. 'Has he – has he taken Wedren Lan's death badly?'

'I fear so,' he replied unhappily. 'He seems calm, but inside – how could he not take it badly?'

She was glad of Tean Mon's arm to lean on as they made their way to the Hyalon's chambers. Her maids had dressed her in an elaborately pleated and sashed robe of pale yellow, covered by a billowing coat of gold filigree. The colour made her pallor look truly ghastly, but she had not had the energy to insist on changing. Vanity had become pointless. The pastel glory of the palace drifted past them as they walked the long corridors, but even that beauty suddenly seemed hollow.

At the entrance to the main salon, Tean Mon left her alone, placing a hand briefly on the small of her back to reassure her and propel her into the room. She looked at him anxiously, but he shook his head and withdrew, closing the doors behind him.

Her brother, the Hyalon Elatiat Harn Neatru, stood waiting for her. He appeared to be alone. She was glad. There were so few chances these days to see him without a mass of courtiers and servants in attendance.

The salon was bright with electric lamps, whose artificial glare she hated. The ceiling was a soaring translucent dome, with painted birds flying across the panels. The whole room, with its slender pillars and rich draperies, was sky-blue and gold, the favoured colours of the god Eyos. The Hyalon's robe was the pure clear hue of a sapphire, but he seemed rather small and unimposing against the room's extravagances.

Shai Fea went towards him slowly, feeling sick and faint. He was no taller than her, but overindulgence in wine had fleshed him out and given his face a bloated look. His hair was deep bluish-grey, his eyes as pale as fog under bushy eyebrows. They were strange eyes, but kind, she had always thought.

'At last,' said Elatiat Harn. 'I thought you were never coming, Fea.'

She bowed as protocol required. 'I came as soon as I was summoned, your Majesty.' She kept her tone neutral but she could feel tears welling. They had been so close, in the days when their parents were Hyalon and Hyalana. It was only since Elatiat Harn became Hyalon that he had changed. He was still kind to her, but he had become so distant, and she felt that she no longer knew him.

'It seemed a long time. You look unwell. I'm sorry I had to make you walk all this way; I would have come to you, if court protocol allowed it.'

'I – I don't feel very well. I've been awake all night, since . . .'

'Of course. I understand.' Suddenly his arms were round her, and she was cradled against his shoulder, her tears staining the fine silk of his robe. It was the first time he had hugged her in years. 'Oh, Fea. Poor Fea,' he said. 'I'm so sorry.'

'It was a terrible shock,' she said, her voice muffled.

'All the deaths have been a shock to me.'

'To all of us.'

'But I am the Hyalon. The responsibility for my family's safety rests with me.'

They looked at each other. There were tears in his eyes and she sensed, as she often had before, the huge, sad weight of the burden he carried. Her fear began to diminish. Why had she been so afraid of her own brother?

Their father had barely entered middle age when he had died of an illness, ten years ago, and it was Neatru tradition that the Hyalon's wife should not outlive him. So their mother, the Hyalana Shai Tialah, had followed her husband to the grave, and Shai Fea had never fully recovered from the shock of her death. Elatiat Harn, on the other hand, had hardly appeared to mourn. It was that, more than his sudden elevation to Hyalon, that had made her feel alienated from him. *But that's been his upbringing, to suppress emotions and attend to his duty,* she thought. *Inside, he cares.*

Holding her hand, he led her out onto the balcony,

which was like a frill of stiffened lace against the façade of the palace. Bell-birds swooped rose and gold against the sky, oblivious to the strangely-coloured clouds that undulated above them. She could not remember the last time she had seen the sun.

'I should like to be married,' said Elatiat Harn pensively. 'I *should* marry, but how can I, while this enemy preys on us? My wife would not be safe. I cannot even protect my closest family . . .'

The large Neatru family who controlled Niankan and the surrounding country, Palan, ruled by inheritance of rank and formed a chamber of nobles who had considerable power but were ultimately subservient to the Hyalon. Over a hundred and fifty members lived in the palace itself, with lesser branches of the families and their retainers forming the aristocracy of Niankan-Siol.

They were the people of the sky, worshippers of the one true god, Eyos. Their religion and society rejected everything of earth as being base and evil. They aspired towards the heavens, and despised those who lived in the under-city, the Pels. This was the natural way of things, and Shai Fea had never questioned it.

A silukian kitten – twice the size of Shai Fea's pet – walked precariously along the balcony rail and pushed its head against the Hyalon's arm for attention. Elatiat Harn stroked the pearl-pink skin, which was no longer quite naked but sheened with down. 'Look, her wing-buds are forming,' he said. 'She will not be with us much longer. Everything that's dear and good comes to an end, doesn't it?' And he gave Shai Fea a long, strange look.

It should not be like this, she thought. Comfortable with the support of a large army and a command of science, nothing had threatened the Neatrus' rule for centuries. Elatiat Harn's reign should have been secure, but instead it seemed to be cursed. An unseen murderer stalked them; what other cause was there for twenty deaths that had no obvious explanation? Some of those who died,

Shai Fea and others had thought privately, were no particular loss; a few she had actively loathed. But her brother had lost three of his closest friends and advisers, and she had witnessed every worsening moment of his pain.

Now a perpetual undercurrent of fear permeated the House of Neatru. Who would be next? After each killing, scapegoats would be found and executed. Flaim-worshipping Pels were blamed, though there was no proof to condemn them, and all the Pel servants had been dismissed from the palace. It was a joke in the lower city that even the servants in Niankan-Siol were aristocrats, a joke not far from the truth. Every precaution was taken against poisoning, everyone was guarded to an almost ridiculous extent, but the slow trickle of deaths continued. Only the Hyalon himself seemed to remain above it, appearing calm and self-contained.

Shai Fea thought, *Only Tean Mon and I really know how much the deaths are hurting him.* As he had said, the family's safety was his responsibility, the need and impossibility of protecting them a massive burden. Shai Fea shared the sense of helplessness, would have done anything she could to help; but with each murder he only seemed to grow a little further away from her.

He spoke, interrupting her thoughts. 'I have done everything I can think of to quell the worship of Flaim. I don't want to be hated. I don't enjoy sending out the Satrans to tear Pels out of their homes, to break up their secret meetings, to threaten and kill them . . . but what else can I do? They all have the choice. Renounce Flaim and worship Eyos, it's that simple. But there is always a core of the stupid, the stubborn and the downright wicked who can't or won't see the truth. The sky is where we belong. The round blue eye of our god. If I could find a way to sever us from the treacherous earth completely, I would.'

Shai Fea was relieved not to talk about Wedren Lan. 'I feel sorry for the Pels, almost,' she said. 'Even the ones

who worship Eyos still have to live on the ground.'
'They can't all live in Niankan-Siol. There isn't room. Besides, it gives them something to strive for, to pray for.'
'But they'll never achieve it.' She spoke wistfully. She did not care about the Pels in more than an abstract way.
'As long as the Flaimians go on practising their evil against me, they have no hope at all. Let's pray together, Fea.'
'If Eyos loves us, why does he darken the sky?' she said.
Her brother's hand tightened on hers until it hurt. 'Don't speak blasphemy, Fea! They are only clouds, the sky is still above them and Eyos will raise us into it – but only if we do his will. Now, pray with me!'
He raised his face to the sky, eyes closed, silently invoking Eyos. Shai Fea tried to do the same but she could not concentrate, and found herself staring out at the dizzying view of Niankan-Siol, her mind blank. Beyond the gleaming city were distant hills, carved into terraced farmland. A blue tower, the Tomb of the Hyalons, glinted against the skyline but she looked away quickly, still unable to bear the sight of it. Instead her gaze came to rest on a dome, a mile or so from Niankan, which bubbled out of the landscape like a vast, half-buried pearl.
The White Dome had always fascinated and frightened her. It was the source of the power that fed Niankan-Siol, and it housed the scientists who made the power possible. It was also a prison for transgressors, who vanished into its depths to be used as slaves in the enigmatic process that generated electricity for the Siols. A skein of cables, like a silver hair, connected it to the city. Few were allowed in, even fewer came out. Even the scientists who ran it, including the Director Iytrel Halia herself, were virtual prisoners there . . . but who was free in Niankan, except the bell-birds?
The White Dome was a mystical place, often haunting her like a great half-moon cresting the edge of her dreams. She stared at it, and in the face of the awe she felt, her

fears seemed petty.

Presently Elatiat Harn finished his prayer and looked at her. 'Do you feel calmer now?'

'Yes.' She almost managed a smile.

'Then you can tell me what happened last night.' He led her back into the salon and sat her on a couch.

'I've already told your chamberlains. I was half the night telling them. Must I go through it again?'

'Please try, Fea,' he said kindly. 'I must know.'

'We retired three hours after dinner, as we always do. We shared a flask of wine. Nothing was out of the ordinary until I – I began to dream.'

'What about?'

She hesitated. 'Mother.'

'Oh dear. Not again.'

'I can't help it. She was our mother, how can I forget her? But this was different. She was by the bed and I think she was trying to warn me. Harn, the murderer must have walked through our room. He could have killed me instead, or both of us!'

He squeezed her arm gently. 'Just go on with your story.'

She told how she had searched the room and found the body on the balcony. Her voice was unsteady and she could feel herself trembling from head to foot.

'So you were the last person to see your husband alive,' he said. 'And when the guards entered they found him outside on the balcony, the windows locked and the key in your hand. How do you explain that?'

'I can't. I don't know how it happened. I was still half-asleep and in shock. I remember trying to open the windows, so I must have pulled the key out of the lock then.'

'That is one possibility.'

'Is there another?'

'Poor Fea,' he sighed. 'I remember you weeping on my shoulder before your wedding, cursing tradition. It is a dreadful thing to be married to someone for whom you feel nothing, isn't it?'

His voice was soothing. 'Yes,' she murmured without thinking.

'I do not blame you. I am only . . . sad. Heartbroken, Fea.'

'Why?' She looked at him in surprise. 'You never liked him either.'

'Not sad for him . . . but for what you've done.'

It occured to Shai Fea that she had not been hearing what Elatiat Harn was actually saying. Her heart kicked in her throat, making it hard to breathe. 'For what *I've* done? I don't understand.'

'Come now, Fea. How it was done is unimportant; a poison in the loving cup of wine, perhaps. And really, 'Why?' is no mystery. But I still have to ask you, *why*?'

Her lips parted, but the words congealed somewhere in her throat. His gentle tone and the words he was uttering were so incompatible that she could not believe her ears.

He went on, 'Did you not stop to consider what this would do to me? That you were hurting me as much or more than you hurt Wedren Lan? You never did think through the consequences of your actions. You imagined that you could hide this behind all the other killings. But you were bound to be found out! Fea, I love you and I thought you loved me. So how could you do this to me?'

At last she forced her dry tongue to work. 'You – you cannot be accusing me – no, Harn, don't joke about this –'

'It's not a joke, Fea.' He stroked her shoulder, as he had stroked the kitten. 'Eyos, I wish it were.'

'No, you have it all wrong! I didn't hate Lan and I didn't wish him dead. I – I know how it looked, but don't you think, if I'd really wanted to murder him, I'd have found a way that didn't make me look guilty?'

'But that was always your way as a child, don't you remember? You would create mischief, then make such a fuss about it that no-one believed you could possibly have been responsible.

Her voice was becoming high and breathless. 'Yes, but I was just a child –'

'And you still are, in many ways. I want to be angry with you but I can't, Fea. However wicked your action, it wasn't your fault. I just feel so sad. If you could do it once, perhaps you could have done it many, many times . . .'

'What are you saying? That I'm responsible for all the murders?'

He leaned forward slightly, one hand propped on his thigh; a thoughtful pose he often assumed in the Chamber of Nobles. It usually meant he had made up his mind and would not be swayed by any more arguments. 'I hate to think it, but I've exhausted every other possibility.'

It was so outrageous, so nightmarish that she could not find words to defend herself. A black whirlwind was spinning in her mind and she could not get her breath; the palace, the world itself, were collapsing around her.

'Why? he said again. 'My own dear sister. Little Fea. Why?'

'I'm innocent!'

He took her hand, and a tear made a silvery trail down his cheek. 'I couldn't bear to make you face a trial and execution, public disgrace. It's better that you remain under house arrest for a while.'

'How long?'

'Until it is time for you to disappear. A sudden illness. Yes.'

A wild thought came to her, that either he or she had misundertood tradition. 'No – no,' she began breathlessly. 'The tradition only applies to the wife of the Hyalon. No other woman has to follow her husband to the grave, does she? She doesn't, it's only the Hyalon's widow!'

She might have been a bird cheeping for all the impact her words made on him. 'You are confused, Fea,' he said abstractedly. 'This is nothing to do with that. I am talking about punishment for the most serious of crimes.'

'I'm innocent, *innocent*!' she cried until her voice began to fail. Suddenly, in the midst of her panic, the thought came to her, *He is mad. I never saw it before, but he is mad!*

The Hyalon called out, and four Satrans stepped from curtained alcoves around the room. Their sky-blue enamelled armour had always reminded her of the beautiful beetles who sunned themselves on her balcony in fine weather. Guards meant safety . . . but these were moving to surround her.

'You can't! I want my own Satrans. This is ridiculous.'

The Hyalon stood up to face her, and she had never seen such sorrow in his face before, even when their parents had died. Her soul curled into a cold, grey knot.

'How did they infect you, sister?' he said.

'Who?'

'The Pels. The Flaimians.' He ran a finger down her cheek. 'I don't condemn you, but I have to do this. It's for your own good, little one. You do understand, don't you?' He looked at the Satrans. 'Take the Hyalet back to her own chambers. And remember that her arrest is to remain secret.'

'No!' Shai Fea glared at the guards, daring them to touch her. They looked embarrassed, but she knew that if she did not go willingly, they would use force. 'I beg you, Harn. You can't do this! A trial would find me innocent. Even – even if you kill me, the murders will go on, because I did not commit them!'

'You have friends, Highness. Your life will be bearable. It will not be so different from before, except for not being able to leave your chamber . . .' Lord Tean Mon trailed off. He was doing his best, but the words were hollow.

'Yes, but how long will my life last?' Shai Fea said softly. She lay curled up on her bed, her head on her Uncle's knees. Her maids waited in her dressing room; Satrans guarded the door and the balcony windows. She and Tean Mon whispered so they would not be overheard. 'My brother has lost his mind. It must have been happening for years and I couldn't see it . . .'

'I did my best,' said Tean Mon. 'I reasoned with him for as long as he would listen, but it made no difference. He is convinced that you are guilty. He's suffering from a very serious delusion, but no-one will ever believe us, not as long as his behaviour appears rational to others.'

'I'm his sister, I should have known.'

'I did see the signs, but I ignored them,' he said heavily. 'His shows of strength, the purges of the lower city; they aren't the actions of a strong Hyalon. He is a very frightened man.'

'Whoever is committing these murders, that's what they wanted. To drive the Hyalon mad. My poor brother, I could weep out my soul for him. If I ever found those who'd done this . . .'

A spasm of emotion shook her. Tean Mon stroked her hair, tucking the stray strands behind her ears. 'Hush,' he said. 'Don't worry about the future. He loves you, he'll see reason.'

'This reminds me of when I was a little girl. You used to tell me stories when mother and father were too busy to put me to bed. I wish I were a child again. I felt safe then.'

'I have no stories to tell you now, Fea.' Her Uncle's face had the papery look of an old man's, and his eyes were so weighed down with tiredness that they were hardly more than slits. 'What a world Jhensit is. Do we try to find out the cause of our ills and do something to remedy them? No. Instead we blame the gods and flee into the sky, like ants crowding into the top of a flooded anthill. If we deny the ground, we reason, it cannot hurt us. Eyos will lift us into the sky before Jhensit vanishes completely.'

His voice soothed her. She was not really listening to the words at first. 'But we are living on dreams,' he went on. 'We cannot leave the ground. Niankan-Siol is firmly rooted there, however tall we build the pillars. We cannot exist without the earth. What fools we are, cursing all animals except those that fly. We profess to despise all growing things, yet we imitate them. Cold flowers made of glass. No colours except those of the sky. But where does glass come from?'

'Don't, Uncle!' Shai Fea opened her eyes, suddenly realising what he was saying. 'I've never heard you talk like this before. It's blasphemy! You're scaring me.'

'Forgive me, my dear. I'm no companion for you, I'm too melancholy. Shall I send in your maids instead?'

'No,' she said quickly. 'I want you to stay with me. But what's wrong? If you've lost your faith, if you've changed, I couldn't bear it.'

'I haven't changed. I am only saying the things that have been in my heart for years. After what has happened today, I feel too weary to keep them secret any longer. I am really not what you think me. I am a terrible coward.'

'Don't say that! You're all I've got. If I can't trust you, who can I trust?'

'Oh, you can trust me, that I promise with all my heart.'

'Then don't say these awful things! I need you to be the Uncle I've always known . . .' But as she spoke, she felt something changing within her mind. All her life she had thought Tean Mon strong and wise; now he was telling her that he was weak. The whole day had been filled with betrayals, with the distress of finding that nothing was what she had thought it. Yet just as she felt she could take no more, a wordless inner voice began to speak.

I have lived all my life with the illusions of childhood. Now is the time to grow up. It's Elatiat Harn who's deranged, not me; he is the true victim. It's my responsibilty to save him.

She sat up, feeling the floor very cold against her feet.

'Help me escape,' she said.

'What?' He looked alarmed.

'I mean it.'

'It would be madness.'

'Everything around me is madness. How can it be any worse?'

'There's nowhere for you to go.'

'There must be somewhere!' she whispered fiercely. 'Will you help me or not?'

He hesitated. Then his shoulders slumped, and his face took on a resigned look. 'Of course I will. My dear, I – I never thought you would have the spirit to consider it.'

'You think I have no spirit?' She looked at him, terrified that it was true, but still dismayed that he had said it. 'The fact that I'm afraid doesn't mean I can't try to be strong. I must do what mother would have done. There's no-one to help my brother except me.'

4

Emissary of Flaim

The Way between worlds distorted time and perception.

Ashurek had passed through Ways before, but he had never experienced one quite like this. While he was aware that his physical self still hurtled through the whirling, buzzing tunnel, his mind rose out of his body and passed into another plane.

He was hanging in space, staring up at the black disc of a planet. He felt that he had always been there and always would be, a speck against the infinite curve of the void. There was no past and no future. Jewelled light rimmed the upper half of the planet, but the sun that created the corona would never rise.

There was a face on the disc. The light misted his eyes, and all he could discern on the blackness was an olive-green shimmer on brow, lips and cheekbones. It was a ghost mask looking down on him with the utter insouciance of the universe itself.

The lips moved, like the slow shifting of a mountain range.

'I am here and I will always be here, inside you and outside. You have known this forever.' And it seemed to Ashurek that he knew what the Face was. The knowledge was agony. The only reality was the endless chasm in which he hung, and its depthless cold was petrifying him and cracking his bones.

Time folded in on itself.

It happened so swiftly that he could not pinpoint the moment of change. Perhaps it took place outside time, like a dream. He was standing on solid ground, and the ghost-face had vanished as if it had never existed. He had the impression that he had simply stayed in the same place while the Way changed everything around him.

He stood in a deserted city. Massive stone towers the colour of iron soared around him. The broad paved road between them was weathered and criss-crossed with fissures, but there were no weeds growing in the cracks. The street ran straight into the distance, offering an endless perspective of domes and colonnades, all of the same brooding aspect.

The sky was a luminous green, with no cloud and no sun. It looked flat and changeless but for a yellowish glow where the street dwindled into the horizon. Distant towers were silhouetted against it, their windows unblinking topaz eyes.

Ashurek turned round slowly. There was no sign of Silvren. A cold stream of fear ran through him, and rage both at himself and at the High Master. Had Gregardreos managed to snatch her back from the Way at the last instant, or was she lost somewhere in this strange dimension?

The air was dry and silent, as if nothing had moved in it for centuries. *There is no life here,* he thought. A necropolis? But somehow he knew that there were no dead either.

Ashurek began to walk along the street. The atmosphere was one of incalculable age, and he felt that the city had stood from the dawn of time and now waited with infinite patience for time to end. The stone towers were shells with nothing inside, some so decayed that they were no more than façades. Yet the ruins would endure for ever, as if they had come into existence exactly as they were now.

He stopped near a wide, shadowy portico and inhaled

its sepulchral mustiness. There was a double row of columns and, in the wall behind them, a line of arched windows with no glass and nothing visible inside the building except a blackness which he had no wish to investigate. The city seemed to be holding its breath. Ashurek's senses were sharp to the point of prescience, but he possessed nothing approaching a sorcerer's far-sight. For the first time, he wished that he did. Was this all there was to Jhensit – emptiness? If so, why had a Way from Jhensit been haunting Ikonus as if pleading for someone to discover it? A cry for help, perhaps, which no-one had heeded – and now it was too late.

He walked on, wondering how much exploring he was required to do before Gregardreos considered it a satisfactory punishment. He was tempted to return to Ikonus immediately; Silvren's safety meant more to him than the High Master's laws. *I should have told him to be damned, taken Silvren and Mellorn away at once . . .*

A sudden sound interrupted his thoughts and he stopped. It was soft but piercing in the stillness, like dry leaves or a leather glove scraping along stone, and it came from the portico he had just passed. He turned back slowly, his hand on the jewelled hilt of his sword.

Moving until he could see between the columns, he caught his breath. Most of the windows were still dark, but one was brightly lit with a view of another landscape, all ochre and acid-yellow.

He was looking at a bizarre desert, and in the centre of the arch, staring out at him, was Silvren.

With a cry he ran between the first row of columns towards her. Was she really there? She did not react at once and he thought she could not see him after all, but when he was half-way across the portico she cried, 'Ashurek, no!'

He paused and heard the dry scraping noise again. From behind the column nearest the window the tip of a limb appeared, longer than a human leg yet slender as an insect's. It tapped delicately at the stone as if tasting it, then rose into the air, pointing at Ashurek with a slight, involuntary jerking motion.

He watched with horrified curiosity as the whole creature edged slowly into view. Ashurek had noticed nothing before; could it have been crouching in the shadows? It was a blood-red monstrosity, with a mass of filamentous legs which seemed to support the plated carapace of the body by sheer numbers rather than strength. It was as high as his waist and perhaps five feet long, the gleam of pinkish slime on its surface giving it a translucent look. Several of its forelimbs pawed at the air as if beckoning to him. Worst of all was its head, which resembled the long head of an animal with all the flesh stripped from it; a scarlet skull with black, empty eye-sockets. Two prongs of bone pointed down from it, fangs or mandibles, dripping a greenish-black fluid that turned Ashurek's stomach.

Now it stood between him and the window. It seemed to have no intention of moving, but Ashurek had even less intention of being prevented from reaching Silvren.

'Ashurek! Oh ye gods, don't!' she cried.

'Don't fear, Silvren.'

She showed no sign of having heard him. She was reaching out to the window and moving her hands as if against glass.

'Can you hear me?' he shouted.

No reply. Then she cried, 'Help me. I don't know where . . .'

Her voice faded. She was gone, and he had only blinked. The yellow desert still glared through the archway, but it was empty.

Ashurek stared grimly at the monster and it stared back, as expressionless as a machine yet unspeakably malign. 'I do not know what degree of intelligence you possess,' he said, 'but if you can understand me, I request you to stand aside and let me pass.'

The creature sank down, its jointed legs bowing beneath it. Not giving way, he realised, but gathering itself to spring – and the next moment it was flying towards him like a clenched fist.

His sword was already out of its scabbard and the blade sliced the air with a hiss as he swung it two-handed, stepping aside in the same instant to chop the beast from the air in mid-flight.

A shock shuddered through his arms, numbing them. He staggered back, his cloak flapping around him. The creature hit the stone flags but scrabbled to its feet, uninjured, and scurried towards him.

Revolted, Ashurek stabbed straight down into its domed back. The blade slid in, but it was like stabbing leather and no blood came out, only an oozing clear fluid. The creature staggered and righted itself with no sign of pain, then lunged at him with its bony fangs.

Ashurek leapt back, striking at its skull to no effect. Its flesh seemed hard as iron, yet soft and papery, impervious to steel. Was it even alive? The tang of blood filled his nostrils and with it came an overwhelming feeling of despair, as if the smell were drugging him.

He moved back swiftly, trying to clear his mind. Could he lure it away from the window then dash round it? As he withdrew, it came with him, but it marked him too closely and its red limbs were everywhere, preventing him from slipping past.

Ashurek began to work his way round in a circle, trying to put himself between it and the window. It followed him with ghastly, mechanical persistence and the blows he struck to its head and limbs were purely defensive. If he turned his back on it for a second it would be on him, the sharp prongs penetrating his cloak and injecting their poison.

Where was its vulnerable spot? Perhaps where the carapace joined the underbelly, but he could not gain a low enough angle to strike it there. He jumped to one side and made a second cut in its carapace.

The beast reared, lessening the impact of the thrust. Again there was the feeling of stabbing leather, no seeping of body fluids. Ashurek was beginning to despair of harming it, when something strange happened.

There was a soft noise like a pod bursting, and the carapace split open to reveal something undulating inside, glistening pink and raw. *Human shoulders*, Ashurek thought. That was what it looked like, muscled shoulders struggling and writhing to break free, except that there was no head between them.

Thrown off-balance by shock he moved too late, and the pliable limbs were folding themselves round him, dry as grass-reeds yet unexpectedly strong. He was jerked off his feet, felt his tunic tear and the spikes of bone grazing his skin, sticky venom flowing across his stomach. In desperation he brought his sword round and thrust upwards, beneath the skull, feeling a soft crunch as the blade entered the soft mouth parts.

The creature became completely still. Had he killed it? It showed no reaction, no pain; it simply stopped moving. Frantic to escape the poison, he began to wriggle from underneath it, tugging his sword free. As he crawled away, gasping with revulsion, it remained staring at nothing from its empty sockets.

As he stood up he saw that the only part of it still moving was the strange undulating mass in its carapace. He watched, and to his horror an arm shot out, a human arm, slick and bluish-red like a new-born baby.

Just as quickly the arm was withdrawn, but it had dropped something. A book!

Ashurek glanced at the window. The desert landscape remained, Silvren was still nowhere in sight. The creature was like an ugly blood-red sculpture, gleaming moistly in the shadows. Not wanting to go near it, but unable to resist the compulsion, Ashurek edged round and picked up the book.

It was a small volume, bound in black leather. He opened it and the first page showed an exquisitely stylised illumination, all glowing colours and gold leaf, of a palatial chamber. There were rich draperies and a magnificent bed, in shades of sky-blue, and in a chair next to the bed sat a splendidly-robed man, also in blue. The man was staring at a shapeless white figure which stood at the chamber door; not so much a figure as a nothingness, a gap in the illumination that had a human shape.

It meant nothing to Ashurek. He turned the page quickly only to see the same picture repeated. Impatiently he began to leaf through the pages, finding the same illumination again and again – except that, on each successive one, the white figure was slightly closer to the man in the chair.

His stomach tightened. He knew that when the figure reached the chair, the man would die. He wanted to throw the book away but he could not, he had to keep turning the pages – and when he reached the last page, a hot wave of horror went through him and he cried out hoarsely.

The colourless figure had been replaced by a red, hideously-jointed insect, and the one in the chair was Silvren – Silvren with her head back, her mouth stretched in a scream, her eyes wide with agony. The creature was rearing up onto her lap and its venomous fangs were buried in her chest.

Ashurek flung the book away in horror, but Silvren's screaming seemed to fill the air, a shrill note vibrating just above the range of hearing. Glancing wildly around him he dropped his sword into its sheath and ran at the bright window.

Hands outstretched, he made to leap onto the sill but something stopped him. Not glass, a softer membrane like the skin between air and water. He pressed his hands to it and the whole landscape beyond seemed to waver and distort before springing back into place.

'Silvren!' he yelled, and flung himself full length through the archway. The soft membrane caught him, and gave way beneath him – the whole dimension nothing more than a painting on film, nothing within the window except emptiness. There was a feeling that the whole universe was collapsing on itself, rushing downwards and inwards to a single white dot.

Ashurek lay still for a long time in half-darkness. His body throbbed. He could not seem to raise his consciousness to a level which would allow him to move.

'Silvren?' he murmured.

There was no reply.

He had the impression that he was still in a city, though one that was subtly different from the first. Buildings like mausoleums towered around him, but these were mushroom-beige, not grey. And they were not ruins.

He blinked up at the sky. It looked wrong, flat and pale with an oddly artificial glow. Against it he saw a long, slender vehicle cross the gap between the top of the buildings. It seemed to move on a cable, humming metallically and showering sparks as it went. It was gone so swiftly that he might have imagined it.

There was something he needed to find. 'The book . . .' he murmured. He had to see it again, but there was only dusty, cold stone under his hands. Then a warning screamed in his mind and adrenalin rushed through him. He was instantly alert, as if he had been woken from a deep sleep by cold water.

He stood up quickly, disentangling himself from his cloak. His head swam so wildly that he could hardly see, but he heard a murmur of voices, growing in volume.

He was surrounded by a crowd of people. They had formed a wide circle round him, as if they were wary of approaching him too closely. They looked human, at least from a distance; light-skinned, dark-haired dressed in leggings and long tunics of thick, greyish-black fabric. They were about a head shorter than him, on average. Those at the front were staring at him, murmuring to one another. Some had fallen to their knees. Further back, men and women were jostling to get a better view, while the edges of the crowd were seething raggedly as more and more people ran to see what was happening.

Damn Gregardreos! Where the hell is this place? If he's tricked me, he'll pay . . . Ashurek felt there had been another time distortion. Whether these folk had surrounded him as he lay semi-conscious or whether he had suddenly appeared from nowhere, he did not know, but they plainly could not believe their eyes. He must have looked demonic to them.

There seemed to be no way to escape, unless they would let him pass without hindrance. He took a couple of steps but the circle moved with him, those in front backing away and those behind him closing in.

A faint chanting began. It sounded like a name, spoken over and over again. '*Flaim. Flaim. Flaim . . .*' Again he tried to move. Again the crowd flowed with him, effectively imprisoning him. They seemed over-awed rather than aggressive, and he had no wish to hurt anyone. His only hope lay in trying to communicate with them.

He stood still, looking around him. He noticed one who was not kneeling or chanting, but watching him with quiet intensity; a lean and graceful man, with long dark hair and a look of intelligence that marked him out from the others. Ashurek met his eyes. The man glanced from side to side, then began to walk slowly forward.

His action seemed to break the spell that lay on the crowd. Two women ran towards Ashurek from another direction. Others followed, trying to pull them back, but that was enough to begin it. Suddenly people were rushing in from all sides, falling round his legs, grabbing at his cloak, wailing.

Ashurek fought to shake them off with bitter annoyance. He did not want to use his sword against unarmed people. As he struggled, a louder commotion began several yards away.

There were soldiers ploughing into the fringe of the crowd, their armour brilliant blue among the drab civilians. That instant told him almost everything about the world he had entered. He saw the glint of strangely-glowing swords and he saw men and women struck down and dragged away, screaming.

Panic spread. People were clawing at Ashurek in supplication. 'Back!' he yelled, sweeping his cloak in an arc. They fell over themselves to avoid him, and he seized the opportunity and began to force a path through them.

Through the confusion, he became aware of someone hanging onto his arm. He looked round angrily and saw it was the man who had started to approach him.

'Trust me, my lord, I'll take you to safety,' the stranger said, with a brief bow. 'My name's Jaia Keorn Silail.'

The language sounded strange and rough to Ashurek's ears, yet he understood it. At least Gregardreos had not let him down in that, he thought grudgingly.

'Quickly, then,' said Ashurek. Instinct told him that the offer was genuine; if not, Jaia Keorn Silail would soon regret it. And he needed a guide in this strange world.

'Follow me, my lord. Stay close.'

People moved out of their way as they went, but not fast enough for them to make much progress. Ashurek drew his sword and the effect was miraculous. A path melted before them, closing up again behind to hamper the soldiers, who seemed too busy with the crowd to have noticed Ashurek. Jaia Keorn led him into the shadows that sliced between two tall rows of buildings and the shouts and screams faded.

A few people tried to follow but a meaningful glare from Ashurek saw them off. Jaia Keorn wove through the back streets until they came to a narrow alley, where he led Ashurek down a flight of steps that ended at a door under a stone arch. From the barrels that almost concealed it, it appeared to be the cellar of an inn.

Jaia Keorn produced a key and unlocked the door.

'Inside, quickly,' he said.

'You first,' said Ashurek, ever cautious. Jaia Keorn obeyed and Ashurek followed under the arch. Darkness swallowed them, but chinks of faint light revealed that they were in a low stone passage, thick with dust and blocked at the far end by a stack of barrels. Jaia Keorn locked the door behind them, then met Ashurek's eyes. 'I'm keeping others out, not locking you in, my lord,' he said hurriedly.

'I gathered that. How long do you anticipate hiding in here?'

'As long as necessary,' he replied. 'I'm forced to live here, no-one's found me yet so I trust in Flaim that you will be also be safe from discovery.'

He went to the end of the passage and hauled one of the barrels aside. He squeezed through the gap and motioned Ashurek to do the same, then dragged the barrel back into place behind them.

Beyond was another door. It opened onto a cellar, lit only by a grey glow falling through a grille at street level. The air was thick with the smell of damp stone. There was a dull metallic thud as Jaia Keorn swung the door shut and locked it.

The cellar was some fifteen feet square, with a wooden screen across one corner, a mattress on the floor, an ancient cupboard and a table standing below the grille. On the opposite wall there was a mirror, opaque with age, hanging in a shallow alcove. Ashurek looked around with mild disgust. He had seen dungeons that were more habitable. In another corner there was a cage in which a creature mewed and fluttered. He immediately remembered the scarlet creature with an echo of dread, but this animal, although he could not see it clearly, seemed birdlike and roughly the size of a small child.

Ashurek took all this in and said quietly, 'Perhaps you will now explain why you took the trouble to help me.'

He turned back to Jaia Keorn and saw that the man had prostrated himself on his stomach and was lying flat out at Ashurek's feet.

'What are you doing?'

'I welcome you, my lord emissary of Flaim.'

Ashurek was silent for a moment. Then he said, 'Please stand up. I do not require obeisance.'

The man obeyed, rising with quick grace. 'Then tell me what you do require, my lord.'

'Enlightenment,' Ashurek said drily, half to himself, but Jaia Keorn took him literally and went to the table to light a fat candle. In the sudden flare of light, Ashurek saw him clearly for the first time. He was a head shorter than Ashurek and slightly round-shouldered, though his leanness gave an impression of height. There was a feminine grace in the way he moved, despite the look of poverty and toughness in his face. Ashurek judged him to be in his thirties, by Earth reckoning. Blue-black hair drifted to below his shoulders, while his eyes, though set in tired, pouchy flesh, were large and brilliantly blue.

They looked at each other for a few seconds until Ashurek broke the silence. 'You gave the impression that you know something about me. Do you know my name?'

'No, my lord,' he said apologetically. Although Ashurek would have defined his accent as low-caste, he spoke with the preciseness of one who had tried to educate himself out of poverty.

'I am Ashurek. Does that mean anything to you?'

Jaia Keorn looked confused, as if he was not sure how to answer. 'Forgive me, I only knew of your arrival, not your name –'

'Stop,' said Ashurek. 'Let us begin again. I want to understand this. First, tell me where I am.'

'In Niankan-Pel.'

'Which is where?'

The man seemed more taken aback than ever. 'It is the capital of Palan.'

'And Palan is on a world named Jhensit?'

'Yes.'

'Ah.' He breathed out softly, thinking, *So Gregardreos finally sent me to the right place . . . but what was that other city?* 'Your countrymen out there were behaving as if I were some sort of god, one they knew. Can you explain that to me?'

'They thought you were Flaim himself.'

'Flaim?' he said, hoping Jaia Keorn would elaborate.

'My lord, you appeared from nowhere, with a face and form that belong to no mortal we've ever seen, the face of the god; they can hardly be blamed for making that assumption.' His lips twitched with a brief smile, a hint of superiority. 'I believe I'm privileged to know better.'

'Indeed? And what is it you know?'

'That you are not Flaim, but his emissary, sent in answer to our prayers.'

This answer shocked Ashurek, but he was well-practised in hiding his thoughts and remained expressionless. 'How did you come by this information?'

'I had a vision last night.' Jaia Keorn swept his hair over his shoulder, an affected gesture that seemed a habit. 'I saw a figure, all burning black around the edges, and the knowledge simply came to me; Flaim was sending his messenger to us! But I may not be the only one who had the vision. That was why I wanted to be there to meet you before anyone else realised! The others too busy being terrified to understand what was happening –'

'But you knew the truth,' Ashurek said drily.

Jaia Keorn nodded, unable to hide his sense of self-satisfaction. 'I pray so, my lord Ashurek.'

Ashurek walked slowly across the room, pulling off his gloves and dropping them on the table as he did so, and went to look out of the grille. He could see nothing except the base of a grey wall, but distant shouts and screams floated from outside. His appearance had started a riot, which was apparently continuing. The thought depressed him. Turning away, he seated himself on a bench and leaned on the table. 'Jaia Keorn Silail –'

'Just Keorn, my lord. I hope to prove a friend.'

'Very well. Keorn, imagine that whoever I may be, I know nothing of Jhensit or the gods you worship. How would you explain things to me?'

Jaia Keorn nodded slightly, as if telling himself that although Ashurek's behaviour was unexpected, Flaim's emissary was hardly likely to behave predictably and must be humoured. 'Look at this.' He lit another candle and went to the alcove in the opposite wall. At his touch, the age-spotted mirror swung aside to reveal a door of metal filigree over a dark cavity roughly eighteen inches wide and two feet high. Light flowed into the cavity and Ashurek saw that it was a shrine.

Inside was a statue, an image of a god that bore some physical resemblance to Ashurek. The face was dark as earth or thunder, slender and savage. Lightning forked from the fingers, black clouds swirled round the body and the feet were tree roots.

'This is the god Flaim, who rules the earth and the weather. We are forbidden to worship him, but I have always been his loyal servant and I shall remain so.' He bowed, then closed the shrine and returned to the table, blowing out the second candle as he sat down opposite Ashurek. A skein of white smoke coiled from the wick, oily-fragrant.

'Why is your god forbidden?' Ashurek asked.

'The Pels have to worship the Siol's god instead, Eyos, the god of the sky. That's the Hyalon's command.'

Ashurek did not believe in gods as such, but he reserved judgement. He had seen too much of supernatural beings to assume that Jhensit's deities were only figments of the imagination. 'The Hyalon?'

'Our ruler. He lives in the upper city. You are in Niankan-Pel, my lord; the Neatru family who rule us live in Niankan-Siol, as near the sky as they can manage.' There was scorn in his voice. 'The Siols believe that the sky is clean and pure; earth is filthy and demonic, and so are we.'

'So,' Ashurek said thoughtfully, 'they regard Flaim as a demon and those who follow him as devil-worshippers?'

'Exactly.' Keorn looked at him with startled eyes, as if he could not believe he was having to explain this. 'It wasn't always like this. The Siols used to tolerate us, as long as we worked and didn't complain. It's only in the last ten years, since the new Hyalon took the throne, that we must renounce Flaim and follow Eyos, on pain of punishment . . .'

'And you do not believe in this god of the sky?'

'Eyos!' Keorn seemed to forget his reverence for Ashurek in a rush of bitterness. 'They worship the sky and pretend it's a god! But Flaim *rules* the sky as well as the earth, how can they be separate? But that's the way things are. Anyone suspected of worshipping Flaim is beaten or arrested, or worse. The Pels are the Siols' slaves, and if the earth is a hell it's because *they've* made it so.'

It was a story all too familiar to Ashurek. He had himself been the instrument of such oppression in the Gorethrian Empire, to his bitter regret. 'You cannot stop people believing in something by making laws against it. It can have the opposite effect.'

Keorn nodded eagerly. 'My lord, you understand, don't you? I can see why Flaim would be angry with us, turning away from him, but it is under sufferance and there are many who still keep the faith in secret. I have never been disloyal, I hide myself away rather than lie to the damned Siols! But now you are here.'

'So it seems.' Ashurek folded his arms, distancing himself from Keorn's growing fervour. 'And why do you imagine I have come here?'

'To help us!' The Pel leaned forward and clasped Ashurek's arm. His eyes were feverish, his touch hot and unduly familiar. 'Flaim has listened, he's sent you to lead us and overthrow the Siols, bring the Neatrus and their stinking city down into the dirt!'

The words hit Ashurek like vitriol, a cold shock followed by a slow, vicious burning. It was just such violence that he had foresworn, and the prospect of such help being expected of him was unspeakably repugnant. Was it coincidence or had he been manoeuvred into this nightmare by Gregardreos? No, the High Master was not that subtle.

Ashurek said nothing. He looked at Keorn's hand and then at his face. The Pel suddenly saw something terrible in the ice-green light of Ashurek's eyes, and he withdrew his hand as if he had been burned. He was trembling slightly, his fervour doused and his confidence shaken.

'Forgive me, my lord,' he whispered. He shifted restlessly on the bench. 'I – I – you must think me a bad host. I can only offer poor food and wine, but anything I have is yours.'

'Some refreshment would be very welcome.'

Keorn looked mildly surprised that a god's emissary would accept the offer, but he stood up quickly, glad of a chance to ease the tension. As he busied himself between the cupboard and the table, setting out a meal, Ashurek brooded on what had happened. The simple fact of his appearance in Jhensit had already provoked a riot, perhaps deaths. And worst of all there was Silvren; he could not forget that last, ghastly painting in the book. Had he been mockingly tormented about her fate or merely shown the truth?

He was in a maze and there was no simple way to the centre. He knew that the only way to find her was by following his 'agreement' with Gregardreos, and in that the help of someone like Jaia Keorn could be invaluable. There was nothing to be gained by alienating him. Despite the Pel's religious fanaticism, his wild assumption that he had been 'chosen' by Flaim to take part in some great design, Ashurek did not actually dislike him.

There's an advantage in letting him believe that I'm some kind of demi-god. That would be an easy way to control him . . . but not an honest one.

Keorn fussed over the meal to such a degree that Ashurek almost expected a banquet. What he was eventually served was a cold mash, possibly of vegetables and meat, although it was too heavily spiced for him to be sure. With it there were leathery circles of bread and a goblet of thick, bitter wine. The food was not to his taste but Ashurek was hungry and, as long as it did not poison him, he would need the strength.

In the shadows, the animal in the cage mewed faintly and plucked at the bars.

Ashurek took a long draught of the wine and looked at the bubbles floating on the dark surface. 'You mentioned a vision, Keorn. Do you have such visions often?'

The Pel looked uneasy. 'No. Very rarely, and this was the first clear one I've ever had.'

'So you could accept that although you correctly predicted my arrival, you could be wrong about who I am?'

'I– I'm not sure of your meaning.'

'What would you say if I told you that I am not Flaim's messenger, I am only a man, and that I know absolutely nothing about your gods except what you have told me?'

Jaia Keorn paused with a piece of bread half-way to his mouth. 'It would depend why you were saying it, my lord.'

Ashurek smiled thinly. 'Because it is true. I came from a world called Ikonus because a Way from Jhensit was haunting our world. I wished to see if Jhensit meant us any harm.'

It was a gross simplification of the truth, but he had no intention of telling Keorn everything. The man went on staring at him, tiny candle-flames burning in his irises. 'I'm sorry, my lord, but I don't know what you mean.'

'You know nothing about the Way between our worlds?'

'No, I've never heard of such a thing.'

'This, then.' Ashurek proceeded to tell him about his arrival in the deserted city, his fight with the creature and the strange book it had produced. As he spoke, Keorn stopped eating and went increasingly pale.

'I have never seen or heard of the things you describe,' he said when Ashurek had finished. He swallowed some wine, then pushed his hair out of his face. 'Now I feel like an ignorant fool, and not fit to be your helper. No. My father was a mystic, he could have answered these questions, but I inherited only a hundredth of his talent.'

'Where is your father?' Ashurek asked, expecting to be told that he was dead.

'Miles away, at the – well, a very long way from here. I haven't seen him for years, he may not still be alive.' His voice was razor-edged with bitterness. 'He had to flee Niankan because the damned Siols believed his skills meant he was a witch – a devil-worshipper, as you said. Damn the bloody Hyalon!'

'Is there anyone else who would know?'

'Not that I know of.'

'Never mind. I need you, Keorn, to guide me round the city and the customs of your land, but I wish to be honest with you. I am human, even if I appear otherwise. I wish no harm to your world, only to find Silvren and return home. I can take no part in any uprising against your rulers; that is none of my concern. With this in mind, are you still willing to help me? If not, I shall leave at once and find what I need elsewhere.'

He saw several changes of expression pass over Jaia Keorn's face. There was consternation, then a kind of withdrawal, his lower lip thrust out sulkily for a time. Finally his eyes cleared and he gazed at Ashurek with what resembled, disconcertingly, adoration.

'I don't know whether you are testing me, Lord Ashurek, but my mind was made up to serve you as soon as I saw you and that hasn't changed.' He smiled. 'If you say you are a man, I believe you. It may be that Flaim hasn't revealed his purposes to you, and you don't yet know who you truly are!'

With the unrest on the streets and the difficulty of Ashurek going unnoticed, they could not go out before nightfall. Jaia Keorn gave up his mattress to Ashurek and lay on the bare floor, wrapped in a cloak.

Ashurek was suddenly aware of how much the transition between worlds had exhausted him, yet he could not sleep. The Pel's words kept echoing through his mind; he was obviously determined to believe what he wanted to, whatever Ashurek said. Yet there was the sinister, nagging fear that Keorn might be right.

Eventually Ashurek slipped into a half-doze beset by unpleasantly vivid dreams. There was a face sketched in olive-green brush strokes across the whole universe, and he was suspended for eternity under its mocking gaze. Silvren was rushing towards him across the void, her arms outstretched, but just as she came close enough to touch him she fell into nothingness. Somewhere below him, Mellorn had become a grown woman, dark-skinned and golden-haired, and was striding across an infinite range of black mountains . . .

He was woken by a faint cry, repeated over and over again; a pitiful animal noise that was almost human. No daylight fell through the window grille. There was a candle burning in the alcove, and against the light he saw Jaia Keorn standing at the open shrine, with the cage in front of him.

Chanting in a whisper, he reached into the cage and hauled out the struggling animal. Feathers fluttered in the light, but its shape seemed wrong for a bird. It fought him, but with the dexterity of practice Keorn pinned it down on top of the bars with one arm.

In his other hand there was a strange, two-pronged weapon the length of a dagger. It gleamed like oil as he raised it, outlined by coppery fire. With a swift movement he brought it down on the creature's chest, but there was no sound of metal crunching into flesh; only an sharp, fierce *snap*. Blue sparks showered into the air. In the brief incandescence, the animal convulsed, uttered a scream and died.

Ashurek was not unduly shocked by the sacrifice. He had seen far worse things when he had been an officer serving in the Gorethrian army, and unspeakable obscenities perpetrated by demons. But there was a coldness in the pit of his stomach as the creature, now lifeless, was bundled back into the cage.

'Flaim, accept this sacrifice.' Keorn's voice was audible now and he sounded breathless with emotion. 'We beseech you, reveal your will to your emissary Lord Ashurek, let him lead us and save us. We are unworthy but do not destroy us. We aren't the ones who've turned our faces against you in favour of the false god. We are the faithful. Preserve Jhensit. Do not let us all vanish into the maelstrom.'

And the image that came into Ashurek's mind was that of demons from his own Earth; creatures of malignant evil with which he had been forced to bargain to his cost. That was another vow he had made, never to summon the help of such vile creatures, however great his need. But would he break that vow too, if Silvren's life depended on it? It seemed that despite all his good intentions, at heart he had not changed and perhaps never could.

He leaned up on his elbows and said, 'You are a fool, Keorn.'

The Pel started, then looked round with a strange half-smile. 'Why do you call me that?'

'Because you don't know what you're playing with. You worship Flaim, sacrifice to him and invoke him. What will you do if he answers your summons? Stronger men than you have been destroyed by asking the help of such beings.'

Jaia Keorn came to his side, knelt down and ran his finger along Ashurek's dark, slender hand. 'But Flaim *has* answered my prayers,' he said softly. 'He has sent me you.'

5

In Flaim's Domain

'Shai Fea, what's wrong? Keep walking, you mustn't stop!'

Her uncle's voice sounded thin and distant through the roaring of her fear. Shai Fea could not reply. Terror had rushed up at her out of nowhere and she was paralysed, clinging to the handrail with every gust of wind threatening to fling her out into space.

The glowing structures of Niankan-Siol were massed above them, the hard crust of the earth floated beneath. and in between there was only, the vertiginous gulf of darkness. *A Hyalet of the Ruling House, afraid of heights?* It was unthinkable. She had lived with the height of Niankan-Siol all her life; the fear of falling had only been an abstract one, and official trips to the lower city had been made in the safety of a lift. But now she was fleeing for her life, and the only escape route was this staircase, plunging in a seemingly endless spiral around an outlying strut. If she had anticipated the dizziness that would seize her, she would never have begun the descent. Now it was too late, they were half-way down and the stair had become a helix in which she and Tean Mon were doomed to circle round and round forever.

Thoughts swam through the blinding vertigo. *I wish I'd never left the palace. If I'd known this would happen . . . What made me think I had the courage?*

Tean Mon had engineered her escape within a day,

making her swap places with a maid. He knew which of her servants were most loyal to her, which guards could be bribed to turn a blind eye, and he had rearranged the duty rosters so that they were placed all along his planned route. Later, when the Hyalet's disappearance was discovered, they would be punished; but they had wanted her to escape. They loved her enough to take the risk.

All the way through the long corridors of the palace and the walkways outside Shai Fea had gone with her heart pounding thickly in her throat, expecting to be challenged at any second. Normally they would have used a sky-carriage to make such a long journey, but tonight that was too much of a risk. When a carriage had skimmed past on its cables Shai Fea had almost leapt out of her skin. The city had crackled and shone around her; her home no longer, it felt as cold and indifferent to her as she knew the lower city would feel. They had reached the spiral stair safely, yet it was her own faint heart that betrayed her.

I belong nowhere, she thought, hanging onto the rail as the fear plunged though her. *If I move, I'll fall. I'd like to die but I'm scared. I'm scared . . .*

'Take my hand,' said Tean Mon. 'Follow me, one step after another . . .'

She must have obeyed him, although she remembered nothing about the rest of the descent. The next she knew she was stepping onto firm ground, drenched with cold sweat and almost weeping with shame.

'I'm sorry, Uncle, so sorry,' she said. 'I don't know what happened to me.'

'Are you all right, my dear?' said Tean Mon. 'You are as white as a ghost.'

'I'm much better now.' She tried to smile, to reassure him as he had reassured her, but the thread of terror was still inside her and she knew she would never be quite free of it again.

They were at the base of the strut, within a high wall. The two guards did not seem surprised to see them, but were ready to help them swap their blue Siol cloaks for ones of a drab Pel style. Then the guards unlocked the gate and let them through without a word.

They were free. The night air throbbed and sighed around them, carrying the rank scents of the lower city. Shai Fea felt as if the darkness were blowing right through her and she knew that she was a fugitive, that she could never go back. All her life she had been treated as if she were a bird made of spun glass; delicate, beautiful, existing at the centre of the universe. Now she felt anonymous and very vulnerable.

Her uncle put his arm round her shoulders. His face was hidden by the hood of his cloak.

'So far so good, but we must make haste.'

'Where are we going?'

He was reluctant to answer, she could tell. He led her away from the high wall that enclosed the strut and along a deserted street. The slabs reflected the diffuse glow of the upper city, but the buildings towering around them were lightless. This must have been a magnificent city once, before the sky-city was built. Now it was falling into ruin and the stench of the streets filled her with disgust. This was Flaim's domain, dark and terrifying.

'Niankan-Pel is not an easy place in which to hide, not for Siols,' said Tean Mon. 'You must understand, the place I'm taking you to, I have no choice, it's the only place that's safe.'

She hung onto his arm, but there was something in his tone that only increased her alarm. Although she had passed through the lower city in royal processions, it had never been on foot, and now she walked gingerly as if the earth's poison might soak through her soles. The streets were almost deserted but for the occasional hooded figure, rushing along surreptitiously. Once they saw a group of soldiers crossing the street in the distance, but Tean Mon pulled her into the darkness of a doorway until they had gone. The atmosphere was so thick and silent that she could hardly bear it.

'Why is it so quiet?' she whispered.

'There is a curfew.'

'Why? Because of me?'

'No, no. There was a disturbance in the city earlier, some fanatics of Flaim started a riot.'

She shuddered. 'But there are people breaking the curfew.'

Her uncle shrugged, 'As they will. As we are doing.'

'I am more afraid of being in this place than of being captured,' she said, angry with herself. 'Why? I have seen Niankan-Pel before, it is not so terrible . . . is it?'

Tean Mon understood her feelings, though he did not seem to be suffering in the same way. He said gently, 'Fea, the part of Niankan-Pel that you have seen when riding in processions is not the true lower city. Those streets are where the merchants live and they are kept pristine for the Ruling Family's use. This is the real lower city and it is poor and dirty, I'm afraid. But no, it is not so terrible.'

Only then did it strike her that Tean Mon, who had no more cause to be familiar with the lower city than she, knew exactly where he was going. 'Uncle, how do you know your way about? Have you been here before?'

'Yes, many times.'

'Why?'

He sighed. There was more to his uneasiness than the anxiety of being followed. 'Fea, listen to me. There's only one hiding place for us, but when I take you there, I fear you will lose all the love you have for me. You may hate me for it. Even if you could forgive me, certainly you will never respect me again.'

'You're talking nonsense, Uncle,' she said nervously. 'How could a place make me hate you? Don't be silly!'

'Believe me, it can.' He sounded weary, and he pressed the back of his hand to his cheeks as if they were burning. 'But your safety is more important to me than anything else.'

Eyos help me, she pleaded silently. *Please give me strength.*

He led her deeper into the backstreets, through twisting alleys where the darkness was chill and heavy as mud. She could hear the river, which she had only seen from a distance as a sluggish brown snake. Surely they would not have to cross it? But no, Tean Mon was leading her towards a tall, narrow house, squeezed in between others. She could see no detail in the darkness, only the glint of arched windows. It looked cold and hollow, a hovel after the luxury of the palace, but all she could hope for was being taken to a warm, dry room where she could lock herself away and rest.

Tean Mon, however, avoided the front door and led her into a narrow alley running between that house and the next. Shai Fea let out an exclamation of disgust. There was mud and vegetation under her feet, and the stench of the river made her feel sick.

'Hush!' he said. 'What's wrong?'

'I can't walk on the bare earth! It's like touching the devil himself!'

'Oh, Eyos.' He sounded as if he were almost in tears. 'Fea, it's all right, it can't hurt you. Think of your brother.'

It was the right thing to say and it steadied her. Only for Elatiat Harn's sake could she bear this.

The back of the house was fused into a mass of rock in which, concealed by an overhanging bush, there was a door. He tapped on it in an odd rhythm, like a code. There was a pause, then a voice, muffled by the thick wood, called, 'Who's there?'

'You know who it is, Tsin Liah. Open up, quickly!'

A skein of light crept out, and with it a stink that made Shai Fea cough. It was the smell of wet earth, of vegetation, animal excrement and the rankness of flowers.

A woman's face appeared in the aperture. She was a Pel, tall and plump, with hair scraped back from a round, slightly wrinkled face. 'Come in, quickly. I can't believe how many of you have ignored the curfew! Did you hear about the riot? They're saying Flaim manifested himself right in the middle of Ochre Street – never heard such rubbish, but they don't need much to set them off, do they?'

Shai Fea was shocked to hear a Pel address her Uncle with such familiarity, showing no deference whatsoever. Tean Mon ushered her through the doorway and Shai Fea found herself in a low, narrow cave, the air chilly and thick with the awful earth-stench. Her mind recoiled. She hugged herself, silently invoking Eyos. If she tried to speak she would scream.

The woman shut and locked the door behind them. 'Well, my lord, this is a surprise. Can't stay away, can you?'

'I'm not here for pleasure, Liah. This is far more important. We need somewhere to hide, and this is the only place I have.'

Pleasure? Shai Fea thought incredulously. *What enjoyment could he find here?* She had heard sickening stories that some nobles had Pel mistresses, but she had never believed them. Tean Mon would not do such a thing.

'Something to do with this young lady?' Tsin Liah's rough accent grated on the Hyalet's ears. 'Good Flaim, she doesn't look like a bad girl, but you never can tell. What's she done?'

Shai Fea was stunned. She was a Hyalet, no-one spoke to her like that! 'I have done nothing!' she snapped. 'And I would thank you not to speak of me as if I were a child!'

'Fea . . .' said Tean Mon soothingly. 'Please, Liah, there must be no questions. You won't even know we're here, but if you could bring us some food . . .'

The Pel's Plump face creased in a smile. 'No trouble. You can please yourself, of course, but you're going to be awfully uncomfortable down there. How long is it for?'

'I wish I had a choice,' he said, shaking his head unhappily. 'And I don't know, I just don't know.'

He placed a hand on Shai Fea's back and began to guide

her along the cave, which curved down into a roughly-hewn flight of steps. She held her cloak over her mouth, trying not to breathe the miasma. Tsin Liah remained by the door and when they were out of earshot, Shai Fea said, 'She knows you very well, doesn't she?'

Tean Mon avoided her eyes. He looked desperately ashamed. 'Yes. She's a good woman, a good friend.'

'I am not a fool,' she hissed. 'I am not that innocent. She is your mistress, isn't she?'

He looked startled. 'Oh, my dear. No, she isn't, she only keeps the door. This is far worse than that.'

'Worse? I don't understand. What is this awful place?'

'Try to understand,' he said weakly.

The steps led down and down, lit by a dim green light filtering from below. They were underground, inside the devil's realm. Only Shai Fea's upbringing enabled her to control the hysteria welling in her stomach.

The stairs ended. A verdant glow flooded her eyes, and the air was thick with odorous dew and sinister rustling noises.

Shai Fea stood with her hand clutching her chest, unable to breathe. Some sort of cave. . . She had never seen anything like it before and it made no sense. Why were there trees here? The cave ceiling was thick with foliage and hanging vines, through which electric lamps shone like a multitude of moons. Their soft light illuminated everything that Eyos had taught them to shun and revile, all the creeping, crawling, sap-filled life that belonged to Flaim.

Banks of grass and moss undulated away through masses of shrubs. Their leaves were dark green mottled with gold, sharp as daggers, dripping water. Everything shone and sparkled. A chill draught stirred the trees, and she could hear the distant trickle of water.

And there were flowers. Not the brittle, scentless glass ornaments that adorned the palace, but livid blooms hanging on stems, purple and brown and feverish red. The purple ones were like open mouths with lolling yellow tongues. Yet there was a man actually on his hands and knees among them . . . digging?

Unseen creatures rustled in the undergrowth. She thought she caught a glimpse of a hairy four-legged thing, rooting in the grass, and her stomach turned over. This was a nightmare. All this talk of Flaim appearing, and now she was suddenly in the devil's domain . . .

'Is she all right?'

Tsin Liah's voice reached her through an echoing tunnel. Her uncle's arms were round her and he was lowering her gently to the ground. She retched drily then began to cough, fighting for breath.

'I feared this might happen. It's the power of Eyos's teaching over the mind. Can you bring some water?'

When her head cleared, she found herself lying on a mound of moss, her uncle sitting next to her. Tsin Liah had gone, but Tean Mon was holding a cup to her lips. She sat up and sipped at the water, then bowed her head onto her knees, shuddering.

'What is this horrible place?'

'Fea, don't you know?' he said, upset and concerned. 'It's a garden.'

'A garden? And you come here for pleasure? I don't believe it! How could you, how could you?'

'I said you would hate me for this.' He sounded deeply ashamed.

'I don't hate you,' she whispered. 'How could I hate you? I just don't understand. I thought you loved the sky-god. Sometimes I think there is no-one left who will not betray me, in one way or another.'

'Dear Eyos,' he said wretchedly.

'You cannot be a Flaimian, you *can't*!'

'No, I don't worship Flaim! This is nothing to do with that. I so want you to understand, but it's hard to explain. Call it my weakness, but I cannot believe that the good earth belongs to the devil. I need . . .'

'What?'

He looked away. His shoulders were slumped. She had

never seen this him like this before, and it terrified and revolted her. 'We live in a cold place, all crystal and metal,' he said. 'No living thing is allowed there, except birds and silukians. It is unnatural. I crave to touch the grass, to smell the scent of real flowers and stroke the animals. To feel under my fingers not the naked skin of some creature that will grow wings and fly away, but soft fur . . .'

'It is disgusting.'

'I can't expect you to understand. But, Fea, this place is not the only hidden garden in Niankan-Pel. And I am not the only Siol who comes in secret to touch the earth. Look around . . .'

There were two or three figures moving through the garden, and despite their dark cloaks she could tell by their bearing that they were Siols. Anonymous, disguised, finding surreptitious pleasure in breaking the commandments of Eyos.

'It's perverted. It's heresy. If the Hyalon knew . . .'

'Exactly. That's why the gardens are so well hidden. I'm not proud of it,' he said unhappily. 'I would have done anything for you not to have found this out. Have you nothing to say to me?'

'You are not the person I thought you were,' she said in a small, icy voice.

'No. I am not.' Absently, he pulled a tall, pendulous flower towards him and breathed its scent. A large insect fell out onto his lap, and he brushed it away onto the ground. 'Perhaps one day I'll be able to explain it in full. I – I had cause to deal with Pels once, and they became friends. I realised there was nothing evil in the earth, the god they worship isn't a devil . . . We are all on the same world, Pels and Siols. There is no separate salvation for the privileged.

'In truth, my dear, I am a terrible coward. I live a double life and I close my mind to the things I cannot bear. I am not the only one, but that's no excuse.'

Shai Fea wanted to ask why he had worked with Pels,

but she had had too many shocks. Nothing was what she had thought it, and even Tean Mon, her rock, was falling apart before her eyes.

'I thought I knew you, Uncle, and now I find out it was all a lie,' she cried. 'I'm completely alone!'

'No, Fea, please.' His voice sounded old and cracked, as if he were dying. Who was she to criticise him for being weak, when she was no stronger herself? She still loved him. That was why she felt so hurt.

She turned away from him and stared into the depths of the garden. 'But what am I going to do? I can't stand this place and you say there's nowhere else. How can I help my brother?' She rubbed tears out of her eyes.

When he did not reply, she swung round to look at him. He was leaning forward, one fist pressed to his chest, his eyes closed and his face the colour of wet ash.

'Uncle!' she cried. 'What's wrong, is it your heart?'

'No,' he said, swallowing hard. 'It is nothing – just tiredness.' He sucked in a huge breath and relaxed. His eyes opened, pale blue and watery. He patted her hand. 'I am all right, my dear. Listen, I must go and speak with Tsin Liah for a few minutes. I won't be long, try to rest and don't worry.'

She gripped his thin fingers. 'Please hurry back,' she said.

Shai Fea did not know she had fallen asleep until she woke up suddenly, with no idea of why she was lying on a soft green surface under a scattering of dim lights. She could hear a voice, her mother's voice, whispering, '. . . and it would take only one Siol to decide that his loyalty to the Hyalon is greater than his desire to keep this place secret, only one anonymous message to bring the Satrans here. And Tean Mon thinks you are safe? If only I could . . .'

The voice faded and Shai Fea sat up with a cry, confused. The figure beside her was the Pel woman, not her mother.

'It's all right, it's only me, dear,' said Tsin Liah. Her round face had a kindly expression.

'I thought – I thought my mother –' She looked around wildly. 'I must have been dreaming. I didn't know where I was.' Taking a deep breath, she noticed that the green scent no longer seemed quite so unpleasant.

'You're safe. You've been asleep hours. You must've been exhausted, poor thing.'

'Hours? Where's my uncle? He is here, isn't he?'

'No, dear. He went out last night, and he hasn't come back yet.'

Shai Fea stared at her in disbelief. '*Went out?* He can't have done! He wouldn't leave me alone here!' She remembered the terrible cold things she had said to him. Had she hurt him so much that he had simply abandoned her in despair? 'He said he was going to talk to you, so what have you done with him?'

'Now, now. Give me a chance. He couldn't tell you he was going out, because you'd never have let him leave, would you? Look, he lives in the upper city, surrounded by Siols, people like glass spikes he calls them, having to watch every word he says to them. He can never say what's really on his mind. So why do you think he comes here? He can say what he likes to me and all I'll do is shrug and say "Never mind". He can tell the animals what he likes and they won't answer back!'

'Just tell me what he said. Please,' Shai Fea said faintly.

'All he would say was that he had . . . how did he put it? Received some information, which he had to go and investigate. You weren't to worry. He'd be back as soon as he could, so I said I'd take care of you in the meantime.'

Shai Fea took this in incredulously. What did it mean, how could he desert her? 'But it's been hours . . .'

'Then you'll have to be patient. Now, I'm going to bring you something to eat, then I'll show you round the garden. Flaim knows what these Eyostians teach you up there. You'll like it when you've got used to it.'

'I doubt it.' The garden seemed so moist, so *alive*. A silvery-grey animal with long ears was grazing its way towards her and Shai Fea watched it with a mixture of fear and fascination. 'I couldn't eat anything that grew in this dirty place,' she said. 'Please leave me alone.'

Tsin Liah stood up, shaking her head good-naturedly. 'I don't know where you Siols think food comes from. Do you think the cooks spin it out of air? However fancy it looks when you eat it, there's only one place it comes from, and that's out of the earth. I'll be back, and you'll be glad of a meal.' With that she walked away.

Shai Fea felt damp and dirty and she ached all over. *I have been a complete fool,* she thought bleakly. *I imagined, if I could only get away, I'd find the person who killed Wedren Lan as if by magic.* But the city was huge and she felt like a lost child, without the faintest idea of how to begin. And her uncle was risking his life for her sake. *How could I be so stupid?* Pulling her cloak round her, she huddled herself miserably on the moss to wait for Tean Mon to return, trying not to think of the words her mother had said in the dream.

She waited a long time.

6

The Garden of Blood

Almost from the moment Ashurek stepped into the street, he felt that he was being followed. He scanned the shadows between the buildings, but he could see no-one. It was more a feeling of being haunted than of a physical presence.

Jaia Keorn did not seem aware of it. 'They've called a curfew, so we shall have to be careful,' he said. 'I know the pattern of Satran patrols. I used to be in the Satrans myself.'

'A deserter?' Ashurek suggested mildly.

The Pel grimaced. 'The day they dispatched me to arrest a member of my own family, I deserted without shame. Now I try not to show my face in daylight, if I can avoid it.'

Inconspicuous in hooded cloaks, Ashurek and Jaia Keorn moved through the towering shadows of Niankan-Pel. A diffuse pearly light from above lit their way. Ashurek looked up and saw, not the open sky, but a layer of mansions and palaces floating several hundred feet above the rooftops. The translucent, resinous-looking material of which they were constructed gave an impression of airy delicacy, though he swiftly realised that they were not defying gravity but resting on stilts rooted in the ground. The area covered by the upper city was far smaller than the sprawling city below, perhaps two square miles, but the effect was awesome. The ethereal halls glowed with pale tints of aquamarine, blue and soft yellow, with here and there a blush of rose. Complex walkways threaded between them. There was an alien quality to the radiance, akin to the energy of sorcery. But unlike sorcery, this light was flat and unchanging. Once or twice a shining carriage slid overhead with a metallic hiss, scattering sparks.

Ashurek could not help comparing it with the city of his birth, Shalekahh, which had been all sparkling white elegance. The resemblance was superficial – his own city had been built firmly on the ground with no aid from sorcery and with, to his mind, infinitely more taste – but he sensed a similar philosophy in the construction. A display of confident superiority.

'That's Niankan-Siol,' Keorn said as they walked, 'where the Ruling Family and the aristocrats live. The city of Eyos.' He pointed up at a pale blue-green structure of breathtaking size and delicacy, soaring high above the surrounding mansions. Even its massive base was decorated with elaborate symbols of blue, gold and white, and was studded with small windows – spyholes for the Rulers to watch what went on beneath? 'That's the Hyalon's palace, the House of Neatru. You can't see from here, but directly underneath, on the ground, are the Satrans' barracks.'

'I am impressed,' said Ashurek. 'There is obviously great skill and learning in Jhensit. Even my ancestors never thought to build a city in the clouds. But why *was* it built?'

Jaia Keorn gave a short laugh. 'A mixture of skill and learning, arrogance and stupidity. Three hundred years ago there was only the lower city. There are hills all round us, which were forested once, but had been cleared to make farmland. At some stage, they cut down one tree too many. There was a huge rainstorm and all the mud came sliding off the hills and flooded the city. Thousands drowned. The Flaimians said it was the revenge of Flaim on the worshippers of Eyos; the Eyostians said it was

Flaim's doing, because they regard him as the devil.'

'It seems that Flaim takes the blame for everything, ' said Ashurek. 'I begin to sympathise with him.'

The Pel gave him an odd glance and went on. 'Afterwards, the Ruling Family ordered the creation of a new city above the ground.'

'Would it not have made more sense to build a new city elsewhere?'

Keorn pulled a sour face. 'That's the one thing they've never had, the Siols, sense. It was their chance to prove a point, that they were superior to the Flaimians. They raised themselves above the mud, left us to wallow in it. That was the real beginning of the separation between us, and our slavery to them.'

'In my world, we only enslaved other races, not our own people,' Ashurek said with dark irony.

Jaia Keorn frowned, and Ashurek feared his chance remark would spark off questions which he had no wish to answer. But the Pel only said, 'But you must believe that slavery is wrong.'

'Oh yes,' said Ashurek. 'I agree completely.'

'The clearing of the old city and the building of the new expended thousands more lives. Once they were content to work us to death. Now we've all got to worship the right god as well, and even then they're not satisfied . . .'

Ashurek listened indifferently as Keorn went on. Although he needed to learn about Jhensit, he had no wish to involve himself in its problems. He was convinced that Jhensit's connection with Ikonus was linked to Silvren's fate; once he had solved the mystery he could set about searching for her in earnest. Nothing else mattered.

The houses soared around them like row upon row of decaying cathedrals with eyeless sockets for windows. The roofs were dusted with opaline radiance. A few curfew-breakers darted from shadow to shadow, but otherwise the streets were so quiet that he could hear the faint hum emitted by the upper city.

A breeze sprang up, carrying the stench of sewage, wet stone, and alien vegetation. Ashurek wondered what lay beyond the city.

Jaia Keorn took a road that wound uphill and gave onto a wider vista of Niankan-Pel. A river lay below them, wide and sludge-brown, with dwellings crowded chaotically on the banks. Silt lay in the streets, and the atmosphere of dilapidation and desertion was overwhelming. The windows were square mouths, silently exhaling lost histories, lost lives, of which Ashurek knew nothing.

The edge of Niankan-Siol just spanned the river, standing in sublime detachment above its squalor. Across the river valley, beyond the city, hills massed against the sky. No moon or stars shone through the clouds, which seemed to have a weird, purplish aura. The sky felt wrong, although Ashurek could not define why.

'Ochre River,' said Keorn. 'This part of the city took the worst of the mudslide, and has been flooded on and off ever since. No-one much lives here now, only beggars, hermits, people who've given up on life.'

'I would have thought this a safer place to hide than your cellar.'

Keorn snorted. 'Nowhere less safe. The Satrans are round there all the time, hunting Flaimians. They've a hold on this city like a fish in an aueret's beak.'

'Are the Satrans Pels, or Siols?'

'Both. Officers are mostly Siols, the men all Pels. If you see any in sky-blue and gold, they're all from the upper city, the Hyalon's personal regiment. The rest wear deep blue.'

Ashurek said thoughtfully, 'But the Siols' power is obviously more than military. What of the sorcerous power that lights their city?'

'I don't know what you mean by sorcerous. If you mean you don't understand it, neither do I. There's a place called the White Dome . . .' The Pel sounded vague, then disgust came into his voice. 'But that's a prison, though the Siols try to pretend it isn't. It's where I'd be sent if I were ever caught, and no-one who goes in ever comes out.'

'Where is this White Dome?'

'Outside the city. We're on the wrong side to see it.' He added shortly, 'There are people I know in there.'

Ashurek was silent for a few minutes, looking around him. 'There is a great sense of age on this city, of imminent death. I think the grip your Hyalon has on this place is not so much a show of strength as a sign of absolute terror, and there's something you're not telling me. What is the truth about Jhensit?'

The Pel looked away across the river. There was no sound except the gurgle and slap of the water. His lips thinned, and eventually he said, 'Only Flaim knows that.'

He began to walk on but Ashurek paused, again feeling that there was a presence watching them, stalking them. He caught up with Keorn.

'There is someone following us.'

Jaia Keorn raised his head and listened. 'No. If there was something there, I'd have known by now.'

'There is someone, and they've followed us since we left your home. I thought you were the prescient one.'

Keorn looked up at the tall Gorethrian, his eyes glittering blue under the edge of his hood. 'My talents are very minor. I believe you, my lord. Where are they?'

The Pel drew a weapon from his belt, the strange two-bladed dagger with which he had made his sacrifice to Flaim. For a few minutes they went on in silence, keeping to the shadows. It seemed to Ashurek that the presence was ahead of them now, preparing to step out into their path.

He grabbed Jaia Keorn's arm.

There was a scuffling noise ahead. A figure in a voluminous cloak fled out of an alley, hood back and hair flying, only to be pursued and seized by six others robed in black. They closed round him in a circle and began to inflict a vicious beating. The victim was lost to sight in their midst, but his cries of pain rang out through the air.

'They're villains, river filth,' said Keorn. 'They'll rob or kill anything that moves.'

Ashurek had already started towards them, his hand on the hilt of his sword. He heard Keorn whisper urgently, 'Don't, my lord, they're murderers!' but he ignored the warning.

Drawing his sword, he took one of the attackers from behind with a swift, easy thrust under the ribs.

The others took a second to register that one of their number had fallen dead. Then they straightened up and stared at Ashurek. They were Pels, squat and dark-haired, with soulless, embittered eyes in young faces. The weapons in their hands were stones.

'As you see, I am not a man of honour,' said Ashurek. 'But then, neither are any of you.'

Their expressions turned to astonished terror as they took in his tall, forbidding figure, his eyes burning green in the coal-dark face. They turned and fled.

As their footsteps faded, Ashurek quickly cleaned and sheathed his sword. The thug he had killed had fallen across the victim of the attack, so he hauled the corpse aside and knelt down beside the injured man.

The man was thin, with a pale, lined face and ash-grey hair. He was conscious, but his mouth opened and closed wetly and he was barely able to speak. His forehead was sticky with blood.

'Old fool,' said Keorn, bending down to look at him. 'He should know better than to walk the streets of Pel after dark.' Then his expression changed to one of shock. 'By Flaim, it's a bloody Siol!'

The man clutched at Keorn's arm. 'Mercy – don't hold that against me,' he wheezed.

'We'll have to take him back to your home,' said Ashurek.

'Not a Siol! I can't take an Eyostian in!'

'I believe this man's health is more important than your religious sensibilities,' Ashurek said icily.

'It's not just that!' Keorn broke off, not wanting to incriminate himself by saying too much in front of the Siol. He chewed his lip. 'I suppose we can't just leave him. Those villains, were they the ones you sensed following us, my lord?

'No.' Ashurek began to lift the victim carefully. 'It was this man. I believe he was about to confront me when those rogues set on him. Good sir, can you hear me? Am I right?'

The old man nodded convulsively. Finally his voice rasped from his throat. 'Yes. Yes. I saw a vision, I know where you're from. Help me . . .' His head fell to one side and his eyes closed.

Ashurek met Keorn's startled eyes. 'Another who seems to have unexplained knowledge of my presence. You said there might be others.'

'Yes, but Pels, not Siols!' Keorn sounded deeply resentful. 'It's impossible, I don't understand.'

'Then the sooner we restore him to health, the sooner he can explain himself to us.'

The Siol lay on the mattress in Jaia Keorn's cellar, his face the colour of wet paper, scored with lines deepened by worry or illness. His breath rustled moistly in and out of his lungs, and from time to time he groaned and cried out.

'Shai Fea, Shai Fea . . . No, no, I know you are not guilty. I'll help you. Eyos, I must help her . . .'

Ashurek paused in bathing the man's forehead and looked at Keorn. 'The name he keeps saying, Shai Fea – does it mean something to you?'

'It's the name of – no, this is impossible.' Jaia Keorn's fine, dark hair kept falling over his face and he kept pushing it back, seeming irritated and distressed.

'What's impossible?'

'I – I think I recognise him. I can't be sure because I've only seen him from a distance, in processions, but I think it's Lord Tean Mon Neatru.'

'Who is he?'

'Only the Hyalon's uncle! How could we have brought a Neatru here? I might as well have knocked on the barracks door and given myself up!'

'And Shai Fea?' said Ashurek.

Keorn met his eyes and became more subdued. 'The Hyalon's sister, if that's who he means. But how did he know where to find you? You see, this – this psychic gift that some of us possess, it's the gift of Flaim, no Siol should have it. Is there nothing they won't steal from us?'

Ashurek found this tirade grotesque, directed as it was by a fit, energetic man to one lying helpless. Yet his own motive was no better; he wanted the Siol alive to answer his questions. He went on bathing Tean Mon's head, expecting every breath to be his last.

For the rest of the night and most of the next day, Lord Tean Mon lay semi-conscious. His colour improved slowly and he grew less restless, eventually falling into a deep sleep. As darkness fell, his eyelids flickered open to reveal irises of a piercing pale blue, and he asked for water.

Jaia Keorn grudgingly brought a goblet, then resumed his position, squatting with his arms wrapped round his knees. Ashurek knelt by the Siol and helped him to take a drink, but as the man lay back again he stared at Ashurek as if really seeing him for the first time. He had an expression of alarm common to those who had never seen a Gorethrian before.

'Dear Eyos, it was no dream,' he said. 'You have come from the sorcerers, haven't you? Who sent you? Was it Alat Ryn? I have spent so many years wondering what became of him, praying that he'd outgrown the wickedness of his youth.'

'I do not know anyone called Alat Ryn,' said Ashurek.

Tean Mon's face changed as if he had remembered something. He clutched Ashurek's sleeve, trying to sit up. 'My little girl . . . How long have I been here?'

'A night and a day.'

His face fell in shock. 'I left my niece on her own. I must go to her.'

'There's no question of you moving,' Ashurek said firmly.

Tean Mon fell back on the mattress, his face wrinkled with pain. 'But she will be frantic with worry. I cannot leave her in that place any longer.'

'Is she in danger?'

'I don't know. I thought she was safe but I've had such awful dreams that someone might betray her.'

'Such dreams are understandable, if you're anxious about her.'

'But they were so real!' Tean Mon exclaimed. 'It was my sister, Shai Fea's mother, telling me I was a fool to leave her there, that I couldn't rely on the unspoken law . . .'

'Don't upset yourself,' said Ashurek. 'A few minutes will make no difference. I must know where you think I come from.'

'The world of the sorcerers. Ikonus.'

Shock and excitement speared through him. So, these people did know of Ikonus! Ashurek was eager to pursue this first tenuous connection between the two worlds, but Tean Mon seemed to misread the intensity of his gaze. He shrank away and said with fragile dignity, 'Sir, I know nothing about you, but you are well-spoken and obviously of noble birth. I am completely at your mercy. I can only hope you will respect my weakness and, for the trust I am obliged to place in you, treat me kindly.'

Ashurek was not swift to feel pity, but the man's pain and dignity moved him. 'Of course,' he said, taken aback. 'I wish you no harm. I have not come to Jhensit as an enemy. My name is Ashurek.'

'And your companion was right, I am Lord Tean Mon.'

'Why were you looking for me?'

'It was last night, a vision came to me out of nowhere.' He looked at Jaia Keorn, who was still crouching on the floor and regarding the Siol with suspicion. 'You say the gift of prescience is a Pel one. Nevertheless, I also possess it. I wish I did not. To a Siol it's not a gift but a curse, something I have to keep hidden lest I be accused of being tainted by Flaim.'

'Tainted! The gift's ours, our secret, not to be degraded by damned Siol interference!' Jaia Keorn said viciously.

Tean Mon became angry. 'Don't use that tone to me, boy! There are many things I could tell you, if there was time, but know this: Pel powers are no secret to me and never have been, and if I chose there would be many more sweating their lives away in the White Dome! But I respect the Pels. I do not betray them. Enjoy your freedom and remember that it is by my grace!'

He collapsed back, exhausted. Jaia Keorn swore venomously and marched away to sit at the table, his back to them.

Ashurek held the water to Tean Mon's lips, then pressed a cold cloth to his brow. 'Please continue, if you can.'

'Yes.' The old man drew a shaky breath. 'I've tried to suppress the visions and I thought they'd stopped, but last night . . . I was talking to Fea, I remember, and it made me think of the past and the vision of you came like a maelstrom. I knew that you had come from Ikonus and that I must come to find you. It was very important, if only I could remember why . . . forgive me, my head aches and I can't hold onto my thoughts.'

'Please try. It's essential you tell me how you know of Ikonus.'

'I want to, but I can't concentrate, I can't think of anything until I'm with Shai Fea. I implore you, Lord Ashurek, bring my niece to me. I can do nothing until I know she's safe. What if someone *does* betray her? Please . . .'

It was obvious that Ashurek would get no sense out of Tean Mon until he was reunited with Shai Fea. The Siol was too valuable to lose. 'Is she far away?'

'Not far. In the lower city. But it's a secret place, you

must swear to me you will never reveal it to anyone else.'

'I swear,' said Ashurek. He glanced at Jaia Keorn's rigid back, and decided that it was definitely unsafe to leave him alone with the Neatru Lord. 'Listen to this, Keorn. You can guide me there.'

Tean Mon smiled gratefully at Ashurek. 'Ah, you are no creature of Flaim. There is humanity in you. When you come back we can talk as much as you wish.'

They left Tean Mon more cheerful and well on the way to recovery, but Jaia Keorn remained in a vile mood. As they made their way through the streets he wasted no time in voicing his resentment.

'After all I've told you about Siols, you start helping them? Members of the Hyalon's closest family, no less! How dare that old man lay claim to you? *I* found you! I can't believe this is happening!'

At least Keorn had the spirit not to treat Ashurek with obsequious awe, but this stream of acrimony was becoming equally tiresome. Ashurek stopped and gripped the Pel's shoulder, almost lifting him off the ground. 'It must be the will of Flaim,' he said. 'You offered to serve me. If you've changed your mind, it would be no loss.'

The threat was more in the tone than the words. Jaia Keorn looked into the Gorethrian's menacing face and saw that Ashurek was deadly serious, that he would dispose of him without a thought if necessary. Shaken, he fell sulkily quiet.

'I will say this for you,' said Ashurek. 'You are no hypocrite; you are as offensive to the Siols' faces as you are behind their backs.'

It was dark, but tonight the curfew had been lifted and the streets flowed with life, as cloaked Pels went about their business with scurrying nervousness. Satrans were everywhere and the sky-blue armour of Niankan-Siol was much in evidence, but Keorn and Ashurek were careful to avoid them. Many of the officers were mounted on huge flightless birds which were pallid shadows in the gloom, appearing to float rather than run.

'What are those creatures called?' Ashurek asked.

'Auerets.'

'Do you not ride four-legged animals?'

Keorn gave a short laugh. 'Creatures with four legs are of the earth; the Siols will only touch feathered or flying beasts. Talking of hypocrisy, there are plenty of Siols who only pretend to share the official Eyostian view.'

'In what way?'

'Well, the place Tean Mon's sent us to is a garden. I know these hidden gardens exist because my mother worked in one until she died, and they are not there for the Pels' benefit. It's only Siols who visit them. In public, they profess to loathe the earth, but secretly they love it. The attraction of the forbidden, I suppose. And that, to them, is blasphemy.' Jaia Keorn spoke with an edge of humour to his voice, as if he could not quite believe the Siols' eccentricity. For that matter, neither could Ashurek. 'I tell you, he wouldn't be so enthusiastic about soil if he had to live in Niankan-Pel!'

Keorn found the way easily to a row of tall, narrow houses, with a thin alley running towards the river bank and a mass of rock at the back, just as Tean Mon had described. But the overhanging bush had been torn aside and the door stood ajar, the threshold scattered with leaves.

'Something's wrong here,' said Keorn.

'Be careful,' said Ashurek, drawing his sword.

'That's a metal weapon, isn't it?'

'Yes, what of it?'

'Only that metal blades are forbidden,' Keorn said, shrugging. 'But then, I should not have this, either. A souvenir I kept when I left the Satrans.' He took the two-pronged, glowing dagger from his belt. 'It can kill with a touch, and so can the heat-swords that the Satrans carry.'

'I appreciate the warning,' said Ashurek.

As they pushed open the door, the cold scent of earth and greenery coiled out to meet them. The narrow cavern inside was dark and silent.

'There should be some stairs,' said Keorn, moving towards the rear of the cavern. 'Yes, here . . .'As they descended the stairs, faint sounds drifted up to them; shouts, perhaps the clashing of weapons. A shiver of involuntary excitement went through Ashurek, belying his conscious loathing of violence. It was something he had not felt for a long time, but it returned sweetly as if it had never been away; anticipation of battle.

An emerald glow flooded up to meet them, growing deeper and stronger. They reached the base of the stairs and stepped into the strange, rich light of a garden within a cave.

There was activity among the trees, some yards away, but the first thing Ashurek saw was a woman, crawling about on the moss and trying over and over again to rise to her feet. She was shouting hoarsely, 'Bastards! You bloody bastards!'

They rushed to her and helped her to her feet. Her face was plump and lined, her hair dishevelled, and there was a flower of blood on her temple. She was hysterical and did not realise that she was being helped.

'I'll kill you for this! Siol filth!'

'Hush, hush. We're friends, ' said Jaia Keorn. He supported her with an arm curled around her broad back, in complete contrast to the way he had behaved with Tean Mon.

'Is this Shai Fea?' said Ashurek.

'No, this woman's a Pel. She might be Tsin Liah.'

'Stop them,' the woman gasped weakly. 'Bloody swine!'

Ashurek took the scene in with a swift glance. Satrans in sky-blue were rampaging across the garden with drawn swords, slashing randomly at the vegetation, uprooting shrubs, gouging holes in the grass. There was an element of hysteria in their destruction. They shouted as they hacked at the trees, and their glee was hot and vicious. Three or four unarmed men in drab cloaks – Siol visitors, presumably – were making futile attempts to restrain them, but the soldiers only laughed and drove them back with their glittering, crackling weapons.

Ashurek seized Jaia Keorn and the woman and pulled them into the cover of some bushes from which they could view the cavern.

In the centre of a mossy hollow, twenty yards away, a single Satran stood with his back to them. As he shifted position, Ashurek saw that he was holding onto a slender, cloaked figure, gripping her above the elbows so hard that she was bent over with pain.

Already much of the garden was ruined. Muddy water was rushing through an open sluice gate in a culvert, pooling on the lawns and splashing up under the Satrans' feet. A tree rocked to and fro, showering leaves everywhere, as two soldiers struggled to uproot it. Flowers lay crushed on the grass, animals were screaming pitifully.

Jaia Keorn had spoken of the garden with amused cynicism. Now, however, he looked stricken, white with rage. 'Bastards!' he spat. 'They don't know what they're doing.'

'Oh, they do. ' The Pel woman was weeping. 'They know exactly what they're destroying.' She looked from Keorn to Ashurek, and turned pale. 'Who are you?'

'Don't be afraid,' Ashurek said. 'Tean Mon sent us to fetch Shai Fea. Are you Tsin Liah?'

She nodded. 'Someone must have recognised her and betrayed her. I don't know who, it could have been anyone. The Satrans forced their way in and I couldn't stop them –'

'Try to calm yourself, there was nothing you could have done. Wait here. While they're occupied I'll fetch the Hyalet and we'll go out the way we came. Be ready to run.'

'Flaim help me, I'll kill them,' said Jaia Keorn.

Ashurek placed a hand on his shoulder, holding him down. 'Don't be a fool. Confront them and you'll get us all killed.'

Ashurek's tone was dangerous and Keorn subsided, swallowing hard. 'There may be more of the pigs outside, waiting for us.'

'We'll worry about that later,' said Ashurek.

He sprang to his feet, ran towards the guard holding Shai Fea, and took him through the neck before the man even realised he was in danger. The Hyalet, already terrified, cried out with horror as the guard collapsed and she saw Ashurek's face.

He seized her and clamped a hand over her mouth. 'Forgive me, madam, but if you make a sound it could prove fatal. Your uncle sent me for you. He's safe and I'll take you to him, but we must make haste.' Gripping her wrist, he began to make for the entrance, but Keorn intercepted them.

'My lord, there are more Satrans coming, they must have been watching the door!'

They ran back into the cover of the foliage and watched as four brightly-garbed soldiers came out of the stair-tunnel and positioned themselves there. They stood nonchalantly, and seemed to find the destruction of the garden highly amusing.

Keorn let out an exclamation of disgust. 'Now what do we do?'

'Is there another way out?' Ashurek said calmly.

'No,' said Tsin Liah. 'Only the culverts.'

'Where is the nearest?'

She pointed behind them, through a glistening tunnel of foliage towards the unseen cave wall. 'That way.'

'Come on, then,' said Ashurek, but Keorn and Shai Fea were staring at him in disbelief. 'I have no intention of trying to fight my way through so many men if it can be avoided. Come!'

They obeyed hurriedly, but when Keorn tried to lift Tsin Liah, she fought him off. 'Don't be ridiculous. I'm staying here to salvage what I can. They won't drive *me* out!'

'Then take my advice, madam,' said Keorn. 'Pretend to be dead and they'll leave you alone.'

The culvert was two feet high, the floor thick with mud and veined with trickling river water. The Hyalet stared at it with an expression of utter revulsion.

'No – no, I cannot crawl through there! I can't, don't try to make me!'

'You must, and quickly, unless you'd rather be captured,' Ashurek said impatiently.

'I would!' Shadow figures were crashing about in the undergrowth, moving nearer by the second.

'It's up to you, but this is the only way you will see your uncle again.'

These words reached her but she still wavered, looking white and sick. Ashurek took her wrist in a firm, impersonal grasp and guided her towards the culvert. 'Keorn, go first,' he said.

The Pel did so and Ashurek followed, manhandling Shai Fea into the wet, dark tunnel. Stinking mud oozed about them. The Hyalet's fear became full-blown panic and she tried to turn round, crying out incoherently, her eyes sightless with terror. Ashurek attempted to push her forward but she fought back with inhuman energy. His boots skidded in the mud, he could not get a purchase, and for a few terrible moments it seemed they were both trapped. Then he managed to pinion her arms and through sheer determination began to haul her bodily along the culvert. It took all his strength and he was soon breathless, mud-soaked and angry.

At last, several endless minutes later, they were emerging onto the darkness of the river bank. Dim yellow light shimmered on the water and the night air blew sharp and cold on their mud-spattered skin. The Hyalet shivered in Ashurek's arms, blank eyed and almost out of her mind. Ashurek's anger faded as he realised that her reluctance to crawl through the earth had not been fastidiousness but an actual phobia. Some Eyostians really believed the earth itself was corrupt.

'I know that was difficult for you, my lady, but there was no choice,' Ashurek said gently.

Her shallow breathing slowed down, and she began to regain control of herself. 'Who are you? Where's my uncle, what have you done to him?'

'We found him injured, but he's recovering. You'll see him soon. There's no need to be afraid.'

Shai Fea did not look convinced. Keorn gave her a scornful look, greatly indignant at getting himself covered in mud for her sake. 'At least there are no guards on the river bank,' he said flatly. 'Let's hurry before they realise we've gone.'

It had been a good fifteen minutes' walk from the cellar to the garden; the way back seemed twice as far, and their cloaks were stiff and heavy with mud. As they went, Ashurek tried to calm Shai Fea by explaining how they had met Tean Mon, but he was not sure how much of it she was hearing.

At last they were in the alley, hurrying down the steps as Jaia Keorn fumbled for his keys and opened the door. The barrels concealing the inner door fell over with a crash as he tried to move them too quickly. He swore and began to stack them again.

As Ashurek went past him into the cellar, Shai Fea slid from his grasp and half-ran across the room, looking wildly around her.

'Uncle?'

A candle flickered on the table, filling the cellar with huge, jumping shadows. The Hyalet saw Tean Mon on the mattress, and fell to her knees at his side with a soft cry of relief. A moment later her cry became a scream. *'No!'*

Ashurek knew instantly that Tean Mon was dead. But he could not believe it, not until he knelt down beside her and saw for himself. He felt for the man's pulse but it was no use; the Siol lord stared sightlessly at the ceiling and he lay neatly, as if he had composed himself for death. Shai Fea collapsed across his chest, uttering agonised, wrenching cries.

I don't believe it, Ashurek thought helplessly. Tean Mon had seemed well on the way to recovery when they had left; had he really died of his injuries? He could not put the blame on Jaia Keorn, but there was still something strange about it.

The Pel came rushing in. 'What's wrong?'

Ashurek stood up slowly. 'Tean Mon is dead.'

'Oh, Flaim help us,' Keorn said, so artlessly shocked that Ashurek was convinced that he had had no hand in it. The Pel went to pour out three goblets of wine, embarrassed by Shai Fea's grief and not as callous about it as Ashurek would have expected.

Ashurek felt a leaden sense of failure creep through him as he watched Shai Fea, unable to help her. Now his questions would not be answered, Silvren seemed further from him than ever; but that was only a vague distress, eclipsed by Shai Fea's misery.

Eventually her sobs began to subside and she turned a ghastly, red and white face to him. 'You said he was recovering. You said he would be well.'

He took a goblet from Keorn and handed it to her. 'Before we left, he did seem much better,' Ashurek said quietly. 'His injury must have been worse than I realised. I am sorry, my lady.'

'He looks like Wedren Lan did – just lying there – no, it can't be! What are you?' she hissed. 'What in hell are you? Devil! Why do you hate my family so much?'

Ashurek was not altogether sure what she meant, although she seemed to be hinting that other members of her family had died in a similar way. The mystery deepened. He said, 'I do not know your family and I have done them no harm. I was trying to help Tean Mon. I failed and I am sorry.'

She wept again, more quietly now, and Ashurek decided to leave her with her grief. They were strangers, and any attempt to comfort her would only distress her more. Keorn had returned to the corridor to struggle with the barrels, so Ashurek sat alone at the table, drinking the wine and trying to shake the dried mud out of his clothes. Did Shai Fea share her uncle's knowledge of Ikonus? Somehow he doubted it. One thing was certain; they could not stay in the cellar much longer.

Ten or fifteen minutes had passed when there was a heavy pounding on the outer door. Ashurek leapt up, just as Keorn came running into the cellar, shouting, 'Someone's breaking in!'

There came the sound of wood splintering, then the outer door burst open with a crash and a wedge of brilliant light sliced through the doorway. The Satrans had found them.

Ashurek drew his sword, and on impulse seized a heavy jug from the table. 'We'll have to break through them, ' he said, crossing to the inner door. 'Be ready to follow me, and bring Shai Fea, whatever it takes.'

The light in the corridor was blinding but he lifted the jug and flung it straight at the beam. Glass cracked and the light died, and now Ashurek could make out the silhouette of a Satran, outlined by the pearly gleam from the street behind him.

'Halt!' the Satran shouted, flinging the dead lamp aside. He started forward, but Ashurek did not pause. The soldier was taken so much by surprise that he could not defend himself as the Gorethrian's blade sliced through his throat. A red flood darkened his shiny breastplate as he collapsed across the threshold.

Ashurek found himself facing two more Siol guards, staring from their comrade's body to him in shock. 'Eyos, all that blood,' one of them muttered, as if he had never seen a corpse before. They held their swords defensively – heat-swords, Jaia Keorn had called them, double-pronged weapons of a translucent substance in which spots of colour shifted. They emitted a faint buzz and he remembered Keorn's warning that they killed with a touch.

The other Satran found his voice. 'In the name of the Hyalon, I order you to surrender!'

'I don't wish to shed any more blood,' Ashurek said evenly. 'Step aside, or you'll join your companion.'

Behind him he heard a shuffling of footsteps, Shai Fea protesting indistinctly.

The Satran looked at Ashurek's sword and his lips tightened in a satisfied smile. 'You do not stand a chance with that weapon. Touch it to my heat-sword and you'll die. Now give up –'

Ashurek did not wait for him to finish speaking. He lunged, but the soldier was ready and Ashurek had to twist aside to avoid the lightning-curve of the heat-sword. As it whizzed by his ear he felt his hair stand on end, and a painful tingling sensation spread over his neck and shoulder. His muscles jumped, paralysing him for a split second.

He recovered his timing but he was shaken. Whether the power was sorcerous or scientific – if there was any difference – the sword contained the fire of lightning and he no longer doubted that its touch would be lethal. If he tried to deflect the blade with his own, the sinister power would surge into him.

He began to feint and dodge, misleading the Satran with phantom strokes. They fought awkwardly with the corpse between them, and the doorway gave Ashurek an advantage; the Satrans could only attack singly but it was almost impossible to avoid the heat-sword completely without retreating into the corridor. With every near miss he felt the deathly crackle of power sweeping over him.

He had never known such a keen sense of danger in a one-to-one fight. Icy sweat burst from his skin, yet there was a peculiar exhilaration in this strange battle, coupled with the frustration of being unable to land a blow. Angered, he thrust at the soldier's side. His sword made contact with the enamelled armour, a piece of which broke off.

'Drop your sword, you don't stand a chance!' said the Satran through clenched teeth. His eyes shone in the glow of his blade.

It was a rare swordsman, Ashurek thought, who could fight with absolute concentration and speak at the same time. The Satran was over-confident. Ashurek used the moment to begin a false stroke, and as the heat-sword came hissing down, he severed the man's sword-hand at the wrist.

Blood arced from the stump as the man fell backwards and passed out with shock. The other Siol took his place and attacked with manic bravery, his face a mask of rage under the blue and gilt helmet.

Now Ashurek had learned several things. The Satrans were too reliant on the invincibility of their weapons, at the expense of skill. His ability was greater, his reach longer. It was also obvious that their armour was designed to insulate them from attack by other heat-swords – not to protect them from steel.

Now he understood why metal weapons were forbidden.

He increased the pace of the fight, taking greater risks as he sidestepped and ducked. Several times his sword made contact with armour, shattering it and drawing blood. Weakened by pain, the Satran allowed himself to be forced back to the base of the steps and now he was on the defensive.

One last time Ashurek felt the whiplash of lightning down the side of his face and body, then he thrust into a place on Satran's side where he had already struck once, leaving the armour like crushed egg-shell. Dark blood rushed out, and the soldier fell.

Ignoring his dying groans, Ashurek turned to see Keorn stripping the heatswords from the other two Satrans. Shai Fea cowered in the doorway. Ashurek ran up the steps to find the alley deserted, except for two auerets, long-legged birds with chalk-white plumage. They were as stately and graceful as flamingos, and they looked disdainfully down their long, hooked beaks as he approached them.

He picked up their delicate reins and led them to the top of the steps. 'Quickly, while we have the chance.'

Keorn and Shai Fea took their time in complying, picking their way round the fallen Satrans with obvious horror. He had expected that of the Hyalet, but not of Jaia Keorn, who had been a soldier himself. Of course, the heat-swords killed cleanly and bloodlessly; even hardened soldiers here did not expect to see hacked and bloody corpses.

'We'll have to leave the city, unless there's somewhere else,' said Ashurek, thrusting the reins of one of the auerets at Jaia Keorn.

The Pel looked numb with shock, but he replied, 'Nowhere safe in the city after this.'

'What about my uncle?' said Shai Fea. She was plainly terrified of Ashurek, but more terrified of being left alone. There was no time to sympathise with her, though.

'He is dead. His problems are over.' Ashurek took her arm but she recoiled, trying to fight free. 'My lady, I won't harm you. It is me or the Satrans, whichever you prefer.'

The auerets had saddles between their wings, comfortable for one but barely large enough for two. Jaia Keorn seemed to know how to handle the bird; it crouched obediently for him to mount, but once on its back he said, 'Pels don't ride. I've never sat on one of these things before.'

'Now is your chance to learn,' said Ashurek. 'And mine.' The bird, well-trained, folded its legs beneath it and he mounted and hauled Shai Fea up in front of him. She was shaking violently. As he urged the creature to its feet, five soldiers – Pels in deep blue – came running from the far end of the alley.

The bird danced sideways, flapping its wings, but Ashurek swiftly brought it under control and sent it running along the dark street. A soldier caught at his stirrup, but he kicked the man away.

'Which way?' he yelled to Keorn.

'Keep going. Turn right at the next street.' The Pel was clinging to the front of the saddle, staying on by sheer desperation.

The aueret was easy to control, though Ashurek found its two-beat gait unsettling, and the long thin neck tended to obscure his line of vision. For a few seconds they fled along a deserted road, but at the next junction there was another group of Satrans waiting, all mounted. He swung left instead of right and the riders followed, shouting.

A civilisation that could produce the heat-swords, Ashurek knew, was likely to have a system of rapid signalling more efficient than Gorethria's. Even if they outran their pursuers, there would be more of the Hyalon's guards already manoeuvring to block their route.

'This is mad,' said Keorn. 'We'll never make it, whichever way we go.'

'You are the one who knows the city. There must be a way.'

'We'll try the river, then,' the Pel said unhappily. 'We're almost back there, anyway.'

A breeze, thick with the flat organic stench of effluent, blew against them. The Hyalet sat rigid in Ashurek's grasp, her hair billowing. He saw the dull gleam of the river before them, and the crowded buildings, dark as clotted blood, massed along the banks.

The street ahead of them curved up into a bridge, and at the far side Ashurek saw a mass of figures waiting. He might not have seen them, save for a brief wink of light, some soldier turning on a lamp by accident.

The ten riders pursuing them were gaining ground. Ashurek made straight for the bridge, then at the last second swung the aueret round to the right and onto the river bank. Keorn almost lost his seat as his mount was forced round, and swore vehemently. The bank dropped steeply before levelling out into a broad path alongside the water.

Here the ground was soft underfoot, too muddy for them to keep up their speed. Ashurek glanced round. The Satrans were following at an even distance, and they had lit several powerful lamps whose beams wove a dazzling dance in the air. Any chance they had of vanishing into the shadows, Ashurek thought, was as good as lost. Then he heard a cry, and the ponderous *splosh* of turbid river water.

'They've lost a man,' he said.

'Don't sound so pleased, my lord,' said Keorn. 'We could go the same way.'

'Are there any more bridges?'

'Not this way. Shortest way out of the city, but the boundary's guarded. Are you planning to swim to freedom?'

'I've no intention of immersing myself in that filth again,' said Ashurek. 'We'll fight our way through.'

Hearing noises to the side, Ashurek looked up and saw another flock of mounted auerets floating along the roadway above the bank. The Satrans' armour gleamed in the eerie light from the upper city. He began to assess his chances of standing and fighting them and decided that with Shai Fea in front of him, they were minimal.

Above the soldiers' shouts and the squelching of the birds' feet in the mud, there came a thin, metallic voice from the upper city. It seemed to be everywhere at once, a directionless echo repeating the same phrase over and over again. He could not make out the words, but Shai Fea lifted her head and gave a cry of dismay.

'Oh, dear Eyos, no!'

'What is it?'

'Warning of the Maelstrom.'

'What does that mean?'

She seemed unable to explain. He looked round at Keorn, who looked equally alarmed. 'Well?'

'A sort of storm. If we're caught in it, it'll be a waste of breath explaining,' he said.

'How long before it breaks?'

'I don't know,' Shai Fea gasped. 'A few minutes, any second. We must get under cover, we *must!*

She began to struggle as if she was about to dismount in mid-flight, but he held her still. 'Calm yourself, or we will end up in the river.'

The new party of Satrans had been drawing level, but now they checked in consternation at the storm warning. The leader shouted an angry command and they pressed on again, but their obvious fear made Ashurek aware that there must be a very real danger, something worse than a handful of guards.

The river curved slowly to the right, and a few hundred yards ahead stood the now familiar forms of Niankan's military.

Ashurek and his companions were hemmed in on all sides. A swift and desperate thought came to him; if they turned in their tracks and charged straight at the riders behind them, they would gain an element of surprise and scatter a few of them into the water.

He was drawing his breath to tell Keorn when the sky caught alight. One moment it was black, the next it became a lake of mercury, silver-edged, crackling with fire.

There was a sense of dislocation, as if a sheet of glass had come down between him and reality. Through a milky translucence he saw the three groups of soldiers halting, scattering, their mouths wide with unheard screams. They moved in jerky slow-motion, and they seemed no longer solid but empty outlines sketched on the air.

Jaia Keorn had his hands raised as if to ward off an attacker, but he was motionless, a waxwork.

Ashurek could not feel Shai Fea in his arms, nor the aueret under him. The city was fragmenting, falling away in flakes of mother-of-pearl. The ground turned to liquid, the river to hard yellow soil, and the weird silver light writhed and flowed around them like consuming acid.

7

A Bitter Sea

Ashurek willed the aueret to run onwards through the swirling, numbing light, not knowing whether he was going through the actions or dreaming them. The scene rushed past him and became filled with strange visions. Silvren loomed towards him, her eyes perfect circles, her face stretched and furrowed with absolute terror. Behind her came a grinning silver creature with a blood-red mouth, but it drove her towards a many-legged monster with a glistening scarlet skull for a face . . .

Ashurek tried to scream. The past driving her into the future . . . and although some distant part of his mind told him that it was an illusion, the whispering, mocking fear that she was in danger swelled in his mind as if he had never been free of it.

The apparition raced past him, and was gone. Now he clearly saw Niankan to his right, but under the sky's weird radiance the city looked wrong. There was no upper city. The mansions of Pel were encrusted with mud, shadows flickered starkly in the clogged streets. An ocean of mud swamped the city and swept up all round it into solid waves of hills. It was an alien, drowned world, melting and weeping under the eerie storm-light, sinking under its own glutinous weight. Ashurek thought he could hear the cries of those who had been crushed under the landslide. He imagined soil flowing like lava, and layers of bones, brown with filth and age, trapped forever like fossils . . .

He knew he was seeing into Jhensit's past and a compulsive sense of fate stole over him. Observe, the High Master had said. Only observe . . .

The field of cosmic disturbance was losing its strength, and normality began to return. The argent blaze of the sky writhed more and more frantically as it faded, like the colours on a bubble that is about to burst. There was the jolt of ground under the aueret's feet, and he became aware of the creature running beneath him, of Shai Fea slumping forward across his arm. Sound hurtled back like an arrow.

He glanced round and saw Jaia Keorn just behind him, still clinging onto the saddle for all he was worth. He had dropped the reins, but his aueret ran with its wings outstretched, a dancer in a feathered white cloak.

'Where are we?' Ashurek called. 'This is your land, not mine.' The Pel did not reply. His face was blank with terror.

'We seem to be out of the city, at any rate,' Ashurek said to himself, guessing that he was unlikely to get much sense out of his companions for a time. Now the phenomenon had loosed its hold on them, and long experience of the supernatural had given him the ability to regain his bearings swiftly. The dark bulk of the lower city was behind them, with Niankan-Siol shining sublimely above, as if nothing had happened.

In front of them the hills were walls of cinnamon rock scored with shadow. The sky was like black pearl, and lightning – the last remnant of the disturbance – trickled like water across a darkened window.

There was no sign of pursuit. Ashurek slowed the bird to a walk. 'It appears we've shaken them off,' he said to Jaia Keorn. 'You must know roughly where we are. We must find a hiding place.'

Still Jaia Keorn said nothing. His hair had tangled into a wild halo and he had the look of a possessed witch.

Ashurek gave Shai Fea a gentle shake. 'My lady, whatever happened is over. Answer me, what direction shall we take?'

The Hyalet groaned, and muttered something he could not hear. Sighing, he leaned over to pick up the loose reins of Keorn's mount and urged both animals into a lope. He did not know how much stamina they had, so he must find a suitable refuge before they became too tired to go on.

It was then he realised that they were on the far side of the river. It had appeared to turn solid; apparently that had been more than an illusion. Now the sluggish water flowed again, but for a time something had disrupted the fabric of the world.

Ashurek turned away from the river and made the birds climb a hillside. Only a little soil clung to the rocks, a few tufts of grass and shallow-rooted shrubs. As Keorn had said, erosion had stripped the earth away, but the birds climbed surefootedly.

From the peak he gazed down on an expanse of farmland, illuminated by bursts of lightning and the diffuse glow of the sky. In stepped terraces the fields swept down across a valley which gave way to a thick skein of woodland. An erratic breeze buffeted them from all directions, and there was still the taint of wrongness in the air. Ashurek set a swift pace to put the open ground behind them.

Once in the edge of the woods, Ashurek dismounted to rest the aueret and suggested that Keorn do the same. The Pel obeyed, though he still looked dazed. Shai Fea was like a china-faced puppet, moving without any will of her own. She stared straight through Ashurek as he helped her down, and he thought, *if they do not recover soon, I shall have to leave them.* He could not jeopardise his search for Silvren for the sake of these strangers.

The woodland had a sharp-leaved, thorny feel to it. The tree trunks were grotesque and twisted, the spaces between them caverns in which dark shrubs grew. Something wet stroked Ashurek's hand, and he caught the rich, heavy scent of an unknown flower.

After a time, Keorn began to blink and shake his head.

'Where are we?' he asked, raking a hand through his hair.
'In some woodland beyond Niankan,' said Ashurek. 'More than that I do not know. I think perhaps you should explain what your so-called Maelstrom was.'
'I don't know.'
'You must have some idea. There was a warning, therefore you must have experienced such disturbances before.'
Keorn drew a shaky breath. 'Yes, it happens sometimes, but that doesn't mean I know what it is! No-one does – or if the Siols do, they haven't bothered to explain it to us low-lives. I've heard they call it the wrath of Flaim. But my lord, surely you must know – '
'As I told you, I am human, not privy to Flaim's secrets. But it seemed that a different dimension was trying to intrude on this one, or that this dimension was being sucked into another. It disrupted space to some extent, or we could not have crossed the river.'
'We crossed the river?' Keorn fingered his hair nervously. 'What you've said is more of an explanation of it than I've heard in my life. A warning always comes from the White Dome – don't ask me how they know – to give people time to get under cover. That is the first time I've been caught in it – Flaim, it was like all the nightmares I've ever had in one! I can't believe I'm still alive and sane! Perhaps your presence gave us protection, my lord.'
'I doubt it,' Ashurek said shortly. 'But I gathered it is not a good idea to be caught outside in it.'
'I've heard of men going mad, killing themselves,' said Keorn. 'They find bodies in the streets afterwards.' He stopped abruptly and his eyelids swept down over his sapphire eyes. Ashurek guessed that he was remembering the fight with the Satrans.
'Oh no. No,' Shai Fea said suddenly, either in response to Keorn's words or to her own thoughts. 'My uncle, he was covered in blood, they'd cut his hand off . . . and my husband was all soaked in it, his neck was cut . . .

but no, there was no blood on them when I found them, was there? I don't remember . . .'

'Hush,' said Ashurek, trying to still her shuddering with an impersonal hand on her shoulder. 'I also saw things that distressed me, but it's over now and we have worse problems than mere nightmares. We are lost, we have little food or drink, and it may only be a matter of time before the Satrans find us.'

'But they really are dead!' she said savagely, with sudden reason. 'I didn't dream that. Oh Eyos, my poor uncle, dying all alone when I should have been with him . . . ' her voice grew fainter and fainter. 'I want my mother.'

Keorn was staring at her, but her head was bowed and she did not notice. He said, quite loud enough for her to hear, 'My lord, what's the use of taking the Hyalet with us? Unless we can use her as a hostage.'

'I shall forget you said that,' Ashurek said coldly. 'Your mind would be better occupied helping me to find somewhere we can rest and decide what to do. Is the Maelstrom likely to happen again?'

'Not for a good many days,' said the Pel. 'Though they do seem to happen more often lately . . . I should sacrifice to Flaim, to thank him for preserving us and to pray we never get caught in one again.'

Presently they found a knoll, well-screened by bushes, from which Ashurek could see through the trees in all directions. He wondered what the auerets ate, but when he tethered them they seemed content to forage for insects in the bushes. That would sustain them for a time, but they must need larger prey, and water.

The bushes had leaves like serrated knives, and blooms hanging heavy on long stems. It was too dark to make out colour or detail, but the grass felt matted and springy, like a ground-covering herb. It gave off a pleasant sharp fragrance when crushed.

Keorn sat down on the grass at once, and yawned as he pulled the two stolen heat-swords from his belt, the blades now dull and lifeless. He held one out to Ashurek.

'They are easy to use, my lord,' he said. He pressed an indentation on the hilt, and the weapon crackled briefly into life. 'You had better have one.'

Ashurek shook his head. 'What is the point, when the Satrans are armoured against them? I prefer to trust a simple sword.'

Jaia Keorn swallowed uncomfortably. 'I do not mean to criticise the ways of Flaim, my lord – but I was – not prepared for the sight of what your sword could do. Heat-swords kill cleanly, you see.'

That was why Jaia Keorn, despite having been a soldier, had reacted with such revulsion to the sight of the bloodied corpses. Ashurek smiled thinly, feeling a sense of weariness and self-hatred creeping upon him. He had sworn never to fight again, yet once in the wrong situation the old Gorethrian instinct had taken him over effortlessly. Now he had killed three men at least. 'But the end result is the same,' he said, his voice low and dangerous. 'Does your squeamishness lessen the sin?'

Keorn looked shocked. 'I – no – only mean – '

'I have a sword,' Ashurek said. 'Keep one, give the other to the Hyalet.' With that he turned his back on the Pel, not interested in his reaction.

Shai Fea was standing in the centre of the knoll, hugging herself. She blinked, slowly emerging from her shock and becoming aware of her surroundings.

'Sit down and rest, my lady,' said Ashurek.

Her eyes widened. For the first time he had a clear look at her. She was taller than Silvren but her build was similar; slender, very straight-backed. Her face was round yet had the pointed, wide-eyed beauty of a cat's, and her hair was black and fine as down, with a blue sheen even in the darkness.

She looked around at the shrubs, the grass and the trees looming against the sky. 'This is worse than the garden,' she whispered. 'Dear Eyos, help me.' She closed her eyes and her lips moved in a silent prayer.

She was evidently as fervent a follower of Eyos as Keorn was of Flaim, and her rejection of the earth seemed childishly literal. Jaia Keorn did not seem anxious about venomous creatures in the undergrowth, so her religion must be the only basis for her distress.

'You must rest,' he said gently. He touched her arm and she leapt back, her eyes flying open and her breath quickening.

'Don't touch me!' She stared at him as if seeing him for the first time, but now there was regal anger and defiance in her face as well as fear. She had seemed nothing more than a very ordinary and frightened young woman when he had rescued her, but now her nobility of bearing and imperiousness came through. Suddenly she was a presence, a cool shining flame.

He also saw that it was an act, one she played very well and no doubt had done since childhood, but an act nonetheless.

'Who are you?' she demanded. 'I am a Neatru of the Ruling House and I command you to tell me the truth. Did you kill my uncle? You can kill me too if you must, but kindly tell me the truth first!'

'I already have, my lady. He came to find me, and was attacked by ruffians on his way.'

'I don't believe you. If it were true, he would have told me about you.' She backed away a step. 'Fiend! What are you? Dear Eyos, I saw the way you slew those poor Satrans, my own brother's men – I feel sick to think about it.'

Ashurek's green eyes narrowed, shining coldly. 'It was no pleasure to me, I assure you. I broke a vow to rescue you, for Tean Mon's sake.'

'But why? What are you, appearing in this land like a demon? You are no human being! What do you want?' Her voice shook, and she was challenging him more out of sheer terror than bravery. He did not want her to be afraid. He did not wish to be in Jhensit at all.

Jaia Keorn broke in, 'And who are you, my lady? You

call yourself *Hyalet* as if some accident of birth gave you the right of command over us. But you're not in the palace now! And if you knew who Lord Ashurek is, you would not dare speak to him like that.'

'Who is he?' she hissed.

'Just a man,' Ashurek said quickly, 'and I have no ill intentions towards you or your family, my lady.'

Now Jaia Keorn looked furious. He said nothing, but he glared at Ashurek as if willing him to renounce those words and admit that he was Flaim's emissary and the Siols' enemy.

Ashurek looked at them for a few seconds longer, wearied by their fear and their angry, demanding eyes. He wanted nothing more to do with them. Pushing his cloak back from his shoulders, he turned away and began to untether one of the auerets.

'What are you doing?' said Shai Fea.

'I'm leaving,' Ashurek replied flatly. 'If this is how you feel, I shall not impose my presence on you any longer. I am not interested in your fate and I don't want to involve myself in your world's sorry affairs. I have something else to do.'

He began to walk down the side of the knoll. After a moment, he heard the Hyalet's voice. 'Wait.'

He stopped but did not turn. 'Why?'

'Because I am the Hyalet. I command it.'

Now he did half-turn to face her, his expression one of dark and bitter irony. 'And I was a Prince, my lady. I would have been an Emperor now if I had gone back to claim my throne, but I did not, because royal titles and powers mean nothing to me.'

Shai Fea looked like a ghost in the night, pale and graceful and distressed. 'Then – then I ask you as a human being. Can you lay claim to that title, too?'

'Some have said not.'

'I need help.'

Her dignity and vulnerability reminded him of Tean Mon, and they also reminded him of Silvren. Against his better judgement, he went back to her. 'As you pointed out, I have shed enough blood trying to protect you. I don't want to shed any more. Are you sure you want my help?'

'I – I don't know where to begin. Tean Mon would have known what to do. Now I can see how stupid and impossible my ideas were, but he would have thought of something; without him, I feel helpless. Why did he go to look for you?'

'I'm not sure,' said Ashurek. 'I would have found out, if he'd lived, but all he said was that he had had a prescient vision about me. But you knew him, surely you knew that he was subject to these visions?'

She shook her head unhappily. 'There was a lot he didn't tell me. I loved him, but I don't think I knew him at all.'

'Never mind.' Ashurek sighed inwardly. 'I cannot ask you to trust me. That must be your decision. Nor can I promise any help.' He removed his cloak and spread it on the ground. 'But if you sit down and explain yourself to me, at least we might begin to understand each other.'

The Hyalet hesitated, then seated herself gingerly on the cloak. She sat like a child, hugging her knees. 'I cannot tell you in front of this Pel.'

Jaia Keorn looked at her indignantly. 'Excuse me, your *Highness*, but I resent that. I've no love for your family, but I am not a barbarian. It was the Hyalon's men who were trying to arrest you, not Pels!'

She stared coldly at him. 'Perhaps some Pels are not so bad. My uncle said he had friends among them, and Tsin Liah was kind to me. But there is no kindness in *you* – whatever your name is.'

'Jaia Keorn Silail.'

Shai Fea switched her gaze to Ashurek. 'Do you trust him?'

'It would hardly be a recommendation if I did,' Ashurek said drily. 'I hardly know him.'

Keorn gaped at him. 'How can you say that, after all the help I've given you? I haven't let you down, and you thank me by aiding a Neatru and insulting me to her!'

'Enough, Keorn. I speak the truth, that's all. I have tried to explain that I am not what you seem to think. It's up to the Hyalet whether she speaks in front of you or not.'

Keorn's wide mouth became sulky, and he fell quiet, picking at bits of grass. Shai Fea looked at him, hesitated, then said, 'No. I cannot. Not all of it, and what I do say you must swear never to repeat.'

'I swear,' Keorn said sweetly. 'I'm sure it won't be interesting enough to remember, let alone tell anyone else.'

Ignoring his spite, she looked at Ashurek and whispered, 'I have been accused of a crime I did not commit. I have to find the person who was really responsible.'

'Surely it would be enough to prove your innocence, without having to track down the guilty one as well,' said Ashurek.

'You don't understand. It's not that simple. It's more to save my brother than myself.'

Despite his words, Keorn was staring at her, fascinated. The idea that the Hyalon Elatiat Harn himself needed saving was of overwhelming interest. Shai Fea did not notice; her gaze was fastened on Ashurek's and her expression was desperate, as if to say, *I fear you are a demon, but I have no-one else.*

'And how had you hoped to find this criminal?' asked Ashurek.

'I don't know. It must be a Pel, there's a Flaimian curse on – she broke off, afraid of saying too much. 'I need to be in the city.'

'There's no chance of that, unless we all want to be arrested and killed,' said Keorn.

'I agree, but where are we to go instead?' said Ashurek. 'I know how to survive in the wild, but the Hyalet is evidently not used to setting foot on the ground, let alone living off it. Besides, I have more important things to do than waste time in this forest. If I can't ask questions of Tean Mon, I must seek the answers elsewhere.'

'What answers?' said Shai Fea.

Ashurek felt an indefinable change, as if he had been hypnotised and her words had brought him awake. Everything seemed very clear and sharp; he was acutely aware of Shai Fea and Keorn as living beings, their breathing, the rustling of their clothes, their bright and hope-filled eyes. Jhensit meant nothing to him. He should not be here. Observe, and come home; that had been the agreement, but every step seemed to take him further away from Silvren.

He could allow himself to feel no more than a trace of detached sympathy for these people; their suffering only awakened his own bitter memories, and seemed shallow compared with what he, Silvren and others had been through on Earth. He took a breath and exhaled softly. *I cannot afford to care about this world. I do not care.*

Quite gently, he replied, 'I believe you have enough troubles of your own, my lady. I would not distress you with mine.'

She looked at him questioningly – *Do demons have troubles?* – but did not reply. Eventually Jaia Keorn spoke.

'Oh, damnation! I've tried to think of every possible answer, but there's only one thing for it. We'll have to go to my father's house.'

'Where is that? You said he had to leave the city,' said Ashurek.

The Pel grinned bitterly. 'Yes. He lives in isolation and has done for many years, ever since he had to flee one of the Hyalon's purges.'

Shai Fea winced slightly, and looked away.

'How far is it?'

'Quite a way, about five days even on the auerets.'

'Can they manage such a journey?'

'Oh yes, as long as there are streams or lakes for them to feed in.'

'We'll go to your father, then,' said Ashurek, pleased that a decision had been made. 'But you don't sound happy at the prospect.'

'I'm not, and you'll see why,' Jaia Keorn said abruptly. 'But if you want your questions answered, he's the one to do it.'

Ashurek kept watch while the other two rested, planning to set off again before dawn. Shai Fea was finding it impossible to sleep; she tossed and turned in great discomfort, and when she eventually lay still, she began to sob quietly and persistently.

To escape the sound, and leave her to weep in private, he moved a few yards away from the knoll. The two auerets crouched on the ground like ducks to sleep, huddled together with their necks entwined. He smiled as he passed, feeling a certain affection for them. Once he was certain that he could not be seen from the knoll, he reached into his pouch and drew out the three lodestones that the High Master had given him. Placing one on the ground, moving the others in a certain configuration, he began to summon a Way.

Nothing happened. The trees frowned down on him, twisted wraiths bristling with daggers, watched his every move. The cries of nocturnal animals echoed through the branches; the air still prickled with the last remnants of the chaos-storm. *I am too tired, or too half-hearted,* Ashurek thought. *Unless, of course, Gregardreos has given me worthless chips of granite in place of true lodestones . . .*

He uttered a sigh, and put the stones away. He had not planned to leave Jhensit yet; he had only wanted to see if the Way would appear to his command. Apparently, it would not. *If you've deceived me, Gregardreos, you're more clever than I thought: your mask of decency had me completely fooled.*

He began to climb the knoll again, when a faint shimmer of light through the trees caught his eye, moving near Shai Fea. He took cover at once, moving stealthily with his hand on the hilt of his sword until he could see its source.

There was a figure standing over the Hyalet, a woman

in ragged robes that had once been magnificent and still lent majesty to her form. A dull silver-grey radiance bathed her. Her hair was a blue-black cloud, and her face was Shai Fea's aged thirty years, not beautiful but possessing a deeper, more haunting quality. Everything was in her face; suffering, anger, and love, and the impression it made on Ashurek's mind was deep and immediate. It could have been his own mother, looking down at Shai Fea; the form was different but that did not matter, her soul was the same. Strong and loving, but bitter.

He saw that the Hyalet was awake and gazing up at the apparition, but she did not seem afraid. The woman was speaking, and Shai Fea was answering.

'Child, who has driven you out into this hostile forest?'

'It was Harn, mother. But it wasn't his fault. We have so many troubles, I wish I could tell you. . .'

'And I wish I could be with you. More and more I wish it.'

'Mother, it's so wonderful to hear you speak to me. You've never spoken before.'

'Darling Fea. I've always wanted to. It is so hard to watch over you and be unable to touch you . . .'

Shai Fea began to sit up, stretching out a hand. 'Mother, please hold me – '

'No, no.' The woman stepped back a pace. 'I can never touch you, darling. I'm sorry. But no-one will hurt you or make you unhappy, as long as I am there.'

'Please stay. You always go away . . .'

'I must. But I came to tell you this, beloved. Don't fear the earth.'

'But Eyos . . .'

'There is no Flaim and there is no Eyos,' the figure said softly. 'There are no gods. Only . . .'

'What?'

'Only what remains.' The figure turned, but as she did so she looked straight into Ashurek's eyes. The gaze burned through him like a comet trail, drowning him in the cold fire of space. Then she was walking away, seeming to pass through the trees rather than round them, as if both she and they were made of a gelatinous substance. The light vanished with her.

Shai Fea remained propped on her elbows for a few moments, then she lay back again, not seeming unduly distressed.

'My lady,' Ashurek called out softly, trying not to startle her. He emerged from the cover of the foliage and went towards her, and she sat up quickly and wrapped her cloak around herself.

'Oh, Eyos,' she said miserably, shivering. 'I wake up and find I'm still in this nightmare. I was having such a pleasant dream.'

'A dream?' said Ashurek. 'Did you dream that your mother was talking to you?'

She stared at him, round-eyed with astonishment. 'How did you know that? We call Flaim the stealer of dreams . . .'

'You should pay more attention to your mother. She just told you that Flaim and Eyos don't exist. I know, because I saw her.'

'*Saw* her? That's impossible!' Shai Fea was angry as well as incredulous.

'Why?'

'Because – because she is dead. She – she died with my father, ten years ago. She was the Hyalana Shai Tialah.'

'And you do not think that anyone but yourself can see her ghost?'

'I don't believe in ghosts. I dream that she comes to me, that's all. It's my dream, no-one else's!'

'Then forgive me for intruding on it, but I did see her. I do not believe in ghosts either, yet I have known spirits to take a different form after their deaths . . . If you feel there's no harm in her, I'll say no more about it.'

'No, please don't,' Shai Fea said thinly. 'You are made of ice, you don't understand anything about me!'

'I don't presume to,' he replied, moving away. 'But I

know how it feels to lose a mother, to mourn a whole family. Good night, my lady.'

Before dawn, Ashurek shared some of his small store of food between himself and Jaia Keorn. Shai Fea refused to eat. She was calm but utterly wretched, and Ashurek doubted that she had the fortitude to survive for long. He wished she had Silvren's strength, but he tried not to condemn her; she had lost her home, position and family in the space of two days. He saddled the auerets and they rode on, Keorn slowly gaining confidence on the tall bird's back.

There was something about this forest that put Ashurek in mind of Gorethria; a sharp-edged feel, richly-coloured, brooding and ancient. As light glimmered through the forest, it seemed all black iron and bronze and splinters of stained glass, spiky and brittle. The sky looked abnormal; there was no sun and the clouds swirled in strange patterns that could not be caused by any natural wind. Jhensit seemed to be waiting in deathly silence for the blow that would destroy it once and for all.

When they had ridden for three hours or so, they paused to rest and Ashurek asked Keorn to draw him a map.

'I have nothing to draw with,' the Pel replied.

'If you sketch with a stick on the ground, that will suffice.'

'We don't need a map, I know where I'm going.'

'But I do not,' said Ashurek. 'I'd like to be better acquainted with the geography of your world.'

'I've had no education, my lord, I can't draw a map!'

'But you told me you were in the army . . .'

'We just do not draw maps!'

Ashurek thought he was overreacting to a simple request, but he turned to Shai Fea instead. 'Surely you must have been educated, my lady.'

'The earth is foreign to me,' she murmured. He sensed that he was touching on a deep fear, something to which they were closing their minds.

'But surely one of you has some idea . . .'

'There's no point in maps!' Keorn turned away in exasperation.

'He is right,' Shai Fea said quietly. 'But I'll try to draw what I know.' She picked up a twig and moved it across the springy grass, leaving a faint impression where it flattened the blades and the tiny beige flowers. The herb scent rose around them. 'Here is Niankan; the land around it is called Palan. Then the ocean, and islands . . . I can't remember all of them.'

What Ashurek saw, though roughly drawn, was almost identical to Ikonus; a large continent with smaller lands straggling along its edge.

'Are there no other lands across the ocean?' he asked. She shook her head. 'And what of peoples other than the Pels and the Siols?'

Keorn answered. 'There were others once, but they're all gone now.'

'How? Wars, or plagues?'

Ashurek's persistence seemed to aggravate Keorn. The Pel turned from him and mounted his aueret, startling the creature so much that he had a struggle to stay in the saddle. 'Why do you demand to know so much about us, when you say nothing about yourself in return? The faster we ride, the faster you'll have your damned answers!'

For the first three days they passed through farmland, laid out in the characteristic pattern of Palan; strips of fields radiating from a stone manor, surrounded by clusters of cottages.

'Siol lords control the farms,' Keorn told Ashurek. 'And Pels work the land, naturally. The best food goes to Niankan-Siol, and we get what's left, if we're lucky.'

Shai Fea gave him a cold glance, but did not deign to reply.

As they rode, Ashurek studied the sky at regular intervals. The strangest thing about Jhensit was its weather, or lack of it. The sun never showed itself through the high, swirling bands of lavender and silver, which were too eerie to be beautiful. Rain clouds gathered a couple of times, low and grey, but when they dispersed, the upper atmosphere still undulated with phantom colours.

Shai Fea often looked at the sky, Keorn never, but neither made any comment about it. Perhaps it was natural for Jhensit, but it did not feel so to Ashurek.

The auerets skimmed like herons across the landscape, running so smoothly it seemed they might take flight at any second. Shai Fea told Ashurek that she was deeply glad at not having to walk. She had ridden auerets many times in royal processions through the lower city, and sometimes out into the countryside; the birds kept the Siols from unwelcome contact with the earth.

'Now if I close my eyes, I can pretend that this is only a pleasure ride, and I can imagine my family all around me, the bright colours and the laughter . . . but then I open my eyes and here I am with strangers, and so far from home I can't even see the highest tower of the palace.'

Ashurek made a minimal response to these confidences, maintaining a courteous distance. She was still afraid of him, he knew, but she kept the fear under control and he tried to do nothing that would exacerbate it. When she spoke, it was as much as to herself as to him.

Later she said pensively, 'I've tried and tried to understand why Tean Mon needed the garden. He wasn't a Flaimian, I'm sure. The strange thing was, after I'd been there for a time, it didn't seem so terrible after all. The flowers were prettier than the glass ones in the palace. It was almost pleasant, and when the Satrans came and destroyed it I wanted to stop them. It was as if they were destroying my uncle! But perhaps that's the secret of Flaim's evil. The earth is not fearsome and dangerous, but seductive . . . How can I tell what is right?'

'I wish I knew,' said Ashurek. 'Or at least, I wish I imagined I knew, as priests do.'

They kept their distance from the farms and stayed in the cover of trees as much as they could. The area round

Niankan was heavily populated, and they saw many Pels working in the fields. By the fourth evening, however, the farmland was deteriorating into wilderness, and Ashurek felt renewed excitement at the thought of entering this unknown region.

There were green and amber hills, fretted with dark lines of woodland, glowing in a mellow twilight. It had a peculiar, untidy beauty. Shai Fea grew very uneasy at being taken even further into Flaim's domain.

'The further we go, the safer we'll be,' said Keorn. 'No-one comes this far from the city, not even the Satarans. If they think we've come this far, they'll assume we've committed suicide.'

'What's the danger?'

'None, really, as long as the ground is still here,' Keorn said cryptically. 'Isn't that right, your Highness?'

Shai Fea's eyes went oddly blank, and she did not reply.

'But this land was farmed once,' said Ashurek. 'Why was it abandoned?'

'You'll see soon enough.' Jaia Keorn spoke brusquely, but he was pale. 'My poor father has great courage living out here, but at least he knows they'll never come out to look for him.'

They sighted an old Siol manor, deserted and overgrown with vines. There were fruit trees around it and a stream running nearby. Ashurek suggested that they stayed there for the night; it would be luxury after nights of sleeping rough.

As they went towards the house on foot through a belt of trees, they came upon an animal limping in circles on the ground and mewing piteously. It was a lean creature like an elongated cat, its body covered with a pale blue-green down, and feathered wings springing from its shoulders, tipped with bright azure. As they went closer, they saw that one of its legs was staked to the ground.

With a cry of disgust, Shai Fea started at once to release it, but Keorn said, 'Leave it.'

'Don't be ridiculous! It's a silukian, we keep their kittens as pets.' Ignoring Keorn, she spoke gently to the silukian, calming it until it would allow her to untie the string from its leg. It seemed to know she only meant to help it; its mewing deepened to a throaty warble, and it gave her a long glance of its golden eyes. Then it darted away through the trees, took wing and was lost to sight.

'Who would be so cruel as to tether that poor creature here?' she said turning to face Keorn. 'Why did you tell me to leave it?'

'Because, my lady, you are robbing Pels of their livelihood.'

'Let us go to the house,' Ashurek said. 'If anyone does venture out into this region, I don't particularly want to meet them.'

'What do you mean, livelihood?' Shai Fea said as they went.

'Isn't it obvious?' said Keorn, with blatant callousness. 'They tether a silukian to the ground, the others hear its cries and fly down, and the Pels catch them in a net.'

'That is the most disgusting thing I've ever heard,' Shai Fea whispered.

Keorn raised his eyebrows and went on cynically, 'Why do you care? I thought Eyostians hated animals, nasty filthy things.'

'Not birds, and not silukians.'

'Ah. Of course, they can fly.'

'It must have been such a creature that I saw caged at your home,' Ashurek said off-handedly. 'The one you sacrificed to Flaim.'

Shai Fea stared at Keorn, livid. 'That's why they catch them, to sacrifice to Flaim? You disgust me! Of all the things I have ever heard about Pels, this is the worst. When I go back, my brother will know about this, he'll stop it –'

'Dear Flaim, what a hypocrite you are!' Keorn raised his voice suddenly. 'Don't lecture me about sacrificing a few animals, when the Siols think nothing of killing thousands of humans. It's not cruelty, to make a sacrifice to appease Flaim and help Jhensit! What have you ever done? And where do you think the Neatrus get their precious pets from? The Pels sell them the kittens. Without that money they'd starve. Just stop and look at your own family, your Highness, before you call us disgusting!'

The night they spent in the deserted house, with beds to sleep on and fresh fruit to eat, was their most comfortable physically, the most unpleasant in other respects. Keorn and Shai Fea lapsed into hostile silence, and Ashurek had no particular wish to speak to either of them. He knew he had worsened the argument when he might have been more conciliatory, but he did not care. His only interest was meeting Jaia Keorn's mysterious father, Jyel Vanan Silail.

One more day's travel, and Keorn announced that they were near his father's house. He seemed uneasy, and his tension communicated itself to Ashurek and Shai Fea, worsened by the strange fog that swirled on the hills, obscuring the vista. There was something unnatural about the fog, Ashurek thought. Odd tints of colour moved through it like insubstantial snakes. Half a mile away, a dark roof, shining with moisture, appeared from the grey-white drifts.

'There it is,' said Keorn. 'Still there, thank Flaim.'

Shai Fea looked at Ashurek, almost smiling for the first time. 'I never expected to be grateful at the prospect of entering a Pel's house,' she said softly.

Keorn dismounted from his aueret, gave the reins to Ashurek, and strode towards the house with renewed energy. Ashurek and Shai Fea followed, also on foot. For a few minutes the house was out of sight in the mist, then it reappeared like a dark ghost, several hundred yards ahead.

Jaia Keorn stopped very suddenly and gave a hoarse yell. He sank to the ground, and as Ashurek caught him up the mist thinned, and he saw the reason for his shout.

They had come to the edge of the world.

The little dark-roofed house they had seen was now on an island that floated, impossibly, in a chasm of nothingness.

'Oh, dear Flaim,' Keorn gasped. 'I knew he shouldn't have stayed here, I did warn him, over and over. Stupid stubborn idiot!' He sank to the ground with his head in his hands.

Leaving Shai Fea to hold the auerets, Ashurek went forward to the very edge and looked down. His stomach swooped. The chasm dropped vertically below him, a thousand feet of powdery-brown rock, falling and falling until it vanished into a dizzying haze. On either side of him, the edge curved away as far as the eye could see, not clean-cut but ragged as if it had been carved away with a fretsaw. There was no far side to the chasm.

They were on a rim of land beyond which the laws of physics ceased and there lay only the mist and strangeness of another dimension. Ashurek felt tiny as a fly poised over the infinite abyss, as if the slightest breath or movement would dislodge him. Slowly, he raised his head to look at the impossible island.

It was perhaps a quarter of a mile across, and its surface was level with the cliff on which they stood. It was detached from the mainland by a two-hundred yard gulf. Beneath its broad, flat top, its bulk tapered for hundreds of feet into a narrow stalk of rock, brown and rough as a fossilised bone. But there was no bed of rock for it to rest on; it simply ended in mid-air, a thin violet sea.

'The last time I came,' said Keorn, 'my father's house was on solid ground and this Edge was five miles away.' His voice was full of quiet despair. 'Now you know why we don't bother with maps any more. They say Jhensit was spherical once. Every time there's a Maelstrom, a little more land vanishes and the Edge creeps further in. You wanted to know the truth about us; well, here it is. Jhensit's dying, my lord, that's all.'

8

The Island and the Unheard Cry

Silvren stood alone in a desert.

A vortex was rotating around her – the last of the Way that had brought her here – but through its transparent walls she could see a landscape the straw-gold of plasma. It resembled sand and rock, yet it was in constant motion, a sentient sea thrashing in agony.

Her senses were numb, her head spinning. The last she remembered was Ashurek stepping into the Way, in the soft Ikonian dawn – then the Way flashing out to swallow her. The shock of passing between worlds was disorientating. She knew Ashurek should be with her, but he was not and there was no sign of him. How could they have been separated?

Alarmed, she tried to move, but the wall of the vortex buffeted her and she could not pass through. As she touched it a hazy window opened onto a distant scene . . . Ashurek in an ancient city, being watched by a hideous creature of which he seemed unaware.

She felt as if she were on the edge between dreaming and waking, not quite in control of herself, overwhelmed by a terrifying sense of danger. She was crying out to him, trying to make him hear, to help her, to help himself . . .

And now he was battling the red creature. She tried to summon power but it was as if she had only dreamed she was a Sorceress; power fell like dust through her hands. As she watched in horror, Ashurek went down beneath the monster's claws.

Silvren made another desperate attempt to push through the transparent barrier, and this time it gave. Stumbling through, she regained her balance but the image had vanished and there was nothing around her but the restless, groaning desert. Her contact with Ashurek was lost.

She tried to far-see. The constant movement of the landscape sent a sickening dizziness right through her, and the effort only brought painful stars to her eyes. *If I came through the Way with Ashurek we should have remained together. How could Gregardreos let this happen?*

She swallowed against the dryness of her throat, trying to orientate herself. Her sorcerous training had taught her to control fear, and she needed every atom of that strength not to panic.

Did I see Ashurek, or was it an illusion? No harm can have come to him. Gregardreos would not have allowed it! Concentrate . . .

She stood still, closed her eyes and forced her mind into a calming trance. It was like trying to force a cork underwater. Her anxiety kept springing back to the surface, but at last she felt the blue darkness close over her head and she began to See . . .

She saw chaos, the savage currents in the centre of a storm made visible in wild burning colours; a storm perpetually consuming itself, perpetually refuelled by the world on which it fed.

This was wrong. She had lost her powers, or perhaps she had no power in this place; she was not far-seeing, only looking at the unformed depths of limbo.

Shuddering, she tried to force herself through it. She focused her mind on Ashurek and groped blindly through the bursting colours. Her Sight began to clear. She could see shapes moving beyond the chaos now, and she felt the cool fingertips of understanding touching her mind. Jhensit . . . why did that name seem so familiar, like something she had once known and forgotten?

Then the darkness slammed down. Worse than being blinded, it was a black shutter cutting across her brain. She staggered with the shock, but she knew exactly what it was; a block, inflicted by a superior sorcerer.

She opened her eyes and found herself looking into Gregardreos's golden-bearded face.

'Silvren, are you all right?' His large hands clasped her arms and he looked desperately concerned, 'I'm so sorry, I thought I'd lost you. I didn't mean this to happen.'

The last of the Way dissipated in a whisper of sand. The ochre plain rose and fell noisily around them and the ground shook under their feet. The sky was festooned with streamers of yellow cloud.

'Gregar, I'm just glad to see you!' she gasped. 'What *did* happen?'

'I lost control of the Way. It seized you so I had to follow.'

'But Ashurek's not here! What's happened to him? I tried to use my far-sight, but –'

'I don't know where he is, but I'm sure he's safe,' Gregardreos said quickly. He did not quite seem his normal self, but she put that down to anxiety. 'I believe he was delivered safely to Jhensit.'

'But I saw –'

'Whatever you saw, Silvren, may not have been real. Trust me, I'm sure he is all right; it is we who have cause to worry. This is a disaster.'

'Where are we, then?'

'I – I am not sure. It's obscure . . .'

'But it's obviously a place of chaos,' she said. 'I was trying to far-see, but all I saw was entropy and I don't know whether it was external or just the failure of my power. But when I *did* begin to See more clearly, you placed a block on me! What possessed you?'

'Forgive me, but I had to.'

'Why?'

He looked about him, a lion scenting the air. 'Because

this place should not exist and there is something very wrong about it. I could not let you try to See into it, Silvren, it is too dangerous.'

'But I was just on the edge of discovering something! I feel as if I've heard of Jhensit before. You shouldn't have stopped me. I have to try again, I was so close to finding Ashurek –'

'No! If I know nothing of Jhensit, how can you have heard of it?' There was a sternness in his voice that he had not used on her for years, which he reserved only for wrongdoers or the most difficult of students, 'I won't let you risk it, and if you try again, I shall block you again.'

Silvren was shocked, and a little angry. The thought crossed her mind that if Gregardreos had not come after her, she could have acted independently and done what she thought best. She felt a touch guilty at the thought – he was only trying to protect her, and as her High Master she must obey him – but when Ashurek's life was at stake she could not back down.

'What are you afraid of?' she said.

'Are you questioning the need for caution? I thought I'd taught you better than that.'

'You also taught me to look after myself. How do you think I managed when you were not there to coddle me?'

'Silvren, Silvren –'

'Ashurek could be dead! If you won't let me act, what do you suggest we do about it instead?'

Gregardreos looked away, rubbing distractedly at his neck. 'I am sure he's not dead. There's no reason for us not to return to Ikonus, as long as we can summon another Way.'

'I'm not going back until I find him.'

'You're so gentle, Silvren, it's always a shock to me to find how stubborn you can be. If we go back, everything will be as we planned in the first place . . .'

'I didn't plan any of it!'

'Silvren, there is no point in us staying here. Why

turn this into greater disaster than need be?'

'Because it's too late. We *are* here and we have to go forward, not back. Ashurek came here for you, we can't just abandon him!'

The High Master did not reply. 'Speak to me!' she said, but still he said nothing, only turned slowly in a circle. He was growing paler and paler, and it suddenly struck her that he was not merely anxious, but ill.

'What's wrong?' she said.

'Jhensit,' he gasped. 'Ah, this place, this poor world, I didn't know . . . Let me go, no . . .'

His skin was washed-out jade, sheened with sweat. She wondered if he had been struck by a far-vision, and was seeing the terrible thing from which he had wanted to protect her. She went to support him but she was too late and he collapsed to the ground. Words wheezed from his lips but he was speaking to something unseen.

Silvren watched in horror as his body jerked in the sinewy rhythm of a fit, and his eyes rolled back in their sockets until only white crescents were left.

'Let me go . . . I didn't know, I swear,' he groaned. 'No, no, I'll stay . . .'

The island floated on the ocean of vapour, untouchable and sublimely beautiful. Its nearest edge was two hundred yards from the rim of land on which they stood, and between there was only the swelling mist and the void falling away into infinity.

The tops of other such islands could be seen floating in layers of vapour which undulated like a gossamer sea. Twilight lent it a murky violet hue. Perhaps it really was a sea of some unknown gas, Ashurek thought, which bore up those inverted mountains.

'Father knew the danger!' said Keorn. He was shaking. 'I can't believe his house was spared. But how are we going to get across? It's impossible.'

'There is also no point, unless we know your father is still alive,' said Ashurek.

'They say the Maelstrom over Niankan is only an echo of what it is at the Edge. He may not have survived it.' Keorn rubbed his eyes with the back of his hand. 'But he is tough, and perhaps Flaim showed him mercy.'

There was no sign of life on the island. Rough grass straggled over its edges. A lake gleamed in front of the house, black as peat and fringed by a mass of spidery trees. Coils of mist quested through the vegetation.

'It's a shame the auerets can't fly,' said Ashurek. 'But if this haze can bear up a massive piece of rock, it might also bear our weight. We could float across.'

'Oh yes?' The Pel gave him an unamused look. 'Who is going to be the first to try?'

Ashurek picked up a stone and threw it in a gentle curve over the edge. It arced downwards. They watched it fall until it was lost to sight, then Keorn stood back and cupped his hands to his mouth.

'Jyel Vanan!' he yelled at the top of his lungs. 'Are you there? It's me, Jaia Keorn!'

For the space of a few breaths there was no response. Then a sound began, the soft beating of wings like a flock of birds all taking to the air at once. Spots of colour whirled into the drab landscape; six creatures, blue and pearl-pink and gold, came flying towards them. Ashurek realised they were silukians, like the one Shai Fea had rescued. They resembled elongated, exotic cats, and their wings shimmered like shot silk.

Keorn began to draw his heat-sword, but Shai Fea seized his wrist. 'Don't!'

He shook her off angrily. 'They don't stay kittens, you know. They can be vicious.'

'Only to those who harm them!' He gave her a dark look, but sheathed the weapon.

The silukians swooped to the ground on the rim of

the island, picked up something in their mouths, then took to the air again and flew to the Edge. Behind them two ropes looped out like spider silk to span the void. They landed at Shai Fea's feet and dropped the rope ends, then flapped their wings as if saluting her, chattering and mewing. She bent down and reached out to them but they would not be touched. They drew away and skimmed back across the gulf, offering no further help.

'Intelligent creatures, my lady,' said Ashurek. 'Could they know that you saved their fellow?'

'Oh, they are more than animals,' Shai Fea replied, glancing at Jaia Keorn.

'And well trained,' the Pel said without inflexion. 'There's obviously someone on the island . . .'

'Who wishes us to go across.' Ashurek picked up the rope ends and took up the slack, finding that they were firmly attached on the far side. He went to a sturdy tree a few yards from the Edge and looped them round the trunk, pulling them tight with a vision of hauling the whole island against the Edge like a great ship against a quay. But the island remained firmly where it was. He secured the knots and checked them for strength.

Turning round, he found Keorn and Shai Fea watching him with expressions of disbelief and apprehension. Well, shall we go and seek Jyel Vanan?' he said.

The Pel went to the Edge, looked over and stepped back quickly. 'I don't think I can,' he murmured.

'There's no other way,' said Ashurek. 'I have made the ropes as taut as I can. We'll have to trust that they're as securely tied on the far side. I'll go first.'

'And I last,' said Shai Fea. 'I – I am used to heights.'

'I wonder if this can be considered a height, if it truly is bottomless,' Ashurek remarked.

'That's not very reassuring, my lord,' said Keorn.

'What would be the use of pretending it's less dangerous than it is?'

Ashurek had tied one rope higher than the other, so

that they could walk on the lower while holding on to the upper. Taking a firm grip on the precarious bridge, he stepped off the Edge.

It was worse than he had anticipated. The ropes gave as they took his weight, and he swayed dangerously, suddenly suspended in a roiling, depthless sky. Beneath him was nothingness; before him, the rough face of the island-stalk plunged vertically until it dwindled to nothing hundreds of feet below. Vertigo swept through him like uncontrollable nausea and sweat broke from his pores, making his palms slip on the rope. He forced himself to look straight ahead and find a slow rhythm one step at a time, to carry him across the chasm.

An eternity of minutes later, Ashurek was scrambling onto the rim of the island, taking deep breaths to steady himself and savouring the feel of rock and vegetation under his hands. As he gained his feet, he saw Keorn already beginning the precarious crossing. The Pel's face was deadly white, but he crossed swiftly and was soon reaching out for Ashurek's hand, trembling and moaning with relief as he reached comparatively solid ground.

It was Keorn who had expressed the most fear, but it was Shai Fea who froze, half way across. The ropes were bowed into a V-shape under her weight and she was as tiny as an insect caught on a strand of cobweb, helpless in the abyss.

Ashurek waited for her to move. Several seconds went by and he knew that she could not, that if he left her she would fall. With a grim glance at Jaia Keorn, he grasped the ropes and edged out over the soaring drop again.

Shai Fea must have felt him approach, but she did not see him. Her eyes were tight shut and she was paralysed, completely rigid. Tears were running down her cheeks.

'Shai Fea,' he said softly. 'I want you to let go of the rope and hold onto me.'

Her voice emerged in a high-pitched, strangled gasp. 'I cannot!'

It was Gorethrian nature to have little sympathy with

fear, or at least with the inability to conquer it. Ashurek had known men and women who had faced worse predicaments with far greater courage, and he felt little for Shai Fea other than impatience, though he did not show it. 'You can, and you will,' he said in the same even tone.

'I can't . . .'

Her hands were locked with fear, but with difficulty he prised them off the rope, first the left and then the right. When she had transferred her convulsive grip to his shoulders, he looped his left arm round her back and slowly began to edge along the ropes, forcing her to go with him.

She dragged her feet and slipped. For a wild moment they hung off balance, swaying dizzily, then Ashurek managed to pull himself upright. 'If you cannot walk, take your feet off the rope and hold onto me.'

She did so, clinging to him with both arms and legs as he edged slowly along the up-slanting rope. She was slight, yet her rigid body was a dead weight dragging on him. At last he reached the island, where Keorn helped to pull Shai Fea onto the rim of land.

As soon as she touched the ground she collapsed, shuddering violently. The silukians circled round her, uttering plaintive cries of concern, but they scattered as Ashurek approached. He looked down at her impassively, waiting for her to recover.

'I thought you said you were used to heights,' he remarked.

She pushed back her tangled hair from her pallid, sweating face. 'I thought I was, but – but not like that, I don't understand what –'

Ashurek cut her short. 'It doesn't matter. Now we're here let us not waste any more time.'

He began to turn away but Keorn, strangely, looked embarrassed and stretched out a hand to help Shai Fea to her feet. For a moment he seemed to have forgotten that she was a Siol and seen her as she was; a human being in need of help. She accepted his hand, but once on her feet she distanced herself from him, hiding her shame and anger behind her mask of dignity.

The silukians were strange silken butterflies swooping around them, but all else was black and brown. The peat-lake gleamed like polished flint. As Ashurek began to lead them around the shore, their reflections moved with them, black wraiths.

Ashurek thought he could feel the ground moving under them as they walked, as if the pressure of their feet was enough to shake the floating island. He dismissed it as imagination, lingering dizziness. Mist snaked around his face and hung in the trees like veils of net.

He felt Keorn pluck at his arm but he had already seen a figure emerging from the dark house. The man walking towards them moved very slowly and deliberately on long, thin legs, as if walking on knives. He was wearing only a pair of loose trousers. A cloud of white hair floated around his head, wild and uncombed, and his long beard straggled across a chest that was emaciated to the point of concavity.

Keorn stopped, stared at him and shook his head. 'It's father, but he's changed. He looks so old.'

He went forward. He and Jyel Vanan looked each other up and down, but they did not touch. Ashurek sensed the unease between them, any affection they might feel too bound up with pain to be shown. Finally Keorn said with an uneasy laugh, 'Well, Father, I don't suppose you expected to see me.'

The old man lifted a bony, swollen-jointed hand to his son's face, but the fingers hovered there without touching him. 'I knew you were coming, of course. I only wonder that you took so long.'

'You're so thin! Why don't you look after yourself?'

'I am a branch of the tree of Flaim' said the old man. 'A branch needs no flesh, and the roots sustain it. Flaim sustains me.'

'But – but you could get off this island. Why do you stay here, right on the Edge like this? It's a miracle you've survived at all!'

'Just so.' Jyel Vanan smiled thinly. 'Flaim preserved me in this place, therefore I have no reason to leave.' He looked at Ashurek and Shai Fea without discernible surprise, as if he had been expecting them too. His eyes were clear and blue, so tranquil that they were almost vacant. 'Come into the house.'

Keorn gave Ashurek a look, plainly thinking that his father had lost his mind in his enforced isolation. Ashurek reserved judgement.

The house was of an odd style, built all of dark tiles, with an ornate, curved roof that shone darkly with moisture. Ashurek wondered if they had crossed a border into another country – which, apart from this fragment, no longer existed.

At the threshold Jyel Vanan paused to sketch signs in the air and murmur a chant, then led them into the dark interior. At a second door, the ritualistic behaviour was repeated before they could enter.

'Why all this, father?' Keorn said with a touch of impatience.

'Did you come here to question my behaviour?' the old man said mildly. 'Everything I do pays reverence to Flaim, and I do nothing without showing my reverence.'

Ashurek began to see, then, that Jyel Vanan had not so much gone mad as saved his sanity by giving himself completely to his god. The rigid religious customs – or superstitions – brought sense and shape to his life. Ashurek looked round at Shai Fea, pausing until the others had moved out of earshot.

'Do you wish him to know who you are?' he said softly.

She glared at him. 'As what I wish means nothing to you, tell him what you like! I don't want to stay in this house of blasphemy. I expect he would enjoy flinging an Eyostian to her death, and you would no doubt enjoy watching!'

Ashurek did not reply, but stood aside to let her enter

before him. She seemed on the verge of losing control and causing a scene, but instead she fell silent and retreated into her protective layers of regality.

Inside, the house was all red and black, luxurious once but now faded with neglect. The atmosphere had the eerie brooding quality of a deserted temple, heavy with dust, coloured by the strange auras that flickered beyond the island's rim.

The thin hermit turned to face them and bowed solemnly. 'You are welcome to my house, your Highness, Lord Ashurek, Keorn my son.'

'You seem to know everything,' said Keorn, half-affectionate, half-resentful. He put his hands on his hips. 'Is there any point in telling you why we're here, or do you know that too?'

Jyel Vanan spread his hands. 'Flaim gave me these gifts, but by his will they have a limit. I saw you coming, I know your companions' names. I do not know why you are here – but I am glad. I am afraid I have forgotten how a host should behave – if I ever knew – but my son knows his way around my house. Keorn, would you show them where to bathe and rest, while I give thanks to Flaim for your arrival? You are welcome to share what food you can find in my kitchen; the silukians bring it for me.'

Shai Fea turned to face him, her eyes hard. 'So, the silukians serve you, and you thank them by taking their lives?'

Keorn sighed and folded his arms, but Jyel Vanan only smiled at her, his eyes kind. 'I don't sacrifice any creature to Flaim. There is no longer any need. I am so perfectly in tune with the earth-god that I sacrifice only myself, each and every day.'

'Oh.' She seemed surprised and embarrassed.

'And other Flaimians will find their way to higher wisdom in time.' He glanced at his son, who now looked more sullen than ever. 'Go along, Keorn. And hurry, I'm eager to talk!'

Ashurek found the prospect of stripping off his dusty garments and washing extremely welcome. Jaia Keorn led him up a winding staircase of black wood, and opened the door to a small room with a single chair and a bed that looked as if it had not been slept in for ten years.

'There are only two spare rooms,' he said. 'Two of us will have to share.'

'Then Shai Fea and I will have one each, and you can share with your father,' Ashurek said indifferently. Keorn acquiesced, but his eyes lingered on Ashurek's face and he seemed disgruntled.

Some time later, when they had refreshed themselves and had a frugal meal of fruit and water, Jyel Vanan took them into a large room which must once have been a living room. Now it had more the air of a crypt, and there was no light except the Maelstrom-fires. Ashurek would not have been surprised if Shai Fea had stayed in her room but apparently she did not want to be alone, nor to miss anything.

They seated themselves on dark, dusty chairs, automatically sitting as far away from each other as they could. Jyel Vanan sat cross-legged on the floor and murmured a prayer. Keorn prayed with him, but the moment it was over he said, 'What happened here, father? When we came and saw the Edge, I was sure you must've died. I can't believe you're still here! You've got to come away from this place.'

The hermit's eyes snapped open. 'When have I ever heeded or needed your advice? The Maelstroms here are far worse than any in Niankan-Pel. Many times I thought I would lose my life, or my mind . . . but Flaim preserved me, as you see. There is no more to say about it. Again I ask, why have you come?'

For a few moments, no-one spoke. Ashurek felt an odd respect for Jyel Vanan, his self-containment and absolute faith. Or was it envy?

'I need certain information, which your son believed you would be able to supply,' Ashurek said, leaning forward.

'I cannot pour light into darkness,' said Jyel Vanan.

'Ah.'

'You are a strange presence here. You wish to take without giving, but you cannot. Not here. Before I can give you the help you want, you must tell us what you want from Jhensit.'

Ashurek sensed the others' eyes on him burning torches of anticipation. He had known this moment would come eventually. 'So,' he said, 'if I tell you why I am here, you'll promise to answer my questions in return?'

'As far as I am able. That is fair.'

'Very well. I assume you know something of Ikonus.' Jyel Vanan nodded. 'I have come from there. I am not a native of that world but I live there now, and although I'm not a sorcerer I am well acquainted with them.' He made the story as skeletal as he could, instinctively feeling that Jyel Vanan knew exactly what he was talking about. 'There was a Way from Jhensit haunting Ikonus. The High Master feared some kind of danger from it and sent me to find out if it was real.'

Jyel Vanan tipped his head back and uttered a dry, staccato clicking noise. It took Ashurek a moment to realise that he was laughing. 'Jhensit, a threat to Ikonus! If only!'

'But people of a doomed world might seek to invade another,' Ashurek said.

'Perhaps so, if we only had the power. But if Flaim chooses not to give it to us, how can we go against his will? Forgive me, Lord Ashurek, I don't think you're telling us the whole truth.'

Ashurek's eyes took on a menacing glint. 'I do not care to be called a liar. However, there is something else. I believe the High Master may have deceived me and put someone I love in danger. I must understand Jhensit in order to find Silvren.'

'Who is Silvren?' Shai Fea broke in.

'A Sorceress,' Ashurek said flatly. 'And she is lost somewhere between our two worlds.'

The old man regarded him shrewdly, then his face changed, as if it were about to collapse into grief. 'I knew you were not the saviour we've been praying for, but the knowledge still hurts . . .'

'I see no point in pretending a philanthropic attitude. Jhensit has been used as an instrument to disrupt my life. I simply want to find Silvren, return home and settle my score with the High Master.'

'No!' said Keorn, so vehemently that even his father stared at him. 'No – I mean – what we talked about when you first arrived, Lord Ashurek, you can't have forgotten it!'

'What did you talk about?' said Vanan.

Keorn lowered his voice, but his tone was intense and he fidgeted with agitation. 'Ashurek was sent by Flaim but he won't admit it. For some reason the god has not revealed his purpose. My lord, please try to understand! We *need* you. You talk about using – by Flaim, do you think you're so far above us that you won't even stoop to help?'

Ashurek turned towards him, the light in his eyes glacial and blinding. 'You don't know what you are asking. In the past, people to whom I owed everything needed my help, yet against my will I failed and destroyed them. So what help do you imagine I could give to you, people to whom I owe nothing?'

There was a terrible silence. Even the imperturbable Jyel Vanan seemed to shrink away, as if Ashurek's shadow had filled the room and blocked out the light of Flaim. Eventually the Gorethrian said softly, 'I am not Flaim's. I have told you my story and now it's my turn to question you. You know of Ikonus; I would like to know how.'

The old man's shoulders rose and fell, and he murmured a prayer. 'If you want the whole story, it will take a while to tell.'

'I have time.'

'So. Did you know that Pels are sometimes born with strange powers? It is an ability to "see" things that are far away, sometimes a dark fire or energy inside.'

'It sounds much like the power of sorcery,' said Ashurek.

'A similar thing, perhaps,' Vanan said sadly. 'Such Pels are possessed by the fire of the earth, the spirit of Flaim, and whenever the Siols discover such a child they take it away to the White Dome – as if it were a criminal! That is how much the Siols fear the power, though it has never done them harm.

'I have the power too, but I managed to keep it secret. When I was young I could sense it in others, so I devoted my strength to helping them stay hidden. Ten of us formed a secret circle to find out all we could about this power. We spent years praying to Flaim, seeking an answer to the mystery. Sometimes even the hidden ones would be found, because there was always one Pel or another willing to be bought by the Siols, and to use the power to betray us. Our circle became more and more secret as we learned to use our powers to prevent discovery.

'One day a stranger came to a meeting. We knew he had the power but we could sense nothing else about him, until he unmasked himself and admitted he was a Siol. The others were for killing him, but I stopped them. He gave a false name but it wasn't hard to guess who he was.'

'Lord Tean Mon Neatru,' said Shai Fea. Her eyes were wide, her face grey and set with grief.

'Yes, your Highness. He was not what I had expected of a Siol; he was gentle and thoughtful, very troubled. An Eyostian with the powers of the Devil! He would be troubled, wouldn't he?' Jyel Vanan seemed to be issuing a challenge to Shai Fea, trying to shock her, but she remained impassive, as if nothing he said could make things worse.

Keorn, however, did seem shocked. 'You knew him, father? You never told me!'

'He had found out our circle, but he didn't want to

betray us, only to work with us, to try to find out what the power was.' Vanan looked at his son, who was frowning and shaking his head. 'I know you must think we were fools to trust him, but Flaim told us we could. The power made him one of us, in a way. And he brought the Siol intellect; he thought about things the rest of us tried not to. "It's only superstition makes us call this power evil," he said to me. "This ability should be used for the world's benefit, not for selfish reasons. If Jhensit dies because we were afraid to ask questions, everything will have been wasted."

'So we worked with him, trying to find out what our powers could do. Dangerous, the things we tried. But eventually, by combining our powers, we created a tunnel that led to another world.

'A brave man volunteered to be sent through. The drain on our energy was enormous, and we didn't know what fate we'd sent him to. Several years went by, and we were sure he was dead, until one day he returned. The effort of coming back had left him close to death, but he lived long enough to tell us what had happened.

'He had been to a world called Ikonus, he said. It was a sibling to this, as golden as Jhensit was dark. Strange powers were common there, and there was a School of Sorcery where latent sorcerers could go for help. But his own powers hadn't been strong enough, and they'd made him leave.

'Despite his death, it was exciting news. Tean Mon said that where the first man had failed, others would succeed and one day a real Sorcerer would come back and save Jhensit. That seemed a vain hope; I saw it as an escape route for those who would otherwise be taken away by the Siols. But it was no easy solution. Ikonus didn't turn our folk away, but they gave us no help to send them there either. They had enough latent sorcerers of their own and couldn't give aid to outsiders. The making of the Way was so difficult that we could only create one perhaps once a year, and such a drain on our energy that some members of our circle would be made ill for months afterwards. So the making of the Way had to be planned very carefully. The latent who was to be sent through had to be carefully selected. His power was not enough; he must be completely trustworthy and he must promise not to return unless he became a true sorcerer and believed he could find a way to help Jhensit.

'We did not send many, only six . . . no, seven.'

'So, did anyone come back?' Ashurek asked.

'No-one. There was silence from Ikonus, and eventually we had to abandon the effort. The last of the young people we tried to send . . . Leahn Gwal, we'd put so much hope in him, his power seemed so strong. His family were Pels, of course, but the father held a high administrative office in the Satrans. They lived and behaved almost like Siols, gave themselves airs. They had two children, Leahn Gwal and his younger brother, Alat Ryn, who had no power. It would've been a disaster for the family, if the Siols had found out about the older boy, so they were grateful for the chance for Leahn Gwal to be sent to safety.

'It all had to be arranged in such secrecy that even the parents couldn't be told where Leahn Gwal would be sent, or by whom. They were distraught at parting from him, but we needed the boy and he was a danger to them, so it was the only answer.

'The day came. Leahn Gwal was brought in secret to the circle and the Way was made. He was about to step through, when another boy appeared from nowhere with a knife in his hand, stabbed him through the neck – 'Jyel Vanan grew animated, indicating the actions with his hands. ' – and as Leahn Gwal fell to the ground, the other lad leaped into the Way and vanished.

'Poor Gwal was dead. It was his brother Alat Ryn who'd taken his place. He had no power of his own, but he couldn't bear all the attention his brother had had, all the conspiracy and secrecy. So he usurped him out of childish jealousy.'

The old man sighed, flexing his crabbed hands. 'We never knew how Alat Ryn had managed to follow us. He was only twelve, but a clever child, obviously. Now a lad had been murdered, the Way wasted on someone who had no power. The circle were left completely dispirited and we disbanded not long after that, though a few of us still held out hope for a sorcerer to come from Ikonus. It's been so many years, a lifetime . . .'

'How long have you lived here?' said Ashurek.

Jyel Vanan looked at his son. 'Ten years, is it? Since the new Hyalon came to power, and Pels started vanishing, whether they had the power or not. Tean Mon said flee, he'd stop them from following me, so I did. Ah, Keorn, what a world this is . . .'

'Tean Mon helped you escape?' said Keorn. 'If I'd known . . .'

'Would you have treated him differently?' said Ashurek. Keorn did not reply, so he turned to the hermit. 'Jyel Vanan, do you know why there was still a Way from Jhensit haunting Ikonus?'

'No. It is many years since the circle disbanded, so it cannot have been their doing.'

'Do you know who did make it?'

The old man shook his head. 'My faculties are not what they were. I have no answer.'

'And have you ever been visited by anyone from Ikonus?'

'No, only the first Pel who returned to us. No-one else until you. If they had only sent someone, things might have been different.'

'Perhaps it is the Way you made all those years ago that still haunts Ikonus,' said Ashurek. 'Some remnant of its energy remains, which was why we called it up so easily.'

'Or there is a link between our two worlds; how else could we non-sorcerers have found a Way there?'

'Twin worlds, perhaps,' Ashurek murmured, thinking of the map that Shai Fea had sketched for him.

'Tell me now, what became of the Pels who went to

Ikonus?' The old man leaned forward, his eyes eager. 'You said you know the School and the Sorcerers, so you must know them.'

'I'm sorry to disappoint you. I have never seen anyone who resembles a Pel on Ikonus.'

'No-one? What about Alat Ryn?'

'Tean Mon asked me the same question, but I had never heard the name. There are no Pel sorcerers, Jyel Vanan. The name of Jhensit was unknown on Ikonus until the Way was discovered.'

'Oh, dear Flaim.' His webbed lids fell shut and his forehead wrinkled with pain. 'Perhaps we sent them all into nothingness, after the first. All that false hope, but we were working in the dark, we didn't know what we were doing. And we just sent them to their deaths.'

Ashurek was quiet, letting him recover. Presently the old man opened his eyes and said, 'What will you do now, Lord Ashurek?'

'I shall look for Silvren, as I said.'

'If you went back to Ikonus you could tell them what's happening, get them to send us help . . .'

It seemed a perfect solution; find Silvren, return to Ikonus and inform Gregardreos that Jhensit was no danger. Then it would be the Sorcerers' responsibility to decide what to do. In reality it was not that simple; Ashurek had tried to summon a Way once, and the lodestones had failed. 'Aye, and if I can, I shall.' Ashurek said quietly. 'Unfortunately, returning to Ikonus may not be easy. Jyel Vanan, could you create a Way?'

'You can't ask that of my father!' Keorn broke in heatedly. 'You heard what he said, it was hard enough to do with ten young, strong adults. Do you want to kill him?'

'I fear my son is right,' said Jyel Vanan. 'Flaim intended our powers for something, but not for us to be Sorcerers.' The look in his strange, calm eyes struck a pang of guilt through Ashurek. 'If ever you see your High Master again, tell him that the Way was not a threat. It was a cry for help!'

9

'You will never find her'

Ashurek stood at the window of the small bedroom, watching darkness fall over the region of mists. By night the void glowed with mysterious colours. Ropes of holly green light snaked through layers of ivory and deep gold, while violet and crimson vapour billowed like clouds, peeling back now and then to reveal a sparkle of brilliant, breathtaking blue. The effect was hypnotic. He felt that Silvren was somewhere in that sea, calling him to join her, and it would be easy and pleasant simply to drift away into the mist . . .

There was a knock on the door, making him start, and Jaia Keorn entered. He was wearing loose white trousers, presumably borrowed from his father, and his newly-washed hair drifted about his narrow shoulders. He closed the door and leaned against it.

'My father agrees with me,' he stated.

'About what?' Ashurek turned his head but remained by the window.

'That you were sent to help us. That you *must* help us!'

'And I told you that I cannot. You want me to lead some small and savage revolution to bring the Neatrus down? What use would that be, when the world is still crumbling about you? I am no Sorcerer and no demi-god, and I do not know how to save your world.'

'So you are going home?'

'If I can.'

'Please,' Keorn whispered. He crossed the room and he hung onto Ashurek's arm with both hands. There were tears in his eyes, glittering with the multi-coloured fire of the Maelstrom. 'Please don't leave us. I have never seen anyone like you and I simply *know* Flaim chose you. How can you be so sure it's not so? If I've spoken harshly to you, forgive me, it was only frustration that made me angry. Don't you know what pain and fear we're in? Can't you *see*?'

And Ashurek could see, and all the pain from his own past welled up in empathy. Jaia Keorn was desperate, not only for himself but for his people, enslaved and doomed. He could not be blamed for clutching at straws, reading miracles into Ashurek's presence.

And perhaps I should help, Ashurek thought distantly. *History need not repeat itself. On the contrary, perhaps it would begin to atone for the mistakes I have made in the past.*

'Do not become involved', the Sorcerers had instructed him. That had been a condition of the bargain, and if he broke it they might refuse him entry to Ikonus. Was that why the lodestones had failed? He was already far more deeply involved than he had intended to become, and he cared nothing for the High Master's strictures.

But Silvren . . .

'I'm sorry,' said Keorn, wiping tears from his cheeks. 'I've no right to press you about it. But stay a few days, rest. Perhaps Flaim will speak to you.'

'And will Flaim speak to Shai Fea?' Ashurek said drily. 'You obviously have no love for each other, but I would like some assurance that she will be safe with you, whatever I decide to do.'

Keorn looked offended. 'I wish she wasn't here, I admit, but I wouldn't harm her. Do you think, if I'd wanted to kill her, I couldn't have done it already? I speak my mind to her, that's all.'

'But she is not responsible for her family's tyranny. If you would forget what she is and treat her as human, it would help her. She needs friendship.'

The Pel laughed, astonished. 'You tell *me* that, after the way you have treated her?'

'Friendship I cannot give,' said Ashurek.

'You are cruel,' Keorn said softly. 'I wonder what has happened to make you so harsh. But I'll do anything you ask, if you only stay.'

Ashurek sighed. 'A few days, I make no guarantees.'

'Thank you.' That, as far as Ashurek was concerned, was the end of the conversation, but Jaia Keorn remained with his hands on Ashurek's arm, stroking the sleeve as if he were trying to calm a savage animal. Ashurek looked round, his eyes frosty under demonically-slanted brows. 'Good night,' he said coldly. Keorn released him at once and backed hesitantly towards the door, his wide blue eyes holding Ashurek's gaze without wavering.

They remained on the island for several days, as far as Ashurek could judge the passage of time. In spite of their bizarre situation, poised in a weird ocean that might swallow them at any second, he felt no real sense of danger. Keorn seemed quite at home there and even Shai Fea, though she hardly spoke to anyone, seemed much calmer than she had been. The tranquillity that Jyel Vanan had found infected all of them with a sense of timelessness, and Ashurek understood why the hermit was so content to stay there.

Ashurek often walked around the rim of the island, as close to the edge as he dared, and the billowing, strangely-hued vapours brought him a strange peace. His sense of urgency to find Silvren was lost. He felt that the weird sea was hypnotising him, deluding him, yet he could do nothing to shake off the feeling of lassitude.

Silvren . . . is this to tell me that I really have lost you this time, that I must forget and begin again? Where is the anger that I should feel? I must find you, yet . . .

Yet he had never felt further away from her, both spiritually and physically.

Somewhere in that other-realm there might be an

answer, or there might be death. Jyel Vanan's wisdom came only from his own experiences and his beliefs; he knew no more of the truth than did Ashurek. He seemed happy now to talk for talking's sake, and although Ashurek drew as much information from him as he could, it was still not enough.

'How did Jhensit's disease first begin, and when?' Ashurek asked. The four of them were walking through the dark trees, while the 'sea' and the sky alike danced with ripples of purple, silver and blue.

'No-one in Niankan has ever known,' said the old man, 'We were never a widely travelled people. It must have started as a small spot of canker in some far distant land, spreading slowly over the centuries until it approached the borders of Palan.'

'You must have had warning of it.'

'They say that many refugees came into Palan, but the Neatrus sent them back into their own countries by force.'

'Presumably to be swallowed up by the Maelstrom when it came,' said Ashurek. Keorn made a noise of disgust. Shai Fea gave Jyel Vanan a sideways glance, as if angry that her family's behaviour was being called into question yet again, but she said nothing to deny it. She walked with them, even took her meals with them and seemed to have lost her horror of the ground, but otherwise she remained aloof and rarely spoke.

'So if they weren't spared, why should we be?' Keorn said bitterly. He kicked at a stone, and it arced over the rim and vanished into the mists. 'Everyone can only die once, anyway, so what does it matter?'

'If we gave ourselves up to what Flaim wants, instead of fighting it,' said Jyel Vanan, 'how much the happier we would be.'

'It seems to me that you've already done so, father,' said Keorn.

'I try, but still . . . I feel I cannot bear to die without knowing the answer.'

Ashurek smiled to himself. That was what mattered; to know *why*.

'I thought your faith had already given you the answer,' said Shai Fea acerbically. 'That it is Flaim's revenge on the arrogant Eyostians, to destroy the whole world.'

'And what answer does you faith give you, your Highness?'

The Hyalet bowed her head. 'I have no faith. I was taught that the earth was evil, but I've found it isn't so. Tean Mon lost his faith and now it's happened to me. My mother told me there were no gods.' She looked at Jyel Vanan defiantly. 'No Eyos, and no Flaim!'

She turned away and walked off on her own, locked in her own misery and trying to disguise it as haughtiness. It was not in Ashurek's power to console her, and the less contact there was between them, the better it would be for both of them.

Nevertheless, the sight of her small and lonely figure affected him. He had been here four days; nothing had changed. Jyel Vanan occupied his days with endless religious rituals; Keorn joined him in some and spent the rest of the times shadowing Ashurek, saying little, just watching him with a strange, soft gaze.

And meanwhile I stay here, drifting as if ensorcelled . . . I have wasted enough time.

At twilight, Ashurek slipped out of the house alone and went through the trees to an open stretch of ground. He took the three lodestones from his pouch. Perhaps he had delayed this moment because he had simply been afraid of another failure, but now the decision was made. He would return to Ikonus and if Silvren was not there, he could begin to search for her in earnest.

He began to summon the Way. No vortex answered his summons, but something happened; there was a green ghost face hanging before him, almost kissing him as it breathed the words into his mouth: *'You will never find her. One brief moment of dissatisfaction, of wishing you were somewhere other than living in peace with your beloved, brought you to this. Now your wish is granted! She is gone but I am still here, waiting . . .*

He dropped the lodestones as if they were hot coals. The face vanished and the spell of tranquillity broke; he pitched forward in the grass and despair flooded him. He would never find Silvren and his own foolishness had lost her, an unthinking whim that had destroyed his life and hers. Beyond weeping, he groaned, but there was no expression of grief that could shift the leaden heaviness in his soul.

The Face was not real. He could not let himself believe that it was real, nor that it had spoken the truth . . .

Regaining control he sat up, and was startled to find himself looking into Shai Fea's eyes. She was some yards away, standing in the fringe of the trees, with silukians all round her.

She must have come out of the house to be with the creatures; her only comfort, and better friends than he or Keorn had been to her. They mewed and chittered, flapping their bright silky wings as she went towards Ashurek.

By the time she reached him he was on his feet, and she made no comment on what she had seen. She looked up at him, and she was pale with anger.

'I want to talk to you,' she said stiffly.

They went back to Ashurek's room, Shai Fea holding a candle whose glow made her form seem the more ghostlike in the gloom.

'Sit down,' Ashurek said politely, closing the door. She perched herself on the edge of the bed, so he seated himself opposite in the only chair.

'You were trying to leave, weren't you?' she said in a low voice. 'My poor uncle dies and you seize me, bring me to the Edge of the world, where I am a million miles from finding my husband's killer – and now you want to leave! If it wasn't for you I wouldn't be here, I wouldn't have almost fallen –' She broke off. 'You gave your word to help me.'

'I promised you nothing.'

'I was under the impression that you did. If you had any sense of decency –'

'I make no such claims,' he said evenly. 'To look for the person you say is guilty of a crime you did not commit, we would have to return to the city and doubtless we'd have to flee again as quickly.'

'So you won't do anything, then?'

'Listen, my lady. Have you not seen the Edge of the world with your own eyes? Look out of the window. What use is it to hunt one criminal, when the whole of Jhensit may soon cease to exist? The Siols are ensuring their own doom. They can build their cities up to the very clouds if they like, but it will not save them. Whatever you do you will remain bound to the earth. That applies to birds, silukians, even the clouds themselves.'

'I can't bear this,' she said. She pressed her fingers to her face. 'I'm so frightened. I just don't know what to do.'

In the candle's warm light, Ashurek began to see the qualities in her that made the Jhensitians different; only small differences, but enough to emphasise that they were alien. Her hair was thick but as fine as down, a near-black that verged on midnight blue. Her fingers were long and thin. He noticed the colour of her eyes as she looked up at him; green round the pupil, blending to a dark blue rim round the iris, flecked with shades of those colours like multi-layered jewels.

She went on, 'I – I wanted to explain why I was so afraid on the rope. I have lived all my life in Niankan-Siol, but it was always safe, you see. When I was escaping with my uncle, he took me down one of the struts and I suddenly knew, for the first time, that it was not safe, there was only space underneath me and this awful fear just rushed up at me out of nowhere. On the rope, it was the same. I couldn't help it . . .'

'And I told you, it doesn't matter.'

'It matters to me!' She met his gaze briefly and looked away. 'You are right, of course. What right have I to expect anything of you? I was trying to find hope, that's all. As Keorn's spent every moment of the journey telling you how despicable the Neatrus are, I suppose you think we are not worth helping. But he's wrong,' she said bitterly. 'We are not the vicious tyrants the Pels try to make out.'

'Why would they lie?' Ashurek asked sardonically.

'Jealousy! They have decided to hate us and they'll invent anything to justify their hatred. But we're not like that, we're the people of the sky. Eyos teaches us to be gentle. My parents may have seemed frightening to people who served them, but within the family they were the kindest of souls. The Siols love beauty, they are the most civilised people you could hope to find.'

'Of course,' said Ashurek. 'Gorethria was also a civilised country. There never was such a race for correct etiquette and aestheticism.'

She frowned. 'What do you mean?'

'That the veneer of civilisation was only the manifestation of extreme arrogance. Their arrogance led them to believe themselves to be superior to every other race on Earth, with the right to prove it as often and as viciously as they considered expedient.'

Shai Fea's eyes hardened. 'It seems to me that you describe yourself,' she said tightly.

The remark surprised Ashurek. He met her eyes, and this time she did not look away. 'Perhaps I do,' he said softly. 'Sometimes I think my purpose in this life is to be a living warning. Unfortunately, few interpret what they see correctly.'

Now she seemed taken aback. She shook her head slightly, and tendrils of her hair floated out and settled slowly back into place. 'I have never met anyone like you before,' she said.

'That sentiment is mutual.' He stood up brusquely and went to the window. 'But I think I understand you. I was like you once. I believed my family could do no wrong; the fact that they presided over a brutal Empire was the natural way of things. And I know the excruciating pain of having those beliefs destroyed. You have to cling to them, Hyalet. The truth would tear you apart.'

She was silent. He turned and saw her twisting her delicate hands together, her head bent. 'You understand nothing,' she whispered.

Tears would not have moved him. But he could not stop thinking of Silvren and in Shai Fea he saw similarities. Her extreme vulnerability was combined with an inner strength that never broke, however fragile it became. In that moment, the attitude in which she sat, staring at the floor, struck through him like a sword of fire.

'What do I not understand?' he said. He sat opposite her, watching her, his eyes glowing with a cool green light.

'You are so cold. How can anyone be as callous as you?'

'Does that matter to you?' The tenderness he felt for her disconcerted him; he kept his tone impassive. 'Shai Fea, I am beyond being shocked. You can tell me anything you wish, and I shall never repeat it or use it against you, if that's what you fear.'

'I'm not afraid of you,' she said. 'I was to begin with, but I have worse things to fear than you. You have saved me twice, though I don't know why. I think . . . I think you are not cruel, but that you don't care about us, either.'

'I am listening to you.'

She tried to smile. 'I suppose that is enough. Nothing has been the same since my mother and father died. I never told you what happened to them, did I? It's all I can do to speak of it, but my father died of an illness and the Hyalana is not allowed to outlive her husband. They buried her alive.' Shai Fea stopped, her face frozen as she fought against tears. After a minute she went on, 'It seemed a golden age, when they were alive . . . and I expect you will tell me that was an illusion of childhood, but it's more than that. As soon as my brother Elatiat Harn became Hyalon, there was a different atmosphere in the palace . . . A sort of greyness, not fear exactly, but as if the rooms were full of ghosts, waiting for something to happen.

'And then members of the Ruling Family, my family, began to die. I mean something apart from the deaths you would expect, of illness or old age. There was a murderer walking among us. Living among us. Twenty have died in ten years, but no-one has ever been caught in the act or even seen. We surrounded ourselves with guards, then looked at the guards with suspicion. My own husband was slain in our bedchamber, while I slept through it and heard not a thing.'

'I am sorry.'

'Don't be. I didn't love him . . . but I'd grown used to him and I didn't wish him dead! The most terrible thing is that the murders have driven my brother mad, and I didn't even realise, I didn't understand what had happened to him until he turned round and accused me of my husband's murder. It breaks my heart to think of him. With every death he would gather a new group of people to accuse and execute, initiate a new purge on the lower city. I never questioned his actions. I was not brought up to think. I didn't realise how things really were until I met Keorn . . . Oh, Eyos, what am I going to do?'

There were pearl-grey shadows circling her eyes. She pressed a hand to her cheek, pausing until the spasm of emotion passed away. Ashurek had a powerful desire to hold her, as he would have held Silvren when she was unhappy. In an effort to control the impulse, he said more harshly than he intended, 'One thing is certain, you will achieve nothing by pleading ''What shall I do?'' and giving into terror at the slightest crisis.'

Shai Fea glared at him, suddenly angry. 'Yes, I am a coward! I don't deny it. I'm a coward, and so was Tean

Mon, and Elatiat Harn the entire House of Neatru start at their own shadows because of these murders. Only a creature with no soul wouldn't be afraid, so don't you dare to scorn me for it! You don't know what it is like, you have never felt fear in your life!'

There was a long, long silence. He felt her gaze hot on his face but he did not meet her eyes. Eventually he said in a low voice, 'You are wrong. I have felt fear. I have been imprisoned in a hellish darkness in which I was as terrified as it is possible to be. And never in that terror did I find a comforting wall, a hand at the end of the tunnel grasping mine and saying, "There will be an end to this, you will survive." Never. That is where Silvren differs from me. She has that limit inside herself. The Dark Regions could not break her. She even found something to love and look after in that loveless place. A place that existed solely to cause suffering and terror was pointless, therefore it had no power over her . . . But over me, it was sovereign.'

Her eyes were wide, glistening in the lamplight. 'So how did you survive?'

'By making a bargain with my captors which resulted in horrendous bloodshed. It's a long story, one I have no wish to tell. Suffice it to say that I am not proud of what I did.'

After a time, Shai Fea said very softly, 'That's why you need Silvren. To put a limit on the chaos.'

'Yes.'

'But what if you lose her?'

'When you saw me . . . something had happened to make me believe that I have lost her. If it is so, if I never find her again, my life will doubtless be considerably shorter than it would otherwise have been.'

'No,' she said. 'No.'

Ashurek moved to sit beside her on the bed and put his arms around her. She did not withdraw but embraced him fiercely.

'Do you know what I fear most?' she whispered. 'That

my brother was right. That I killed my husband and all the others as well, and never even knew what I was doing.'

'I can't take away your fears, Shai Fea, any more than you can mine,' he said into her ear. 'But at least there is comfort in sharing them.' Her hair clung to his hands, heavy and soft as the finest silk, and her mouth opened beneath his, a flower of red warmth in the darkness.

Brightness woke him. It was not coming from outside but from inside the room, and he knew at once that it was unnatural. A halo of acid yellow was creeping over the side of the bed like a tiny sunrise. Its edges flared silver, painting the ceiling with a misty aurora as it flowed upwards into a luminous pillar.

Ashurek watched it, unable to move, yet not feeling greatly alarmed. He tried to speak, to wake Shai Fea, but her eyes were already open and sparkling like crystals under the strange radiance.

The pillar became a human figure. Not solid, not a ghost, but liquid; flowing water filled with light. It was Shai Fea's mother, the Hyalana Shai Tialah. She addressed her daughter, but her hands hovered over Ashurek and her eyes, brimming with diamond tears, were on him.

'No-one will ever hurt you, my daughter. Anyone who hurts you – anyone who even tries – they shall pay the price.'

And Ashurek saw what lay at the centre of the light, and he screamed.

He woke properly then, to find the room in semi-darkness and Shai Fea shaking him, alarmed.

'What's wrong?' she cried.

'Your mother – I saw your mother . . .'

'Yes, so did I, but why did you cry out? She is kind, she only comes to comfort me.'

He lay back, pulling her against his chest. 'I know. It was just a dream I was having.'

'But –'

'A dream,' he insisted. 'I have nightmares sometimes, Fea. I should have warned you.' And trying to forget what he had seen he calmed her with kisses, until she relaxed and responded to his embrace.

After breakfast, while Jaia Keorn and his father were at their prayers, Ashurek and Shai Fea walked along the rim of the island. Jhensit still turned and the sun still shone above them somewhere, its light sifting through the vapours of the Maelstrom. Everything glowed lavender and cinnamon.

Shai Fea seemed glad that Ashurek was with her, and slid her arm through his. After a time she said, 'I cannot believe I was afraid of the earth and the things that grow on it. It seems as if that happened to another person, someone who'd lived all her life in a glass bubble . . . When I was a child, I thought my father knew everything. I thought my family were so great and brave, building a city in the sky, like bell-birds singing their supremacy over all the little people grubbing on the ground. Until recently, I still thought my brother knew everything. He must, mustn't he, if he was Hyalon . . .?'

'And now?' said Ashurek.

'I realise they know nothing at all. It was as my uncle said, they were just crowding up and up into the sky out of terror because the world was disappearing beneath their feet and they didn't know why, didn't know how to stop it, didn't know anything . . . Now even the sky is betraying us. The Maelstrom is all round us, but I can remember when the sky was blue and the sun shone. So if it has grown worse so quickly, it cannot be long before the end, can it?'

She sounded desolate. He stroked her hair. For the first time he could see no future beyond staying on this island forever, or until the Maelstrom consumed them at last. He wondered if the other victims had felt so calm at the end.

'Sometimes there is a point to being afraid,' he said. 'It forces you into action.'

'Or it can paralyse. Like my poor brother, running in circles like a tethered silukian. What if there isn't an answer? What if we never know?'

They walked on without speaking for a long time, turning their backs to the straggling trees and the dark-roofed house and watching the ever-changing beauty of the Maelstrom. Long skeins of cloud – violet, deepest blue and crimson – rose up though the mist and fell again, like slow-moving serpents in an ocean of blurred light. The calmness had settled on Ashurek again and now the thought of fighting it did not enter his mind.

A cry from the direction of the trees startled them. 'My Lord Ashurek!'

'Who's that?' Shai Fea said, her hand flying to her throat. 'Oh, it's only Keorn.'

Ashurek was annoyed at being disturbed, but he did not let it show. With one hand resting lightly round Shai Fea's shoulders, he waited for the Pel to come towards them. 'Good day, Keorn,' he said.

'Is it?' Jaia Keorn stopped in front of them with his hands on his hips. 'For you no doubt it is.'

'Is something wrong?'

Keorn was clearly furious. His lips were thin, his eyes narrow. 'I thought you were Flaim's apostle, his creature, our saviour. Instead, this.'

'What?' said Ashurek coolly. He was beginning to realise why Keorn was angry, but he could not quite believe it.

The Pel half-turned away, talking a few steps to the very edge of the island and teetering there until Ashurek feared he would fall. 'After everything I told you about the Siols, the evidence you've seen with your own eyes! You promised to stay, to help *us* not them!'

'Is this true?' said Shai Fea. 'You promised to help the Pels against us?'

'I promised nothing to anyone,' Ashurek said, more

wearied than shocked by Keorn's outburst. 'I warned you many times not to leap to conclusions.'

'By Flaim, I wish I'd listened!' Keorn was shouting now, demented. 'But I couldn't believe it, I *can't* believe you'd refuse to help once you understood. More fool me!' He pointed at Shai Fea. 'I thought you hated her.'

'You were mistaken,' said Ashurek.

'No, this is impossible. You were Flaim's. You came to *me* and now you betray me, taking this Neatru filth to your bed!'

'How dare you!' Shai Fea exclaimed. Her delicate hands became fists.

'Ah, so that is it, Keorn,' said Ashurek. 'I didn't think you had been provoked to such rage purely by concern for your people.'

Jaia Keorn's lips stretched in savage grin. 'Say the word. Jealousy, yes, jealousy!' He moved in a graceful half-circle round them, his hair floating back from his pale, wild face. Now they were between him and the island's edge.

Shai Fea looked stunned. 'I don't understand, you don't even like me –'

'Not you! Idiot, you think I wanted you?' He stretched shaking hands towards Ashurek, half-laughing and half-crying. 'I said I would do anything for you, my lord. I would have been yours, I thought –'

'You dreamed,' said Ashurek. 'I have always been honest with you. It is not my fault that you have deluded yourself.'

With a cry of anguish, Jaia Keorn flung himself at them, swift as a dark whirlwind. His face was twisted, his hands outstretched, and before they could react his hands slammed into them with the full impetus of his body behind them. There was the superhuman strength of fury in the blow. Like twigs hit by a gust of wind, Ashurek and Shai Fea were thrust over the edge of the island and sent plunging like stones into the Maelstrom.

10

The White Dome

The High Master lay white and sweating, oblivious to Silvren and to the unstable landscape around him. Pressing her hands on his chest, she reached into him with her higher senses to discover what was wrong, but she met only impenetrable grey barriers. He had protected himself so well against others' far-sight that he had also sealed himself against help. Her healing aura slid off him like water off oiled skin.

'Gregar,' she whispered. 'If you can hear me, please open up to me.'

Had something about Jhensit struck at a weak spot within his soul? She remembered how badly affected he had been when Ashurek first summoned the Way, and this was far worse. She could not touch him, all she could do was to wait and hope.

The ground shuddered under them, and in every direction ridges of lemon and ochre rock marched towards the horizon. But those ridges rose and fell like waves, sighing and groaning.

Eventually, to her immense relief, the High Master's colour returned and his eyes focused on her. He sat up, hauling in deep breaths.

'Silvren, how good it is to see your sweet face,' he said. 'Why do you look so worried?'

'Don't you remember what happened? You had a kind of fit.'

'Did I?' He massaged his forehead. 'Yes . . . yes, I remember. But it's all right, I'm quite well again now.'

'I tried to heal you, but I couldn't reach you at all,' she said reproachfully.

'Silvren, I'm sorry.' He touched her arm gently. 'That must have distressed you, but every sorcerer must have safeguards against his soul being invaded by others.'

'Yes, but do you need such strong walls that people can't help you either?'

'I was not ill.'

'How was I to know? I thought you were going to die! Was it a far-vision?'

He took a while to reply. It alarmed her to see him like this, like a powerful beast brought down by a hunter's arrow.

'Yes . . . and what I saw was a very great shock. This world is dying.'

'This world? But where are we?'

'On Jhensit, in a way. Rather, we're stranded in the entropy that is consuming Jhensit.'

'Oh, gods,' Silvren said under her breath. 'What about Ashurek? Did you find him?'

'I'm afraid not. Listen, I know I said we should go back to Ikonus, but after what I've seen I can't. It is my duty to do what I can to help. You must go back, though, there is no need for you to be involved and I don't want you to be put in danger.'

'No,' she said firmly. 'As long as you and Ashurek are here, I'm staying too.'

He gave her a long, regretful look, then exhaled softly. 'I can see that nothing I say will change your mind. I wish you wouldn't –'

'You need me.'

'I cannot argue with that.' Gregardreos smoothed back his braided hair, rose to his feet and shook the creases out of his robe. 'Very well. Let's see what there is to find. I sometimes wonder which of us is High Master, my dear; I never can refuse you anything.'

'Not when it really matters,' she said with a smile.

Gregardreos chose their direction, and they began to walk with difficulty across the undulating surface, arm-in-arm to keep their balance. Streaks of yellow cloud hung above them, ominously still, but the ground writhed continuously, throwing up pillars of outlandish shapes and swallowing them again. Silvren felt sick and off-balance. The perpetual mournful groaning of the desert was heart-tearing.

Again she tried to look deeper and further than the surface of the alien realm, and again she met the dark barriers of the block.

'I wish you would let me far-see!' she said angrily.

'It's too dangerous.'

'For me, but not for you? This is ridiculous. You've told me the worst, it wouldn't be a shock to me.'

This time it was the High Master's turn to be obstinate. 'It's more than that. These are unstable dimensions, even I cannot See clearly through them.'

'But you've discovered something, I don't understand why you're hiding it from me.'

'Hiding?' He sounded shocked.

'Yes! How do you know which way to go?'

'Ah. Forgive me, I should have explained. We must go to the centre of the chaos, for our own safety and to find out if my vision was a true one.'

'And what is the centre?'

'When we get there, you will see.'

'Why the mystery?'

He looked at her, stern and almost angry. 'Because I find it hard to talk about, that's all! We need our energy for travelling, not talking. Silvren,' he said more gently, 'bear with me. It will become clear. Until then, please trust me.'

'All right,' she sighed. 'Who can I trust, if not you?'

They walked without stopping for what felt like two days, although there was no way to judge time. Any method of travelling more swiftly would have been too dangerous in that unstable region. Sorcerous energy sustained them, as it could in emergencies, without the need for food or water; but the High Master insisted on his power protecting them both, saying that the energy-field was too alien.

'So you won't let me use my own powers at all?' she said incredulously.

'Please do as I say. It's for a good reason, believe me,' he replied.

'It had better be! I don't think you know the difference between being cautious and ludicrously overprotective.' She went on arguing, but in the end she had to defer.

Colours changed without warning; the desert flashed from yellow to murky blue, then to pinkish-beige. It could no longer strictly be called a desert, for now its look was velvety and pitted like the surface of a mushroom and felt disturbingly spongy beneath their feet. Chasms split the ground without warning, several times nearly swallowing them. At others, the ground would swell up beneath them and throw them off their feet, or sink and leave them with a steep slope to climb. The more tired they grew, the less Gregardreos was able to anticipate these dangers.

'How much further?' said Silvren.

'Not far now,' he said. He was pale with exhaustion, but he still would not let her help. Despite the block on her higher senses, a feel of the place seeped through the barrier. It was not real. It was a dimension that had been curdled by weird forces and was now struggling to reassemble itself in whatever form it could achieve.

They stopped to rest for a time, though without much relief as they dared not sit down. As they paused, Silvren noticed a pearly glow lapping at the sky.

'What is it?' Instinctively she reached out towards it with her prescient sense, only for the High Master's barrier to fog her mind at once. Frustrated, she waited for an answer at second-hand.

'We are almost there,' he said, sounding anxious.

'Thank goodness! Or is there something else to be afraid of?'

'Perhaps.' He smiled but it was a mask and she was not sure what lay underneath. 'Come on, my dear.'

Soon they saw the source of the glow; a silvery hemisphere hanging from the clouds. It was almost transparent, delineated by a shining crescent of light.

It seemed vast. As they drew nearer, Silvren noticed that the disruptions of the ground were lessening. For the first time, they could walk without stumbling every few steps.

'It's quieter,' she said. The landscape and the sky had changed to washed-out violet, and the half-sphere hung above them like an awesome planet of crystal.

'The eye of the storm,' said Gregardreos. 'Quite where we go from here I am not sure, but we should be safer for a time.'

They walked with their eyes on the sky, until a movement caught Silvren's eye and a sour breath of danger went through her. In the same second, Gregardreos put a protective arm around her.

'By the Sphere,' he said. 'I knew there was something, but this is worse than I – ' he broke off, almost choking.

Hideous creatures were moving alongside them. There was a human torso, glistening watery red as if it had been half-melted in a fire, dragging itself along on spindly arms. Its head was back, its mouth open around needle-sharp teeth. There was a domed thing, headless, that stumbled along on tentacles, another like a skinned dog with eight long legs. Others resembled the creature that Silvren had seen attacking Ashurek, and all of them were the colour of blood.

She stared at them in pity and disgust. 'If they meant us harm, they would have attacked us already,' she said shakily.

Gregardreos drew a breath, steadied himself. 'I hope

they don't attack us, for their own sake. It is a risk, destroying or even injuring creatures of which we know nothing. We don't know what balance might be disturbed by it.'

Silvren almost laughed. The cold Sorcerer's logic of his words was reassuring, simply because it was so typical of him. 'Then we had better go on our way, and try to ignore them. Gods, what are they?'

Gregardreos did not answer. Perhaps, thought Silvren, he simply did not know. No Sorcerer was omniscient, not even the High Master.

He created a protective aura to shield them as they went, but it was a colourless, fragile caul within which Silvren felt no less vulnerable. She did not want to look at the deformed creatures, she wanted to run, but she forced herself to watch them with an objective eye. What they emanated was not evil but a kind of mindless yearning that was no less chilling.

Soon they saw another mass of the creatures ahead, bunched like squabbling pack of dogs. For a moment Silvren thought her eyes were playing tricks, but they were not; there was a human figure in their centre, under attack.

Silvren pulled at Gregardreos's arm. 'Someone needs our help.'

'No, don't run!' he said. 'They might take it as a threat.'

'But if we don't hurry, we'll be too late!' Exasperated, she broke away from him and ran towards the knot of creatures.

They undulated like raw flesh around a small, slim woman who was keeping them back with sweeps of a glowing sword. It was a two-pronged weapon that hummed and left streaks of blue fire on the air. The monsters obviously feared it, but she was tiring and her eyes were wild with desperation.

She saw Silvren, stared.

'Help me!' she yelled. 'For Eyos's sake, do something!'

Silvren heard Gregardreos's voice behind her, shouting

'No, Silvren, don't!' but it was too late, she had already decided to disobey him.

She gathered power into her body and discharged it in a perfect arc of fire that seared the creatures and left the woman standing, untouched and astonished.

It was over in a second, but Silvren stumbled back, staring at her hands. The fire had been black. It should have been golden, silver or blue – pure, as it was on Ikonus. But it had been smoke-black, lightless, and it left her feeling drained and dirty.

The air filled with vile fumes as the red creatures smouldered and collapsed into mounds of ash. Their fellows, the ones that had been following her and the High Master, had halted and were waiting in brooding silence, but Silvren ignored them. Gregradreos's hands were on her shoulders, comforting, but she went on staring at her hands.

'I did warn you,' he said.

'The power – did you see? There's something wrong with it. It felt so dark . . . Horrible, I can't explain how horrible it was.'

'I know,' he said. 'It's the nature of this place; you cannot draw pure power from a corrupt source. Are you all right?'

She nodded, swallowing hard. The woman was picking her way towards them over the slimy, smoking remains.

'I don't know who you are, but I owe you my life!' she called. She was tiny, clad in a tight-fitting uniform of blue and white, her torso protected by a shell-like moulded breastplate. Her hair was white, cropped short, and although she was old she had an air of sprightly energy. Her eyes were deep blue, hooded but intense. The crackling weapon was still in her hand, but the light vanished with a click as she sheathed it in her belt. 'I am Iytrel Halia, Director of the White Dome, and I thank you. But who are you, what are you doing here? Don't you know what danger you're in?'

Silvren automatically waited for the High Master to

answer, but he said nothing. He was gazing back at the scarlet creatures and she guessed he was trying to perceive their true nature.

'My companion is Gregardreos, the High Master of the School of Sorcery on Ikonus, and I am Silvren, a Sorceress. As to why we're here, I'd rather Gregardreos told you that.' She shook his arm and he looked at her vaguely.

'No, you tell her,' he murmured. His eyes were clouded, and a touch of foreboding went through her. He seemed sunk in exhaustion, almost beyond communicating.

'We came to your world unintentionally, and we mean no harm,' Silvren said quickly. 'It's a long story –'

'In that case, it will have to wait until we are out of the Maelstrom, and safe from the Muridonu.' The deformities were moving restlessly, and there were twice as many as there had been a few moments earlier.

'If they attack again, I can defend us,' said Silvren.

'No doubt, but the danger's worse than you realise. If we stay here too long, we'll *become* like them.'

Silvren gaped at her, then glanced at Gregardreos. 'Did you know?'

'This is a chaotic dimension that warps everything,' he said woodenly.

'So you must come with me,' said Iytrel Halia. Her tone was imperative.

'Where?' Silvren's sense of foreboding grew. For all she knew they were being taken prisoner, and meanwhile the Muridonu watched her with empty eyes and Gregardreos had become a sleep-walker, a different person at her side.

The woman pointed to the shimmering bowl of light above them. 'To the White Dome.'

Silvren could see no way to reach it, but she followed Iytrel Halia to a point directly below it. The High Master did not move, and she had to take his arm to make him walk with her. She asked what was wrong, but he only murmured, 'Nothing.'

'I have never seen anyone with golden hair before,' remarked Iytrel Halia. 'You are both so golden. Did you say Ikonus?'

'Yes, do you know of it?'

'I have heard the name,' Iytrel Halia said cryptically. 'A name I thought was a foolish superstition, so I am greatly humbled. But you must understand, it is my duty to find out who you are and what you want with us.'

'Of course, ' Silvren said uneasily. 'As long as you help us. I'm worried about Gregar.'

'Why? He just looks tired to me.'

'Maybe, but this is so unlike him. Something about this place has affected him very badly.'

Iytrel Halia snorted. 'The Maelstrom would affect anyone.'

'So why are you here?'

'I am a scientist, I take these risks in the name of research. But I'll tell you more above. I can't think straight here.'

Now they were directly beneath the hemisphere, which from below was almost invisible except for a faint, glassy sheen and an unpleasant pressure, as if the atmosphere itself was distorted and pressing down. Even deprived of true far-sight, Silvren was aware that it was a delicate skin at the intersection of two dimensions.

'Careful,' said Iytrel Halia, slipping a hand through her arm. Silvren began to ask how they could possibly reach the dome, when she felt a sudden grinding dizziness, and the ground turned liquid under her feet.

One instant she was looking up at the sky, the next she was pressed against a strange surface, plastic, warm and yielding. The dizziness worsened; she was weightless, with no idea of up and down. Then she knew; she was on the skin of the Dome and it was absorbing her . . .

She felt the silent snap of transference into another dimension, which was delicate yet cut right through the depths of her soul. She was in a still, hot darkness that weighed on her like the depths of the ocean.

'All present and correct?' said a dry voice in the darkness. A lamp flicked on. Gregardreos was at Silvren's side, Iytrel Halia in front of her, and they stood in a dark shaft that soared upwards into blackness. The floor was slightly concave, and there was one spot that gleamed with spirals of iridescence. 'That is the way through to the Maelstrom, to be avoided if you do not wish to repeat the experience. Now, I have a problem; I'd rather not have to explain you to anyone else before I know more about you, but there's no way through without being seen. Damn . . .'

Silvren said, 'If it is so important, I can protect Gregardreos and myself against being seen.'

'Make yourselves invisible, you mean?'

'Not as such . . . the effect is that no-one will remember having seen us. ' Gregardreos made no objection; she was not sure he had even heard her. She wove a net of power – steeling herself against the unfamiliar and unpleasant darkness of it – and saw Iytrel Halia's mouth fall open.

'Where are you?'

'Still here,' said Silvren.

'I know you're there but I feel a kind of pressure in my head, as if I can't quite see properly . . .' She sounded shaken.

'I'm sorry, but it won't harm you. And I give my word we will stay with you by our choice.'

'Very well.' Halia pushed open a door in the side of the shaft and led them up a narrow staircase. 'Welcome to the White Dome!'

'White?' exclaimed Silvren.

'Hmm.' The scientist gave a quirky smile. 'Named by those who have never been inside, you see.'

They walked along dark corridors which were lined with doors and lit only by dim red and green lights. The substance of which the Dome was built was something Silvren had never seen before, a greyish resin with a metallic sheen. The effect was grim and depressing.

Forlorn human cries shattered the silence, and at the junctions of corridors were guards in uniforms of glowing blue. They saluted Halia as she passed.

Once they were out of earshot, Silvren whispered, 'This is a prison, isn't it?'

'Not entirely,' the scientist replied in a tight voice.

There were three levels of cells, and then they came to a massive, locked door, at which Halia had to show a badge of authority to be allowed through. As it opened, a wall of noise greeted them; a piercing, electric vibration. Silvren pulled Gregardreos through quickly before the guards slammed the door on them.

The area in which they stood could not have been a more awe-inspiring contrast to the prison below. It was a cavernous space, so vast that she could not see the ceiling or the far walls. Five huge cylindrical structures loomed above them, vanishing into the misty heights. They were manned by a mass of dark-haired people who climbed ladders and walkways around the machines, their bodies half-naked and slicked with sweat as they went about obscure tasks. A crawling white light played over everything and the air was dense and needle-sharp with energy. On the floor, several men and women dressed similarly to Halia were walking about, supervising, and blue-clad guards were positioned at various levels around the area.

Silvren watched with horrified fascination, struck dumb by the assault of noise.

'This is the centre of the Dome, where power for the city is generated,' said Halia. Silvren stared up at the central machine, the largest of the five, and saw three stars winking high up on its slick surface; one blue, one green and one red. She felt overwhelmed and desperate to escape.

It took time, however, to work their way through the chamber of generators. Iytrel Halia led them along twisting walkways and up precarious flights of steps, saluted by guards as she went. Weird misty lights swelled around them, bursts of sparks shone briefly in the half-light. At last they were passing through another huge door, and the noise was left behind.

The levels above the centre were brighter and more peaceful, and Silvren caught glimpses of workshops, where more of the dark-haired workers were making weapons, like the one Halia carried. Each level was lighter and smaller than the one below, and Silvren realised that the Dome was actually a sphere. They were almost at the top. Here it was clean and quiet; daylight fell through a curved, translucent wall and there were no workers (slaves? prisoners?), only men and women in blue and white and a handful of guards. All greeted Halia deferentially as she passed, but took no notice of Silvren and Gregardreos.

The scientist led them into a large, light room and closed the door behind them.

'My living quarters,' she said. 'We will not be disturbed here.'

Silvren dropped the guise of invisibility with relief, feeling drained by using the alien sorcery, and looked around. There were no windows, but light fell through walls that were decorated with delicate paintings of birds and softened by silver-blue draperies. The contrast between this cool luxury and the fiery darkness below was stunning. She looked at Gregardreos.

'Gregar? Are you feeling all right?'

'Perfectly,' he murmured, though it was obviously not true.

Iytrel Halia gave them a long, appraising look. 'Now, where do we begin?'

'With the High Master,' said Silvren firmly. 'Is there somewhere he can rest?'

'Of course, this way. Is he your husband?'

'Goodness, no, nothing like that,' Silvren said quickly.

'Forgive me, it's so obvious that you care a lot for him.'

Silvren smiled faintly. 'He's a dear friend, and a father to me in everything but blood.'

In another room, smaller though no less exquisite, they took Gregardreos to a bed, and he obediently lay down and closed his eyes. 'By the Sphere, I hope he is only tired,' said Silvren. 'I've never seen him like this before.'

'Well, Silvren of Ikonus, let's sit with him while you tell me your story, then I'll decide how much to tell you of mine,' said Halia. If Gregardreos was listening, he gave no sign.

'Those who have the knowledge can make Ways between one world and another,' said Silvren. 'Someone on Ikonus made a Way to Jhensit, unintentionally, as if it was already there and they merely found it. The High Master insisted we investigate, in case Jhensit was a threat to Ikonus.' In not telling the full truth Silvren only meant to simplify, not to dissemble. Halia looked at her through narrowed eyes, a shrewd and intelligent gaze, as if to say, *There's more to this than meets the eye, but let it pass for now.*

'You can be sure, we have too many problems of our own to be a threat to any other world.' Iytrel Halia began to tell Silvren about Jhensit in a direct and business-like way. She told her of Palan, the last fragment of land left in an ocean of instability, of Niankan-Pel and Niankan-Siol and the Hyalon, Elatiat Harn Neatru. Silvren said, 'The Hyalon himself has not heard of Ikonus, yet you have. How?'

'A rumour that permeated from the Pels years ago, some nonsense about a secret circle who knew the way to a golden world from which Sorcerers would one day come to save us.' She grinned. 'Well, would you have believed it?'

'I would have tried to find out if it was true,' Silvren said, smiling.

'Eyostians do not deign to listen to Pel superstition – and how wrong we are! This place Ikonus exists and you *are* Sorcerers, apparently. But will you save us? That's the question.'

She spoke tongue-in-cheek, but the question was serious. Silvren sighed. 'I don't know how much more

Gregardreos would want me to say. When we were in that dreadful place, the Maelstrom, he said that we must help; but he's kept me in the dark about what meant by that. There may be nothing we can do.'

'You have already saved my life. That's a start.'

'And you saved ours,' said Silvren. 'But why were you in the Maelstrom at all?'

'I go there sometimes, unofficially, just looking for answers . . . clues . . . Not even that, just asking questions. You may have noticed, the White Dome is actually a globe, half above the ground, half buried below it. So, underneath there should only be earth and rock, shouldn't there?'

'Yes.'

'The shaft we entered goes right up into the centre of the main generator,' Halia went on. 'It channels energy from the earth, the generators refine it and direct it to the city. No-one enters that shaft, simply because there's no reason to, there's nothing there, but when I was made Director I was not going to leave any part of my domain unexplored and I found that spot, an aperture which led not into earth but into the Maelstrom. It is beyond science. What does it mean? That the Maelstrom is not only eating the edges of Jhensit but is under our feet as well? And here we are on a little raft of land, counting the days until we sink.'

She fell silent. Silvren asked, 'Why was the White Dome built at all?'

'It was constructed to house the power source that feeds Niankan-Siol. The Siol scientists live and work in the upper levels; we run the place, in theory. The folk you saw on the generators are Pel prisoners. Some are criminals, others guilty of being "cursed by Flaim" with unnatural psychic gifts.' She looked askance at Silvren. 'Not unlike your powers, perhaps, though much less potent. They certainly can't walk through walls or they'd all be gone!'

Silvren did not laugh, and Halia looked slightly

embarrassed. She cleared her throat. 'Well, their gifts are useful to us in one way; they seem to have a rapport with the Maelstrom, and they can predict its strength and warn us of storms.'

'That's their only crime, to be prescient?' said Silvren.

'But it's the curse of the devil – so Eyostians believe, at least. They seem fairly harmless to me. Damn it, I may be a Siol but I hate the way things are! I feel sorry for the poor bastards.'

'So why don't you do something to change it?'

Halia's lips thinned. 'I know I appear to be in charge, and nominally I am. But you have seen the guards everywhere – they are the Hyalon's men, and in effect my scientists and I are as much prisoners as the Pels. We are more comfortable, certainly, but even I cannot come and go without permission. If I tried to change anything, I would simply be removed from my post and things would grow even worse. Even my sympathy for the Pels could get me dismissed.'

Silvren decided to reserve judgement. 'You don't sound over-fond of the Hyalon.'

'Mmm.' Halia looked down at her hands. 'I should hand you over to him, of course.'

'Is that a good idea?' Silvren said apprehensively.

'It's my duty. It may not be the wisest thing to do, however. He's too capricious. I feel inclined to keep you as my secret, for a little while at least. Do you mind?'

Silvren liked Halia and felt she could be trusted. She looked down at the unresponsive High Master. 'There's no point in rushing into anything,' she said.

Iytrel Halia stood up and patted her on the shoulder. 'You look exhausted. It's reassuring to find that Sorcerers are human, after all. Look, through that alcove is another bedchamber; go and rest, and I'll sit with him.'

Silvren argued, but the Director was insistent and she was glad to give in. Night was falling. A cool flat light – which she now knew was produced by the White Dome's generators – illuminated the outer rooms, but

Silvren lay down in welcome darkness. She had been so concerned for Gregardreos that she thought of nothing else. Now, alone, it occurred to her to test her power of far-sight. She thrust her mind outwards but the blocks rolled down like banks of cloud, heavy with rain.

Her eyes flew open and she shivered.

The High Master's far-vision must have been worse than he would admit. If he was now losing his mind because of it, she could understand why he had wanted to protect her. Yet he had thought himself strong enough to face it, and he had been wrong.

She fell into a long, deep sleep, haunted at the edges by a single dream; Ashurek, flicking slowly through the pages of a book. And the book terrified her, and she tried to tell him not to look at it, but he only stared at her and shook his head.

She woke up with a start, sweating. There was someone in the room with her. She looked up, alarmed, and found Gregardreos bending over her, a lamp beyond the alcove rimming his profile with gold and glittering in the stray strands of his hair. His fingers touched her cheek, but he withdrew them quickly when he saw she was awake.

'Gregar,' she said, sitting up, cold and irrationally afraid. But he smiled at her; a weary, resigned smile.

'Hush, it's all right,' he said. 'I'm quite myself again. I'm sorry to have given you such a fright.'

'Thank goodness.' Tears came to her eyes. She reached out to hug him, but he drew away. There was an awkward moment, and she decided to be direct. 'Whatever was wrong with you?'

'I had another vision, when we were in the Maelstrom,' he said. 'It was rather a shock. I had to delve very deep to understand it, which made me rather uncommunicative, that's all. I'm sorry.'

'It doesn't matter, as long you are all right. Halia was telling me –'

'I know I appeared to be elsewhere, but I heard every

word of your conversation. It has been very hard to make this decision.'

'What decision?'

He gazed at her for a few seconds, as if plucking up the courage to speak. 'Silvren, I have a confession to make. I – I knew of Jhensit before.'

She had not expected this. 'How?'

'It was a few years ago – a faint message came to the Chamber of Sight, someone in Jhensit asking for help. But the message faded and I could not recapture it. I was so busy with the School that I never tried to find Jhensit again nor see why they needed our help. I have felt guilty about it ever since, but I always put it to the back of my mind. That's why I sent Ashurek. I didn't want to see the result of my own negligence.'

He sounded so distressed that Silvren could only leap to his defence. 'Perhaps you did wrong, but it wasn't your fault –'

He cut across her. 'Then when I did come here and realised just how bad things are, it was an appalling shock. That's what caused my apparent fit; shock. I could not speak because of what I have seen.'

Her throat felt constricted, 'And what did you see?'

'That the White Dome itself is causing the Maelstrom.'

Iytrel Halia reacted with stunned incredulity as the High Master explained what he had discovered. It was early morning, and soft light sifted through the walls, turning the room palest blue and silver. Her white hair sparkled under the light and she frowned, shook her head and twisted her hands together as she listened.

'The power produced by the White Dome is drawn from Jhensit itself,' said Gregardreos.

'I know that.'

'It's a similar principal to sorcery, but we are only humans, we only take a tiny fraction of the energies within Ikonus. You are doing the same thing but with vast machines and it is too much. Your world can't sustain it. You are bleeding Jhensit dry.'

'This is too incredible.'

'The White Dome sucks the energy out and all that's left is a husk, without structure; entropy. The Maelstrom. You are destroying your own world.'

'No!' The Director leapt up and vanished into one of the other rooms. They could hear her pacing about and talking to herself; after ten minutes or so she came back, calm but grim-faced.

'I don't want to believe you, but it rings ominously true,' she said. 'You've told me your theory; now convince me.'

They talked for a long time and the Director was a merciless inquisitor, but in the end she was convinced. Gregardreos was completely in control again, leonine and assertive, every inch the High Master. Silvren had never met anyone – with the possible exception of Ashurek – who could resist his confident authority.

Iytrel Halia looked straight ahead of her, her blue eyes introspective. 'The White Dome has caused the Maelstrom,' she said softly. 'So, High Master of Sorcery, what do you suggest?'

'There's only one thing to do, and that is to shut down the White Dome.'

'What? The Neatrus would never let us do that in a thousand years! The Hyalon would never believe you. He'd go mad, he'd have us for high treason!'

'Let me talk to him,' Gregardreos said reasonably.

'I doubt that he'd even see you. You don't know him; believe me, any breath of this and we'd all be down in the dungeons with the Pels, or worse. It's completely impossible.' She strode round the room.

'Do you know how to shut the machines down?' said Gregardreos.

'Of course I do! It's not easy – it's designed not to be easy, but I can do it.'

'In that case, I advise you to act without your Hyalon's permission.'

She stopped her pacing and turned her intense eyes on him. There was denial in her expression, Silvren noticed, but also a spark of rebellion. 'It would be a complete disaster. It's not just a matter of switching off a light, it's as good as full-scale rebellion!'

'There will be a worse disaster if you don't.'

'Listen to him, Halia,' Silvren broke in. 'What's more important, one city or the whole world? Jhensit can only start to heal itself if the machines are stopped.'

'I can't make this decision alone. I could get my scientists on my side, but the guards would stop us the instant they knew something suspicious was happening.'

'The guards,' said Gregardreos confidentially, 'need not be a problem. Do you have the courage to do it, Halia? To defy the Hyalon and save Jhensit?'

He hit the right note; suddenly there was the excitement of conspiracy and revolution in the air, but Silvren felt chilled by it.

Iytrel Halia gaped at the High Master, then broke into a wide and savage grin. 'Eyos, we could do it. Perhaps you wondered why the Hyalon treats the Dome with such caution and keeps us under close guard? They need the knowledge and power science can provide, but it's that very knowledge that makes us cynical about Eyos, less obedient to authority. I really used to resent that fear, that lack of trust, but do you know? I would just like to look him in the eye and say, "Yes. Yes. You were right to be afraid." '

11

Into the Maelstrom

Ashurek and Shai Fea tumbled through a depthless sky.

Layer after layer of violet cloud rushed up to meet them, folded softly around them, let them slip through. Ashurek was ready for the impact of solid ground, for sudden and merciful blackness, but they went on falling as if the gossamer ocean were infinite.

Soon it seemed to him that they were not falling but floating – travelling horizontally, or upwards? Ugly colours assaulted his eyes and he could find no sense of direction, no reference point. The air was thickening, bearing them up; they sank as if through water. He struggled for breath. A red mist blurred his vision and he raised a hand to rub his eyes, only to realise that the redness was external.

The atmosphere was thick with snow, blood-red snow.

Ashurek did not feel the impact of landing; his body was received painlessly by a drift as soft as feathers. Shai Fea was beside him. He fought to escape the suffocating mass but he could get no purchase to free himself. Cold red flakes clung to his skin and found their way into his throat, melting there and releasing a metallic tang.

Blood. He understood then. He lay in the blood of all the thousands whose deaths he had caused, the lives that had seeped out and been left to lie until the world itself froze over. Like water it evaporated into the sky and fell as snow, over and over again, onto the arctic waste of death.

No! The Serpent caused those deaths, not I. I was its instrument, I did not . . .

Out of the scarlet blizzard came figures, formed of blood. They were the ghosts of everyone he had ever slain, directly or indirectly. His brother and sister were there, dead by his hand; and his mother and father, whose deaths he might have prevented, if only he had acted before it was too late. Sins of omission. A terrible throng come to claim their revenge, which they had already claimed a thousand times over in the burning torment of guilt.

'Leave me!' he roared. Somehow he was on his feet, swaying and stumbling in the soft surface. His sword was in his hand. How could his guilt be alleviated by slaying them a second time?

He flung the weapon away from him with a shout. 'Back! Leave me alone!'

The ghosts paused, watching him. This should be a nightmare but it was not, he was awake, they were real. But now he realised that they bore no resemblance to anyone he knew, that they were not even human. Some were vaguely man-shaped but horribly deformed, others insectile or formless, like torn scraps of flesh that still breathed, moved and suffered. Their faces were plates of bone with black holes for eyes, and their bodies gleamed like newly-cut meat.

'What are they?' Shai Fea was clinging to his arm, and he could feel her shaking from head to foot.

'So, you can see them too?' he said with difficulty. She nodded. 'I don't know what they are. I thought –'

'What? Why did you throw your sword away?'

Ashurek forced down his sense of horror, just far enough for him to regain control. Without answering, he went forward slowly, wading knee-deep through the red drifts. Although he knew where his sword had fallen he could not see it, but his boot struck steel and he bent to retrieve the weapon.

Never taking his eyes from the creatures, he wiped the

blade on his sleeve and sheathed it. They watched him in utter silence; nothing moved except the bloody flakes drifting down around them. Then Shai Fea came stumbling to his side, catching his arm to stop herself falling.

'Ashurek, don't leave me,' she gasped.

He put an arm round her shoulders. 'This is your world, Fea,' he said quietly. 'You must have some idea of what these beings are, if only from myth.'

'No – no, I swear, I've no idea.'

'Then they must be my ghosts.'

She looked at him in horror. 'Eyos, what sort of ghosts do you . . .?' Her voice died, and he did not even try to answer.

'Speak!' he shouted in anguish. 'Tell me what you want of me, or let us pass in peace!'

The scarlet throng stirred and began to murmur. They all seemed to be saying the same thing. It was hard to distinguish the words, but as they repeated them over and over again Ashurek began to discern their sense, '*We are the Muridonu. We were human once. We were flesh and blood and we committed no sin to deserve this. But it is your fault we are here, your fault, the damned family of Neatru in their crystal city who condemned us to this. When we sought refuge they turned us back . . .*'

'Oh, dear Eyos,' Shai Fea cried. 'They're talking to me. They are not your ghosts, they're ours!'

'*We wanted life and we were sent to death, this walking death in the Maelstrom . . .*'

Ashurek remembered what Jyel Vanan had told them, that refugees trying to escape the Maelstrom had been turned away from Palan's borders by the Siols. He turned to Shai Fea. 'They are not spirits. They are still alive in these distorted forms.'

She was shuddering, catching her breath as she hid her face against his shoulder. Eventually she said, 'When the Maelstrom touches Niankan, those caught outside often go mad. All those people who must have vanished into it over the years, no-one has ever returned. What if they're not dead, just wandering about here forever . . . changed, mad?'

'I have no doubt that that would be worse than death.'

'Ashurek, did you hear what I said? No-one has ever returned! We will be in this terrible place forever, with those –'

Her voice was rising. He gripped her shoulder, hard. 'And we will not escape by panicking.'

The Muridonu edged forward through the red gloom, sighing and groaning, but they halted as he raised his arm. He remembered the creature that had attacked him and prevented him from reaching Silvren when he had first come through the Way, the venom flowing from its spiny fangs. These creatures were pitiful but they were also red-edged with danger.

'Stop! Stand aside and let us pass!'

'Wherever you go, we shall follow. Lead us, Ashurek. We shall be your army, if you take us to freedom. Lead us, lead . . .'

He listened in dismay. More beings asking his help? Even these wretched, doomed things that would doubtless tear him to pieces given the chance?

'I cannot help you, and I will not lead you,' he said. He regarded them grimly for a few moments, then turned and began to walk away, with Shai Fea at his side. The Muridonu followed. When he halted, so did they; when he went on, they were behind him, a silent flock of sheep.

'Eyos, why won't they leave us alone?' said Shai Fea. Angry as well as frightened, she turned and said imperiously, 'I command you not to follow us!'

Her words had no effect. The red figures simply stared blankly at her.

'There seems to be nothing we can do, short of slaying them,' said Ashurek, 'and I have no intention of doing that. As long as they offer us no harm, we must tolerate them.'

He spoke without emotion, but inside he was burning. In the disorientation of the Maelstrom he had seen the

Muridonu as the past come back to haunt him, and no amount of logic could rid him of that impression. He could not harm them. They demanded help; everyone on this cursed world demanded his help, and all the time at the back of his mind were the High Master's words, 'You are only to observe, not to become involved.'

Damn you, Gregardreos! Damn your vindictiveness, your carelessness in putting Silvren in danger, he thought savagely. *If I ever return to complete my 'penance', is this what you want to hear? That a sad, small world is dying while Ikonus basks complacently in its own power like a gorged lizard?*

It was impossible to move with any speed through the sanguine storm. The endlessly whirling flakes were hypnotic, bringing a sickening sense of claustrophobia.

'This is hell,' Shai Fea said in a low voice. 'It's Flaim's domain. What if there's no end to it?'

Ashurek no longer had the heart to condemn her pessimism. She was no Sorceress, she had neither Silvren's power nor her training, and she had every reason to be afraid. He pulled her closer to him. 'I thought you had lost your faith and decided Flaim does not exist,' he said gently.

'Now I feel that Flaim was there all the time, and Eyos has deserted me. Flaim is the only god and he hates us, he can't be content with killing us, he must drive us mad first. What have we done to deserve this?'

'I have been in places such as this before,' said Ashurek. 'Illogical places, where the laws of nature cease. There is sometimes a centre to them, or an intelligence behind them . . .'

'How do we find it?'

'I have no idea. And this may be an exception, chaos without reason. But at least we are still alive, and uninjured.'

'I feel safe with you, Ashurek. If I was on my own, I'd die.'

A sudden instinct that something had changed made both of them turn round. With astonishment they saw that the Muridonu had stopped following them; the ghastly red shapes were motionless, almost invisible through the blizzard.

'Thank goodness!' Shai Fea exclaimed.

Ashurek did not share her relief. 'There must be a reason for them to have stopped. Wait a moment . . .'

He strained his eyes and through the bloody half-light he saw a grotesque shape. It was another of the Muridonu, one that was not pitiful but purely malevolent. It was much like the first one that he had encountered, but twice the size, as tall as Ashurek. He studied it and he knew it did not intend merely to fall in with the flock that were following him.

'Stay here,' he said, loosening his sword in its sheath. 'I have fought one of these things before.'

It crept towards him on a multitude of jointed legs, the eyeless mask of a head fronting the dark bulk of the carapace. Ashurek went to meet it with more confidence, knowing its vulnerable spot, anticipating the moves it was likely to make.

As it approached through the red storm it came into horrific focus, and he could see the long, bony mouthpieces, wet with poison. A fleeting idea crossed his mind, that its venom did not kill but simply transformed humans into Muridonu, mutated half-beings. Then the creature was upon him, and his sword was sweeping down to meet its armoured foreleg.

There was a dull crack, and the creature jerked back with its leg dangling uselessly. Ashurek would have preferred it to become incensed by rage; its insectile blankness was far harder to deal with. He had the ghastly impression that if he hacked it to bits, the remains would still be writhing in an attempt to attack him.

Two more limbs came thrusting at him. He struck at them hard, almost losing his balance in the soft surface. Once he had disabled the four front legs, the creature would be less able to protect its vulnerable mouthparts. One thrust should finish it swiftly.

Something strange happened to him then. He began to feel fear. Not the straightforward instinct for self-preservation that quickened his reflexes, but real, strength-sapping terror.

He felt sweat trickling down his back as he fought, and the fear fed on itself. Usually in battle, his apprehension transformed itself to anger and strength; this sudden weakness dismayed him, lying sick and cold in his stomach. His limbs were trembling. What was wrong? After all these years had he lost his nerve, fallen victim to the cowardice he so despised in others?

Furious with himself, he fought back more viciously. Three of the creatures' legs were cracked now, still groping for him but with little strength or accuracy. He prepared to go for the kill.

As he did, something bulged in one of the creature's black eyeholes. Something round, shiny and yellowish. Ashurek stepped back, thrown off his stroke. A head came thrusting out of the hole, a human head crowned with golden hair –

Silvren's head.

Ashurek staggered backwards, crying out with horror. The head was alive, its lips were moving. Silvren. Had it attacked her, absorbed her, what? He could not slay it now, how would he know he was not killing her, or what was left of her?

He lost his footing and fell. The creature loomed above him, and two faces stared down; the red skull-mask with its mouth parts glistening, champing in anticipation – and worse, far worse, Silvren's sweet face bulging grotesquely from the eye-socket.

Ashurek groaned, waiting for the end to come. The next he knew, there was a humming, crackling light somewhere above, red snow hissing away into vapour as a figure dashed past him. He saw the swirl of a cloak, a dark flame of hair. Shai Fea rushed at the creature with the heat-sword held two-handed, and plunged the weapon straight into its empty eye.

The air fizzed with blue sparks. The beast lurched backwards, wrenching itself free, but too late; smoke poured from its face and a flat whining noise issued from its carapace; not a cry of pain, but hot air escaping.

The fire caught. Flames roared up, blinding white. The creature collapsed in on itself and began to shrivel in a cloud of noxious gases.

Ashurek lifted his head and saw Shai Fea stumbling towards him. She lost her footing and floundered waist-deep in the red drifts, but she could not stand up; she went on sinking, and then Ashurek felt the ground falling away beneath them, and he looked down and saw a mouth, a mouth opening up beneath him, and the drifts were flowing into it like snow into a chasm, and he and Shai Fea were sliding into the darkness . . .

He was inside the stomach of a huge beast. He could feel the slow rumble of its heartbeat, the heaving of its lungs, the rivers of blood gushing through its veins. Some distance from him in the wet, purple darkness he could hear the High Master saying that there was only one way to destroy the beast: to crawl through its arteries and stab it straight through the heart.

'No,' said Ashurek. 'If you stab it it will spill its lifeblood on the ground and poison us all.'

But the High Master would not listen and he was gone into the swollen darkness with a shining green sword in his hand . . .

Only when Ashurek jerked back to awareness did he realise that he had lost consciousness for a second, and in that second he had had a complete and unpleasant dream. There was no beast, no dark mouth; instead, the surface beneath him was grass . . . pale green-gold grass, starred with tiny beige flowers. Columns of pink and gold light hung in the air, rippling softly like veils in a breeze; silent, beautiful, but wrong.

'Where are we?' Ashurek heard Shai Fea's voice, lifted his head and saw her crawling towards him, dishevelled and dripping crimson fluid onto the ground. He sat up and she crawled into his arms.

They remained for a long time without speaking, clinging to each other until the shock subsided. A hundred yards away, blurred by the curtains of light, was the fretted Edge of the world, and beyond that the roof of Jyel Vanan's house just visible as a dark smear.

Eventually Ashurek said, 'I could not have seen Silvren. I will not believe it was real.'

'No, no it wasn't. I saw such awful things, I saw my husband and my uncle, and my poor brother was with them, he was dead too . . . No, it was only that creature, feeding on our fears.'

'Yes. An illusion.' He drew a deep breath that vibrated through his whole body. 'You acted very bravely, Fea. If you hadn't done as you did, we would have died or joined those wretched half-beings. I have misjudged you; I ask your forgiveness for that.'

She shook her head, seeming embarrassed. 'No, I – I did it because I had to, it wasn't brave. I wish –'

'What?'

She bit her lip and it turned deep red. 'That I could do something to ease the pain you're in.'

Ashurek met her beautiful eyes; blue-green, flecked with jewels. There was nothing he could say. They both knew that his pain could only be healed by Silvren's return, and that in turn would hurt Shai Fea. Neither of them could win.

'You do ease the pain,' he said softly. 'And that is something very few people in my life have ever managed to do. Anything I can do to help you, I will.'

'But you said –'

'Forget what I said.' He kissed her, then helped her to her feet. 'It seems we are out of the Maelstrom, though we're still near the Edge of Jhensit. I wonder how we escaped?'

'Thank me for that,' said a deep, female voice.

Coalescing out of air was a tall, pale figure; Shai Fea's mother, the Hyalana Shai Tialah.

Her face was so like Shai Fea's, round yet delicate, with the added depth of wisdom and age. Even the raggedness of her garments lent a wild majesty to her form, and the veils of rose and gold light seemed part of her, like an ever-moving ethereal cloak.

Another illusion?

'Mother, oh, mother!' Shai Fea exclaimed. She started forward but the Hyalana raised her hands as if to ward her off. Ashurek was stricken by the impression that there was a black, burning halo around her fingers.

'Dearest child,' said Tialah. She looked at Ashurek, challenging but not unkind. 'Why did he bring you into this dreadful realm?' She shone with maternal love, with strength and a dreadful hidden pain; too real to be no more than a spirit.

'Ashurek? He didn't,' said Shai Fea. 'It was – it was an accident. No-one's fault. What are you doing here, do you know where we are?'

The Hyalana spoke slowly, as if in a dream. 'I watch over you, dearest, whenever I can and wherever you are. I have brought you back to the Edge of the world. I will not let anyone harm you.'

Shai Fea's painful joy was almost unbearable to watch, and Ashurek wished he could avoid witnessing it. Yet at the back of his throat was an odd sensation that he could not identify; a sour taste of corruption. Something made him look round and with dismay he saw a half-circle of Muridonu, watching, silently imploring, *Lead us. Lead us*.

'Don't leave, Mother, stay with me,' Shai Fea was saying. 'It means so much to see you, when I thought I'd lost you.'

Intent on her mother, she had not seen the creatures, but Tialah had. She gave them a long look before turning back to her daughter. 'I would do anything for you, my love. I would have done anything to spare you this, but how can we escape the circumstances to which we are born? If I'd known, I would never have borne you or Elatiat Harn.'

'Don't say that! I don't understand you.'

'I wish I had never been born myself. Or at least, I wish I had died when I should have died.'

The colour bled out of Shai Fea's face. 'What do you mean?'

'What little of me there is left survived for your sake, Fea, yet the price was too great.'

The Hyalana glanced at Ashurek, and in that instant there was deeper understanding between them than there had ever been between her and Shai Fea. Her eyes were proud and stern, yet they were brittle glass through which he glimpsed a soul screaming for help.

Then she walked slowly past him, towards the Muridonu. They reared up to attack; a mass of bony arms and insect legs, claws and poisoned fangs, but she showed no fear. She reached out as if to pet them, and each one she touched fell dead.

When she had finished she came back to Ashurek and Shai Fea. 'No-one and nothing is allowed to hurt my daughter,' she said.

'In that case, madam,' said Ashurek, 'I suggest that you tell your daughter the truth. It seems to me that you are hurting her more than anyone.'

Shai Fea was wide-eyed. 'What do you mean?'

'Does your mother know what happened to your husband, and the purpose for which you asked my help?'

'Of course!'

'Tell her again.'

She made a weak noise of protest, but his tone was imperative. 'Wedren Lan was killed,' she stammered, 'and I have vowed to find the murderer . . . but you were there, mother, the night he died! You warned me and . . . and you know how badly it affected Harn.'

'I know all of this, child.' The Hyalana's eyes became icy. 'But it is your brother's fault you are in this situation.'

'I know, but only because he's not himself. I have to prove my innocence and find the real killer for his sake, to save his sanity.'

'Have you thought that his sanity might be beyond saving?' said the Hyalana. There was no flicker of response on her face, only the steady, cold stare.

She was going to admit nothing; perhaps she could not. As gently as he could, Ashurek said, 'Don't you understand yet, Fea? She is the murderer.'

Shai Fea jumped as if she had been stung. 'Who do you mean?' Her face turned ivory-grey. 'Not my mother. No. How dare you!'

'Let her deny it then. Speak to your daughter, madam, but tell her the truth.'

Still Shai Tialah's face did not change. She said evenly, 'Everyone that hurt me, and everyone that hurts you, dear Fea; what do they deserve, but death?'

Ashurek held Shai Fea, one arm round her back, the other gripping her hand. She was shaking violently.

'Think,' he said. 'Who were the people who died?'

Lips parted, she stared blankly at the shimmering, semi-solid form of her mother. 'People you hated,' she whispered. 'My father's councillors, friends of Elatiat Harn that you didn't like, and Wedren Lan . . .'

'If you had loved him, I would have spared him. But you did not and I couldn't bear to see you bonded in such a miserable marriage.'

Shai Fea shook her head in convulsive denial. It was all she could do to speak. 'But you are dead, you are a ghost, how could you have –? I thought you came to comfort me. No, I don't believe it, I *won't!*'

Now her mother looked sad. Her desolation cut right through Ashurek; he kept seeing his own mother in her deep eyes. 'Of course I came to comfort you. But to protect you as well.'

Shai Fea was weeping openly now, her cheeks glazed with tears. 'I don't understand. How could you do this? Are you dead or not?'

'Did you never wonder what it was like for me, being sent alive to join your father in the tomb?'

'Don't, mother. Of course I wondered. I had nightmares for years!'

'Then I'll tell you, child, that no nightmare could touch the reality of it. I stood on my balcony on the day of your father's funeral and it was one of those rare days when the sky was clear of all traces of the Maelstrom. It was so thin and clear, like a lake, the round blue eye of Eyos. But where was our god that day? Mocking me with tradition. I was still young and strong, it was not my fault that my husband had died before his time and not my sin to be punished. The air was so sweet that day . . . Do you remember?'

'No, I was thinking about nothing but you,' Shai Fea sobbed.

'But I noticed everything, because it was my last day. Lovely Niankan-Siol, all blue and jade and palest yellow. I did not want to leave. I was not in the right frame of mind at all; I should have been calm, pious, resigned, accepting my husband in death as I had in life. Instead, I was furious and terrified.

'I tried so hard to behave as the Hyalana should, when they came for me, those damned men who insisted on tradition. But I lost control and I shouted at them. "Why must I die, just because my husband is dead?" "Tradition," they replied. "Tradition, tradition. The Hyalana cannot outlive her husband." Only Tean Mon and some of my friends spoke for me. And I hated the rest, men I had always respected, my own cousins and uncles; I hated them.

'My last meeting with you was unbearable, Fea, but with Elatiat Harn it was worse. Did he ever tell you?'

Shai Fea shook her head wordlessly.

'He feigned all the correct emotions, regret and sadness, but what he really felt was impatience. I could always read that boy like a book. The faster his father and mother were interred and forgotten, the faster he could be crowned. Oh, we parted with many rancorous words. I begged him to break tradition, you see, and let me live.'

'Damn him, Eyos and Flaim curse him,' Shai Fea cried. 'Why couldn't he have listened to you?'

'He said my remarks were unworthy. "Do you wish history to remember you for cowardice, when the rest of your life has been unimpeachable?" he said. "You have always known this would happen, you have had all your life to prepare for it."

'I could have told him, ten lifetimes were not enough to prepare. But I only had one, one little life which he would take away from me, sever me from my daughter . . .' The Hyalana broke off, then went on more calmly, 'Certainly he made me ashamed. When I saw he and the councillors wouldn't be moved, I went to the funeral bier with dignity. No Satrans would lay their hands on me!' She held out the hem of her tattered robes. 'These are the clothes I was buried in. All saffron and eggshell blue, do you remember? And gold filigree over it, and the little glass birds in my hair. Dressed as for a wedding. And it was such a beautiful day . . . Don't cry, Fea. Didn't you do enough crying then?

'The procession through Niankan-Pel was like a dream. If only I'd thrown myself from the balcony and cheated them of this! All those crowds with sombre sad faces, and not a soul there who could reach out and help me. I was alone. I was not even allowed to see you or Tean Mon. I felt I was riding on a great wave of silence, miles above the world and for a time I thought, perhaps it will not be so bad, perhaps Eyos will take me into the sky after all . . .

' "Consign the body to the earth and the soul to the sky," the priests say. But my husband's soul had already fled to the sky, while mine was still below, and it was the earth I feared. The Tomb of the Hyalons is a very beautiful thing, a great azure tower, but it is a lie.'

'What do you mean, a lie?' Shai Fea said faintly.

'There are no Hyalons inside it. A door opens in the

side, like a black mouth, with a groaning of cogs and gears. The bier bearing the dead Hyalon slides in, followed by the one bearing his living wife, tied down lest she try to escape at the last moment. And the door slides shut and they are sealed within their tomb.'

'Leaving you to die of starvation, presumably,' said Ashurek.

'So I had imagined, but that was not the end of it. Another mechanism started up, the floor of the tomb split open, and I was plunged down into the disgusting soft soil. All my life I had been taught to believe that the earth was vile, and I believed it. But now I was buried in it and my husband's body fell on me, soft and cold and heavy.

'The dead do not return to tell their stories, do they? They keep the inside of the Tomb pristine, like a palace, while all the dead rulers moulder in the earth beneath.

'The soil seemed full of movement, I remember, as if a machine was churning up the earth to bury us. With the last of my breath I cursed the Neatrus. And I said to any god that would listen, "Spare me. I would do anything not to die." Then my nose and mouth filled with the stuff, the bitterness of mud and decay, and I died.

'I seemed to be travelling down an infinitely long black tunnel, yet I could still feel the weight of soil on top of me. *Pour bronze into this space,* I thought. *Let my body be vaporised and a statue left in my place, something for them to remember me by, something that does not feel . . .*

'When I reached the end of the tunnel, the face was waiting for me.'

Ashurek stiffened. 'What face?'

'More a mask; the green face of Flaim, I thought it was. It said, "Would you truly do anything not to die?"

'I wasn't afraid. I felt nothing at all, I was in a dream-state in which all emotion and conscience had ceased to exist. I said "Yes."

' "Would you exchange your life for that of another?"

' "To let someone else die in my place?" I said. And

it replied, ''Not just one other, but many others.''

'And I said, ''Yes.''

'Then the Face poured a fluid into the space where I was, melting my flesh but replacing it with a finer substance. I began to breathe again. I breathed earth as if it were air, and I passed through it as if I had become liquid.

'But the Face had cheated me. I was not truly dead, nor was I truly alive again. I could never go back to my real life, I could only haunt the edges and take my revenge on those who had forced me to this. That is why, beloved daughter, I can never touch you. If I touched you, you would die.'

Shai Fea recoiled from her, eyes round with horror.

'Don't look at me like that!' the Hyalana cried in anguish. 'It is all I have left, your love! If you take that from me I'll have nothing left but revenge!'

'Mother, this is evil,' Shai Fea said hoarsely. 'You cannot believe it's right.'

'I believe nothing.'

'But you've brought disaster to our lives!'

'How can I bring disaster to a world that is almost dead?'

'You've destroyed Elatiat Harn.'

'But he destroyed me! And now he's destroyed you!'

Shai Fea lifted a hand which trembled in mid-air like a white leaf. 'Please, please tell me that you did not kill Tean Mon.'

'That is the only one I regret. But he let you down, my love; he thought you were safe when you were not.'

With a thin, heart-rending groan, Shai Fea sank to the ground and hid her face in her hands. The Hyalana went on, 'And the one who pushed you into the Maelstrom – should he escape punishment?'

To his astonishment, Ashurek – who was kneeling beside Shai Fea – glanced up and saw Jaia Keorn standing rigid and white with dread a few feet from the Hyalana, as if bound there by her aura. He was staring at Ashurek, almost out of his mind with shock. Three ghosts, returned from their graves to exact an unthinkable revenge.

Shai Fea looked up. 'No, mother. Please spare him. I – I'll still love you, but only if you spare him!'

Jaia Keorn's eyes widened. The Hyalana waved a careless hand at him and he fell loose-jointed to the ground – not dead, but freed from her aura. He began to crawl away.

'I spare him because he is nothing, he had no reason to care for you. But your brother – he should have cared! Oh, I should have done this a long time ago. I hesitated because he was my son, but he is my son no longer. I could allow him to hurt me – but to hurt you, my sweet daughter, never.'

She turned away, and her body seemed almost as insubstantial as the rippling columns of light through which she walked. Ashurek got swiftly to his feet, lifting Shai Fea with him.

'Mother, no!' She turned frantically to Ashurek. 'She's going to kill Elatiat Harn. We must stop her, we must!'

Ashurek watched the Hyalana walk away, and she was already far from them; a figure so pale that she was not a solid shape in the landscape but a nothingness, a gap. She looked back once before she vanished, and he heard her voice, faint but clear.

'You are a fire, Ashurek. The fire that burns away everything but the truth.'

12

Ice in the Rain

Where the Edge of the world met the Maelstrom, curtains of light swayed like an aurora, shot through with slow-rolling fireballs of red, gold and purple. There was a distant, ominous rumbling. Shai Fea was already hurrying in the direction that her mother had taken; Ashurek went with her, with a powerful feeling that they must get away from the Edge as swiftly as possible.

'We'll never catch her,' Shai Fea said breathlessly. 'How fast can she travel? It will take us days, and she could be there in an instant.'

'Save your breath to run,' said Ashurek.

Glancing back, he could just see the island through the rose and golden veils; the dark roof of the house and the straggling crescent of trees. It seemed to tremble. Jaia Keorn was running after them, a scarecrow silhouette in the mists.

'Please wait!' the Pel was shouting. 'My Lord Ashurek, please!'

Reluctantly, Ashurek slowed down and waited. Shai Fea was out of breath, and could not have gone much further without a rest, so she stopped without protest as Jaia Keorn came running up to them. He skidded onto his knees, almost cowering before them.

'Please,' he stammered, 'I'm unworthy even to look at you, I know, but I must speak. I should have known that even the Maelstrom could not destroy you.'

Ashurek's face was impassive, his eyes cruel as winter thorns. 'I suppose you will now claim that you tried to kill me to test my divinity. Are you satisfied?'

'I acted in rage,' Keorn said thickly. 'I let my personal feelings take possession of me and that was wrong, stupid, unforgivable –'

'In that case, you will not expect us to forgive you,' Ashurek said icily. 'What do you want of us? We must make haste and this is wasting our time.'

He felt Shai Fea touching his arm. 'Don't be so harsh with him,' she said quietly.

'I – I wanted to ask why you spared me,' said the Pel. 'I don't know what that pale woman was but she had death in her hands and she knew what I'd done.'

'It was Shai Fea who told her to spare you, not I,' said Ashurek. 'You're still alive. Be satisfied with that.'

Ashurek started to turn away. The distant rumbling grew louder and the ground shook slightly. Snake-tongues of colour licked at the sky.

'Wait! I have more to tell you –'

'There is no time,' said Ashurek, and he began to run again, pulling Shai Fea with him. 'The Maelstrom is spreading; save yourself!'

Jaia Keorn stood up, suddenly realising the danger. 'Father!' he shouted. He sprinted back towards the Edge and was swiftly lost to sight amid the curtains of mist and light.

Ashurek and Shai Fea ran on, but it was as if they ran through clear tar, and the visions of madness began to torment them, gorging on their fears.

'Illusions!' he shouted. 'Hold onto reality!'

Now the sky was roiling with pearl and silver, streaked with veins of purplish-black. A shower of silukians came hurtling overhead, flecks of vivid colour, uttering piercing cries.

Ashurek fought against the nightmare images and they receded, gibbering and clawing at the periphery of his thoughts. He looked back as he ran and saw Jyel Vanan's island tipping crazily then careering towards the Edge, carried by the momentum of its vast bulk. There was a deep, rolling sound of collision, a cascade of disintegrating rock, then the island bounced away and began to lose height, rotating slowly as it sank into the void.

Through the numbing wind of illusions he and Shai Fea ran, while the Maelstrom came in like a tide behind them and the land began to melt into streamers of fire. The air was thick with the whispering voices of the Muridonu, *We were human once. We were flesh and blood. Wherever you go, we shall follow . . .*

The storm was brief. The sky went on thrashing violently above them, carrying the shockwaves on towards Niankan, but the landscape faded back into a strangely flat solidity. The nightmares vanished like bubbles.

'I can't go any further,' Shai Fea said, doubled up and sobbing for breath.

'I think it's over.' Looking back, he saw that a new Edge had formed, perhaps half-a-mile behind them. It was only intermittently visible through great silvery banks of vapour which rolled and thundered, lit by flashes of acid-green light.

'Poor Jyel Vanan,' said Shai Fea. 'And Jaia Keorn went straight back into it.'

'They may have survived, but they will be trapped in the Maelstrom as we were,' said Ashurek. 'Don't think of it. We've a long journey back to your city.'

But as he spoke, three figures came rushing out of the clouds, delicate and attenuated against the light; Jaia Keorn, leading two auerets which stepped out like long-necked, long-legged dancers.

'I found them for you,' he said. 'My father's gone. I couldn't reach him. He's dead.' He tried to contain his tears but he could not and he turned his back to them, sobbing.

Shai Fea touched him gently on the shoulder. 'Now you know how I feel,' she said, but her voice was kind. 'Now we understand each other.'

* * *

Thus they journeyed back to Niankan as they had come; Ashurek and Shai Fea on one aueret, Jaia Keorn on the other. They had additional companions, three of Jyel Vanan's silukians, which had attached themselves to Shai Fea and now attended her devotedly. They helped take her mind from her own troubles, for which Ashurek was glad. One was deep blue, one white with turquoise wings, the third pale rose deepening to magenta. Their colours were stunning against the landscape, which was all amber veined with black; dying in beauty, like autumn.

They came to the deserted farmhouse where they had rested on their way to Jyel Vanan's house. The evening sky was honey-coloured, the fruit trees spiky jet sculptures around the overgrown building. Ashurek tethered the auerets and they went inside to rest and eat.

None of them could relax. Ashurek was haunted by the feeling that the Muridonu were still pursuing him, but he saw no sign of them and he kept the fear firmly to himself.

Shai Fea looked pale and drawn in the pearly half-light, all energy drained from her. She sat on the edge of a chair, hugging herself, too wrung out to cry any more. Jaia Keorn, seated on the floor with his arms round his knees, was closed in on himself with a mixture of grief and shame. A subdued air hung over them all, despite Shai Fea's desperation to reach Niankan-Siol. Presently Keorn said, 'You didn't answer my question, my lady. Why did you have me spared?'

'Because it's my brother's answer to everything,' she said with a venom that surprised Ashurek. 'If someone is caught doing wrong, they must be executed. I don't want to be like him.'

'I'm glad to hear it,' he said. 'I want to help you.'

He was speaking to Shai Fea more because he was almost too afraid to say anything to Ashurek. Ashurek paused in polishing his sword and said, 'Why? I would have thought it was in your interest for the Hyalon to die.'

'That's not fair! You don't trust me!' Keorn jumped to his feet and stalked towards the door.

'Don't take it personally,' said Ashurek. 'I trust almost

no-one. It will not help your case to take offence so easily.'

'I am going to fetch some water,' Keorn said tightly.

While he was outside, Shai Fea said, 'You know, it is an illusion, being a Hyalet. I thought I had power – but now I see I have no power at all. I was living in a cage, protected. Outside it, people like Jaia Keorn do not obey me or even respect me. Not that I care – It's all a lie, an illusion, everything the Ruling Family stands for. Ashurek, would you have helped the Pels?'

'Perhaps, if circumstances had been different,' he said candidly.

'Different, how?'

'If I had not met you and your mother.'

'You would have helped them?' You would have dragged the Neatrus down into their dirt? That's what the Pels want, to reduce us all to their own level . . .'

'You contradict yourself. You just said that your family stands for a lie, so I would only have been destroying a lie.'

'You're mocking me.'

'You are tormenting yourself.'

'What do you expect me to do?' she said heatedly. 'How would you feel if your mother – if your mother –'

Ashurek stood up, lifted her from the chair, and embraced her. Her voice was muffled against his chest. 'I don't care what she's done, I still love her. I can't bear to see her suffering, I'd do anything to save her from it . . . Oh, dear Eyos, what if we're too late?'

'You must prepare yourself for that possibility. But we must try.'

'It's – it's not so much wanting to save my brother – although I do, of course – as wanting to save my mother from the act. Do you understand? I feel that if she kills him, they will both be damned, and so will I.'

He said nothing, only held her tighter. Jaia Keorn came back in and looked sourly at them. He ladled out some goblets of water and flopped down in his place on the floor, but only when Shai Fea was stronger did Ashurek let her go.

'You said you had something else to tell us, Keorn,' he said, drawing his chair closer to Shai Fea's and sitting next to her.

The Pel nodded. His face was half-averted, his eyes grave. 'My father punished me for what I had done and he put me through what we call the purging of Flaim. I won't describe it to you, but I learned something from it. I understand now – Flaim is not a separate entity, Flaim *is* Jhensit. We've been praying to Flaim to save us while all the time it is we who should save the earth. Flaim is the earth *and* the sky. They are one. Eyos and Flaim are the same god!' He looked sideways at Shai Fea. 'Could you ever believe that, my lady?'

He obviously expected a vehement refusal, but she said, 'Perhaps. It seems completely ridiculous to me now that I was ever afraid of the earth. There's nothing evil in it. The only evil is in the Maelstrom, and this division between the Siols and the Pels . . . I think it only gives the Maelstrom more power.'

Shai Fea and Keorn stared straight at each other, and Ashurek felt very much an intruder, not part of their concerns. Yet he was involved, and far more fully than he had ever intended.

The tenderness he felt for both Shai Fea and her mother disconcerted him to the bone. For years he had little love to spare for anyone except Silvren and his daughter; his love for his own family in Gorethria had not saved them from disaster. Now against all instincts and common sense, he shared Shai Fea's longing to help her mother. *This concern I feel, can it be genuine? Or simply a way of trying to recompense my own family for failing them?*

He had no answer.

When they came within a day's ride of Niankan, they saw a troop of Satrans in the distance; a white-winged flock of auerets, the gleam of sky-blue enamel.

'Decide now, Fea,' said Ashurek. 'Do you really want

to go back to your city? If not, we have to flee now before they see us.'

'I made my decision at the world's Edge. I'm past being afraid, Ashurek.'

'If you are sure.'

Her voice and her bearing were dignified but forlorn. 'It's my home, my family. There's nowhere else for me to go.'

For himself, Ashurek had no fear, no feelings at all for the Hyalon and his Satrans. If anything, he was curious to meet Elatiat Harn and to see Niankan-Siol at closer quarters. His spirits rose and he urged the aueret into a rolling, two-beat run.

The Satrans saw them. There was a hum and crackle of sparks as their heatswords sprang into life, and they closed in to surround the three fugitives. They moved warily, undoubtedly having heard how dangerous Ashurek was.

The captain halted and looked Ashurek up and down, as if he had been unable to believe the stories until now.

'Surrender! You are outnumbered!' he shouted, his voice almost breaking.

Ashurek smiled. 'My sword is in its sheath, as you see, and will remain there. We are giving ourselves up.'

The captain let out a breath, but did not look much happier. 'Your sword, please, sir.'

Ashurek gave him a dark stare. 'Is it not enough for you that I have given my word not to use it?'

'It is an offence to carry a metal weapon. I have to insist you relinquish it.'

Ashurek grudgingly unbuckled the sheath and handed it to him. Then the captain turned to Shai Fea and bowed. 'Your Highness, it is my grievous duty to arrest you and take you straight to the palace.'

'Captain, answer me a question first. Her face was pale, one hand half-raised towards him. 'His majesty the Hyalon – is he well?'

The Satran frowned. 'Yes, perfectly well, ma'am.'

'Thank Eyos.' She slumped on the aueret's back.

'Your pardon, ma'am, that I have to do this . . .'

'It's your duty, captain.' She was half-laughing and half-crying with relief, causing the Satrans to give her curious looks. 'Please take us straight to his Majesty.'

The route by which they entered Niankan-Pel gave a false impression of the city, Ashurek thought. There was a broad thoroughfare, spotlessly clean, almost worthy of Shalekahh; the buildings were graceful, their mushroom-grey stone polished to a semi-precious shine. But this was a route for the Siols, to save them having to abase their eyes on the poverty of Pel. The three silukians wheeled away, unwilling to go deeper into the city, and Shai Fea watched them wistfully as they dwindled to specks against the pale, troubled sky.

They were taken through a tall gate into the barracks, where in the centre of a square, a strut soared to the upper city far above them. Its base was guarded by a high wall, painted with the blue and gold symbols of Eyos. On the captain's instructions they dismounted from the auerets. A second gate opened and Satrans in the sky-blue of Siol ushered Ashurek and Shai Fea through, but stopped Jaia Keorn.

'No Pels are allowed to enter the upper city,' said the captain.

'But I am not an ordinary Pel, I have been with them since – ' The Satrans began to pull him away but he went on protesting. Ashurek shook his head.

'Do as they say, Keorn.'

Keorn looked indignantly at him, as if he were being betrayed yet again. Shai Fea turned to the captain and said, 'Make very sure that he is well looked after. I hold you responsible!'

'Yes, ma'am,' said the captain, paling slightly. 'Now, if you will step into the carriage. Please.'

At the base of the strut waited a cage of pearly-pink glass. The captain and three Satrans – there was not room for more – accompanied Ashurek and Shai Fea into the cage, deeply uneasy at their close proximity to this tall, demonic stranger. The door closed, and one of the men released a lever.

With a shower of white and blue sparks the capsule began its smooth ascent of the strut. As it rose, Ashurek was transfixed by the sight of the city slowly spreading out below him. The streets wove crookedly between the high stone houses; the roofs shone dull pewter, almost beautiful in a faded way. The Ochre River appeared, a serpent wreathed in mist, then the distant brown hills rose into view. On the skyline was a single azure spike which he guessed, from the Hyalana's description, was the Tomb of the Hyalons. Closer to the city, roughly a mile away, was a smooth pale hemisphere, a pearl exuded from the dark guts of the earth.

'What is that?' said Ashurek.

'The White Dome,' Shai Fea replied. 'That is where the scientists create Niankan-Siol's power and light. I have never been there.'

'Keorn seemed to think it was a prison,' Ashurek remarked.

'No talking!' the captain snapped, as if they were touching on an uncomfortable subject. The ascent was completed in silence.

Despite his natural cynicism, Ashurek's breath was taken away by the sheer beauty of Niankan-Siol. They stepped from the capsule onto a guarded platform, and from there onto a flimsily-railed walkway, the surface of which was yellow flecked with gold, shiny as glass.

Fantastical buildings rose around them, all of a delicate resinous material that looked as if it would shatter with one blow of a fist. There were shades of pastel blue, jade, primrose and pearl, stretching as far as the eye could see and melting into a water-ice sky. Walkways threaded between them, with branches leading to doorways, but between the buildings and the walkways there were heart-stopping drops to the city far below. There was an audacity in this disregard for safety that appealed to Ashurek.

Before them was an aquamarine palace which, despite its vastness, seemed as light as air, only resting on its struts because it was tethered there. It was too delicate to be real, a feverish fantasy.

'The House of Neatru,' Shai Fea whispered. 'I'm glad I've come home.'

Vertigo touched him, and his perception changed. The palace seemed the epitomy of Jhensit's sickness. The top crust was still there but everything beneath had collapsed away, ice eaten by spring rain; and those who remained were a people under siege, isolated and afraid, ever more vicious in their desperation to retain their power.

The guards took them through a towering doorway. Inside, the palace was no less exquisite, all eggshell fragility, spun glass and images of birds. A sense of weariness descended on him. Shai Fea's face was taut with anxiety, but when he touched her shoulder she managed a weak smile.

All along the corridors, Siols in elaborate silk robes stood aside for them, staring incredulously at Ashurek. At last the captain brought them to an antechamber and began a long, whispered exchange with a guard and a thin, pale-faced man dressed in blue silk.

When they had finished, the man in blue came forward and bowed to Shai Fea. 'Welcome home, your Highness. We are glad to see you.'

'It is good to be home, Tir,' she responded.

The man's face was tight and hard, his blue-grey hair cropped short. Ashurek instinctively disliked him, though there seemed to be genuine warmth in his words to Shai Fea. Now he turned to Ashurek. 'I am Cilit Tir Neatru, Counsellor to the Hyalon Elatiat Harn. He has agreed to see you both in his private apartments, if you will be so good as to step this way.'

Double doors opened onto a high, lavish chamber all draped in celestial blue and gold. Ashurek froze. It was the chamber he had seen in the mystical book, down to the last detail. He should know, he had seen page after page of the same illustration, with only the figure of the Hyalana – the figure of nothingness – moving inexorably towards the man trapped in the blue and gold chair. And the man, he saw with less surprise, was Elatiat Harn.

The Hyalon, Ashurek thought, was not an impressive figure, despite his magnificent garments. He was small and the stiffened robes made him seem squat against the soaring background of the chamber.

'Your majesty, allow me to present her Highness the Hyalet Shai Fea and – er – Lord Ashurek,' said Cilit Tir. He withdrew, leaving the three of them alone, though there must have been guards concealed within earshot. Elatiat Harn and Shai Fea stood facing each other, a gulf of floor between them. Neither made a move to close the gap. Eventually the Hyalon spoke. 'You look like a Pel, Fea.'

'So would you, if you had been forced to live like one for days on end.'

'I am glad you've come back.' His voice was measured and calm, but his self-control was belied by his appearance; his hair was tousled, his eyes rimmed with scarlet, and his demeanour of barely controlled restlessness. 'You should not have left, but you know that; I don't blame you. I am just so glad you have come home safely.'

She took a step forward. 'But I've got so much to explain, about why I had to leave and why I'm here now. I've seen such terrible things. I am innocent, Harn. I had to prove it but it hardly seems important now, I know who is responsible for the murders and I can hardly bear to tell you but I have to, you're in terrible danger –'

He raised his hand, silencing her. 'There's no need, Fea. I know what you are going to say.'

'How?' Her jewelled irises were circled with white.

Elatiat Harn glanced at Ashurek. He had a distracted look; Ashurek could well believe Shai Fea's assertion that he was bordering on a breakdown. If anything, he looked worse than her description. 'Mother has appeared to me, every night for five nights.'

'What – what did she say to you?'

'Nothing.' He blinked. His eyes were pale coins, floating in blood. 'She first appeared as I lay in bed, on the far side of the room. She stood completely still, like a statue, with one hand raised. She didn't speak, she just watched me and then vanished. I tried to tell myself that it was only a nightmare, but I knew, I knew it was more than that. I have not slept since.

'The next night I sat up in a chair and left the lights burning but she came again, just standing motionless, pointing at me. Every night she appears, a little closer to me each time.'

'And she says nothing?'

'She does not need to. I know, Fea. ' He went to a desk and leaned heavily on it. 'I know that when she reaches me, I shall die.'

'Dear Eyos, help us,' Shai Fea whispered.

Elatiat Harn took a deep breath and mastered himself. 'I know you are innocent. I do not know how to begin to say I'm sorry. I don't understand what I've done to deserve her wrath.'

'You made her go to her death with father! Then you blamed me for her – crimes,' Shai Fea said bluntly.

The Hyalon showed no sign of taking in what she had said. He held his arms out stiffly, not moving, just waiting for her to go to him. Perhaps he could not move. Shai Fea ran to him and they embraced awkwardly, swiftly drawing apart.

'I've so much else to tell you –' she began.

'Not now,' he said. 'I want to talk to you, dearest, I want to hear the things that happened to you, but I can't yet, I have too many other things to deal with.' He glanced at Ashurek, apparently including him in the catalogue of problems. 'Go and rest; I'll send your attendants to you. You are no prisoner now, everything will be as it was before. Welcome home.'

She kissed him on the cheek and looked at him gravely. 'I'll do as you say, but you can't cut me out of your concerns as you used to. We have to fight these things together now.'

She walked away, pausing as she drew level with Ashurek. She looked drained with the shock of relief; she had expected a hard battle of wits and instead she had met understanding and reconciliation. But that did not remove the danger that haunted them.

'Please go, Fea,' said the Hyalon. 'I wish to talk to – ah, Lord Ashurek, alone. If he will permit me.'

There was a touch of sarcasm, conscious or unconscious, in his tone. Ashurek inclined his head. 'Your Majesty, I am honoured to be granted an audience,' he said without inflexion.

With a final pale glance at him, Shai Fea left the chamber.

Ashurek wondered how safe he was, alone with Elatiat Harn. The Hyalon was jumpy and volatile; one word out of place and Ashurek was likely to find himself surrounded by guards, even slain on the spot. Nevertheless, he decided to be direct. He took the offered seat and stretched out his legs, giving the appearance of being more relaxed than he was.

'I have heard a great deal about you,' said Elatiat Harn. His pale gaze darted restlessly around the room, meeting Ashurek's eyes only briefly now and again. 'I have heard that you appeared in a column of smoke like Flaim appearing from the underworld, that you slew several of my best soldiers, that you are a demonic emissary of Flaim. You have caused great trouble in my city. Now I wish to know the truth of it.'

Ashurek explained what he had told Jyel Vanan, this time putting in rather more detail. As he spoke, Harn alternately sat on the edge of his own chair and got up to pace about the room, as if he could not bear to be still. Ashurek could not be sure that the Hyalon believed him or was even listening properly.

'But what are you?' he said, when Ashurek had finished.

'I thought I had made that clear. I am of a different race and a different world, but I am a man, that's all. I had never heard of your gods before I came here, still less been sent by them.'

'But you have strange powers!'

'No,' said Ashurek.

'But some of the Pels do have strange powers!'

'What has that to do with me?'

'I don't know!' Elatiat Harn put a hand to his head, leaving his hair in disarray. He seemed to be making misconnections because he was under stress, his thoughts racing ahead of themselves. He sank back into his chair again and said, 'You must excuse me. I have so many problems. I have not slept for five nights. I do not know where to begin to solve them. Everything seemed easy once . . . I am strong, I have always been strong, but the answers just keep slipping out of my grasp, every time I feel I have found the truth it slides away from me again and changes into something different. Like Shai Fea; Eyos, it seemed so perfectly, coldly clear that she was responsible . . . How could I have thought that? Was I mad?'

He stood up again and made another circuit of the room. 'Now I find out that it is our mother, that she is neither dead nor alive . . . Dear Eyos, either the world has gone mad or I have.'

Ashurek saw that the Hyalon was, in a strange way, quite sane. If he had been a stronger or a more callous man, he might have coped better, but he had a great sense of responsibility, and he had been driven to this state of desperation by terror of failing in his duties.

'I have never envied rulers,' said Ashurek. 'It is a vast burden to bear, and few are equal to it.'

'My father was!' Harn said emphatically.

'And mine. Or do we believe that simply because we think our fathers can do no wrong?'

'You are also the son of a sovereign?' Elatiat Harn leaned forward, his eyes widening a touch, as if he had found an equal, someone in whom he could confide.

Ashurek nodded curtly. 'Something I wish to forget. But think, your Majesty; was your father truly such a great man, or did he achieve that impression simply by closing his eyes and mind to your world's real problems?'

'The Maelstrom,' Elatiat Harn said quietly. 'I remember

when the skies were blue and we thought Eyos would save us. Now the Maelstrom is eating the sky as well as the earth. How can we escape? Is there any point in trying?'

'Better to die fighting than wondering what would have happened if only you'd had the courage to try.'

The Hyalon was quiet for a time, staring broodingly out of the windows to the balcony beyond. Ashurek watched him, wondering if the Siols feared falling to the city below. Was it something he was considering now, an escape from unsolvable dilemmas and from the relentless advance of a malign ghost? Presently Harn moistened his lips and said, 'I know nothing about you, yet I almost feel that I know you. It is in your eyes, that you have suffered many troubles and found a way to vanquish them. With your powers, you could help us.'

Ashurek felt a dull sense of resignation, something heavy falling inside him. 'I told you, I have no special powers,' he said distantly.

Elatiat Harn did not seem to hear. 'Perhaps it was mischance that brought you here, as you claim; mischance to you – but not to us. I feel that you were meant to come here . . .'

'Only observe; so much for that vow,' Ashurek said to himself. The Hyalon seemed to be in a dream, but when he suddenly looked at Ashurek his eyes were alert and intense.

'If you do not help us, you must be against us, on the side of the Pels!'

'I am on no-one's side. And the Pels are your subjects as much as the Siols. Perhaps if you attempted to unite them instead of persecuting them, you would find out the root of Jhensit's doom.'

A spasm of fury crossed the Hyalon's face and vanished as quickly. His face smoothed into a smile that was more a grimace. 'People have died for lesser insults than that,' he said. 'But you are no ordinary man. From you, it does not seem an insult. I would give anything to have your help . . .'

Now Ashurek fell into meditative silence. He could see that if he antagonised Elatiat Harn beyond a certain point, he was likely to be fighting for his life against a mass of Satrans. Yet he was not concerned. The Hyalon needed him more than he needed the Hyalon. What chilled him was the knowledge that a trap was closing around him, propelling him along a path that he had not intended to take.

'I am not to be used,' he said thinly. 'And I am not to be bought. If I help you, it will be because I wish to; not because you have asked. And do not speak of rewarding me; there may be a price to pay that you cannot guess.'

Ashurek lay on a silken bed, staring at the canopy and trying not to make comparisons with the more restrained opulence of Shalekahh. He closed his eyes. Exhaustion had hit him and he was glad of this chance to rest and gather his thoughts. He had arrived as a prisoner and was now being treated as an honoured guest, although he doubted that any attempt to leave the palace would be welcomed by the Hyalon.

He had escaped both the Jyel Vanan's island and the Maelstrom itself, yet he felt further from Silvren than ever. His thoughts turned to the White Dome. Scientists . . . could it be that there were people there with arcane knowledge that even Elatiat Harn or Jyel Vanan did not possess? Yet from what Keorn had told him, the place was inaccessible.

Yes, he was being channelled into making the only choice he could. The High Master had insisted that he do nothing, but what would that achieve? Only by acting would he stand any hope of finding Silvren. The Siols were not evil, as Jaia Keorn had tried to make him believe; they could not hold a candle to Gorethria in that respect. They were simply desperate.

He heard a whisper of movement in the room, and felt the other side of the bed dip.

'Why didn't you come to me?' said Shai Fea.

'I hardly think I would have been allowed into the

Hyalet's private chambers.' He smiled, pulled her to him, and kissed her. Her fine hair clung to his skin; she smelled sweetly of silk and perfumed oils.

'What did my brother say to you?'

He told her. He held her as he spoke, aware of the bow-string tension still in her body.

'What will you do?' she said at last.

'I shall try to give the help you both need.' The wave of relief that went through her was palpable, making her suddenly warm and soft against him. 'And may your god help you, too,' he added. 'Fea, you seem to be under the illusion that I can solve all your problems. I cannot. I have little idea of where to start, and whatever I do is out of selfishness, not philanthropy.'

'Do you feel nothing for me and for my mother? You care about us a little, at least. I don't care what you say, Ashurek, you are not as cold as you pretend.' Not waiting for him to respond, she went on, 'My mother will appear again tonight. I am going to insist that Elatiat Harn lets me sit up with him. Will you wait with us?'

'Yes, of course. But what do you intend to do if she appears?'

'Talk to her. She will listen to me. Oh, gods, I'd do anything to save her but I just don't know what to do.'

Ashurek looked into her jade and sapphire eyes, unsure whether to say what was in his mind.

'I wish to save her too, for your sake,' he said softly. 'If there were any way, I would do it.'

Her eyes were dark with pain and hope. Suddenly a great wave of dread went through him and he brought his mouth down on hers and kissed her savagely until she gasped for breath.

'Ashurek, what –'

'Forgive me.'

'No,' she said, putting her fingers to his lips. 'Love me.'

And some dark foreknowledge in the back of their minds imbued their love-making with fierce desperation, as if they both knew it was to be the last time.

13

'This walking death'

Gregardreos could sense Ashurek's presence, somewhere in Palan; a dull, constant pressure like a bruise. He tried to See more clearly, but the energy field of the White Dome affected his sorcerous sight and the picture remained blurred. Or perhaps he simply was not trying hard enough; there was always the vague hope that if he ignored Ashurek for long enough, Ashurek would cease to exist. He said nothing to Silvren, but the bruise in his mind persisted.

Within the very top of the Dome, blue-white light filtered through the curved roof and fell on the rectangular table where Gregardreos, Silvren and Iytrel Halia sat, with five of her scientists. The room was bright and airy, but a perpetual dull vibration permeated from the lower levels, a reminder of darkness and ominous powers. It was oppressive, but Gregardreos tried to ignore it and concentrate on the meeting.

He and Silvren had been in the Dome for several days, but so far Halia had only let her five most trusted colleagues in on the secret of the High Master's plan.

'The fewer people who know, the better,' said the Director, 'but eight is the minimum to cope with shutting down the generators and keeping the Pels in order. Did you notice, when we were in the generator chamber, that there were three coloured lights near the top of the central machine?'

Silvren and Gregardreos nodded.

'Those are the levers for closing the power down, but it must be done in a special order. First the red lever, which unfortunately alerts the Hyalon that the Dome is being shut down. Then nothing more can be done for two hours, to give the Neatrus time to come here and see what is going on.'

'So it's impossible for us to do anything without the Hyalon knowing anyway?' said Gregardreos.

'I'm afraid so. There is only one way into the Dome, which we can seal from inside, but they may break through it.'

'One thing at a time,' said Gregardreos. 'What's the rest of the procedure?'

'After two hours, the four outer machines must be cut off simultaneously. Another hour's wait, then the last two levers on the central generator can be switched off, the blue and finally the green, which completes the process. But as I say, by that time we may have been invaded, and even if we are not, there are still our own Satrans to contend with.'

The High Master stroked his beard. 'You say there is only one door.'

'Yes, near the top of the Dome where the sky-carriage comes from the upper city. Easier to keep control of those coming in and out, you see.'

'If you can seal it, I can use sorcery to make it impervious,' said Gregardreos. 'Our guards I can persuade to our point of view, as it were, also using my powers. I can do the same for every single person in the Dome, come to that, and even give the Pels the strength to fight off an invasion if the Hyalon's men should break in. Enough to give us the time to complete the shut-down.'

Halia's deep blue eyes gleamed and she leaned forward, folding her hands on the table. 'How soon can we do this?'

'It will take me a few days to work on the guards and

the Pels.' In fact he had already begun – unknown to Silvren – walking through the cell levels late at night, changing the guards' memories and loyalties, looking into the Pels' minds. 'Sealing the door is a matter of minutes.'

'In that case, it had better not be sealed until the very last moment. We'll arouse suspicion if we do it too soon.'

'Agreed,' said the High Master.

One of the other scientists, a stocky, moon-faced man, said, 'Are you seriously proposing to do this without telling the Neatrus?'

'We must! The fact that it's for Jhensit's good will fall on deaf ears. Deprive them of their light and comfort? Never! They won't agree to it, Verin, you know that.'

'Exactly! What you are proposing is an act of rebellion! If you think we can all go back to normal afterwards, you are out of your mind. It will be us or the Hyalon.'

Iytrel Halia did not seem at all perturbed. A slow smile spread across her face. 'Perhaps. But the old order is sick. Imagine sweeping it all away and starting again!'

There was an atmosphere of shock and electric excitement. She had expressed the thoughts that had only been half-formed in her colleagues' minds, too treacherous to voice. Gregardreos shared the excitement. He glanced at Silvren but her face was averted and she looked deeply troubled.

When the meeting ended, Silvren walked away on her own and he had to hurry to catch her up. He could not bear to see her unhappy.

'Silvren, is anything wrong?'

They entered Iytrel Halia's rooms and seated themselves at the small table where they took their meals. The Director had gone about her duties and they were alone.

'Yes,' she said. 'I'm worried. You are doing so many things that are dubious, to put it mildly. You are deceiving the ruler of this land, whom you haven't even met. I could not believe my ears when you said you would manipulate the guards' minds, and what did you mean about the Pels?'

'Many of them have a small psychic ability, enough for me to make them minor Sorcerers for a time by channelling power through them.'

'That's what I thought,' she said grimly. 'And you're not only doing these terrible things to them, you are making them liable to an attack from outside.'

'There will be no attack. The Dome will be sealed.'

'But if the Hyalon's soldiers can't get in, why is it necessary to use the Pels?'

'It is a safeguard,' he said.

'Don't sigh like that and look away! That's what I can't bear, the way you're excluding me! It's not that I don't believe you, but if only you'd let me far-see for myself I would understand the situation properly, and if you'd let me use my own power I might find a gentler way –'

'Silvren, Silvren.' He closed his large hand on hers. 'I'm fully aware of what you're saying. I am doing things that could be considered wrong and I am dangerously close to breaking my Oath. This is a desperate situation, and at such times Sorcerers must live by a higher Oath, which is to do what is right, however it must be achieved. But that's why I can't let you be involved, so that if anyone tried to say that I was doing wrong, no blame and no responsibility would attach to you.'

He expected her to be even angrier, but surprisingly, her eyes softened. His genuine, heartfelt desire to protect her had touched her. His heart warmed in response. Since he had recovered from his initial shock on entering Jhensit, he had been increasingly carried away by a crusading fervour, a compulsion thrusting him with increasing speed along the path he had chosen. *I should have done this years ago, but now I have a second chance and this time – this time –*

The time seemed to be right for more than settling his debt to Jhensit. Silvren held his gaze and her eyes were so warm, afternoon sunlight slanting through golden crystal – surely he could not be misreading the look she gave him? Words that had so often risen to his tongue, only to be swallowed, now rose again and for the first time he could not hold them back.

'Silvren, we shall go back to Ikonus when this is over and – and we could be together.'

Her expression changed imperceptibly – just the flicker of a frown. 'Of course we'll be together, why should things be different?'

She could not have misunderstood him. 'No, Silvren, that's not what I mean – oh, there is no subtle way to say this! That's why I've never presumed to try before, but I feel different now. The past will be gone and there'll be a fresh start. I love you, I always have loved you.'

She did not mistake his meaning this time, that was certain. She stared at him, parted her lips to speak, closed them again. And she did not need to say anything; her expression was enough to turn his heart to lead.

Finally she said, 'You never said anything.'

'I couldn't. I was too afraid of being rejected.'

'But – I – oh gods.' She stood up and went to stare at a painting of birds on the wall. Her shoulders rose and fell. 'I didn't realise.'

'I don't see how you could not have guessed.'

'That's the strange thing,' she sighed. 'Someone else did see it, but I didn't believe them. Perhaps I didn't want to.'

'There's no hope for me, then,' he said quietly.

She went to him and now he could not bear the dazzling light of her kindness. He wished she would scream and shout at him instead, but that was not her way. 'I don't know what to say,' she said helplessly. 'I'm sorry. I never thought of you as – as a lover, and I don't think I can. It doesn't mean I don't still care for you –'

'As a friend and a father. That's what you told Halia.' Pain lanced through him at the memory and he closed his eyes. 'I should have listened, I heard how quickly you denied that I was your husband.'

'I think we had better stop this conversation,' she said.

'Yes. And forget that it ever took place.' When he looked up she had gone.

He felt bleak and humiliated to the core. Now he knew why his instinct to say nothing had been right. *If I had spoken years ago, before she even knew Ashurek, would it have made any difference?* She had not mentioned Ashurek's name once. Had she done that deliberately, to avoid hurting him? Or to say obliquely, *'If Ashurek were not with me it would make no difference. I still could never love you.'*

Pain and anger bubbled up inside him; all the pain of his past, like talons gouging slowly through a quagmire, all distilled in that single flicker of her eyebrows as her true reaction betrayed itself. Not surprise, not even shock, but something infinitely worse, unbearably, mortally wounding: disgust.

Electric lamps and candles blazed in the Hyalon's bedchamber, but no amount of light could drive out the inner chill of the hours before dawn. Elatiat Harn had dismissed all his guards, to the dismay of his counsellors, then sent the counsellors away for the same reason; their own safety.

'If the Hyalana appears, there is certain to be one fool who tries to protect me,' he had said. 'Anyone who touches her will die – like *that*. He snapped his fingers at them and they recoiled and filed out, white-faced.

They had left their fear behind them, though, like a blanket of ice. The whole palace was full of fear. Even the light seemed to radiate needles of frost that stiffened and hung heavy on the air.

Now only Ashurek and Shai Fea sat with Elatiat Harn, and it was exactly like the painting Ashurek had seen in the book; the blue luxury of the room and the terrified man in the chair. Only the colourless figure was missing.

They had passed most of the night playing a game with glass pieces on a hexagonal board, Elatiat Harn trying to maintain a false atmosphere of gaiety. As the hours wore on his veneer of calm stretched thinner and thinner, until he lost concentration completely.

'Let her come, then,' he said under his breath. 'I'm not afraid. Let her come.'

Ashurek and Shai Fea went on with the game, but they were playing mechanically now, cold and heavy-eyed. Shai Fea actually nodded off to sleep over the board, only to awake with a start, exclaiming, 'She's here!'

Elatiat Harn sat forward in his chair, his hands gripping the arms like white spiders. Ashurek looked round the room but there were only the blazing lamps and the shadows pooled in the silken draperies.

'There's no-one,' he said. 'You were dreaming.'

'No.' Shai Fea leaned forward, listening. 'I can feel her. I know she's here.'

A moment later she appeared; a pale figure gleaming with a weird phosphorescence that was faint yet undiminished by the light in the room. And she was standing right over her son, who screamed and pressed himself against the chair back.

'Mother, no!' cried Shai Fea.

The Hyalana paused. She looked round with wide, glistening eyes that were terrifying, not because they were evil, but because they reflected and magnified the fear in the room.

'Dear child, I waited for you,' she said.

Shai Fea took a step towards her. Ashurek also stood up, wary in case she went too close. 'Mother, you can't harm him. We both love him.'

Shai Tialah smiled. 'I know. That's why I waited.'

Then she stretched out an arm – which seemed twice its natural length – and touched Elatiat Harn on the throat. She did not even look at him. A green-black aura sprang out around her hand. Her fingers barely brushed his skin, but the effect was instantaneous; his mouth opened, his eyes bulged out of his skull and the skin around them stretched and turned purple.

Then Tialah took her hand away, stroking his cheek as she did so in an almost affectionate gesture. Elatiat Harn slumped in the chair. There was no visible injury on him but he was dead, as the others had been, killed by a single touch.

Shai Fea stood and stared, completely paralysed. Ashurek put an arm round her in case she fell but she was rigid, hardly breathing.

'All those I hate,' said Tialah, 'and all those who have hurt you, my love.'

'Even your own son,' said Ashurek. The Hyalana's voice was calm but there was a trapped soul behind her eyes and the fear in her face was a trembling light that seemed to breathe its chill into the very room. Ashurek felt the bleakness of distant landscapes whispering across his mind, draining strength from his bones. The power within her could not be defeated by sword or by reasoning; it was beyond even sorcery, and there was nothing he could do to overcome it.

'Your son, your brother Tean Mon,' he said, keeping his voice level. 'Why stop there? Here is your daughter, who surely has no wish to go on living with a murderer for a mother.'

The change in Tialah's face was ghastly. It was as if all the buried terror rushed to the surface and distorted the muscles into a grotesque mask of horror.

'Help me,' she said hoarsely. 'I cannot stop this thing. It will be fed . . .'

'Do you want it to stop?' said Ashurek. 'Did you plan to spend eternity like this, or do you want to be free of your bargain?'

'I am in hell,' said Tialah. Shai Fea shuddered, but she still could not speak. 'Death could not be worse than this. I would do anything to be free.'

'I would like to help you.'

Her eyes narrowed and he poised himself to leap out of range – if it were possible to evade her lightning touch. But she did not move. 'No-one can help me,' she said bleakly. 'I have tried to kill myself, many times, but I cannot. I am already dead.'

'Are you sure?'

'When I wanted to live, I could not. Now I want to die, I cannot.'

'Listen to me. There is something I want you to do,' said Ashurek. He took Shai Fea to a chair, where she sat ice-cold and shaking. Then he turned and faced the Hyalana again. Through the fear he still sensed a fellow feeling with the Hyalana, and poignant regret for what their friendship might have been. He knew he would do whatever it took to save her. That decision made, he moved beyond fear. 'Do you have contact with the being with which you made the bargain?' He spoke softly, hoping Shai Fea could not hear.

'I can speak to it, yes.'

'Then tell it that I want to take the bargain from you. I don't think it will refuse.'

It was the first truly human reaction he had seen in her; complete amazement. 'I do not know . . . I do not know if it could be done.'

'Nor I, but I am willing to try.'

The look in her eyes softened. She frowned. 'I don't understand. Why would you want to do this for me?'

'I cannot answer that. Perhaps I am not doing it for you, but for someone else. My own mother, my own brother and sister. I know how it is to see people I love possessed by evil and to be unable to help, too late to help . . .'

Suddenly she was fully human. He lost all sense of danger. 'So you would make a mad sacrifice to atone for something that happened long in your own past?'

'I would have done this for my own mother. Would that I could have done so little.'

'What about the family you have now?'

He tried to visualise Silvren and Mellorn, but they seemed so distant that he could not even conjure their faces, let alone feel anything. A thick grey veil had come between him and everything but the present.

'They would understand,' he said.

They held each others' gaze. Eventually she said, very softly, 'I would like to embrace my daughter again . . .'

'Take my hands,' said Ashurek. 'If I die, then we'll know this was a vain hope. But if the Face will listen . . .'

They stretched out their hands – hers white as pearl, his a deep violet-brown that verged on black – and touched.

He had made a mistake. He felt death rushing up to claim him. It began as an inky flame that flowed from her hands into the centre of his soul, and then it grew in intensity until it became the darkness that lay not outside but inside his soul, utterly lightless, utterly limitless. The only true eternity was death. And his soul was being borne away on it, shrinking and shrinking until he almost ceased to exist.

Almost . . . but now he was conscious again, and still in the Hyalon's chamber, as if nothing had happened. The lights blazed. He was alone, and outside the window there was complete blackness.

'Light?' said a voice. He turned and saw a figure sitting at the table where – an eternity ago – he had sat over a boardgame with Shai Fea. Now the table was empty, except for two wine goblets and a decanter.

'Do sit down,' said the figure. 'I have waited such a long time to have this talk.'

Ashurek seated himself opposite the figure and accepted the goblet that was pushed towards him. The wine within sparkled like sunlight on a waterfall, and despite himself he drank deeply of it. It had no taste at all, like diamonds.

'I want to talk to you about a certain bargain that you made with the Hyalana Shai Tialah,' said Ashurek. 'But you speak as if you already know me.'

'I know everyone who is interesting.' The figure was tall and languorously graceful, but his face – like the wine – was a featureless blur, light on moving water.

'Are you Flaim?'

The being laughed. 'It depends who you mean by Flaim. The earth-god of the Pels, or the devil of the Eyostians?'

'I incline towards the devil theory,' Ashurek said drily.

'Do you think I am a devil?'

'I don't know. I'm trying to find out.'

'A devil or *the* devil, the ultimate evil. Do you believe in such a being, Ashurek?'

'No. There are too many shades and degrees of wickedness. Perhaps I did once. I thought that the Serpent was the ultimate evil, but when it had gone the corruption was still there – in another form. Strip the evil away and there's another layer underneath.'

'Ah, there you have it exactly!' The being banged his goblet on the table and leaned forward. His face shimmered disconcertingly. 'Something worse. Something more primeval. So, Ashurek, be evil! Seal the surface with your own wickedness, evil that you can understand. Keep the real darkness at bay.'

'Are you giving me an instruction, or mocking me?' said Ashurek, coldly dispassionate.

The glittering blur seemed to quirk into a smile. 'More light?' He lifted the decanter and poured a stream of pure sparkling liquid into Ashurek's goblet. 'Call it advice. You can call me Flaim or Eyos if it makes you feel better, but if those gods exist, it is only as blind and dumb powers. The earth. The sky.'

'So what are you?'

'One who cares for you, Ashurek. It is an absolute pleasure to find you so eager to take over the bargain I made with poor Tialah; you are more precious to me by far. I will not give you the powers of bodily transference that she had, because I know you would spurn them and you are far more interesting to me as your true, flawed self. You will receive only the power to take life with a touch, and immunity to death.' The being enunciated each word with delicate precision, savouring them. 'So, feed me with souls, but remember; I only need them because they are what binds me to you. What I feel for you is pure and perfect love.'

Then the being reached out and put a finger onto Ashurek's chest and straight through his breastbone. He felt something slide quietly into his heart, like a sigh of satisfaction, soft and evil. For a split second Ashurek knew he had made a mistake and he was filled with despair and horror; he had sworn never again to bargain with such creatures, yet he had fallen knowingly into the same trap. But the horror slid away and he could find no emotion, there *was* no emotion to match the enormity of what he was doing.

The being sat back, pleased. 'A small token in return,' he said, and placed a small, black-bound book on the table. Ashurek dreaded what was in it but he could not resist the compulsion to open it.

He saw a picture of a flower; a closed white flower whose stem went into another world and drew water from a foul grey river. The perspective of the painting hurt his eyes and conveyed a meaning that was more than visual. A tiny golden figure approached the flower, step by step, and in the penultimate image raised a sword with a leaf-green blade to sever the bloom.

The last illustration showed the flower lying dead, its petals splayed, and all the poison on which it had fed flowing from its centre like purplish-black blood.

'I do not understand,' said Ashurek.

'You will,' said the being. 'It is symbolic.'

'I gathered that.'

'Layers of meaning, you see. I hate simplicity. My idea of heaven is to strip away the layers for eternity without ever finding the truth at the centre.' And the being raised long, sharp-nailed fingers to his own chin and began to peel back his shimmering mask.

Beneath was a face that Ashurek had seen before and hoped never to see again. Only the olive green shimmer on the highest contours delineated the features; all the rest was a void, a darkness that went back and back like the infinite oblivion of death. The Face filled the universe and he hung forever under its expressionless gaze, waiting in agony for it to speak.

I am here and I will always be here, inside you and outside. You have known this forever . . .

'What are you?' Ashurek screamed. The lines of the Face lifted into a minimal smile, but it made no reply.

Ashurek was falling through stars. He was bitterly cold yet burning, a comet streaking through the void . . . and he was screaming to be free, asking himself why, why, why, when he knew that bargains with evil could only bring greater evil, he had let it happen again . . .

And as he fell he saw Jhensit below him, tiny and perfect in detail; a fretted raft of rock, like Jyel Vanan's island on a greater scale, floating on a sea of entropy which gnawed at the edges of the land and spat them into the Maelstrom. Both at the centre of Jhensit and the centre of the Maelstrom stood the White Dome, and slowly he began to understand what the flower in the book had symbolised.

In one brief, curving wave of witch-sight Ashurek saw this, and then the shutters of human awareness closed in on him.

He was still in darkness, but he could feel his own body again; the pull of gravity, the thudding of blood through his arteries, the touch of silk on his skin. He knew precisely what the Face had given him; no powers of prescience or sorcery, not even the Hyalana's power to vanish and appear at will; just the hideous ability to kill with a touch, and the inability to die. Otherwise he was still himself, still human – if he could ever feel human again.

Ashurek opened his eyes. The room blazed with light, Elatiat Harn was slumped, twisted and lifeless, in his chair, Shai Fea still sitting rigid in hers. For some reason he had expected Shai Tialah to have vanished but she was still standing in front of him, the same – yet changed.

She was solid flesh and blood, and her face was bright with amazement and joy.

'I'm free!' she cried. 'And I'm alive, truly alive!'

Shai Fea leapt out of her chair – the chair where the Face had sat while Ashurek was a guest in its dimension – and came forward. 'What's happened?' she said, her voice strained. 'Mother . . .'

Even in the artificial illumination, the Hyalana looked different. There was colour in her cheeks, she had lost the eerie glow and the look of fluidity. Her garments hung wretchedly on her like those of a peasant. She was completely human again.

'It's over,' she said, holding her arms out to her daughter. 'Ashurek saved me. I'm free and I'm still alive!'

Without hesitation, Shai Fea ran to her mother and they locked their arms round each other and wept. The Hyalana kissed her daughter over and over again, while Ashurek watched, separated from them by more than distance.

'Thank Eyos,' Shai Fea sobbed. 'Oh, thank Eyos. But how?'

'Ashurek . . . it was Ashurek.'

Only then did Shai Fea step back and look at Ashurek. He knew he had always looked strange to her, a dark being from another world with preternatural green eyes. Did she see anything else?

Apparently she did not, because she came towards him and he had to put up his hands to ward her off. 'Don't touch me,' he said quietly.

'Why? I don't understand . . .'

'It is simple; I have taken over the bargain that your mother made. Now if I touch anyone, they will die . . . do you see?'

She recoiled from him, never taking her eyes from his face. 'You have become – become what my mother was?'

'I am no danger to you,' he said tonelessly. 'My will is still my own and I believe I can control the power. But you must never touch me. As long as this curse is on me I am not altogether human.'

'But you are still yourself' said Tialah.

Ashurek's lips twisted in a sardonic, bitter smile. 'Yes. Completely myself.'

'How did this happen?' Shai Fea said faintly.

Ashurek tried to explain. She began to weep again. 'You did this – for my mother's sake?'

'And for you.'

How beautiful her eyes were, he thought abstractedly; almond-shaped and clear as jewels. And her hair; blue-black, soft and fine as feathers. Would it harm her if he touched her hair, or even her sleeve? She said, 'This . . . this thing you have taken from my mother. It means no-one can ever touch you, or you they?'

'That's right.'

Her voice trembled. 'But how long will it go on for?'

'For as long as I live,' he said remotely. *I have waited a long time for you* . . . The words echoed like a leaden bell in his mind. 'There is no easy escape, not for me.'

She did not ask him how he knew. Perhaps she could not bring herself to. 'I see,' she said very softly. Her face was blanched and she visibly made the effort to cut herself off from him and hide her feelings as only a Hyalet could. Her mother stroked her hair, her gaze resting on the corpse of her son.

'I should feel regret for this,' the Hyalana said quietly. 'My own son. All those others, even poor Tean Mon, who never hurt a soul except himself. Yes, I could weep for him, but it will be later. At this moment I cannot feel anything except relief.'

Ashurek looked at Elatiat Harn and exhaustion washed over him. He no longer had any sense of purpose at all. What was the point of finding Silvren, when he could never touch her, never be anything to her but a haunting, tormenting demon? He felt nothing beyond a profound weariness. Jhensit no longer mattered to him. Nothing mattered.

In a small voice, Shai Fea said, 'Mother, Niankan has no ruler. What are we going to do?'

'No ruler, and no direct heir,' said Tialah broodingly. 'But I am alive again and I still bear the title of Hyalana. I shall rule.'

'You?' Shai Fea exclaimed. She was shocked, but Ashurek felt no surprise. He had always seen the strength in Tialah, and it was exactly what his own mother would have done, had her circumstances been the same.

'Who else is there? The nearest heir is your cousin Tiun, but he is just a little boy. Let them make me regent if it makes them feel better, but Palan *must* have a strong leader and I am the only one who can unite them. Oh, tell me I have your support, my love.'

'Of course,' said Shai Fea, hugging her. 'But they will oppose you.'

'Who will? They are all gone, remember, the ones who hated me. I did not kill my friends, except poor Tean Mon.' She spoke ironically, and her daughter looked shocked that she could speak of such things at all. 'How much time does our poor world have left? I have seen the Maelstrom with my own eyes, and the –' She met Ashurek's eyes, and although she broke off he knew she was thinking of the Muridonu, the Maelstrom's victims. 'What happened to me is in the past now and we have to make a new start. I've made up my mind. Let us call the Counsellors, tell them everything and let them decide.'

Counsellor Cilit Tir led the delegation of senior Neatrus to the presence of the Hyalana, all of them dumbfounded by the story she told them. Tialah had bathed and changed into fresh robes – palest blue netted with gold – and she sat in state with Shai Fea at her right hand, Ashurek at her left. She was stern and proud, every inch a sovereign.

'Cousins, the events I have related, appalling as they sound, are the absolute truth. The Hyalon is dead, to my eternal regret, but that cannot be changed. We face a dark future and this is no time for squabbling over the throne.'

Strength flowed from her and Ashurek was a dark, ominous figure at her side. His presence, combined with the incredible situation, unnerved the usually self-assured Neatrus, and they were silent and tangibly unhappy. Eventually Tialah leaned forward to address the lean, pinch-faced Cilit Tir. 'Cousin, you were always a good friend to me, one of the few who spoke for me against tradition. What say you? Will you speak on everyone's behalf?'

Ashurek had judged him to be a controlled, clinical man, but loyal to Tialah and not of a devious nature. Cilit Tir said, 'I will gladly be their spokesman, your Majesty, but only after we have conferred on this matter. We beg your leave to withdraw.'

'Granted.'

When they had gone, Shai Fea also excused herself and withdrew to her own rooms. Ashurek was glad. It was all he could do to look at her now; her pain burned him like a flame on raw flesh.

'Well, Ashurek,' said the Hyalana, 'do you think I am doing the right thing?'

'I have no doubt of it, and I wish you well,' he said. 'However, I believe it will be better for all concerned if I leave now. The further I am from other people, the less harm I can cause them.'

Her reaction startled him. 'No, I won't hear of you leaving! You have the strength to control the Face's power, as I never did, and I have faith in you, I believe you were sent to guide me. Please don't leave.'

Her eyes were warm and compelling; he could only admire the way she had emerged from her semi-death strengthened, not broken. He did not want yet another burden of misplaced trust, yet he was too world-sickened to reject it. Turning away, he opened the balcony windows and stepped out, letting the chilly air sear his lungs, wishing it could sear the darkness out of him.

A long, elegant animal was picking its precarious way along the balcony; a silukian kitten, naked and wingless, yet weirdly beautiful. Absently he stretched out a hand to caress its head.

Too late, he felt the swift surge of power flooding through him. It came from a black place that was at once inside him and outside, vast as space yet as suffocating as a grave. A black halo burst from his fingers and swallowed the kitten's small soul. He snatched his hand away but it was too late, the creature was hurtling down towards the lower city, its last mew dying as it fell.

Ashurek was alone, facing the true enormity of the bargain. He thought he had understood what he was taking on; now he realised that he had only just begun to comprehend the smallest part of it.

He was death to anything he touched.

What was the Face? Why had it wanted him so badly? At least it had left him more or less human, his personality and conscience intact . . . but perhaps it would have been better otherwise.

No, he thought savagely, *if this must be, let me be under no illusion about just how damnable it is!*

Then, *I cannot live. But how can I die?*

Cilit Tir came back much sooner than expected, in a great hurry, like a thin, agitated bird. Ashurek and Tialah were waiting in the domed chamber where he had first met Elatiat Harn.

'Well, what have you to tell me?' said the Hyalana.

'Your Majesty, there is an emergency. We have received a warning that the White Dome is about to be shut down.'

Tialah was taken aback. 'Why?'

'We don't know. A party of Satrans were dispatched straight away to discover what was happening, but they found the Dome sealed against them.'

'Sealed?' she said incredulously. 'Wait – was anything known about this before? Had the Hyalon given permission?'

'Certainly not,' said Cilit Tir. 'If there was anything

wrong at the Dome, the Director Iytrel Halia would certainly have informed us and gained consent for any repairs. Something is very wrong.'

'So you have no idea why they've taken this action or what they hope to achieve by it?'

'None, and with the door sealed there's no way to communicate. Perhaps the Pels have taken control or the scientists themselves have begun some sort of rebellion. Both seem impossible, but there is no other explanation. We have less than three hours to prevent the shut-down being completed.'

Shai Tialah gazed at Cilit Tir, nodding slightly as she thought over what he had said. Ashurek remembered the white flower and the vision of the White Dome at the centre of Jhensit. He still did not fully understand it, but of one thing he was quite convinced; it was a warning that if the White Dome's power was cut off, the result would be far more disastrous than the mere loss of electricity to Niankan-Siol.

'We need a decision,' said Cilit Tir.

'From me?' Tialah raised her eyebrows.

'Yes, your Majesty.'

'From that I assume that you have accepted my authority.'

'Yes, your Majesty.' The Counsellor bobbed his head, looking embarrassed. The emergency had forced the family's hand. Someone must take responsibility, so they had pushed it onto Shai Tialah. Ashurek smiled thinly; the Hyalana caught his eye and he could see that she shared his thoughts exactly.

'A word with you, madam,' said Ashurek.

She sent the Counsellor out into the antechamber and gave Ashurek her attention. 'What is it?'

'I know almost nothing about the White Dome, but the Face showed me a vision which I can only interpret in one way. The Dome contains some kind of poison. If it is shut down, the poison will escape and Jhensit will die. Perhaps you already know this.'

'No. I don't even know what you mean. The White Dome is a mystery to me too, only the Hyalon is supposed to share its secrets, but even my husband and my son did not fully understand them. Well, now it's time for me to learn.' She gave him a sombre look. 'There is very little of Jhensit left to die, but I'll fight to my last breath for what is left. I only wish I knew how!' Putting a hand to her forehead, she pushed back a wisp of slate-blue hair, and exhaled softly. 'It seemed to me that I knew much more when I was in that other state, but most of it has gone now. What it is to be human again.'

'I don't know why the Face should have shown me a true vision, but I feel certain that it did.'

'I think it gives glimpses of the future, however unpleasant. But we are agreed, this future must be averted! They must be prevented from shutting down the Dome at any cost, but how are we to stop them?'

'I have no idea,' said Ashurek, 'but I suggest we go and view the Dome for ourselves. Perhaps an answer will present itself.'

'That is the only way in,' said Cilit Tir. The White Dome was a cloud-white semi-circle, looming out of the landscape a mile away. From the lookout point on which Ashurek stood with Tialah and the Counsellor, cable filaments curved out towards the hills and terminated at a point near the top of the Dome. There a long pearl-white carriage, feathered with blue and gold, was suspended alongside a platform where a group of Satrans were trying to break through the door without success. The door itself was barely visible, and there were no other features, not even windows.

Cilit Tir went on, 'Our ancestors who designed the place thought it too dangerous to be placed within the city. They only made one entrance so that no-one could go in and out without supervision.'

'And thus made it easy to barricade,' said Ashurek.

'There is no way in except by the sky-carriage – but who controls the carriage?'

'It is controlled by the driver, and always left on this side after use. Even if they do cut off power from the Dome, we have a reserve of power which will keep the carriage functioning for some time yet.'

Shai Tialah gripped the rail of the platform. 'If this is an act of rebellion, they know they'll be punished. They may choose to remain under siege until they starve, then we'll never know their reasons.'

Ashurek said, 'Would it be possible to break through the walls at ground level?'

'No,' said the Counsellor. 'The substance of the walls is impervious to anything but a very massive force indeed.'

'Your people are obviously skilful, I can't believe it's beyond their capabilities.'

'We might find a way to break through eventually but it would take days and we only have hours,' said Cilit Tir with a touch of irritation. 'There is only one way and that is for the Satrans to force the door.'

'Well, cousin, they appear to have failed a second time,' said the Hyalana. In the distance, the sky-carriage had begun its return journey along the cables. The platform outside the Dome was empty and the door was still sealed. Several minutes later, the carriage slid to a halt alongside the lookout platform and the ten Satrans alighted, looking despondent.

'We have tried everything to break through, your Majesty,' said their leader 'I'm sorry . . .'

He looked nervous, as if anticipating a burst of wrath, but she only said quietly, 'You are dismissed. Await further orders.'

The soldiers saluted and obeyed, looking relieved. When they had gone, Tialah turned to gaze at the impervious pale sphere.

'Damn the fools who built that place. Why didn't they foresee this? If I'd been in my husband's position, I'd have made sure that this never happened!'

Ashurek already knew the only solution, and felt that he had been drifting towards this fate ever since he had set foot on Jhensit. 'Let me try – alone,' he said.

'Alone?' Tialah exclaimed.

'Have someone show me how to control the sky-carriage and I will find a way into the Dome.'

'You cannot go alone, you must take men with you,' said the Counsellor. 'To do otherwise would be suicidal.'

'But I cannot be killed.' Ashurek gave a very thin, very cold smile, but felt no satisfaction at seeing Cilit Tir shrink away from him. 'I took this curse upon myself for your family's sake. Now I intend to make use of it.'

14

The Poisoned Heart

The air was sharp with a dry, peppery cold as Ashurek stepped out onto the platform at the very edge of Niankan-Siol. On one side of him was the sky-carriage, emitting a low hum and an unfamiliar tang of oil; on the other a flimsy rail, beyond which was the ocean of air between him and the lower city. The Dome lay cupped in the distant sweep of the hills, like a cloud that had dropped from a milky-grey sky.

Ashurek had returned briefly to the palace to change his borrowed Siol robes for his own dark tunic, breeches and boots. His sword hung at his side but he wondered if he would need it, now that his own hands were more deadly. The Hyalana, Cilit Tir and a Satran officer were with him.

'If you are ready, sir. . .' said the officer, indicating for him to step into the front of the carriage. Ashurek did so, feeling the contraption shake beneath him, bouncing slightly on its wires. There was a driver's compartment at each end, and the long, narrow interior was decorated in the Hyalon's livery. There were only four seats, presumably for the use of the most important passengers. Others must stand for the journey.

The driver's compartment was separate from the rest of the carriage, with a single seat. Even the levers that controlled the vehicle were inlaid with blue and gold. Ashurek looked ahead at the skein of silver hairs that supported the sky-carriage, his only link with the White Dome.

'It's quite easy to operate,' said the Satran. 'This lever controls the speed, but you must not push it beyond the vertical. This is the brake. Don't release it fully, leave it in this position. Then when you are two-thirds of the way across, begin to apply it again; that's very important. Are you certain you don't want us to come with you, sir?'

'Absolutely certain.'

'Well, you stand no chance of getting in.'

'We shall see.'

'I wish you luck.' The officer saluted briskly, stepped back onto the platform and began to slide the door shut.

'No, leave it open,' said Ashurek. He sensed Tialah's eyes on him but he did not look at her. Standing with his legs braced against the seat, he unlocked the brake and began to slide the speed-lever forward.

The carriage jerked once then began a smooth acceleration. Niankan-Siol was higher than the Dome and the cables angled downwards so that he was effectively travelling downhill. As the vehicle accelerated, there was a sense of falling and a sudden excitement swooped through his blood.

He was suspended in the sky, skimming across the void like a silver arrowhead. The White Dome rose up like a moon before him.

Against the officer's instructions he released the brake completely and thrust the speed-lever forward as far as it would go. Two-thirds of the way across, he made no move to slow the carriage. His face was serene, his eyes unblinking green suns.

The White Dome filled the sky now. He could see nothing but the vast hemisphere, and his ears were filled with the atonal whine of the mechanism. Wind rushed in through the open door. As the carriage raced towards the landing platform it was still gaining speed and even had he lost his nerve he could not have slowed the headlong rush. He flung himself to the floor, braced for the impact. There was a wrenching of metal, cables snapping and whipping through the air as the carriage ripped loose from its bearings and crashed into the side of the Dome.

Impervious except to a massive force, Cilit Tir had said. Ashurek had taken a great risk; the carriage might have been crushed and plummeted to the ground far below. But the dense white resin gave, the carriage plunged through the hole and slid to rest against an internal wall.

Ashurek was flung forward in the compartment and the pain of the crash shuddered through him. The impact would have killed or badly injured anyone he had brought with him, but he was able to climb to his feet at once, clear-headed, with the pain swiftly fading away. He was in a large chamber of silver and pale blue. There were a number of Satrans and Pels pressed back against the walls, while others lay motionless amid the debris of the shattered wall, staining the white floor with their blood.

Ashurek turned slowly, taking in everything. As he looked back into the inside of the carriage itself his heart almost stopped with shock; it had been empty when he began the journey, but now it was filled with the blood-red, shadowy forms of the Muridonu.

The sight of them nauseated him and he almost lost the resolve to go on. 'I do not want your help,' he said gruffly. 'Leave me.'

In reply they whispered, '*Lead us. We will be your army.*'

Dismay crept leadenly through him but he knew he could do nothing to be rid of them – short of slaying them. Turning his back on them, he stepped out of the carriage.

At once the Satrans and the Pels rushed to the attack. *Fighting together?* he thought incredulously. Heat-swords hissed towards him but their lethal power was only the faintest tingle on his skin as they struck him. He did not even trouble to draw his sword. One Satran stared in amazement as Ashurek seized his heat-sword by the blade and flung it aside; a second later the man was dead, slain by the touch of Ashurek's fingers.

Two more died the same way before the rest realised the danger and they began to back away, on the defensive.

The Pels, though, were a different matter. They were unarmed, ragged men and women with the look of slaves, but there was a shimmer of corrupt sorcery about them. Their eyes had a savage glitter, like Jaia Keorn when he had pushed Ashurek and Shai Fea into the Maelstrom. Their hands spun ovoids of grimy energy which buffeted Ashurek like fists, doing him no harm, but keeping him from reaching them. The power of Flaim? The Face had said that the gods were only a superstition, so how had they acquired this supernatural strength?

There was a stairwell at the side of the chamber and instinct told him that he must go deeper into the Dome. He was aware of the Muridonu crawling out of the carriage behind him and fanning out to engage the Satrans and Pels; he could see their insectile limbs twitching, smell the sourness of their venom. They seemed unaffected by the Pels' power; Ashurek's usually strong stomach was turned as the creatures trampled victims underfoot, gouging their flesh blindly, like machines.

'Let us pass!' he shouted desperately. 'Stand aside and you'll live!' But both the Pels and Satrans went on fighting as if under a compulsion.

As Ashurek forced his way towards the stairwell, a woman appeared from it and stood gaping at the carnage before her. She was small, white-haired, uniformed in white and blue. There were more Satrans and prisoners massed on the stairs behind her.

'I'm the Director, Iytrel Halia. What in the name of Eyos is this?' she said, her mouth turning down with revulsion.

'I've come from the Hyalana to tell you that you must not shut down the Dome,' said Ashurek.

'Was this slaughter necessary to tell us that?'

'There would have been no violence, had your guards not been so enthusiastic. Call them off and listen to me!' The woman's deep blue eyes hardened.

'You don't understand. We are shutting down the generators to save Jhensit.'

'And I tell you that if you do so, you will destroy your world, not save it.'

'I don't know who you are or what you think you'll gain by this, but you are completely wrong,' she snapped. She turned and began to push her way back down the stairs, shouting at her guards as she went, 'Take him, don't let him through!'

Four Satrans came eagerly up the stairs towards him. 'If you lay hands on me you will die,' said Ashurek, but they ignored the warning. A pair of hands closed on him, and at once he felt the surge of olive darkness flowing through him, the terrible burning halo that caught the guard's hands and enveloped him like a sheet of invisible flame.

The guard uttered a strangled scream and fell dead. The others leapt away, their blankness momentarily pierced by shock.

Iytrel Halia had paused on the stairs and was looking back, horrified. 'Devilry!' she exclaimed. 'No more, please.' Then to her own people, 'Leave him, let him through!'

She ran down to the next level and was lost to sight, but the Pels remained, blocking Ashurek's path. They were ignoring her command. Some other force motivated them and they advanced on him, faces blank and eyes burning suicidally.

Four scientists stood in position round the generator chamber, one at each of the smaller cylinders. Gregardreos gave the signal for them to throw the switches; the air juddered with the machines' dying roar, and globes of smoke drifted up into the half-lit haze.

He looked up at the central cylinder, towering darkly above them. A blue star winked high on its side, and twenty feet above that the green; the red light was gone, the first to have been switched off. One hour to wait, and the machine would be put to eternal slumber.

That was when the warning screamed in the High Master's mind. The Dome had been invaded. He tried to far-see but he could get no clear picture of the invaders – only a kind of emptiness coming closer and closer – yet a more visceral instinct told him that it was Ashurek. Fury began to build up inside him. *I have not come this far only to be thwarted at the last minute, least of all by him.* He looked at Silvren, but he could tell by her face that she had not noticed anything. *The blocks I placed on her still hold, thank the Sphere!*

Iytrel Halia came rushing down the stairways from the entrance to the upper levels, limping a little as she ran.

'Eyos, I'm too old for this,' she gasped as she reached the High Master. 'We're invaded! It's not the Hyalon's men, it's worse, I can't describe it.'

Gregardreos folded his arms. 'I know,' he said.

Silvren came up behind him. 'What's happened, Halia?' she said.

'Maniacs and monsters – they smashed the sky-carriage right through the outside wall! We have got to stop before they kill us all.'

Gregardreos felt the fury rising a little higher. 'No. We must go on. Our guards and Pels will hold them back.'

'I told them to stop fighting.'

'They won't have obeyed, they're under my command.'

'Then you tell them to stop! You haven't seen what's going on up there, it's horrible! We have got to surrender, at least call a truce so we can negotiate.'

'She's right,' said Silvren.

Gregardreos turned his stern gaze on her. He did not mean to lose his temper with her – it was like physically stabbing her – but the thought of Ashurek was a red-black fire across his eyes and he could not help himself. 'Would you disobey me? The slightest setback and you turn tail and run? No! We must finish this!'

She flinched, her eyes wide. 'Gregar, what's got into you? I've never seen you like this before.'

'Just do as I say, Silvren. Help me.' He went to the central machine and began to climb the steps that curved round it, his eyes fixed on the blue lever high above him.

'You cannot,' said Iytrel Halia. 'An hour must elapse before the shutdown can be completed.'

'We do not have an hour,' said Gregardreos.

'But there is a timing mechanism to prevent –'

'Then I shall use my power to override it!'

Ashurek's advance against the Pels and Satrans was slow, but it was relentless. Level by level he fought his way downwards, with his army of Muridonu streaming behind him like a blood-red cloak. When they came to the huge, sealed door to the generator house the Muridonu simply gnawed their way through, as if their very bodies were formed of corroding acid. Pure poison, Ashurek thought. There was corruption all around him; the scarlet creatures, the dark power of the Pels, the Face inside himself.

Inside the door, sorcery leapt out at him like a mass of black spikes, vicious and venomous. A group of Pels were guarding the walkway, which was suspended over a dim and cavernous drop. A greyish-black glow formed around them, ballooned upwards and detached itself into a wedge of energy that caught Ashurek full on the chest, flinging him backwards. They were more powerful than their fellows on the higher levels; where had they obtained this power? He dragged himself upright, aware for the first time that they might defeat him.

But the Muridonu were with him and they were impervious to the power. Ignoring the oily flares aimed at them, they swarmed forward over the Pels, who were left weirdly boneless and bleached by the monsters' venom.

Ashurek glanced over the handrail and saw the floor of the chamber far below, with a number of small figures dotted about the base of a massive, central cylinder. He saw the white-haired woman who had tried to stop him; he saw several others similarly dressed, luminous in the half-light. There were more Pels, more Satrans, but the scientists were the ones he must reach.

The perpetual deep throbbing of the Dome seemed to grind right through him, like the very heartbeat of the corruption. A maze of platforms and stairs led eventually to the floor; he did not have time to fight his way along every one. Leaving the Muridonu to their battle, he tipped over the handrail and jumped.

He rolled as he landed and folded smoothly to his feet, feeling no pain at all. Massive shapes loomed in the darkness; alien machines, in shadow but for rims of fiery light. Guards were shouting in shock and rushing to attack him, but suddenly a horrible jubilation went through him and he waded among them, feeling the Face – far away in its own dimension, yet inside him – exulting in this feast of life. One after another shrivelled and died in his grasp until there was suddenly a large space around him, the remaining guards and even the ensorcelled Pels backing away in fear.

Then he looked up, past the horrified eyes fixed on him, and he saw her coming out of the shadows, outlined by bluish fire, her golden hair edged with silver.

Silvren. *Dear gods, Silvren.*

She saw him and froze. The moment lasted forever. There was no joy in her face.

The battle-fever died in the light of her eyes; that pure, piercing, golden light that shone full on the corruption of the bargain he had made, revealed it in all its loathsome evil. He went towards her, but she recoiled and he stopped, just looking at her. He felt like dying. The very first time he had met her, she had seen the demonic power that had possessed him then. She saw straight through him and there was no need to explain everything; she already knew.

'Gods,' she said. 'It was you, then. This – this slaughter.'

'What are you doing here?' His voice was brusque because he could not, dared not express any feeling.

'What are *you* doing here?' she said.

Now she did come towards him; fearless, always walking into danger while others fled. He raised his hands and said, 'Don't touch me.'

She stopped, no more than two feet from him. The anguish of seeing her again, being unable to take her in his arms, was unbearable. 'Something's happened to you,' she said quietly. 'I didn't know you were there until I saw you; I should have sensed you but I didn't. Even now it's as if you're not really there – a nothingness. Ashurek, what have you done?'

A small Muridonu was creeping around the hem of her robe, a many-legged thing with a skull-face. Silvren glanced down at it as if it was no more than a friendly cat. It stared menacingly at Ashurek and suddenly he realised that it was not threatening Silvren, but protecting her. A thick, faint whisper echoed inside his head, *We serve you but we serve her too. Do her no harm.*

'As if I would ever hurt you,' Ashurek murmured.

'But you have,' she said flatly. In all his dreams of finding her, he had never imagined this hostility, this mutual despair. 'What evil has possessed you to do this to us? You ask why I'm here. Gregardreos is with me, he discovered that the White Dome is causing the Maelstrom, and that's why he's shutting down the generators, to save Jhensit! You should be helping us, but instead you bring these vile beings – I don't know you, I can't speak to you, Ashurek! Just call off your creatures and let us finish the task in peace!'

As she spoke, Iytrel Halia came hurrying over to them, calling, 'Silvren, what's happening?'

Neither of them answered. 'Gregardreos. I might have known,' Ashurek sighed. 'And is he responsible for the sorcerous power these Pels are wielding? They are possessed. I tried to end the fighting but it was they who persisted! Put as much blame on me as you like, but not all of it.' She flinched slightly, and he went on, 'The White Dome may well be causing the Maelstrom but if the generator is closed down it will cause Jhensit's destruction.'

'How?' said Iytrel Halia. She was frowning and shaking her head.

'There is poison in this place. The whole Dome reeks of it. Can't you feel it?'

'Yes,' Silvren whispered. 'Of course, but I –'

'Shut off the machine and the poison will be released. I'm telling you the truth, Silvren. Who do you believe, him or me?'

She gaped at him. Eventually she choked out one word. 'You!'

'Then help me stop him. Where is he?'

Silvren pointed wordlessly into the air. Ashurek looked up at the cylinder soaring into a powdery-silver haze and saw two blurred stars winking through it; one blue, the higher one green. It was hard to see through the haze but he made out a small figure, high up on a walkway near the blue light. As he watched, the light vanished.

'He should not have done that,' said Halia. 'It wasn't time. We'd better stop him reaching the top lever.'

Ashurek was already sprinting towards the base of the generator. He began to run up the curving stairways, his feet echoing hollowly on the treads. Silvren's face dwindled below him, small and pale. The height did not disturb him but the deep vibration of the machine shook him to the bone, making him dizzy.

By the time he gained the platform of the blue lever the High Master was on the level above him. He was glaring down at Ashurek, his lips twisted in a snarl that made him look crazed, completely unlike himself. He appeared to be holding a glowing, leaf-green sword above his head, just as in Ashurek's visions – but the sword was a lever, attached to the machine, and he was poised to pull it downwards.

'Gregardreos, don't!' Ashurek shouted. 'You're making a mistake. If you switch off the machine, you'll destroy Jhensit.'

The golden-haired Sorcerer blinked. 'You presume to know better than me?'

'I presume nothing. I'm simply asking you to pause and think before you do this. You'll realise I'm speaking the truth.'

'You speak the truth as a fish breathes air! You can't hide the evil in your soul, Ashurek. You were born in blood and you'll die in blood!'

Ashurek started up the next flight of steps.

'Stay back!' roared Gregardreos, a mist of spittle spraying from his mouth. 'You've been a thorn in my side long enough!'

Ashurek paused. 'You are obviously disturbed,' he said levelly. 'Don't act rashly. Come down and speak to Silvren.'

'Silvren? But she agrees with me!'

'Not any more.'

This was probably the worst thing Ashurek could have said, but the High Master was beyond being reasoned with. He seemed swollen with the White Dome's power, a rabid lion. 'Always the same!' Gregardreos exclaimed. 'I speak the perfect, purest truth to her and it's all she can do to trust me – but one poisonous word from you and she is fawning at your feet again. Damn you! If she won't have me, nor shall you have her!'

He stretched up to take a firmer grip on the lever.

'No!' shouted Ashurek. He ran up the last of the steps but a leaden bolt of sorcery came arrowing towards him – he glimpsed the mad gleam of the High Master's eyes, saw the lever straining downwards and the green light dying – then the fire burst in his chest and he was thrown off the steps.

Air rushed past him as he fell. The generator's hum became a falling note. The floor slammed into his back and his whole skeleton stung with excruciating pain, while the note went on falling, deepening into silence.

Ashurek did not lose consciousness. The pain faded swiftly and he stood up as if nothing had happened, aware of Halia and the others staring at him incredulously. He met Silvren's astonished eyes. She had seen him fall, she had not wanted him to die, yet she could not believe he had survived. He would have done anything to be alone with her, to embrace her and to explain.

The fighting between the Pels and the Muridonu had stopped. The dim fires of the generator were fading and the whole chamber was sinking into blackness, filled with a deep rumbling that seemed to be coming up from the roots of the earth.

'Get away from the centre!' shouted Halia. Pels, Satrans and scientists scattered towards the edge of the chamber. Ashurek braced himself for the explosion, he was almost praying for it to be over quickly and for oblivion to claim him. Surely there was a limit to the Face's protection of him?

No longer contained or consumed by the generators, the dark power of the Maelstrom was thrusting up through the central shaft. The floor shook. A sudden pressure hurt Ashurek's ears, but the explosion when it came was strangely slow and muffled. The unseen force pushed up through the cylinder, burst from its summit and went on upwards through the fabric of the Dome itself. Threads of daylight appeared, widening swiftly as the White Dome split like a seed pod and began to peel back on itself.

Cold daylight sifted in. Pieces of metal and resin began to rain down as the walls collapsed. Ashurek saw a grey line shoot from ceiling to floor like a bolt of lightning, widening swiftly to reveal the hillside outside the Dome. A mad dash began to reach the gap but he held back, looking for Silvren. Someone cannoned into him. He twisted round and saw a Satran falling to the ground, eyes glazed, dead before he even hit the floor. Sickened, Ashurek eased himself out of the path of the others and watched them falling over each other in their scramble for safety. *That could have been Silvren . . .*

Then he saw her silhouetted against the daylight, the last to escape apart from him, and he rushed after her with relief. They were out of the Dome. There was grass under their feet, they were free – but even as he thought it, Ashurek saw the shard of metal come spearing down from above, straight towards Silvren. It struck her skull and she fell headlong on the grass.

Ashurek ran towards her, stopping himself just in time. He could not help her, could not touch her.

The daylight was fading and thickening to a grim purple. Regardless of the continuing danger, Iytrel Halia and the others were slowing down and turning to look back, to understand what they had escaped. There was no sign of the High Master anywhere.

The White Dome had opened up like a flower, a huge and livid bloom from the centre of the jungle, with twisted white petals bent back around a glistening, violet-black interior. From the ruined generator – a jagged spike of a stamen – the outpouring of energy continued almost silently, a fountain of bruise-coloured vapour pouring foulness into the sky.

15

Black Fire

Spasmodic shudders racked the ground, while the air throbbed with unhuman groans and sighs. The plum-coloured pestilence that flowed from the White Dome showed no sign of slackening, and soon it would turn the whole sky dark. Jhensit's death would be a gradual suffocation, Ashurek realised, unless the Maelstrom surged in to tear its fabric apart first. *But how much time do we have?*

Silvren was still unconscious, her breathing shallow. All over the drab hillside the Pels and the Satrans, now free of the High Master's control, were falling to their knees and praying to their respective gods for deliverance. Of the Muridonu there was no sign at all; if they had crept away or simply vanished like ghosts, Ashurek had not noticed. His only concern was Silvren.

Seeing Iytrel Halia a few yards away, staring at the ruined Dome, he called to her, 'Help me!'

She saw Silvren lying unconscious and ran towards them. 'Dear Eyos, what's happened to her?'

'She was struck by a piece of debris. Have someone carry her back to the city immediately.'

The Director gave him a narrow, unfriendly look. 'Of course, but why don't you help her yourself?'

'Because if I touched her, she would die,' Ashurek said, his voice dangerously low. 'And if you don't obey, so will you.'

Unnerved but still hostile, Iytrel Halia backed away and summoned two Satrans. They lifted Silvren with nervously exaggerated care under Ashurek's gaze, and he began to follow them back to Niankan through the ominous gloom. Behind him, he could hear Iytrel Halia demanding to know where Gregardreos was.

'No-one's seen him, ' one of her colleagues replied. 'He can't have survived.'

Ashurek grimaced. The High Master was still alive somewhere, he was certain, but afraid to show his face if he had any conscience. *This is his fault . . . and mine too. I should have stopped him and I failed.*

Niankan-Siol stood as dark and quiet as the under-city. The pastel towers which had once been bathed with electric brilliance were grey and dead; sky-carriages hung lifeless on their cables like shed spider-husks; the only sounds were of feet whispering along the shadowy walkways and the murmur of frightened voices.

Down in Niankan-Pel, blood-red shadows moved through the streets, bringing a venomous death to any who crossed their paths. The Pels fled and huddled in their houses, praying desperately to Flaim, but even solid stone walls were no barrier to the Muridonu.

Silvren saw these things as she slowly drifted back to consciousness, involuntary touches of witch-sight, but her head throbbed and she did not have the strength to pursue them. She was lying in a silk-soft bed. In the White Dome? No, that was gone now and this room was more opulent, yet all in monochrome apart from pools of colour where candlelight shone on the blue silk draperies. There were other figures in the room. She recognised Ashurek's voice with relief – then felt an agonising pang as she remembered what had happened in the Dome.

'I failed, Tialah,' said Ashurek.

'So I see.' A stately woman walked from the window and came to look down at Silvren. Her face was stern but attractive and not unkind. 'What will happen now?'

'I don't know,' he said. 'But I think there is little cause for optimism. Jhensit is disintegrating.'

Silvren drew a deep breath. She ached all over, but she made the effort to speak. 'Ashurek . . .'

He leaned over her but did not touch her. 'She's coming round, thank the gods!' he said. 'Lie still, beloved. How do you feel?' Again she had the horrible impression that although she could see him with her eyes he was not really there. She felt too numb too weep, but a spasm went through her, increasing her physical pain.

'I shall be all right.' She did not mean to sound so cold to him but she could not help it; the bloody invasion of the Dome and the evil bargain he had made stood between them like an ice wall. They might as well have been strangers. Ashurek's pain, his yearning to touch her and the impossibility of doing so, were so tangible that she could hardly bear to look at him. 'Where's Gregardreos?' she asked.

'No-one knows,' said Ashurek, 'but I'm sure he's not dead.'

'I would know if he was,' said Silvren. 'I'm still worried about him, though. I can't understand why he acted as he did but I'm sure there's an explanation. I must find him –'

'No, you must rest,' said the tall woman. 'I am the Hyalana Shai Tialah. Ashurek has told me everything that happened. I'm sure you thought you were doing the right thing but your High Master was very wrong not to have spoken to me first. But I don't hold you to blame. Stay here as long as you wish, and welcome.' She moved away from the bed. 'Ashurek, I must go and speak to Cilit Tir and see what the news is. I can't believe it was only a few hours ago that I was talking of making a new start! I wonder if it will be sudden, or very slow . . . like suffocating in earth?'

The Hyalana went to the door and was gone in a swish of silk.

Silvren and Ashurek were left alone. For a time, neither spoke, then Silvren said, 'So you see, even Sorcerers are fallible.'

She almost wished Ashurek would leave; she could not meet his eyes nor say anything remotely warm to him, even though she knew he could not bear it. He said, 'Silvren, do you know what has happened to me?'

'Not really. Gregar blocked my far-seeing sense, but even without it the evil shines out of you.'

'I want to explain.'

'No,' she said. Her head ached with unshed tears. 'I don't want to hear. I'm not ready. Ashurek, please go now.'

'I would like to,' he said, his tone icy and bitter, 'and as soon as you are well again, I shall.'

Another silence fell. She closed her eyes. At once she thought he had gone, there was only a nothingness where his presence should have been – but when she opened her eyes again, he was still there, watching over her with brooding green eyes. Something had changed, though. There was a tension in the air beyond the tension between them; something physical, a thickening. A golden whirlwind appeared in the centre of the room, lighting it up like day.

'A Way!' said Silvren, struggling to sit up. The light faded as swiftly as it had appeared, and from it stepped two familiar figures.

They were Aflouel and Terarct of the School of Sorcery. Her spirits rose at the sight of Aflouel's plump, smiling face, and even Terarct's angularity seemed comfortingly familiar.

'Silvren!' said Aflouel, hurrying forward and clasping her hands. 'What has happened to you?'

'To me, only a knock on the head – but what are you doing here?'

Terarct gave Ashurek a cool look, then turned to Silvren. 'To be brief, such a cataclysm is shaking this world that it reached us even in Ikonus. We had no choice but to investigate. As acting High Master in Gregardreos's absence, it is my responsibility to do so. Aflouel and I pooled our strength to far-see into Jhensit and we have learned some very terrible things – but you already know, of course.'

Ashurek stood up. His face was impassive, and he seemed a thousand miles from her. 'Now that you have friends to take care of you, Silvren, I shall leave.' He went towards the door; she would have done anything to call him back, but she could not. 'Just what we needed,' he added thinly. 'More Sorcerers.'

He left, and she was infinitely grateful that her friends were with her. Aflouel placed her hands on Silvren's forehead, and a feeling of well-being replaced her physical pain.

'Thank you,' said Silvren. She needed to sleep to complete the healing process, but anxiety kept her wide awake. 'I'm so glad you're here. How much do you know? Gregardreos tried to save Jhensit but he failed. Now he's vanished and I don't know why, but we have to find him.'

Aflouel and Terarct exchanged glances. 'You don't know,' said Terarct.

Silvren felt a ghost of foreboding. 'What do you mean? He can't be dead, I would sense it . . .'

'No, he is alive, and we most certainly have to find him, but when you say he tried to save Jhensit and failed – oh no, it is far worse than that.' Terarct sat on the very edge of the bed, smoothing his robe over his bony knees. 'Have you not used far-sight?'

'I couldn't. Gregar placed blocks on my mind when we first arrived and I've Seen hardly anything since. We argued about it but he wouldn't listen.'

'Are the blocks still there now?' said Aflouel.

Silvren closed her eyes, tentatively pushing her mind beyond the physical plane. 'No. They're gone.'

'Look a little further, and you'll understand why he blocked you,' said Terarct.

Silvren looked at him anxiously. 'He was protecting me.'

'No. He was protecting himself.'

Silvren turned her gaze to Aflouel. She knew she must look but she did not want to, she could not bear to believe that Gregardreos had deceived her.

'It won't be easy for you but you must face it,' said Aflouel, taking her hand. 'Come with me. We'll far-see together and then you'll know all the things that Gregardreos tried to keep hidden.'

When Ashurek returned to his chamber, he found Shai Fea there, waiting for him in the glow of a single candle.

'Are you not afraid of me?' He knew he sounded off-hand, but what he really felt was beyond expression.

'I know you would never harm me,' she said. 'I wanted to talk to you. How is – how is Silvren?'

The Hyalet's face seemed very small and pale under the mass of blue-black hair which floated like down in the slightest draught. He sat in a chair on the opposite side of the room, trying to convince himself that he felt nothing. If any emotion came to the surface he would go mad.

'She is recovering,' he said.

'I – I'm glad.' She looked down at her hands and began to speak rapidly, the words stumbling over each other. 'I know we had no future, you and I, I always knew it. I don't even know if I love you or not – I am too afraid, not of *you* but of the darkness inside – nothing to do with what you did for my mother, I mean a darkness that's always been part of you – and I don't think I would have been strong enough to live with it. But, but you have Silvren again now, of course.'

'I have no-one, Fea,' he said tiredly. 'My touch would be fatal to her as it would be to anyone else.'

'I thought – if she is a Sorceress –'

'She is only human, and I am not going to put it to the test.'

'I'm sorry.' She glanced up at him. 'What will you do?'

'Go where there is no-one, so that I can harm no-one.'

'I wish I could do something,' she whispered. She was tormented and he could do nothing, nothing at all to comfort her. 'I would do anything to help you!'

'You have helped me,' he said gently. 'Now your duty is to your mother and your own people. Help her end this division between the Pels and the Siols.'

Shai Fea glanced listlessly at the writhing, bruised sky beyond the window. 'I would, if we had a future.'

Ashurek had to leave Shai Fea; her pain was almost harder to bear than Silvren's. The time was coming when he would have to leave the palace completely, find a barren place where the Face could not drive him to kill. He should have gone already, but as long as Silvren remained there, as long as Jhensit's existence hung in the balance, he could not bring himself to leave. He went to Shai Tialah's apartments and found her with Cilit Tir and several other Counsellors, all looking tired and ashen with anxiety. The Hyalana turned to Ashurek as if he had come bearing answers to all her problems.

'The Counsellor tells me that the streets of Niankan-Pel are full of Muridonu. They are killing anyone they catch and the Pels are terrified.'

'Revenge, I suppose,' said Ashurek.

Cilit Tir gave him a hard glance. 'What?'

'I said revenge. Don't you know what the Muridonu are? They were once as human as you, until the Maelstrom deformed them. And many of them were trapped in it because your ancestors refused to let them into Palan as refugees.'

The Counsellor made a strangled noise in his throat and turned away as if he were struggling not to be sick. The others looked equally stricken, but Shai Tialah only compressed her lips grimly. She already knew. 'And it will happen to us too,' she said. Her voice rose. 'There will be no Jhensit, only the Maelstrom, and we will become twisted mad things like the Muridonu. Where is Eyos now?'

Her attendants shrank away and she bowed her head, making a concerted effort to regain her self-control.

Ashurek said, 'Let the Pels into the upper city.'

Tialah looked at him as if he had gone mad. 'That's impossible.'

'Why?'

'Because they – they are –'

'Not aristocrats? Worshippers of the earth? But you have seen beyond that, Tialah. I suppose you don't want them to soil your pristine city, but without them it would not have been built. They are your subjects and I am suggesting that you protect them because it is what Silvren would ask you to do.'

Cilit Tir and the others looked scandalised, but the Hyalana nodded slowly. 'I suppose you are right, Ashurek. I responded out of habit, but times are different now.' Cilit Tir was beginning to protest and she rounded angrily on him. 'We are all doomed, Counsellor! Can we not at least show some humanity towards our servants in our last few days – or hours?'

'It will take a lot of organisation,' he said sourly. As he was speaking, the double doors to the chamber swung open and Shai Fea rushed into the room, followed by a white-faced Satran. The sounds of a commotion drifted in from the antechamber.

'Mother, they're in the palace!' she gasped.

'What's happening?' said Tialah, going towards her.

The Satran replied, his voice shaking. 'Your Majesty, those red creatures, the Muridonu – Eyos knows how they got up here but they're all in the corridors and they're coming this way. We've killed a few with heat-swords but there's too many of them, I've lost two of my men and we can't stop them. Your Majesty, I'm sorry.'

Shai Fea stared at Ashurek her face ghastly with terror. 'There was one – it just kept coming for me and coming for me, and I was so frightened – oh, please keep it away from me!'

'Try to keep calm, all of you,' said Ashurek. He moved towards Shai Fea then stopped, looking out into the antechamber. He could see nothing, but the sounds of conflict in the corridor outside were coming closer. 'I suspect that their presence is my fault.'

The Hyalana stared at him. She had been with him in the Maelstrom, she had seen the Muridonu following him then. She said quietly, 'What do you mean?'

'I think you know,' said Ashurek. 'They have followed me since the first time I encountered them. They may have come here to find me, and they will only harm those who try to stop them.' He spoke matter-of-factly, but he felt a deep sense of foreboding and suffocation. Was he doomed to be pursued forever by this unwanted army who were obsessed with making him their leader? At this moment he despised them more than he pitied them.

'What do you suggest we do?' said the Hyalana.

'Keep everyone calm while I try to speak to them.'

He began to walk out into the antechamber when the Muridonu appeared; not through the door but all around him, washing through the walls and the draperies like scarlet ghosts. Some dragged deformed bodies along on spindly arms – human beings turned inside out – while others tiptoed on insectile feet or lurched along on pseudopodia. Their eyes were empty, their faces armed with poisonous spikes of bone. Horror overcame him, as if he had never seen them before, and he understood Shai Fea's renewed fear.

Wherever you go we will follow. Lead us. Save us. The words echoed through his mind, but they were empty of hope. These creatures were damned, and they breathed their damnation into the air like a miasma.

'Stop!' he cried, but the Muridonu went on swarming around him and through into the chamber, muttering their incessant and empty litany. He turned. They were swiftly filling the room, glistening like bubbles of blood.

Everyone in the chamber seemed paralysed, except Shai Fea, who broke away from her mother and fled before them.

'Make them leave me alone!' she cried. She struggled frantically with the balcony windows. 'I've got to get away from them!'

Ashurek was already striding across the room towards her when she finally wrenched the windows open and dashed out onto the balcony. From there, everything seemed to happen in slow-motion, a few seconds stretched out over eternity. She was running blindly, too fast. She lost her footing; the rail caught her across the stomach but her momentum was still carrying her forward and she pitched over the edge, arms flailing as she tried to stop herself.

One hand clawed at the top of the rail, arresting her fall for the brief moment it took Ashurek to reach her. He did not stop to think as he leaned forward, seized her shoulders and began to haul her back to safety.

At his touch, she screamed.

For an endless moment he was paralysed; he was aware of what was happening, aware of her mother and all the Counsellors watching in stunned horror, yet he could not let her go.

Black light radiated from his hands. Black fire smouldered on her skin, enveloping her whole form in a funereal glow. As the darkness lapped her throat the scream ended abruptly, as if the fire had melted and sealed her throat. Her eyes remained open, round and white with horror, but the light of life had vanished from them.

At last Ashurek's will overrode the paralysis, and his hands sprang open like claws. Shai Fea fell to the floor, half on the balcony and half in the room and there was a terrible, utter silence.

It was Shai Tialah who spoke first, one soft word: 'Demon.'

Ashurek turned. They shrank away; their eyes glittered

with fear and hatred. No matter that the Hyalana had once been possessed by this curse herself; no matter that he had saved her, that they had all known what was entailed. In this dreadful moment all that was swept away and there was only the shock, the stark fact that Ashurek had killed Shai Fea. In their eyes he had suddenly become wholly evil.

Shai Fea's body was whole and perfect, bearing no trace of the dark radiance that had killed her. For a few moments Ashurek was so stunned that he felt nothing, only a deep coldness in his stomach. But the coldness magnified until it became a fierce pain, ice blazing through his veins.

He could not speak. What could he say to them? With this fell power in him he *was* a demon. No lame expression of regret would help them, nor would it even begin to touch the grief that swelled inside him.

Their faces were ragged masks of emotion, but he remained expressionless, his eyes the green of a frozen ocean. Somehow he found his voice. 'I shall go down to the lower city. The Muridonu will follow me and you'll no longer be troubled by them. Let the Pels take refuge here.'

They fell out of his way as he strode across the room. It was not the first time he had inspired such fear in others, and he loathed it more than ever now. He went on walking through the palace corridors, along the gloomy walkways outside, unchallenged by the Satrans, never hesitating or looking back – but conscious all the time of the Muridonu moving with him, an unwanted, sinister army.

Silvren opened her eyes. She was hanging onto Aflouel's hands so hard that they were bloodless, but it was all she could do to let go. The room looked grey, all shadows, like the grim journey of far-sight from which she had just surfaced.

'Now do you see?' said Teraret.

'The Sphere,' said Silvren. She felt exhausted, as if her disillusionment had drained all the spirit from her.

'Yes, the Sphere.' His face was almost luminous in the candlelight, harsh and oddly eager. 'It is ironic that you were explaining its function to a student so recently.'

'It seems years ago.'

'The Sphere filters the energy of Ikonus, leaving it pure for our use,' Terarct went on, not wanting to be interrupted. 'And it was supposed to absorb the negative, corrupting side of the power. But always, since the Sphere was first created, some of the Flux has leaked into a different dimension and caused the slow destruction of another world.'

Silvren shivered slightly at the memory of what she had Seen; Jhensit, slowly eaten away over the centuries, while the Ikonians had happily gone about their lives in smug ignorance.

'But of course,' he went on, 'only a little of the Flux was escaping. The rest *was* absorbed and that proved a disaster, did it not, when the Sphere was destroyed and all that accumulated darkness was released? So, when the Sphere was reconstructed, it was arranged instead for all the negative power to pass into another dimension, where it could do no-one any harm. But who supervised the reconstruction?'

'Gregardreos,' she said faintly. 'Do you have to go through this again?'

'I want to be sure that we all have the same perception of the situation,' Terarct said crisply. 'Gregardreos, exactly. But the question is, when he rebuilt the Sphere, did he discover that it had been leaking the Flux to Jhensit? Because if so, he never said anything. And did he take care to direct the Flux to empty space, where it could do no harm? Apparently not. Instead he directed *all* of the negative energy to Jhensit, where it could not help but accelerate the destruction of this world. In other words, the Sphere created the Maelstrom; Gregardreos's action made it far, far worse.'

Silvren's throat was so tight that she could hardly speak. He was only reiterating what she had learned – the knowledge that Gregardreos had tried to hide from her – but she still wanted to deny it. She swallowed painfully. 'Surely you aren't suggesting that Gregar did it deliberately?'

'Well, that is something we have yet to discover. Only he can tell us his reasons.'

'I don't know how you can be so objective about this!' she said heatedly. 'It's impossible, he would never do something that he knew would harm another world – it's completely out of character!'

'Silvren, I am as distressed as you about this,' said Terarct. 'But we have to be objective. We all have a degree of responsibility for this, but ultimately Gregardreos must take the blame. If he did not know what he was doing, he most certainly should have done.'

Silvren sighed and lay back. Aflouel stroked her forehead, her rosy face was drawn and sombre.

'So either he was acting in ignorance or he was lying to me,' Silvren said. 'They're both too awful to contemplate. There's something else that feels wrong; I can't understand why none of us have heard of Jhensit before. When I first heard the name it seemed familiar, as if I'd known it once and then forgotten it.'

Aflouel blinked. 'That's strange, I had the same feeling.'

'But Gregar admitted to me that he *had* heard of Jhensit,' said Silvren. 'He said they once sent a call for help but he ignored it and has felt guilty ever since.'

'That's interesting,' said Terarct, leaning forward and resting his chin on his hand.

'But that must be why he lied to me! He told me that the White Dome was causing the Maelstrom, when it wasn't true.'

Terarct said, 'It was obvious to Aflouel and myself that it wasn't true, so there is no way the High Master could have believed otherwise.'

Silvren nodded. 'I know. I saw it at once, when my far-sight returned. But Gregar claimed the White Dome was bleeding Jhensit dry, when all the time he must have known the truth was different. The White Dome was feeding on the Maelstrom; he must have known that closing down the Dome would release the Flux.'

'And you've seen the effects of its corrupting influence.The Maelstrom, the Muridonu, the sorcerous power that Gregardreos lent to the Pels; all had their origin in the Flux, and there's nothing but evil in it. It is dangerous for any of us to use sorcery here, because the energy we would draw is intrinsically bad. We'd all be corrupted by it in the end, as Gregardreos has been.'

'He made a mistake, and he lied because he felt guilty,' said Silvren. 'Perhaps it was too much, that we expected the High Master to be infallible. He tried to do the right things and he failed.' She sat up again, trying to shake off the tiredness and think positively. 'We must find him.'

'Yes,' said Terarct, 'as soon as you feel well enough to come with us. We shall need your help.'

'Gregar needs ours!'

The Sorcerer exchanged glances with Aflouel and shook his head. 'We are not here to help him, Silvren – or rather, not only to help him.'

'Why, then?' she asked, dreading the answer because she already knew what it must be.

'Our duty is to arrest him, and take him back to the School of Sorcery to stand trial.'

The lower city was almost deserted.

The streets were like canyons, cutting through the tall, crumbling buildings. The Muridonu had vanished as Ashurek descended the dizzying spiral stair from Niankan-Siol, but he could feel their presence pressing all around him.

The wall at the base of the strut was unguarded and the door stood open. Ashurek found himself some distance from the Satrans' barracks, but he went straight there, hammered on the gates and waited. He wondered if all the Satrans had fled to the upper city, but after a few moments the gate creaked open and two armed guards confronted him.

'You have a prisoner named Jaia Keorn,' he said. 'I wish you to release him to me.'

The guards stared at him and did not even begin to argue. The world had gone insane, and they had given up trying to make sense of it. A few minutes later, Jaia Keorn was thrust out through the gate. His dark garments were bedraggled from the journey, his hair swept back from his face in a dark tangle, but he walked with an air of defiant and graceful dignity.

'I thought I would never see you again,' he said, staring reproachfully at Ashurek.

'You won't, after this.'

Keorn's face changed; fear glimmered in his eyes. 'What has happened?' He looked up at the stormy, wine-dark sky. 'All I've heard is rumours. I keep praying to Flaim, but he gives me no answers – I don't even think he's there any more.'

'Perhaps he never was,' said Ashurek. 'Many things have happened, none of them good, but I don't want to speak of them. I just came to tell you this; I have persuaded the Neatrus to allow the Pels into the upper city, for their own protection.'

Keorn's blue eyes widened. 'I don't believe it! The Siols would let us up there? It's the perfect opportunity; we'll destroy them!'

Ashurek paused, not responding to this. 'Did you know that the Hyalon is dead?'

'There've been rumours of it. It's true, then? The Siols must be in disarray. This is the best news I could have heard. Oh my lord, you haven't let us down after all – I knew I hadn't misjudged you, that you'd help us in the end. How can I thank you? I wish –'

He started forward, but Ashurek stepped back, holding

up his hands in warning. 'Enough. Don't thank me. The Hyalon is dead, but so is Shai Fea.'

He watched carefully for Keorn's reaction to this. The Pel did not look pleased but completely dismayed. 'How?' he gasped.

'I killed her. It was unintentional, but the blame rests wholly with me. Are you glad?'

'Of course not! Flaim, I can't believe it. She was so young.'

'Then, if you feel sorrow for her, how can you contemplate staging a rebellion against her family? They are as human as she was.'

Jaia Keorn was lost for words. Ashurek went on, 'Your rebellion is just a dream. Face reality, Keorn. You and the Siols are the same people and you are all facing extinction; what will any of you gain by slaying each other? The Siols have made the first step by showing you some humanity and you will only gain what you want by showing some responsibility in return. I suggest that now is a good time to begin.'

Keorn shook his head, still wide-eyed. 'And this – this is what you wanted to say to me?'

'I hold you responsible for the behaviour of the Pels in the upper city. Keep them under control. Negotiate with the Hyalana with the eloquence of which you are plainly capable. If Jhensit has a future, you will be helping to mould a new beginning; if not, you will at least enable the end to be peaceful and dignified. Will you promise to do this, Keorn?'

He drew away from Ashurek, holding his cloak tight round his throat. 'Yes. If it's what you want me to do, Lord Ashurek, I promise.'

'Do it for your own sake, not for mine.'

He began to walk away, but the Pel called anxiously after him, 'Where are you going?'

'I don't know,' said Ashurek, not looking back. 'Fare you well, Keorn.'

As Ashurek went on through the streets he began to

see Satrans, some on foot and some mounted on auerets, riding urgently to and fro. Pels appeared from the buildings, a few at first, then streams of them, all converging towards the centre of the city. An air of subdued fear hung over them, as if they did not quite believe the Satrans meant them no harm but were too afraid to disobey. Ashurek could only hope that evacuation would not erupt into violence. If he looked up, he could already see tiny lines of figures ascending the ladders and stairs towards the opaque and lightless mansions of Niankan-Siol.

He avoided the people as best he could, winding his way though deserted alleys. Corpses were strewn all along the way, presumably the victims caught in the Muridonu's path as they sought Ashurek. He had no particular aim in mind, yet he found himself drifting instinctively towards the Ochre River, and by the time he reached its cold, wet banks, the Muridonu were appearing all around him like blood-clots forming from the blighted air. There had been a few dozen in the palace. Now there were hundreds.

Fitting companions, he thought bleakly. Perhaps it would be a mercy to kill them, but he lacked the stomach for it.

He remembered the deserted city in which he had first arrived through the Way. Like Niankan-Pel it must once have teemed with life, before the Maelstrom came to claim it and to turn its inhabitants into monsters. Now the lower city, too, was dead. Only Ashurek was safe walking there; death haunting his own domain.

He seated himself on a block of stone at the base of a building high above the river bank. The water glimmered purplish-brown, reflecting flashes of fire from the clouds. Although the White Dome was not visible from here, he could tell by the constant, thunderous movement of the sky that the fountain of diseased energy was still flowing. It was almost completely dark, yet it was unlike night; it had a horrible luminosity that made him think of the Serpent's domain, bringing back the despair and depression that he thought he had left behind long ago.

He could not believe that Shai Fea was dead. After he had been so careful to touch no-one, it had taken just one thoughtless impulse, intended to save her. If he had not tried, might she have hung on until someone else had reached her, or would she have fallen to her death anyway? Either way, the blame for her death came back to him. If not for him, the Muridonu would not have been in the palace. And he had won the eternal hatred of Tialah, one of the few whose friendship had meant something to him.

He had known that his love for them would end in disaster. He should have resisted, yet he had not, and they had paid . . . He had lost them, he had lost Silvren, there was nothing left.

'Why?' he said. 'What is this curse that haunts me?'

He could find no answer, inside or outside himself. The blood-red creatures watched him, like dogs watching their master – lifeless dogs, stuffed and stitched to a semblance of life, with soulless eyes. No eyes at all. He could no longer bear to look at them . . .

'Ashurek!'

Silvren's voice. Now he was imagining things. He opened his eyes and saw her standing before him, a slender statue of white and gold, shimmering with light in the gloom.

'Ashurek,' she said again, and he realised she was really there. His heart flickered with hope then turned leaden again.

'You are the last person I expected to see,' he said tonelessly. 'What are you doing here? It's dangerous. I am dangerous.'

'I had to talk to you.'

'Why? I thought we had said all we had to. There's nothing left to say, it's over.'

Her eyes filled with tears; they burned him like acid. 'Perhaps. But I need your help.'

She was reaching out to him. 'Don't touch me!' he

exclaimed. 'Shai Fea is dead. One inadvertent touch and she shrivelled and died at my feet. This is not a nightmare, it is only too real.'

Silvren drew back. 'I know. Tialah told me what happened. She – she explained about the bargain and I understand why you took it on, but –'

'Do you? I doubt it.'

'Ashurek, I can't bear this! How has this happened to us?'

'Ask your beloved High Master. I don't know, but it has. Everything you said to me in the White Dome was justified. I took this bargain on and I can see no way to escape it, unless I am allowed to die. That is the only end for this, Silvren, and Jhensit is also doomed. Sometimes we must accept that not everything can be put right.'

'I can't accept it!'

'This time, you must.'

'No! Ashurek, it's not like you to give in –'

'I was told not to interfere with this world and I chose to ignore that advice. This is the result. If I do not give in, what can I do but cause further disaster? It is over, beloved. Go back home, while you have the chance; Mellorn needs you.'

'How can I go back without you? I know what I said and I meant every word of it, but I still love you. This is killing me. There must be something I can do.'

Her face shone with tears. He swallowed his own grief, not wanting her to see him weep. There was no sound except the distant crackling of the Maelstrom and the mindless whispering of the Muridonu.

'Silvren, please go back to Ikonus.'

'I can't. I have something else to do here first. I must find Gregardreos.'

Ashurek laughed without humour. He reached into the pouch on his belt and took out the three lodestones, holding them flat on his palm. 'Look at these, my love. The lodestones Gregardreos gave me to find my way home. Would you believe me if I told you there is no power in these stones? He did not mean me to come back. He deceived us both.' Ashurek flung the stones, one by one, out into the river. He watched them arc over the water, heard the soft *plop* as they vanished. 'Do you still wish to look for him?'

She lowered her head as if he had made to strike her, but she said, 'I must.' Then she told him what she had discovered with Aflouel and Terarct, but Ashurek felt no surprise at all, and she was infuriated that he did not react. 'Can't you understand that I must find out why he's behaved as he has?'

'What's the mystery? He was jealous, Silvren. He wanted you, so he would go to any lengths to destroy me.'

'You've destroyed yourself!' she shouted suddenly. Her hands became fists and she was fighting not to cry.

'Is it so easy to believe evil of me, so hard to believe it of him?' he asked softly.

She began to back away and he watched her helplessly; knowing he was losing her forever, unable to do anything to bring her back. Silvren, who had never harmed anyone, whose only sin was to trust too easily; what had she done to deserve any of this? Eventually she spoke.

'Please help me now, and I'll never ask anything of you again.'

The forlorn bitterness of her words stung him like knife cuts. He could not refuse.

16

Ghosts

Gregardreos laughed. No-one could touch him now. A weird landscape boiled around him, all pewter and crimson, netted with flashes of blue electricity, but it held no fear for him. He was alone in the Maelstrom and he *was* the Maelstrom, filled with swirling thunderclouds of power in which whips of lightning crackled, clouds that were grim and heavy with blood-red rain. He could no longer tell where the boundaries of his body ended and the Maelstrom began; he was one with the power.

The energy had surged into him when he had shut down the generator, giving him the strength to flee downwards through the ruined White Dome. He knew that it was the Flux from the Sphere that had possessed him but he did not care, he was drunk on it. Unlike the golden, weightless energy of Ikonus, the Flux was leaden and intoxicating, a sickly wine. It took away Gregardreos's conscience, made evil seem a joke, Jhensit's fate a cause for rejoicing.

'Soon, Jhensit, you'll be no more and I shall be free,' he said. Then a dark spike of pain went through him and he clenched his fists, thinking of Ashurek. 'And you will be no more, Prince of evil . . . but I would like to see you again just once, so that I can slay you with my own hands.'

And Silvren?

Another brief stab of anguish, but he felt detached from

human emotions. 'You didn't want me,' he murmured. 'This need not have been, but you made it so. You did not want me . . .'

He only had to wait for Jhensit to die and then he would be free, all-powerful, trailing a cloud of sorcery the size of a world . . . But where would he go, what would he do? He could not think clearly. His mind was reeling. The School of Sorcery was just a blurred patch in his memory and there was no future, only the lurching euphoria of power.

Silvren looked up at the wrecked central cylinder, from which the Flux still poured.

'There must be a way to help Jhensit,' she said. 'If it's the only thing I do, the last thing I do, I have to stop this.'

The three Sorcerers were making their way to the ruins of the White Dome, Ashurek walking some distance behind them and taking no part in their conversation. The Muridonu still trailed after him, but he ignored them. The sky billowed oppressively and a sooty-violet fog hung over the hills, making it hard to see further than a few yards ahead. The twisted petals of the Dome shimmered ghostly white through the gloom.

Silvren led them into the centre and down through the empty prison levels, until they found the door to the central shaft, and the swirling spot that marked the entrance to the Maelstrom. A few seconds of disorientation and they were through the skin and in a realm of wild storms. The ground rose and fell under their feet, insubstantial as a skin stretched over the ocean. The air was thick and malodorous, and livid clouds buffeted them like pillows weighted with iron.

'It wasn't like this before,' Silvren gasped, clinging to Aflouel. 'It's grown much fiercer. Can you sense Gregar?'

'Yes,' said Aflouel. 'But a long way from us . . . if we ever reach him through this.'

'Stay close together,' said Terarct, and the three began to force their way through the Maelstrom. Ashurek pulled his cloak around him and followed, hardly noticing the whiplashes of static that danced on his skin. The Muridonu spread out around him, rising and falling like scarlet flotsam on the surface; seeming to drift away from him, as if by bringing them back to this domain he had somehow defeated them. He watched them and all he felt was a distant sadness.

Terarct and Aflouel cast out a protective net to buffer them from the worst of the Maelstrom, but their only source of energy was the Maelstrom itself. The sorcerous net glowed dull as rusted iron, and gave little comfort.

They were drawn towards the High Master as if he were the magnetic centre of a hyperphysical field, though it took them a long time to reach him. As they went, Ashurek watched Silvren growing more and more drained by the effort of withstanding the malicious darkness of the power. His inability to help her was a torment.

They crested a long, heaving ridge of amber sand and at last they saw Gregardreos, no more than thirty yards away, facing them as if he had known they were coming. He was engorged with power, no longer golden but muddy-grey, like a huge lion soaked with rain and gore. Clouds whirled around him, crackling like heat-swords. Ashurek did not need to be a Sorcerer to see that the Flux which had caused the Maelstrom, and which now filled Gregardreos, was the opposite to the pure energy of Ikonus. Past experience had left him only too sensitive to the rank breath of corruption.

'Gregardreos!' yelled Terarct. 'We must speak to you! It's Terarct and Aflouel from the School of Sorcery.'

The High Master's expression was savage, almost unrecognisable. 'I can see quite clearly who you are,' he said, his voice hoarse but calm. 'Leave me alone. I have to preside over this world's death in solitude.'

'That will not be possible,' said Terarct – pompously, Ashurek thought. 'As you are no doubt aware, it's largely your fault that Jhensit *is* dying. You have broken your

Oath and been guilty of lethal negligence. We are here to take you back to Ikonus to face these charges.'

Gregardreos stared at them. He looked at Silvren, then at Ashurek, but did not acknowledge them. 'What authority do you imagine you have over me, Terarct? Am I not your High Master? The only authority is power, and I have a world of it at my command!'

Rusty snakes of energy sizzled through the air and bit into their skin, driving them all back in pain.

'A corrupt power!' Terarct said, teeth clenched in pain. 'It's the effluvium of the Sphere, it was never meant to be wielded. It will poison you if you go on, and us as well; do you want to be responsible for that?' He held himself straight, and Ashurek had to admire the way he regained his self-containment so swiftly.

'Who do you think you are, Terarct?' Gregardreos gave an unpleasant bark of laughter. 'You think you know everything, yet you understand nothing at all.'

'With respect, Master, you are obviously not yourself. The Maelstrom is affecting your judgement. Let us near you, we are your friends and –'

'Friends!' the High Master cried, throwing his head back. 'Friends who wish to put me on trial? I think not!'

He flung out a badly-aimed curve of fire, but Silvren pushed forward against its dull spikes. 'Gregar, give yourself up. Please, for my sake!'

His grin vanished. He almost looked human again, strained and worried. 'For *your* sake, Silvren? You, who rejected me, ask that? I am not in debt to you. Go back to Ashurek and die in his fond embrace.'

'You don't mean that,' she said uneasily.

'Oh, but I do.'

She froze for a moment then started towards him again. Gregardreos hurled a globe of darkness straight at her, and it struck her first then spread out to her companions, throwing them all off their feet, stinging and burning to the core of their bodies. Ashurek was the first to rise; for a moment he thought the others were dead, but then they began to move, gasping and groaning.

By the time they had recovered the High Master was a hundred yards from them, barely visible in his clouds of fiery shadow.

'How are we to get near him?' said Aflouel.

'If he won't even listen to Silvren, I don't know,' said Terarct. 'The more we attempt to use sorcery here, the more like him we will become. We can't overcome him by force.'

Ashurek walked forward slowly. 'In theory, the bargain I made with the Face means I cannot be killed. He can hurt me, but I don't think he can stop me from reaching him.'

'What good would that do?' said Silvren. 'He has some control over the power. If you try to seize him he may lose control and anything could happen. He may even be strong enough to override the damnable bargain. Look, it's not enough just to arrest him, we also have to find a way to help Jhensit.'

Terarct folded his arms, as if he thought Silvren was being difficult.

'The only way to purge Jhensit of the Flux is for a Sorcerer to take all the power into himself and channel it out and away into space,' he said. 'The High Master cannot do it – he's lost control and become intoxicated by it. I doubt that I am strong enough.'

'Nor I,' said Aflouel. 'And it's not only strength we have to consider, but purity of soul. If any of us has the endurance to withstand the power without being poisoned by it, it's Silvren.'

'And I'll do it, I'm perfectly willing to do it!' Silvren exclaimed. And Ashurek saw hope shining in her eyes; her irrepressible optimism that could turn lead into gold. She was the only clear light in this hellish domain.

That, however, did not stop him turning angrily on the others. 'You cold-bloodedly nominate her to take on this burden?'

'But they're right,' said Silvren. 'If I cannot do it, no-one can.'

'Silvren, I won't let you even consider it! Do you think I can stand here and watch you be destroyed?'

'Don't watch, then!' she exclaimed, glaring at Ashurek. 'And don't you dare try to stop me! If you do, you won't save me – you'll only condemn this world forever. Even if I survive, what have I to survive for – if I can't be with you?' Tears were running down her cheeks.

Ashurek held her gaze for a moment, unable to speak. Then he said, 'Mellorn.'

Silvren turned pale, and looked away. 'There are plenty of people on Ikonus to love her and take care of her. She would understand.'

They were the exact words Ashurek had used to the Hyalana, when he had taken over her bargain with the Face; *Silvren and Mellorn would understand.* He moved away, his throat constricted. 'Do as you will, then.'

Aflouel took Silvren by the elbow, trying to calm the situation. 'The whole idea's only hypothetical, anyway. We couldn't do it without the High Master's co-operation.'

Ashurek sighed. 'As I said, I am willing to try to get near him. But I will not use force; I'll only talk.'

Gregardreos saw Ashurek walking towards him; a tall, lean figure, his chiselled face darker than the storm. His black hair streamed back on the air and his eyes were clear green ice. Gregardreos should have been filled with hatred and fury, but instead he had a strange feeling of helplessness. Angry with himself, he began to shape a sorcerous missile between his hands.

Ashurek stopped some distance from him, and the High Master held the power to himself as if holding his breath.

'I know how it feels to suffer guilt,' said Ashurek.

Gregardreos glared disdainfully at him. 'You do not even begin to comprehend my feelings!'

'Did I say that I did?' The Gorethrian's cool tone was insufferable. *If he cared for Silvren, he could not be so cold!* 'I was describing my own experience. I know how it is to be so racked with guilt that it becomes a madness which can only be purged by destruction. But of course, it is a vicious circle; the destruction only makes the guilt worse.'

The High Master felt a sensation of weakness beginning in his stomach and trickling through him like mercury. He said caustically, 'So, my wise friend, how did you rise above your guilt?'

'I don't think I have,' said Ashurek. 'I don't think I ever can. Either you learn to live with it, or you die.'

Gregardreos went on staring at Ashurek, wishing him dead, willing himself to launch the attack but completely unable to do so. The fogs were closing in and Ashurek seemed to recede. Gregardreos slowly became aware that there were two others with him instead, two white-haired elderly men, one in a long pale robe, the other bearded, bare-chested, with white trousers hanging loose on his spindly legs. He knew them but he denied them. He tried desperately to shake them off; he ignored them, he ran from them, he hurled bolts of sorcery at them that would have crumbled mountains. But when he had finished, the two old men were still there, walking quietly on either side of him as if nothing had happened. Ghosts.

'Do you remember us?' said the robed one. 'My name is Tean Mon. This world was bleeding and weeping to be saved and you turned your back. With all your golden power, all that you could have done – instead you ignored us. What did we ever do to harm you? How have we deserved your bitterness?'

'You speak in riddles,' said the High Master. 'I don't know you. I am Gregardreos!'

'But you do know us,' said the bearded, emaciated man. 'I am Jyel Vanan. We remember a child of a different name – one who committed a very great wrong and instead of making recompense, has since compounded the crime, over and over again.'

'I don't know what you are talking about!'

'Only because you have blocked your mind against us,' said Jyel Vanan. 'Speak your true name and the blocks will come down and you will admit the truth.'

'The truth is that I tried to save Jhensit! Why do you torment me like this? If I have failed, it was not for want of trying.'

'Do you truly believe that?' asked Tean Mon. 'It is one thing to deceive others, another to deceive yourself. I should know. Admit it; you meant to fail.'

'No.'

'Ah yes, you haven't failed; you've succeeded,' said Jyel Vanan. 'Because your intention from the start was to destroy Jhensit, wasn't it?'

'No! Never!'

Tean Mon said, 'You have known for years that the Maelstrom was caused by the poison from Ikonus's Sphere. When you had the chance to make it better, instead you made it worse, and you came here knowing that if you destroyed the White Dome you would destroy Jhensit once and for all. Admit it.'

'It's not true!' Gregardreos cried in anguish.

'Speak your true name, High Master. If you won't, we will speak it for you.'

'Don't.' Suddenly Gregardreos felt his strength returning in a fire of desperation. He felt the muscles swelling in his shoulders, the power surging within him, ready to silence his tormentors. 'You don't know what you are doing.'

'Then you give us no choice.'

'Don't, I beg you!'

But they ignored his pleas and in unison, Jyel Vanan and Tean Mon spoke the name.

The High Master only heard the first syllable before he released the power, but it was enough. A hoarse scream of agony burst from his throat, growing and growing in volume until it was no longer a human voice but a roar of thunder, and in response the Maelstrom began to erupt all around him.

Ashurek saw the High Master turn away, apparently hallucinating, arguing with himself and becoming increasingly distraught. But then came the scream and Ashurek turned and ran, his hands over his ears, tossed this way and that by the wild swell of the ground.

As he reached Silvren, Aflouel and Terarct, the whole landscape was fragmenting, tearing itself into wild streamers of cloud, purple and black and blood-brown. A hurricane streamed past them, spinning round on itself, tighter and tighter until it became a whirlwind. And Silvren was at the centre of the power, a human Sphere, gathering the dark cyclone to her and absorbing it into her slender body.

Ashurek cried out in despair, but the wind carried his voice away. She would be killed and it was too late to stop her; she would sacrifice herself for Jhensit and it was his fault.

Aflouel and Terarct were not helping her. They could not. He understood at once what she was doing; she was channelling the Flux through herself and hurling it outwards, not in a wild mass but in a single, concentrated stream that would disperse harmlessly into space. Her hands were rigidly by her sides and an oily, black jet burst straight from her heart as if she were spilling her own lifeblood to purge Jhensit.

Ashurek did not pause to think. He acted on instinct, because it was the only decision he could make.

If anything was equal to the Face, it was the Flux. He and Silvren would die together. He stepped in front of her, straight into the lethal path of the fire.

The force caught him full on the chest, slicing through him so sharply that he did not even feel it, as if he were made of glass or air or nothingness. Yet the force thrust him out of his body and sent him tumbling through the star-dusted curve of space.

Was he falling, or hanging motionless? A century seemed to have passed and he was spreadeagled like a star on the black void. He looked up and there was the Face, filling half the universe, its shimmering brush-stroke features serene as it gazed down on him. He floated helpless . . . yet he felt the faintest of sensations in his heart, a needle of cold fire, and suddenly he knew that the Flux was still coursing through him.

It burst from his chest like a jet of fire, not black but rust-red against the inkiness of space. Frozen, Ashurek watched it hurtling straight towards the Face's passionless mouth . . .

The lips parted – with surprise, or acceptance? – and the red stream poured straight between them. The Face seemed to drink the Flux, a gargoyle fountain running backwards in time. And as the fire vanished into the mouth, the Face itself began to dwindle . . . now the size of a planet . . . now the size of a coin . . .

Now gone altogether.

17

The Hawk in the Mirror

Ashurek opened his eyes to a clear blue sky.

He was lying on springy gold-green grass that was starred with tiny flowers, and Aflouel was bending over him, her hand on his shoulder.

Her hand – and she was still alive, smiling.

'He's back with us,' she said, turning her head to look at someone beyond his line of vision. Ashurek propped himself onto his elbows with difficulty and he saw Silvren standing over him – his heart lurched with relief but her face was sombre, her eyes veiled and sad.

'You could have been killed,' she said tightly.

'That was what I intended,' he replied. He stood up but she turned away and he dared not go after her, still dared not touch her although Aflouel had touched him without harm.

They were on the hillside outside the White Dome again. The sky was china blue and achingly clear, and the sun floated like a water lily just above the horizon. It was the first time Ashurek had seen Jhensit's sun. Niankan-Siol glowed like a fantastic construction of ice in its rays, and he could see distant flecks of colour dancing above its spires; bell-birds and silukians.

He thought of Shai Fea. He knew he was free of the Face but his relief only felt like lead inside him. Too much had been lost.

The High Master was standing a few yards away, his

head bowed and his blonde hair plastered to his neck with sweat. Terarct was holding his arm, although he looked incapable even of contemplating escape. For the first time, Ashurek almost pitied him.

'You succeeded, then,' said Ashurek, addressing no-one in particular.

Terarct replied, 'Silvren has purged the Flux out of Jhensit and out of Gregardreos. But what of you, Ashurek? Silvren is right, what you did was suicidal.'

Ashurek's lips thinned in a humourless smile. 'The Face consumed the Flux, and in turn the Flux destroyed the Face. I am free of it.'

Out of the corner of his eye he felt that Silvren was watching him, but when he turned his head, she was gazing past him to the city. She said, 'Jhensit is beginning to heal itself. It will take a long time, but it has begun.'

'What happened to the Muridonu?' asked Ashurek.

'I don't know,' she said. 'They vanished with the Flux, so I hope they find peace in death.'

'Does anyone wish to go back to the city?' said Terarct.

Ashurek gazed up at the pale towers of the upper city, thinking of Shai Tialah's face as her daughter's body fell to the floor at his feet; seeing the ice congealing in her eyes as the single word escaped her lips; '*Demon.*'

And Jaia Keorn; had he really seen the wisdom of making peace with the Siols, or would his bitterness make him break his word and bring violence to Niankan-Siol? The Jhensitians' faith in their respective gods, Eyos and Flaim, had been severely shaken. In time they would find ways to rationalise what had happened, and if the old religions were not strengthened, they would only be replaced with a new one. Such was human nature. Ashurek could only hope that Jhensit's narrow escape from doom would end the division between the Siols and the Pels; but however they chose to shape their future, he no longer had any part to play in it.

'No,' he said. 'I have no reason to go back, no-one who would wish to say farewell to me.'

'Then we'll return to Ikonus,' said Terarct. 'Aflouel, help me create the Way.'

Ikonus felt strange after Jhensit, Silvren thought; solid and robust, where the other world had felt fragile and raddled. *Our health at the expense of theirs,* she thought unhappily. She filled herself with the aureate energy to wash away the sourness of the Flux, but every breath brought a whisper of guilt.

They had returned to the School of Sorcery, where the High Master had been placed under house arrest in his quarters. Aflouel and Terarct sat near the bed, Ashurek by the door, two other senior Sorcerers on the far side of the room to bear witness to what took place. Gregardreos had not spoken since the Maelstrom. He lay on his bed under the soft blue-crystal twilight that filtered through the walls, his eyes closed and his breathing laboured. He seemed completely broken.

'It's time to find out the truth,' said Terarct. 'If you would rather not, Silvren –'

'It's all right,' she said softly. 'I think he'd rather it was me, even after what's happened.'

Silvren took the High Master's hands in hers and summoned the gentle energy of healing to pass from her body into his. She had unconsciously gathered her strength as if to thrust against a stone wall, knowing that she probably would not be able to break through his barriers, but desperate to try.

Closing her eyes, she unleashed the energy – and fell, as if the wall had dissolved like sugar beneath her. The High Master's barriers were gone and she was inside his soul, flying and falling with the truth of his thoughts all around her, the essence of who he truly was uncurling before her stunned eyes.

She did not want to See. It would be a violation, an irreparable breach of trust, to spy on him without consent. She withdrew swiftly. The shock of recoil as she returned to the external world left her drained, and she sat slumped against the bed, her head resting on their joined hands.

'Silvren?' said Ashurek.

'I'm all right,' she said. Again, more cautiously this time, she touched the High Master with the silvery aura of healing, and he groaned and opened his eyes.

'You know,' he said. He looked as if all hope had drained out of him.

'Gregar, I didn't want to intrude on your private thoughts. I withdrew without looking, I had no right to spy on you.' She smoothed his forehead with her fingers. 'If I am going to know the truth, I want to hear it from you.'

Pain crossed his face. 'I would have preferred you to seize the knowledge, to save me having to say it.' His voice cracked. 'Of course, you are too honourable for that. More stern than kind, though.'

'What do you mean?'

He moistened his crusted lips. 'You are forcing me to do what is right, to make my own confession, however painful it is.'

She was about to deny this, but something hardened in her heart. 'Yes.'

'Ah, but you are quite right to do so. It's my philosophy also – or used to be, when I knew right from wrong.'

'You owe us the truth,' said Terarct.

Gregardreos glanced at him, as if he had not realised he was in the room. He frowned, then his expression softened. 'I owe all of you the truth. So, let me start at the beginning. I am not a native of Ikonus. I come from Jhensit. I was not even high-born, only a Pel.'

Silvren could not believe it. 'How? You look nothing like them.'

'But I did once. I came from the under-city and I was as slight and dark and round-faced as any of them. My name was –' his voice almost fell to a whisper. 'My name was Alat Ryn. My father was an officer in the Satrans.'

Silvren heard Ashurek make a soft exclamation as if he

had suddenly understood a riddle, but when she looked at him he shook his head. 'Just go on,' he said quietly.

'I was born with the power of sorcery latent in me. I think I always knew what it was, it never seemed unnatural or anything to make a great fuss about. I had a brother –' Gregardreos swallowed. 'A brother, Leahn Gwal. He also had the power to a much lesser degree, but he could not control or hide it.

'I was not a pleasant child. I was arrogant, too clever for my own good. I could control my own energies so perfectly that no-one else knew I possessed them, but because Leahn Gwal couldn't, I despised him.'

'Perhaps you had cause to be jealous of him, too,' said Ashurek.

'He was the one who had all the attention and concern of my parents, damn him!' He looked suspiciously at Ashurek. 'Do you know something about this?'

'I heard a story from a man called Jyel Vanan Silail, about two brothers of those names. He only knew what had become of the older one. The younger one's fate was a mystery.'

The High Master had difficulty continuing. At last he said, 'I have no excuse. There *is* no excuse.'

'For what?' said Silvren.

'There was a secret group of Pels, Jyel Vanan and Tean Mon were part of it, a group who had made a Way to Ikonus. They were going to send my brother through to this mystical place, to become a Sorcerer. I wanted to go in his place, that's all. So I killed him.'

'What?' Silvren could not help herself; she recoiled from him in shock.

'I was a hotheaded boy, I was furious with jealousy, I could only see the most direct way to get what I wanted! I was the one with real power, not him! It was my place, by right.'

Ashurek said, 'Jyel Vanan was under the impression that the younger boy, Alat Ryn, had no talent.'

'Ah, how can I explain? I kept my power secret, out

of a mixture of pride and fear. Others who possessed the power were in constant danger, but I thought, why can't they keep the power hidden? And I realised it was because I was much stronger than them; I could control it and they could not. I concealed it to keep myself safe, I concealed it because that gave me a secret which made me feel superior to others, apart from them. It made me despise them and it justified my despite. And then I had to watch my brother, with his minor gift, receiving all the attention, being sent to a glorious future which should have been mine – but what could I do? Leap up and cry, "Look, you've made a mistake, I am the one who should be sent to Ikonus!"? Perhaps in retrospect that is what I should have done, but at the time it seemed impossible. I already knew of Ikonus, you see; I had had dreams of it, and I knew I belonged there. That, too, was my secret, one I could not share with anyone else. So I could see only one way to get what I wanted; remove Leahn Gwal.

'If my motives sound childish and arrogant, so they were. I was a child. No excuse, I know, and when I look back I loathe myself for that arrogance, the puerile mistakes I made. But I am only trying to explain how things were for me . . .

'I had hated the Siols from the beginning, because they oppressed us. I came to hate my own people too, for allowing it, for their stupid superstitions, worshipping the earth as if it were a god! I hated my own parents for their fears, for the way they crept to the Neatrus for advancement, for favouring my brother . . .'

'Do you still feel this hatred now?' Silvren asked softly.

He sighed. 'I don't know what I feel. When I killed my brother I felt jubilation. It was only when I arrived in Ikonus that I began to have doubts and to worry that my crime would catch up with me.

'I was welcomed at the School, but there were some Pels already there, sent by the secret circle before me, and I became afraid that they would somehow find me out, or that others might pursue me. I had bought my place at the School with blood.'

'So, you set about covering your tracks?' said Ashurek.

'If you must put it that way. I wanted to obliterate the past. My faith in myself was not misplaced,' Gregardreos said ironically. 'I was one of the most powerful latents they'd ever had, a star pupil. But the skills they nurtured in me, I used against them.'

'How?' said Silvren, trying to keep the horror out of her voice.

'I shed no more blood, Silvren, believe me! I was only guilty of deception. It was a slow process, taking years of careful work, but I changed my appearance and my name, making myself as unlike a Pel as I could. I must have been very much a freak, because the other Pels had nowhere near enough power to become Sorcerers. They were all happy enough studying lesser skills at the School – such as the finding of Ways between Worlds. It was not my place to dispose of them but I did; I clouded their memories, made them forget who they were and desire only to use their skills to escape Ikonus. No harm came to them, I simply encouraged them to seek new worlds – anywhere except Jhensit – until they were all gone. I clouded others' minds too, until the existence of Jhensit and my original identity were completely forgotten.'

'You did that to Sorcerers *senior* to you?'

'Yes. I was already more powerful than them.'

'So you became High Master by deception.' She was sitting away from him now as if he had changed into another person whom she could not bear to touch.

'No, I never influenced people to give me advancement! As I grew older I regretted what I had done more and more, and because of that I came to loathe wrongdoing in myself and in others.'

'Quite a reformed character,' Ashurek murmured.

'Yes!' Gregardreos snapped, raising his head. 'It mattered to me that I became High Master on my own merits and that's what I did. Since then I've always striven to prove worthy of the honour. I have never acted in a spirit of cynicism, I have always tried to be straightforward and just.'

In a low voice, she said, 'I never doubted that, until now.'

'Silvren, I am not a wicked man. All I wanted to do was to put Jhensit behind me. That's all. Not to deceive, just to forget the past and make a new life.'

'But if not for that deceit you would not have become High Master.'

He sighed heavily. 'I know. I have broken my Oath many times, and an Oath-breaker deserves to have his white mantle stripped from him.'

'But what about Jhensit?' Ashurek leaned forward, resting his chin on his dark, slender hand. 'The Pels sent people to Ikonus in the hope that they'd return to help their own world.'

'How could I go back?' His voice was harsh with anguish. 'After what I'd done?'

Silvren stared at Gregardreos, her eyes gold ice. 'So you simply locked the door on Jhensit and left them to rot.'

'I knew you wouldn't understand.' He turned his head away.

'I understand perfectly! You have such a powerful idea of right and wrong that you cannot live with your own sins – so you seal them away in a separate compartment, pretend that you are a different person and that they never had anything to do with you! I wish I could say that I can't believe it of you, but the worst thing is that I can, I can!'

The High Master's eyes squeezed shut and tears oozed between the blonde lashes. 'You are right about me. That is what I set out to do and I did it with great success, until Ashurek opened the Way.'

'And that was why it affected you so badly,' said Silvren. 'Guilt?'

'It can be a powerful force,' said Ashurek.

The High Master groaned. 'Yes, I felt guilty, of course I did. I *am* guilty. I'd begun my career with murder, continued it in lies and compounded those crimes with a worse one, neglect. I should have gone back and helped Jhensit. Instead . . .' He turned his head from side to side. 'When Ashurek found the Way I could ignore it no longer. It ripped the old scar open. I couldn't bear it but I couldn't leave it alone either. I had to know what had happened to Jhensit – I just could not face going there myself.'

'And it also gave you the perfect opportunity to get me out of your way,' said Ashurek. 'That would explain how you were able to make me understand the language of Jhensit. I wonder you didn't think to make me forget Silvren at the same time.'

'I did think of it,' Gregardreos said savagely. 'But as High Master I was trying to act honourably and I am still trying to do so.'

Ashurek's eyebrows lifted slightly. 'Yet the lodestones you gave me to make a Way back did not work.'

'There was nothing wrong with those lodestones, only with Jhensit's own field of energy. A Sorcerer would have known the right time and place to use them.'

'I am no Sorcerer, but let it pass. If you were so averse to Jhensit, why did you come through after all?'

'An accident, or so I thought at the time; now I believe it was inevitable. The place was voracious to have me back, I think; it seized Silvren so I had no choice but to follow, and as soon as I arrived there I knew . . .'

'What?' said Silvren.

'Everything. The cause of Jhensit's slow death, which had been a mystery before. It was so easy. Any time, any time since I became a Sorcerer I could have gone through and destroyed the Maelstrom and all would have been well. But I didn't! And that's the worst sin of all. All of this is my fault.'

'True,' said Ashurek. 'But do you really care?'

'If I did not care, would I now be in this state of grief?'

'I have often seen men in a state of grief not for what

they have done, but for being found out. You spoke of despising everyone you left in Jhensit. I have not heard you utter one word of affection for them. Perhaps in your heart you wanted them to die. Perhaps that's why you didn't act, hoping they'd be destroyed.'

Gregardreos's expression was scored with pain, too deep to be feigned. 'You are the last person in existence who has the right to sit in judgement on me.'

'I do not judge you,' said Ashurek, 'but your peers will.'

'He is right.' Silvren folded her arms and she was a carving of white ice, with cold sunlight for hair. 'You know there will be a trial, don't you?'

Gregardreos shuddered from head to foot. His larynx jerked. 'Yes, I – I know. If I have to forfeit my office, I wish it could have been with more dignity and less shame. I only hope that you will all remember that I have been honest in my confession.'

The atmosphere was thick with silence, broken only by the sound of Aflouel weeping quietly. The other two Sorcerers also looked stricken; for a High Master to have fallen like this was unprecedented, and it shook the whole structure of their lives.

Then Terarct stood up and looked down at Gregardreos, his angular face very grave. 'But you have not been completely honest, have you?'

The High Master's eyes opened very wide. It suddenly appeared to Silvren that she and the other sorcerers were dazzlingly bright in the room, yet predatory; angels of vengeance. 'Tell the truth!' Terarct's voice rang sharply through the room, making the crystal walls reverberate.

'I already have!'

'No, you haven't. You have not made one mention of the Sphere.' Gregardreos did not respond, so Terarct went on, 'The Sphere filters all baseness from our power and leaves us only purity. But where does that baseness go? When it was allowed to remain within the Sphere, disaster struck us when a foolish thaumaturge released it. So, when the Sphere was reconstructed it was to channel the base energy into another dimension, a nothingness where it would harm nobody. Yes?'

Still Gregardreos did not speak.

'And you, as High Master, had ultimate responsibility for the reconstruction of the Sphere, ultimate power over where the dark energy was channelled, and exclusive access to the knowledge. Not hard to fool the rest of us about it, when you had proved so adept at other deceptions, was it?'

Gregardreos now lay very still and white, only his shallow breathing showing that he was still alive. Silvren could not bear this, she wanted to deny Terarct's accusations – but she felt dull and cold inside and she could bring herself to say nothing in Gregar's defence.

Terarct continued, 'You knew, from the time you first became High Master, that the Flux was leaking into Jhensit. When you came to reconstruct the Sphere, you deliberately channelled *all* the dark energy there. You say that you wanted to obliterate the past. I suggest that your intention was rather more extreme than that. You meant to wipe out your past quite literally, by destroying your world.'

'No!' Gregardreos cried.

'Yes,' said Terarct. 'You lied to Silvren and the scientists in the White Dome, claiming that you meant to save Jhensit when all the time you had the cold, premeditated intention of destroying it.'

'Not cold,' the High Master gasped. 'Not premeditated.'

He had as good as admitted his guilt. Silvren felt an icy fire rushing up inside her. 'Is this true?' She seized his arm and shook it. *'Is this true?'*

A huge groan burst from his lungs. 'Yes. Yes! But you don't understand, I never planned it, it almost killed me to do it but I had no choice. I know it was wrong, I'd do anything to make amends. Silvren, you must believe me –'

She jerked away from him, shivering from head to foot.

Terarct said drily, 'That is for a tribunal to decide, but the evidence is not in your favour.'

'Will you excuse me?' Silvren said suddenly. 'I cannot listen to any more of this. Gregar, I hope Terarct is wrong, but if he isn't – I shall do everything I can to see that your trial is completely fair; just as you would if our positions were reversed.'

She stood up and walked towards the door, straight-backed and very controlled, not even looking at Ashurek as she passed. But the moment she was in the corridor, out of sight, she collapsed against the wall and began to weep. The sobs were noiseless but they wrenched themselves out of her as if her heart had been ripped in two.

After a few seconds Ashurek came out of the room, shutting the door softly behind him. He watched her but she felt the gulf of all the pain and recrimination that had passed between them, and neither of them knew how to bridge it.

She did not want him to see her grief but she could no longer contain it. She was weeping for what she and Ashurek had lost, as well as for Gregar, and Ashurek's presence – which should have comforted her – only tightened the cruel grip of the talons that held her.

Eventually he said, 'Silvren –'

She cut across him. 'He was like my father, he was my father. I learned everything from him, he was my life and now here it all is, in little pieces.'

'I know.' Ashurek spoke quietly, and his eyes were sad and reflective. 'And I also know that I am no better than him. I was arrogant to assume that everything he did stemmed from jealousy of us; I should have known there was more to it than that. If he has let you down, Silvren, so have I. I don't know how to ask you to forgive me. All I say is that I am still here, and I still love you.'

Then Silvren let the coldness go, went towards him with a sob; and their arms were round each other, her tears soaking into his tunic, Ashurek holding her so tightly that she could hardly breathe. There was no death in his touch, only love; the Face was truly gone.

'I said I would forgive you anything, if you only came back to me,' she said. 'But I am the one who needs to be forgiven.'

It was hard to believe that life on Ikonus had gone on as normal while they had been away, yet it had. Except for the shadow cast by the High Master's impending trial, the world remained sunlit and serene. Mellorn had greeted her parents joyously; although she had missed them and been puzzled by their absence, otherwise she had not been in the slightest distressed. They were glad of their daughter's independent, unsentimental spirit.

Yet that first sight of Mellorn changed something within Ashurek. For the first time he felt that Ikonus was his home. He thought he had felt nothing for this small, well-ordered world, but now he found a sense of affinity growing unbidden within him. Perhaps it was simply realising that Ikonus was not perfect after all, seeing the Sorcerers discover the darkness in their own Past.

For the same reason, he no longer felt any antagonism towards Gregardreos. While not pitying him any more than he pitied himself, he felt a distinct sense of empathy. He asked Terarct what would become of Gregardreos after the trial.

'Oh, nothing terrible,' the Sorcerer replied. 'He will be stripped of his office, of course. Certain restraints will be placed on him to prevent him using his powers and he'll probably be exiled to some island and kept under guard. But he won't be ill-treated: the shame of his disgrace will be punishment enough. We are a civilised people, Ashurek.'

The day before the trial, Silvren went to see the High Master and found him sitting in the corner of his room. A book was open in his lap but he was looking out of the crystal panes at the lush sweep of the gardens beyond.

'Gregar?' she said softly.

He half-turned. Perhaps it was the fall of the light, but his face looked ravaged and red, as if he had been weeping. 'Can you forgive me?' he said tonelessly.

'I – I don't know why people keep wanting me to forgive them,' she said, trying to make light of it. 'Are you ready for the trial?'

'I'm trying to gather my thoughts, but it's not easy.'

'I wish I didn't have to have anything to do with it.' She sat down on a footstool opposite him. 'But you know that the tribunal has to call me as a witness, don't you?'

'Of course.'

'And I have to tell the truth. But I shall make sure they don't forget how much good there is in you, what a superb High Master you were –'

'In the past tense.' His shoulders rose and fell tiredly. 'I'm sure you will be a perfect witness my dear. But you didn't answer my question. I don't care about the damned tribunal! Can *you* forgive me?'

'I don't know.' She suddenly found herself shaking. 'I want to be honest with you. I don't see that I'm in any position to forgive or not forgive. I don't know what motivated you to act as you did, I mean, I know what you told me, but I can't know how it really was for you.'

'Silvren –'

'I – I need time. If my forgiveness truly means so much, I'm sure that in time I'll be able to . . .'

'Silvren, stop!' His hands were fists, his brows furrowed with pain. 'The truth is, I've let you down, haven't I? I am not the person you thought I was. You don't have to explain your pain to me, I know exactly how you feel and I can't bear the knowledge that I've been the cause of it. You thought of me as a father.' He almost spat the words. 'It is as if your own father turned out to be a murderer and liar, isn't it?'

Shocked, she tried to reply, but he did not give her time. 'And I could never tell you that the last thing I ever wanted was to be thought of as a parent to you! Why do I feel so ashamed to say it, even now?'

'I never realised how you felt.'

'What difference would it have made if you had?' He was almost sobbing now. 'You would have been disgusted. When I did tell you, you *were* disgusted.'

'No – only startled.' She shook her head helplessly. 'If I had never met Ashurek, perhaps –'

'No. You could never have loved me.' Light glinted on the reddened rims of his eyes, making them seem full of fire. 'You can only love people like Ashurek, who are flawed, misguided, or even positively evil. I thought I could win you by being noble and honest, I simply didn't understand that only the wicked stirred any response in you.'

Silvren recoiled, completely stunned by the venom of his words. She had never known him speak with such bitterness before, and the allegation hurt her so deeply that she could hardly breathe.

'That's not fair,' she whispered.

'I've hurt you. I didn't mean to.' He leaned forward, his face lined with grief. 'I was only trying to say, can you love me now that you know I'm not perfect?'

She stood up. The last thing she wanted to do was to walk out on him, but she was too distraught to stay. 'Gregar, I can't bear this. I have to go, I'll come back in the morning . . .'

He did not try to stop her, only gazed at her with a terrible expression that branded itself onto her mind forever. As she hurried from the room his voice followed her, anguished.

'You can love any kind of villain! Why not me?'

The day of the trial dawned uncannily like the one on which Silvren and Ashurek had been sent to Jhensit; cool and clear as amethyst. And again they stood leaning on the fence, looking at the horses, and Ashurek's arms were round her.

'You were restless last night,' he said. 'Bad dreams?'

'Awful. I hardly slept. I shall be glad when today is over, and we know the worst.'

'Don't worry, beloved. Terarct told me that at worst he'll only be exiled. He'll live the rest of his life in peace.'

'I know,' she said, shaking her head. 'But still . . .'

A white-robed figure was approaching them through the trees and again she had a feeling of *déjà-vu*; was it Gregardreos moving spectre-like through the dawn, to send Ashurek to Jhensit? Her heart jumped, but this figure was thinner, dark-haired.

'It's only Terarct,' she said, letting out a breath.

'Good morning, Silvren,' he called as he approached, slightly out of breath. 'I'm sorry to call on you so early.'

'It's all right, I'm ready to come to the School. There must still be preparations to be made for the trial, and I wanted to see Gregardreos first anyway.'

His face was very grave. 'There will be no trial,' he said shortly.

She was startled, almost relieved for a second. 'Oh? Why not?'

'This is a very difficult thing to tell you, but I wanted you to know at once.' Terarct's tone was grim. 'Gregardreos is dead. He killed himself last night. We found him this morning, barely an hour ago.'

The landscape turned pale and cold and began to spin around her. 'How? Why didn't someone stop him?'

'No-one sensed anything wrong. There was no mark on him; he simply decided to die. We found this note beside him.'

Silvren took the slip of paper from Terarct, trying to focus on the scrawled, tortured handwriting.

My beloved Sorcerers, my beloved students,

Try to understand.

After the trial, I would have been alive in name only; I am already dead in my heart, so to spare you further trouble and myself further pain it is best I die now. Nothing can repay the wrongs I have done. I ask neither for tolerance nor forgiveness, not even of you, my dearest Silvren. But please believe this: whatever lies I have told in the past, one thing is true; I loved the School of Sorcery more than my life. All the happiness I have ever known sprang from the School and most of all from you, Silvren. I should have been content with such a daughter.

Ashurek, you said of guilt, 'Either you learn to live with it, or you die.' I am not as strong as you.

Gregardreos

'I should have stayed with him,' Silvren said quietly. 'Why was he left on his own?'

'Because he wanted to be. Even as a prisoner he had certain freedoms. We had no right to watch him, nor to breach the barriers he set about himself, if he did not wish it,' said Terarct.

'You must have wanted this to happen!'

'Of course we didn't!' His harsh tone sobered her.

'No. How can I blame you? *I* should have stayed.' She crumpled up the note and stood quiet for a moment. 'What will happen now?'

Terarct cleared his throat. 'A new High Master will have to be elected. I have to tell you that most of the senior Sorcerers want you to consider the position.'

'No,' said Silvren without hesitating. 'I couldn't.'

'Don't decide in haste, there's plenty of time.'

'I won't change my mind.'

'Why?'

'A hundred reasons,' she said. A faint bitter smile shadowed her lips. 'Not least of which is the last thing he said to me.'

'What was that?'

'It doesn't matter. You will make a far better High Master than I would, Terarct. Stand for election and I will support you.'

Only when Terarct left them, in slightly better spirits than he had arrived, did she begin to weep. Ashurek stroked her hair.

'I couldn't take the burden of being High Master, Ashurek, and I know you'd hate it,' she said. 'Whatever you think, you mean far more to me than the School ever can.'

'I know. And you're right, I would have hated it. But why do you want Terarct to be High Master? The man's an automaton.'

'Exactly,' she said. 'As unlike Gregar as he could be.'

That night, Silvren slept peacefully but Ashurek lay wide awake, unable to still his thoughts. Eventually he left the bedroom and went to sit at his desk, with one lamp burning low, making the room a cocoon of amber light and warm red shadow. He and Silvren had agreed only too gladly to forget their differences, without arguments or conditions. Their reconciliation had been joyous, all the more so because now they were certain that their love could survive anything. It would be pleasant to find another house, he thought, further from the School and the village, where they could make a new start . . . but what new start could there be for Gregardreos, or for Shai Fea?

Guilt would not let him sleep, but neither would it destroy him. *Am I stronger than you, Gregar? Or simply more callous?*

A book caught his eye, lying amid the scattered papers. It looked familiar, yet he could not remember leaving it there. Idly he opened it and saw a painting of a deserted city, its ruined walls towering towards a glowing amber sky . . . the city in which he had first found himself when he had been sent to Jhensit.

He gasped in horror and dropped the book, but it was too late; suddenly he was *in* the city, standing on a wide, stone-slabbed street and staring up at the sky. A black planet hung there, rimmed with the merest strand of diamond light.

Was he dreaming? A moment ago he had been wide awake, and it seemed he still was, but he had the dream-like feeling of being drawn towards something unknown yet desperately important. The road converged straight into the far distance, its extreme perspective giving the impression of a painting more real and strange than life. Where it met the skyline he saw a statue silhouetted against the amber dusk.

That was the point he must reach. He began to walk towards it, vividly conscious of the skeletal ruins looming on either side of him, breathing dust and age from their empty doorways. Even a Muridonu would have seemed a burst of vibrant life in this dead place . . .

But he was wrong, there *were* other living beings here . . . Two cloaked and hooded figures were coming along the ancient road, as if they had been walking towards him forever. Feeling no fear, he went on at the same pace, not hurrying. As he reached them, they put their hoods back and he saw their faces.

Shai Tialah and Shai Fea.

Mother and daughter stopped hand-in-hand and gazed at him, no rancour in their eyes.

'I know this is a dream,' said Tialah, 'but it was the only way we could see you again.'

'Why would you wish to see me again?' Ashurek asked quietly.

'Because my daughter has returned to life,' said the Hyalana.

He looked from her to Shai Fea and yes, she *was* alive – her face radiant, her blue-green eyes shining – but this could not really be happening.

'Returned to life . . . How?'

Tialah put her arm round her daughter's shoulders, a gesture that seemed too natural to be part of a dream. 'After the darkness cleared from our skies, she rose from the bier as if she had only slept, and she said that someone had exchanged his life for hers. I thought it must be you, Ashurek – but she said his name was Gregardreos.'

Ashurek stared at them and then at the sky, speechless. *Gregardreos? Can this be real?* At last he managed to say, 'If this is your dream, it is mine too.'

The Hyalana came forward and embraced him. Yes, she was like him, perhaps more single-minded; she had done terrible things, she had killed her own brother and son, yet she was able to leave that dark time in the past and begin again. 'There is no Maelstrom now,' she said as she stepped back. 'Only the future.'

Then Ashurek took Shai Fea in his arms, felt her feathery hair on his hands and her warm mouth under his – for the last time, a last sweet time that he had never expected.

'I will never forget you,' Shai Fea said. She was smiling and her eyes were full of light, yet she spoke with artless irony. 'Nothing you have done will ever be forgotten.'

So I fear, he thought, but he kissed her again and said, 'Fare you well.'

Then Shai Fea and Shai Tialah pulled their hoods over their faces again, and went on their way.

He did not watch them dwindle into the distance; he felt that if he turned round it would break the spell. They were treading their own path now, and he must return to his. He walked on through the dying light until he reached the statue.

It was a carved hawk atop a black plinth – a hawk, dark as obsidian, with outstretched wings and fierce eyes on a level with his – the emblem of Gorethria, his own family's insignia. The statue was his goal, but why? The dream darkened around him and he wanted to escape, but he could see no way out. If he was not asleep, how could he wake up?

'If there is something you wish to tell me, speak,' he said. The hawk remained frozen, its jet-black wings dusted with a faint glow that revealed exquisite detail in the carving of every feather. It radiated absolute coldness, like the universe itself. Ashurek felt the coldness creeping inside him and terror growing, as if he was reliving his first encounter with the Face.

'I have been waiting,' said a smooth voice.

Ashurek jerked round and saw a stone archway barring the road in front of him. A figure stood framed in the arch. It was tall and graceful, human in shape, except that there was a shifting silver light where its face should have been.

Fear almost choked Ashurek. 'You cannot be here. I destroyed you.'

'Ah, you thought you were free of me, my Ashurek?' The being laughed softly, and Ashurek felt the ice in his stomach freezing him from the inside out.

'I had hoped so.'

'Well, and so you are,' said the being. 'Let me explain. You have destroyed the bargain between us but you have not destroyed *me*; nothing can do that. I shall always be here, as I have always been here, waiting for another chance with you. And believe me, dearest Ashurek, my patience is infinite. You have not strayed so very far from the fold.'

Terror overcame him, and he could not speak. The dark city started to wheel around him as the being grasped its own chin and began to peel back the mask of light. He did not want to see the Face beneath but he could not stop himself watching – and as the mask came away, he cried out and thrust out his hands to ward it away.

His hands struck glass. The archway was a mirror, and the Face beneath the mask was his own.

'Ashurek?' Silvren appeared in the glass behind him, and he suddenly realised that he was standing at a window, gripping the frame, staring at his own baleful reflection. He prised his hands away and turned to see her standing in the doorway, her hair tangled and her eyes heavy with sleep; the most beautiful sight he had ever seen. 'What's wrong? I woke up and you weren't there.'

'It's all right,' he said, sounding calm with a great effort. His gaze fell to the desk, and he noted that the book had gone. 'I couldn't sleep, that's all.'

'You look as if you've seen a ghost,' she said, placing a gentle hand on his shoulder. 'Come back to bed.'

Like the sun, Silvren's warmth made ghosts vanish, flooded the darkest shadows with light, filled him with warmth. The fear of the Face receded – but it did not vanish, and he knew now that he would never be completely free of it. He took her hand. In that moment he resolved not to mention it to her; it was his own burden, no need for her to bear it too.

He said, 'I dreamed that Gregar gave his life so that Shai Fea could live again – and I would like to think it was not a dream.'

She looked at him, her golden eyes shimmering. 'If it were possible – I think it's what he would have done. Atonement. Gods, I wish I'd known what he was going through, all those years. There must be something I could have done, to avoid all this!'

'Beloved, don't start blaming yourself. None of it was your fault. What could you have done?'

She sighed. 'Nothing, I suppose. Ashurek, you don't seem to condemn him for what he did, even after the way he tried to deceive us. I could forgive him almost anything, except trying to separate me from you.'

'No, I don't condemn him.' He slid his arms round her slender back and held her tight, but his eyes were grave. 'At least, no more than I condemn myself.'

She pulled back a little and looked at him. 'What do you mean?'

'In essence, I have acted no differently from him. He deserted his home-world in bitterness, turned his back and left it to its own devices, just as I did to Gorethria.'

A touch of fear clouded her eyes. 'You would not think of going back, would you?'

'No, Silvren. I made up my mind to leave the past behind and I shall not change it. Witness what happened when Gregardreos finally went back to Jhensit. But he has died for his mistakes. I am still alive. What right have I to stand in judgement on him?'

'If you can't condemn him, I'm glad. Perhaps you will stop being so hard on yourself.' She smiled. 'We *are* still alive, and still together; what cause have we for sorrow?'

'None,' he said with feeling. 'None.'